Jeremiah M. Pelton

# Genealogy of the Pelton Family in America

Jeremiah M. Pelton

**Genealogy of the Pelton Family in America**

ISBN/EAN: 9783741124303

Manufactured in Europe, USA, Canada, Australia, Japa

Cover: Foto ©Raphael Reischuk / pixelio.de

Manufactured and distributed by brebook publishing software
(www.brebook.com)

Jeremiah M. Pelton

# Genealogy of the Pelton Family in America

# GENEALOGY

## OF THE

# PELTON FAMILY

## IN AMERICA.

BEING A RECORD OF THE DESCENDANTS OF JOHN PELTON
WHO SETTLED IN BOSTON, MASS., ABOUT 1630-1632,
AND DIED IN DORCHESTER, MASS.,
JANUARY 23d, 1681.

By

J. M. PELTON.

ALBANY, N. Y.:
JOEL MUNSELL'S SONS, PUBLISHERS.
1892.

# CONTENTS.



## INDEXES.

# LIST OF ILLUSTRATIONS.

# PREFACE.

As every author is expected to give some good reason for making a book, let us, who bear the name of Pelton, turn ourselves into a family gathering and hear what the compiler of this work has to say for himself.

Born and reared in the township of Warwick, Orange county, N. Y., and his own branch of the family being few in number, he saw few of our name, but through the public journals learned that whether there were few or many of us, the name was widely spread.

Naturally he desired to know more of the history of his race. His grandfather could only go back to his own grandfather, Robert, who came from Long Island, N. Y., to Stamford, Conn., about 1739. Tradition gave us the old story, that three brothers, said to have come from Wales, emigrated to America a short time before the American Revolution. To this was added the further fiction that one of them settled at Saybrook, Conn., a second at New Rochelle, N. Y., and the third at Montgomery, Orange county, N. Y.*

In 1875, being then a business resident of New York, he resolved to look up the history of the Peltons, supposing there might possibly be seventy-five of the name living in America. An examination of

---

* It is true that men of the name settled at these places, but they were neither brothers or immigrants.

"Savage's General Dictionary of the First Three Generations of New England Settlers" showed that our common ancestor, John Pelton, came to Boston very early, previous to 1634; that he removed to Dorchester, Mass., in 1635, where he died in 1681, leaving a will in which he gave the names of his wife, Susanna, and children, John, Samuel, Robert and Mary. An examination of the Family and Land Records of Boston, and a search of a file of The New England Genealogical and Antiquarian Register, published in Boston, followed, and the results collated with inscriptions on tombstones at Essex (Saybrook), Conn., and other records, showed that Samuel[3], oldest son of Samuel[2], second son of John[1] and his youngest brother Benjamin[3], went to Huntington, L. I., N. Y.; that the brothers John[3] and Henry[3], of the same family, went to Connecticut, while Ithamar[3], another brother, settled in New Jersey, followed later by Benjamin[3] from Long Island.

The search thus begun was prosecuted in odd moments of a business life by searches of State, county, city, township, church, cemetery, probate and other records,* examinations of county and township and other histories, including more than three hundred family histories, by the personal writing of more than six thousand letters, sending of circulars, etc., the result of all which is the volume before us.

And now, while we are together, the compiler returns his hearty thanks to all who have assisted him in the work, both men and women, especially the latter, of whom he had frequently to ask assistance when no man seemed able to help him over a difficulty. He also especially returns thanks to the post-

---

* See the Appendix for a list of records searched.

masters of the United States and of Canada and to clerks of townships and of various bodies for their prompt and courteous replies to his letters of inquiry.

He regrets that want of time prevented the gathering of sketches of old homesteads of the race, still standing.

He feels quite sure that but few families have escaped his search, and hopes that a new historian will come forward about ten or fifteen years hence and bring the records down to the then existing date and elucidate a few problems left unsolved by the present compiler.

J. M. PELTON,
246 W. 27th street, New York.

(See page 42.)

# INTRODUCTION.



In the early ages of mankind all names, doubtless
were significant. Names of persons were given
from circumstances attending birth, some appearance
of the child or wish or hope of the parents. As
men became more numerous, and two or more persons had the same name, it became necessary that
some method be found to distinguish one from
another. This was frequently done by a soubriquet
or nick-name, indicating some peculiarity of the person's appearance or character, his occupation or his
residence.

Frequently this second name was derived from the
person's father, whose name with a word signifying
son or descendant added as a prefix or a suffix, as
Joshua, the son of Nun ; Caleb, the son of Jephun-
neh, among the Hebrews; which words frequently
coalesced, as Fitz-Roy, son of the king, and Fitz-
Hugh, the son of Hugh, in old Norman ; James
Petrousky, for James, the son of Peter in Polish ;
Peter Paulowitz for Peter, the son of Paul, in Rus-
sian ; John MacDonald or William O'Hara, in Ireland and Scotland, for the son of Donald, and the
grandson or descendant of Hara, respectively ; David
*Ap*, or Vap Howell, or Ap Rhys, becoming, by con-
traction, Powell and Price in Wales ; and John,
Will's son or Peter's son, becoming John Wilson or
John Peterson in England.

From their predecessors, the Etruscans, with many of their names, the Romans adopted a very complete and precise system of personal designation by three names. The people were divided into large clans or gentes, each of which was subdivided into families. In this system the first name denoted the individual and was equivalent to our Christian name; the second the gens and the third the family. Thus, Publius Cornelius Scipio indicated that this Publius belonged to the great clan or gens Cornelius and to the particular branch or family Scipio of that clan. As nations became more civilized, the necessity of fixed family surnames became apparent. In Europe these came into use from the tenth to the sixteenth century — in some nations by common consent, and in others by legal mandate.

## English Surnames.

In England surnames were adopted to a limited extent in the tenth century. After the Norman conquest, in the eleventh and twelfth centuries, they became prevalent, derived from the owner's location, occupation, office or personal peculiarity. A lord would take as a surname the name of his family seat or manor, while his half dozen sons in the next generation would at their pleasure take as many different surnames. Slowly each family or several related families adopted a fixed surname. But this did not end all genealogical difficulties. Differing languages and dialects, the changing English language, illiteracy and careless spelling caused such a variety in the appearance and pronunciation of the same name that no one but a philologist would dream the numerous forms had come from the same original. For example, the compiler of the Phelps Genealogy found the name in the following forms, viz.: Phelps, Phelips, Phelups, Philps, Philips, Phillips, Felps, ffelleps, ffelpes, Filps, ffilps, ffelleps, ffellips. Guelph, Guelphs, Guelf, Guelfs, Welf, Welfs, and many more, the original, it is said, having been Guelph.

PILDEN, PILTON, PELDON, PELTON, PALTON, PULTON, POLTON, POULTON, AS THE NAME OF A PARISH, MANOR OR PLACE.

The earliest appearance of Pelton or Polton, as the name of a place, found by the writer, is in "Camden's Britannia," vol. 1, p. 19, where it is stated that "about 905, Edward the Elder settled a Bishop's See in Bodman (Cornwall), and granted the Bishop of Kirton three villages in those parts, *Polton*, Caeling, and Landwitham &c. * * Polton is probably Paulton in South Breange, afterwards Pawton."

Pelton, Durham, England, Camden, in his Britannia, gives as a village in the Parish of Chester le Street, situated on the Wear, seven miles north of the city of Durham. Hutchinson's History of Durham, 1787, vol. 2, 401, says: "The village of Pelton is in sight from Lumley Castle." Surtee's Durham, "Pelton a village on high ground a mile to the north-west of Chester le Street. In 1320 Hugh Burdon held half the vill of Pelton of John Haddam, the Superior Lord of the fee, by homage and sixth part of a knight's service. Another Hugh died seized of the same estate in 1350, and in 1395 Agnes, his daughter and heir, wife of the first Hugh del Red-hough, and then of Thomas de Beke Chivaler, died seized of the whole manor of Pelton, held of the Bishop (ut supponitor) by knight's service and suit of court. Thomas del Redhough (Redhugh), son and heir of Agnes, alienated his lands in Pelton to Robert de Whelpington, who was a trustee for the family of Neville, or conveyed to them. In 1426 the manor of Pelton, among the possessions of Ralph, the first Earl of Westmoreland, was included in the forfeiture of the last Earl in 1569. The place is celebrated for its collieries, out of which the Allans of Grange, living in 'The Flatts,' had made a fortune."

PELDON, a parish and manor in Essex, England, the history of which reaches back to the time of Edward the Confessor (1004 to 1066), of which more further on. "PILTON, formerly a distinct estate, held in 1286 by William de Montchensi of Henry de Cramaville, belonged in 1835 to the Bradwell manor" (Wright's Essex, vol. 2, 695, and Morant's Essex, vol. 1, 375). Also a parish in County Devon, in Northampton, and in Somerset. POLTOX, a parish in Kent, Eng. In the "Visitation of Somersetshire," in 1623, by R. Mundy, page 124, we have Palton of Palton.

* Pulton, Manor, Desborough, Northamptonshire (Bridges' Hist. of Northamptonshire). See further on.

---

* As in 1320 Hugh Burdon (see above) held half the vill of Pelton, Durham, and in the reign of Henry IV (1399-1413) the Manor of Desborough passed from the Burdon family to John Pulton, as paramount lord, and became "Pulton Manor," remaining in the family down to the time of Henry VIII (see p. 11), and as John Neville, in 1282, bought a part of the Peldon manor in Essex, and the family of Neville, soon after 1400, came into possession of a part of the manor of Pelton, in Durham, it would be interesting to know whether the Peltons, Poltons or Pultons, the Burdons, and the Nevilles were relatives, and also how long the name of Pelton has existed in Durham. Information as to this last question could probably be obtained by examining the "Boldon Book," made in 1183, which is an examination of Durham, similar to that made of the larger part of England in 1083, and contained in "The Domesday Book." A copy of "The Boldon Book" is in the Bishop's office in Durham.

PELDON, PELDEN, PELTON, PILTON, POLTON, POUL-
TON, PULTON, AND PERHAPS PALTON AS A FAMILY
SURNAME.

Lower, in his Dictionary of English Surnames,
derives Pelton as a surname from the Parish of Peldon in Essex, England. Burke, in his General
Armory, says: "The Peltons and Poltons had their
seats in Essex and Northamptonshire. He gives
their coats of arms, which differ but little (see
p. 14).

In Morant's History of Essex, vol. 1, 417–19, we
find Peldon parish, manor and hall, situated in Wins-
tree Hundred; and that, in the reign of Edward
the Confessor, the lands in the parish where this
manor is situated were held by Turchill, a freeman,
and another freeman, name not given. Peldon Hall,
the mansion house, stands on the north side of the
church. The estate was granted by William the
Conqueror, to William the Deacon, about 1086,
toward the rebuilding of St. Paul's Cathedral, hence
held by the Bishops of London. It was held from
them by a family that, from the manor, took the
name of Peltindone. In 1282 Walter de Peltindone
enfeofed John de Nevill and Margery, his wife, with
part of this manor — three hundred and sixty acres
and a wind-mill, etc." In 1332 it was called Peltyndon, and in 1358 Peltyngdon. The manor has been
known as Peltendune, Peltyngdon, Pellingdon, Peltindone, Peltyndon, Peltindone, Poltendon and
Peldon, and the family name has varied accordingly.

"Dun signifies a hill; a part of the parish is on a
hill."

## PELTON, POLTON AND PULTON HOMES IN ENGLAND FROM 1086 TO 1631.

### *In Essex.*

On October 14, 1066, William the Conqueror fought and won the battle of Hastings. On page 10 we have shown that in 1086 he granted the estate, afterward known as Peldon Manor, to William the Deacon, and that this estate came into the possession of the ancestor of the Pelton family, whose descendants held it down to at least 1358. We also find (Morant's Essex, 1, 113) that Peter Poulton held real estate in Essex in 1568.

### *In Northamptonshire.*

"The Pultons* inhabited Desborough, Northamptonshire, for 370 years. John Pulton, first lord of Desborough, seated at Cransley about 1367, married Jane de Desborough (see marble monument in Desborough church). In the reign of Henry IV (1399 to 1413) the manor of Desborough, Northamptonshire, passed from the Burdon family to John Pulton as paramount lord. In the second year of Edward IV (1463) this manor was in the hands of Thomas Pulton. In the second year of Edward VI (1549) Giles Pulton was seized of a manor called Pulton's Manor. His wife, Catherine, daughter of Thomas Lovett, Esq., of Atwell in Nottinghamshire, died in the 15th year of Henry VIII (1524)." (Bridges' History of Northamptonshire.)

### *In Wiltshire.*

In 1435, the west tower of the church of St. Andrews at Wansborough, Wiltshire, was built by

---

* Burke spells the name Pulton and Pelton.

Thomas Polton and Edith, his wife, as set forth by a brass plate on one of its walls; another brass plate, with an inscription, shows the place of their burial within the church. (See Rickman's Architecture in England, Ed. 6, 1862, p. 405.)

### *Somersetshire and Bucks.*

In the "Visitation of Somersetshire," 1623, R. Mundy, p. 124, we have Palton of Palton.

From "Burke's Commoners," Alban Butler, Esq., of Aston le Walls, married Anne, daughter of Ferdinand Pulton, Esq., of Bourton, Bucks, who died in 1631.

### THE PELTONS OF ENGLAND OF THE PRESENT DAY, THEIR NUMBER, TRADITIONS AND LOCATION.

It is said that the number of persons of any surname found in the directory of London, is a fair guide to the number of that name to be found in the kingdom of Great Britain. An examination of the London Directory, and a personal correspondence with representatives of the name in England, seem to indicate that but few Peltons are now living there, and that they trace their line back, with certainty, for four or five generations only, to Charles Pelton, who, tradition says, came from France, a Huguenot, during one of the persecutions of that people. Tradition also gives it as probable that the ancestor of Charles fled from Pelton Manor, in Durham, to France, at the end of one of the English civil wars. The writer has found nothing to confirm this latter tradition, but thinks it more probable that some of the Peltons of Essex or Northampton went over to France in the time of the Angevine kings, while England was a continental

power and there made their homes.* However true
this return may have been, the writer feels sure that
from 1086 down, there has not been a generation in
which there have not been families in England bearing the name of Pelton, or some of its variants, ready
to fight for the British flag.

Many of the Huguenot immigrants settled in the
Thames valley in England. The reputed immigrant,
Charles Pelton, settled in Brentford near Richmond,
where he was clerk of the chapel for years until he
there died, leaving sons, Charles, Robert, John,
Joshua and Richard, besides daughters, whose descendants of the fourth and fifth generations are now
in London, Croydon, Depthford, Tunbridge Wells
and North Shields, England; in Montreal and
Ottawa, Canada; in France and in Australia.

Quite a colony was in London twenty or thirty
years ago. One of the London Peltons, Samuel,
was made a citizen of that city "for bravery in the
face of the enemy," in one of the Napoleonic wars.† It
is not strange that but few are left in England, con-
sidering their tendency to migrate to new lands, and
to serve their country in times of war.

These Peltons have good mechanical, mathemati-
cal, mercantile and musical talents, and are so much
like our Peltons of America in their mental and physical characteristics, the writer is compelled to believe

---

* The following extract from a foot-note in Macaulay's England, shows
that it was common for Englishmen, in the times of religious persecution,
to leave their country for a long time.

In the controversies of 1686, between Protestants and Catholics, one of the
ablest of the Roman Catholic divines was Andrew Pulton, whose spelling,
after an absence of eighteen years, was so bad, that in a contemporary satire,
entitled *The Advance,* is the following couplet:

> "Send Pulton to be lashed in Busby's school,
> That he in print no longer play the fool."

† Two of Samuel's brothers were serving in the British navy at the time
he was in the army.

that we are descended from the Peltons of Essex or Northampton, they, doubtless, having been closely related, as shown by the similarity of their coats of arms, as given below.

Burke in his "General Armory," and in his "Commoners," says that the Peltons or Poltons had their seats in Essex and Northampton. He gives as coats of arms :

1. "Pelton (Co. Northampton), Or, on a fesse betw. three mullets sa., as many bezants."

2. "Poulton, Pulton, or Polton, Desborough, (Northampton). Ar. fess betw. three mullets sa."

3. "Another. On the fess three bezants."

4. "Pelton or Polton. Ar. three mullets sa, each charged with a bezant." Crest — A hand holding a swan's head and neck erased, all ppr.

5. "Pelton or Polton (Essex). An inescutcheon charged with a bend, within an orle of escallops."

6. "Pelton. Or. six starlings betw. three mullets sa. each charged with a bezant."

7. "Palton (Co. Devon). Ar. Six roses Gu. seeded or, three, two and one."

### *Peltons in Ireland and Germany.*

Thomas Pelton, from Galway, Ireland, the writer saw in New York about 1860. He served in the Union armies in the great rebellion, returned safe, and is now a member of the Grand Army of the Republic. Another Pelton, a few years ago. kept a hotel in Iowa. He was apparently a full-blooded German. Both of these were doubtless of English descent.

Two merchants in Denver, Col., from the continent of Europe, of Hebrew descent, and bearing the name of Pelton, derived their name thus from Palti, one of the chiefs of the tribe of Benjamin

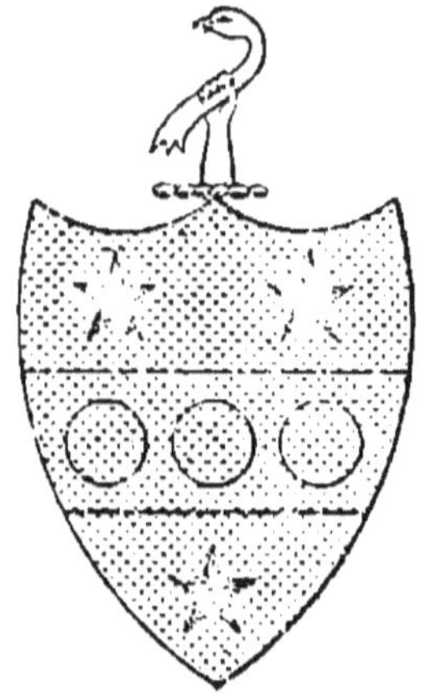

## PELTON, POLTON AND POULTON,

### OF COUNTY NORTHAMPTON, WITH CREST.

(See page 14.)

## PELTON OR POLTON,

### OF COUNTY ESSEX, ENGLAND.

(See page 14.)

(Numbers, ch. 13 : 9). The name in the Jewish vernacular became corrupted in pronunciation and changed to Pelti, which, by the addition of an *n*, became Peltin, the name assumed by their ancestor as a patronymic. In this country they dropped the *i* and inserted an *o*, hence their name Pelton.

## A Few Scraps of History.

1. VIRGINIA.— This name was first applied to what is now Carolina, afterward to territory between Lat. 34° to 45° N. Still later the lands from 34° to 38° N. were granted to The London Company, those from 41° to 46° given to other parties and called New England ; while those from 38° to 41° N. were left open.

On May 13, 1607, 105 colonists sent by The London Company, founded Jamestown. or City, as then called, the first permanent English colony in America.

2. IN NEW ENGLAND, the first settlement was made on the Elizabeth Islands, at the mouth of Buzzard's Bay, in 1602, by Bartholomew Gosland and thirty-two others.

3. PLYMOUTH.-- Nov. 9, 1620, the *Mayflower*, with 100 English puritans, former exiles in Holland, reached Cape Cod, Massachusetts, at a point now Provincetown. Later they sailed across the bay, formed a government and elected John Carver, governor, and landed at Plymouth Dec. 15, O. S., 25, N. S. In 1622, later, colonists settled Weymouth, farther north.

4. SALEM was settled in 1628 by an expedition, led by John Endicott, who acted as governor. In 1629 a reinforcement of 300 men, 80 women and 26 children arrived, with supplies of food, arms, tools, cattle and goats. From this reinforcement a party was sent by Endicott to take possession of the

mouth of Charles river, hence the settlement of Charlestown, July 4, 1629. (Frothingham's History, 1848.) In this year of 1629 a royal charter was granted to the colony of Massachusetts Bay, and the London Company deciding to transfer the government of the colony to America, elected directors from the intending emigrants, with John Winthrop as governor.

5. DORCHESTER, now a part of Boston, was settled by a body of substantial English puritans and non-conformists, urged thereto by Rev. John White of Dorchester, England. They were a body of noble men, superior to the average of emigrants, and came provided with implements and money to prosecute the various trades, and with their ministers ready to form a church in their new home. They sailed from Plymouth on March 30, 1630, N. S., a short time before Gov. Winthrop and his people, intending to go to Charles River, but made land at Nantasket, a short distance south of the present Dorchester, where their good ship *Henry and John*, of 400 tons burthen, landed her 140 passengers, June 11, 1630, N. S. Moving northward a short distance they arrived at Mattapan, as the Indians called it, and finding pasture for their cattle there, stopped June 17, and called their settlement New Dorchester. Here they soon built a church and established a school; built the first water-mill in America, in 1633, and about the same time established the New England cod fishery.

6. BOSTON.—Gov. Winthrop, with his company of about 900 persons, sailed from Yarmouth, England, April 7, 1630, and arrived at Salem, June 12, 1630; John Endicott resigning to Winthrop the governorship. That year, 1630, gave the colony an increase of about 1,000 immigrants in seventeen vessels.

Many of Gov. Winthrop's people at Salem became dissatisfied, and he removed with them to Charlestown. They there found a scarcity of good fresh water. The peninsula opposite, then called by the Indians Shawmut, and by the whites Tri Mountain, had a solitary inhabitant, Rev. William Blackstone, who had lived there several years alone, and had planted an orchard, the first in New England. He heard of their difficulties, visited them, told them he had good land with many springs of good fresh water, and invited them to join him. They accepted his invitation and were pleased. On Sept. 7, 1630, at a meeting in Charlestown, it was voted to remove the governor's house to the peninsula, and that the new town should be called Boston. According to the resolution the governor's house was removed and eventually nearly all the people crossed Charles river to Boston, and there remained.

### *Peltons Who Came to America; When, and Where They Settled.*

The first immigrant of the name known was George Pelton, who sailed in the *Furtherance* to Virginia in 1622, and settled at Burrows Hill, James City. (See Hotten's Original Lists of Emigrants to America, p. 231. Chatto & Windus, London. Bouton, N. Y.)

The writer has learned nothing more of him.

The second was John Pelton, of whom James Savage's General Dictionary of three Generations of The First Settlers of New England says. " Pelton, John. Boston, very early, had an estate, described in The Book of Possessions, removed to Dorchester; his eldest son, John, was baptized March 2, 1645.

In his will of Jan. 3, 1681, proved March 10, following, he names widow, Susanna, sons John, Samuel and Robert the youngest, besides daughter, Mary. To Samuel was given administration of Robert, lost at sea, July, 1683." All Peltons in America, excepting two or three families in Canada, are descended from this John Pelton and from his second son Samuel, as will appear from the record.

## TRADITIONS AND FACTS.

Traditions many and various have been found as to the number who came, the date of their coming and their places of settlement. As to dates given, or approximations thereof, all but one have been wrong, in being too recent. Mrs. Simmons, who died in 1862 in New Hampshire, said her father, John[4] Pelton (second of Saybrook, Conn.), was of the fourth generation of Peltons in America. She was right. Of course we have the common tradition that three brothers came, some say they came from Wales and some from Ireland, that two went by the name of Felton and one by that of Pelton; also that there were Peltons in Virginia whose name was changed into Peyton. Against all these we put these historical facts; that the Peltons came from England, even if some of them sailed from a Welsh port. That the name of John Pelton of Boston and of his descendants was always Pelton. Also that Nathaniel Pelton or Felton, in 1633, then about 17 years old, came to Salem, Mass., that he returned to England in 1634, and came back in 1635 with his brother Benjamin, about 22 years of age, and their mother, Eleanor. Benjamin died about 1689, at about 76; and Nathaniel, July 30, 1705, æ. 90 years.

Public documents and the history of those times show that these men were called both Felton and Pelton. (See New England Genealogical and Antiquarian Reg'r. Vol. for 1849, "ffelton, Benjamin, made a 'freeman' by Mass. General Court at Boston, May 22, 1639.")

In Vol. for 1852, "Early Settlers of Essex and Old Norfolk, Mass.," Felton (See Pelton), Nathaniel, etc., and in Vol. for 1853, "Pelton or Felton," Benjamin, etc., "Early Settlers of Essex and Norfolk, Mass."

We now return to John Pelton of Boston. His name is in "The Book of Possessions." This is the first land record of Boston, and was made by order of the General Court in or about 1634. The description of his property is as follows, viz.: "John Pelton, House and house lot; Owen Rowe, West; Street, North; Cove, South; the marsh, East."

Rowe, Mr. Owen; House and garden, Street North; Cove South; the Marsh East, shows that Mr. Pelton's land, before 1634, (probably in 1631 or '2,) joined on the west that of Owen Rowe, from whom Rowe's wharf was named. The records of the early division of lands in Boston were lost long since. Drake in his "Old Landmarks of Boston," says that, "In the limits of the peninsula the rule was two acres to plant on, and for every able youth one acre within the neck and Noddle's Island (now East Boston)." Judging from the record above, and from the record of the baptism of his oldest child John, March 2, 1645, the writer believes he came over when young and received land as an "able youth." And from records given further on he also believes that he came with or had some older married female relative, or relatives who lived in Boston or Dorchester, during at least a part of the

time of his residence at the latter place. His reasons
for this belief are: 1. That John Smith, quartermaster, so called, married for his third wife "Widow
Katherine Pelton." This must have occurred before
Dec. 30, 1676, as his will bearing that date, and proven
July 25, 1678, mentions "his wife, Katherine, and
sons John and other children." Now, as may be
seen in the body of the work, John[1] Pelton and all
his sons were living at that time, and the further fact
that Samuel Pelton, son of John[1], married Mary
Smith, daughter of John Smith, quartermaster, this
"Widow Pelton" could not have been the widow of
John[1] Pelton, as her name was Susanna. 2. As the
Widow Katherine Pelton (Smith) died in Boston,
July 17, 1710, aged 90, she must have been born in
1620, and 14 years old in 1634, hence could not have
been the mother of John[1] Pelton. In Boston the
land of John Pelton adjoined that of Mr. Owen
Rowe. In Dorchester, to which he removed about
1635, the Peltons were neighbors of the Glovers, one
of the best families there, while Nathaniel Glover,
oldest son of John Glover, and Samuel Pelton each
married a daughter of John Smith, quartermaster,
and each named Mary.*

The "Glover Memorial" shows that on Dec. 25,
1700, Nathaniel Glover, Sen., and his wife, Hannah,
deeded to Nathaniel Glover, Jr., in Dorchester, several parcels of land, among them his house lot of 15
acres, "being butted and bounded on the easterly
end upon the sea or salt water, on the northerly side
by land of Widow Pelton and Joseph Hall; on the
westerly end upon the highway leading to Tileston's

---

* That Mr. John Smith had two daughters Mary, living at the same time,
had escaped the sharp eyes of Mr. Ebenezer Clapp, historian, of Dorchester, until informed of the fact by the writer.

Mill, standing upon Neponsett river, and on the southerly side by land of Mrs. Brick (Breck).

In 1636 the name of John Pelton appears on the records of Dorchester Patent as a proprietor, proof that in character and in religious opinions he was satisfactory. The patent contained then about 30,000 acres, to which additions were made, the whole covering what now comprises the townships of Dorchester, Dedham, Stoughton, Canton, Foxboro and Wrentham, now lying in Norfolk county, Mass. A cursory examination of the Norfolk County Records show the following conveyances and divisions, viz.: Jan. 26, 1699, Susannah (widow of John Pelton, Sen.), Samuel Pelton of Bristol, her son, and Robert, her grandson, to Lyon; Sept. 3, 1707, Samuel Pelton, Sen., and his wife, Mary, of Bristol, New England, convey land; March 16, 1713, Susanna, relict of John[2] Pelton, Samuel Pelton of Seaconk, in New England, son of John Pelton, late of Dorchester, and Robert Pelton of Dorchester, conveyed land in Dorchester; Susanna, widow of John[2], to Samuel Pelton, Jr.; also Susanna, widow of John, with Robert and his wife, Rebecca, to Samuel Pelton, Jr.; Susannah, Samuel, Samuel and Robert, "child of John," to Glover; Robert to Crehore, May 24, 1714; Samuel[3] Pelton and his wife, Sarah, of Nassau (Long Island), in the province of New York, son of Samuel, late of Dorchester, to Gould et als. of Dorchester, for £180, lands in different pieces in Dorchester. The property is described as coming from his father. The deed is long and twice recorded, and it seems to have been a closing-out sale. In 1720, Robert[3] Pelton and wife make three conveyances, to Phillips, Johnson and May. Nov. 9, 1721, Robert Pelton and Rebecca, his wife, convey to Stone. April 24, 1749, Robert Pelton and Rebecca convey to Wentworth. May 10, 1751, Henry Pelton of Groton, Conn., conveys lands in Dorchester that appear to have come from his father, Samuel, and to have been all of his lands there, to Lemuel Pelton (his son) of Middletown, Conn.

After the first allotments of lands of the Dorchester Patent, we find others as follows, viz.: Jan. 17, 1713, to (representatives of) John Pelton and others; Sept. 11, 1717, his name appears with others in the list of proprietors, and about the same date one acre of land is set off to Samuel[3] Pelton and also an acre to Widow Pelton (of John[2]), and another acre to her son Robert. In 1726 lots were set off in Stoughton to Widow Pelton, Robert[3] Pelton and Samuel[3] Pelton; also to the same parties in 1727. In the Suffolk Register are records of various conveyances.

### How the Descendants of John Pelton spread.

We have seen that John[1] Pelton died at Dorchester, leaving children John, Samuel, Mary and Robert. Robert was lost at sea, probably unmarried. John, the eldest, left one son, Robert, who died in Stoughton, Mass. His sons there, died young, unmarried, thus ending the line of John[2] in male descendants. Samuel thus became the sole progenitor in the male line. His sons were Samuel, Ithamar, John, Henry and Benjamin, the latter two born in Bristol, then in Massachusetts, now in Rhode Island.

Samuel went to Huntington, on Long Island, N.Y. His son Robert to Stamford, Conn., whence his descendants spread to Warwick, Orange Co., N. Y., and to New York city; also to Yates Co., N. Y., and Hocking Co., Ohio. Ithamar died in Monmouth Co., N. J., about 1744; no descendants known. John lived, after his marriage, in Connecticut, and died in what is now Portland, then a part of the township of Middletown, in that State, leaving sons, John, James, Phineas, Johnson, Josiah and Joseph. John[4] lived and died in Saybrook or Essex, Conn. His descendants are widely scattered in Connecticut, New York, Pennsylvania, Ohio and Michigan. The descendants of James are found at Clinton, Conn., in Seneca county, N. Y., in Canada at South Gower, and westward in Ohio, in Maryland and in Oregon. Johnson's descendants are in Portland, Conn., in Vermont, in Central New York, and in Michigan. Descendants of Phineas are in Portland and Middletown, Conn., in Massachusetts, in western New York and Michigan. Josiah's descendants are in Portland, Conn., in Cleveland and Vermillion, Ohio, in central New York, in Vermont, in Pennsylvania, in Michigan and in Oregon. Descendants of Joseph are in Portland and Middletown, Conn., in Berkshire county, Mass., in New York city, near Cleveland, Ohio, and in Otsego and Chautauqua counties, N. Y.

HENRY[3], third son of Samuel, lived and died in Groton, Conn., whence his descendants scattered through Chatham and Somers, Conn., Northampton and Berkshire county, Mass., Vermont, Ontario, Canada and Michigan; also, to Horton, Nova Scotia, to Maine and California.

BENJAMIN, also, went to Huntington, Long Island, N. Y., and with his elder brother, Samuel, became one of the progenitors of the Long Island Peltons. He afterward removed to Hopewell, Mercer county, N. J., where he died. His descendants settled in New York city and Ithaca, N. Y., and in Newark, N. J., and are now found on Staten Island, in New York city, in Poughkeepsie and Monticello, N. Y., in Sandusky, Ohio, and in Chicago, Ill.

# SCOPE AND PLAN OF THE WORK.

Scope.—The intention was to give the name, the place and date of birth; if married, the place and date of marriage, with the name of the husband or wife, the name of his or her father, and of what place; occupation and place or places of residence; if dead, the place and date of death, of every person bearing, or who has borne the name of Pelton, now living, or who has lived in America, and descended from John Pelton of Boston and Dorchester, Mass., 1634–1681. Also the names and records of the children of married daughters that have been reported to the compiler.

The fulfillment of this intention has been limited only by the inability of the compiler to find a few persons, and by the negligence of another few who have not answered his letters, or who, in answering, have not given all the information requested.

Plan.—And its explanation.

These records may be said to have been compiled on the perpendicular plan. Those of each branch, and of each family of each branch, being traced down consecutively in a widening stream of pendant, succeeding generations from the first to the last, first through the oldest son, and then through the remaining sons of each family in the order of their birth.*

---

* This the Compiler believes is better and more natural than the much-used, horizontal plan, in which all persons of any generation, as for example, the second or fourth, are grouped together, and all are numbered consecutively from the first to the last.

FIGURES AND NUMBERS AS USED FOR REFERENCES IN THIS WORK.—A small figure or number, over a name, designates the generation to which the person belongs. A number in full-faced figures, at the left of a name, refers to another page where this name may be found.

Such a number to the left of a head of a family, at the beginning of his record, refers backward to the page of his father. If at the left of a married son, it refers forward to that son's detailed family record.

Over the name of each head of a family, at the beginning of his record, is placed a number, in a small figure or figures, that indicates the generation to which the name belongs.

At the right of his name, in small type, are the names of his ancestors, leading back in direct ascent to the immigrant John[1]. To find these ancestors take the number to the left of the name before us, and turning to the page it indicates, we will find the name of his father. The number opposite the father's name gives the page of the grandfather, and thus back to John.[1]

Following a short history of the head of each family come the names of his children, dates of birth, marriage and death of each, and names of husbands and wives.

In this synopsis of family record the known record of each daughter, married or unmarried, and of each unmarried son, is completed without further reference.

As previously stated, the number to the left of a married son indicates the page where the full record of himself and family, in the form above stated, is given as far as known.

Remember that in each family the oldest married son is first taken, and his decendants followed to the

4

last generation. Also that after him follows the second married son, and then the third, etc., all treated in the same manner.

If at any time unable to find a name consult the Index.

Note.—This explanation, too long or useless, as some may think, is given because the Compiler, in his examination of 300 or 400 Genealogical Histories, owing to the plan of a work before him, and the want of an explanation, often found it very difficult, even almost impossible, to trace a line either way.

# JOHN PELTON FIRST OF BOSTON AND DORCHESTER, MASSACHUSETTS.

John Pelton, born in England, place and time unknown, though probably about 1616, and a descendant of Essex Peltons or Poltons (See Introduction), came to Boston about 1630 to 1633, as his name and a description of his property appears in the "Book of Possessions," the oldest land record of Boston, made by order of The General Court in 1634. The record therein on page 91 runs thus: " Mr. Owen Roe his possession in the limits of Boston. One house and garden bounded with the streete north ; the lane west; the Cove south ; and John Pelton east.

John Pelton's possession in Boston. One house and household lot bounded with Owen Roe west ; the streete north ; the Cove south ; and the marsh on the east."

These lands were Lots 104 to 108, on the south side of Essex St., from Washington St., easterly. See Map F. or No. 6, page 74 where Owen Rowe, (as here spelled,) has lot 107 and John Pelton 108.

Soon after, in 1635, probably, he removed to Dorchester, then a few miles out of Boston peninsula, now a part of that city, and which had been settled in the same year but a few months earlier. In 1635 or 1636, he became by grant or purchase a joint owner of the Dorchester Patent, and received his share, as also did his heirs in its many divisions. He was also one of the forty-seven owners of the "Great Lots." (See Clapp's History of Dorchester.) That he was admitted among the very select company at Dorchester, is sufficient proof that his character and religious opinions were considered correct.

In Dorchester he lived by the side of the Glovers and others of the best families, as this extract from the "Glover Memorial" shows. "On Dec. 25, 1700, Nathaniel Glover, Sen. and his wife Hannah, conveyed to their son, Nathaniel Glover, Jr., in Dorchester, several parcels of land, among them his house-lot of fifteen acres, being butted and bounded on the Easterly end upon the Sea or Saltwater, on the Northerly side by land of widow Pelton and Joseph Hall, on the Westerly end upon the Highway leading to Tileston's Mills, standing upon Neponsett River, and on the Southerly side by land of Mrs. Brick (Breck)."

The time and place of his marriage and the maiden name of his wife, are unknown; we learning only from his will that her Christian name was Susanna. They were probably married about 1643, a date that strengthens the opinion (See Introduction, p. 19) that he came to Boston when young, and received his allotment of land there as an "able youth." His occupation and history are unknown, excepting that from his will we learn that he was engaged in the fisheries, then, as now, a valuable business. He died in Dorchester, January 23, 1681. His will dated January 3, 1681, twenty days before his death, proved March 16, following, mentions his wife Susanna, his sons John, Samuel, and Robert the youngest, and his daughter Mary. His widow probably lived until May 7, 1706, and was doubtless the "Old Mother Pelton"

buried May 10, 1706, as given in Clapp's History of
Dorchester, page 282, taken from the records of the
oldest church there, and supposed as such a record was
very unusual, to have been that of a very well-known
person.    Children, born in Dorchester:

29     I John, b., probably early in 1645; baptized
            March 2, 1645; m. about 1673, wife's
            name unknown; d. before 1699.

31     II Samuel, b. about 1647; m. "5th mo." May
            16, 1673, Mary Smith; d. probably,
            1713-14.

       III Robert, born, probably, about 1649-51, at
            Dorchester, Mass.    He was a mariner,
            and on July 7, 1680, he "affirmed the
            loss at sea of the sloop 'Anne and
            Elizabeth' of New York, commanded
            by Alexander Watts." (Glover Me-
            morial.)  He was lost at sea, July, 1683;
            probably  unmarried,  as  his  brother
            Samuel took out letters of administra-
            tion, and no mention is made of wife
            or children.

       IV Mary, born about 1653 or '54, baptized
            Feb. 18, 1654. (Ch. Rec.)  Was living
            at the death of her father; may have
            been older than Robert, as the exact
            order of births is unknown.  Nothing
            is known as to her marriage or her
            death.

30

**27. John Pelton**[1], first son of John[1], born Dorchester, Mass., in 1645, he having been baptized,
(Ch. Rec.,) March 2, 1645.  Married Susanna ——,
time and place unknown.  He lived at Dorchester

and apparently died about 1683,* or certainly before
1699, as in that year his son signs a deed as a representative of his father   Diligent search has been
made to find the date of his marriage and the name
of his wife but in vain, excepting that her name
was probably Susannah; Susannah, relict of John
Pelton, Samuel Pelton of Seekonk, son of John Pelton, late of Dorchester, and Robert Pelton, of Dorchester, having conveyed land in Dorchester March
16, 1713.   Children, born at Dorchester:
36       I Robert, b. Jan. 1, 1675; m. Sept. 2, 1697,
            Rebecca Crehore; d. Sept. 3, 1745.
        II Christien, born June 5, 1678;  no other
            information.
       III Susannah, born Aug., 1680; life and death
            unknown.
        IV Charity, born Jan. 25, 1682; no other in-
            formation.


—    28. Robert Pelton, first son of John², John¹, b.
Dorchester, Mass., January 1, 1675; married at Milton,
Mass., September 2, 1697, by Rev. Peter Schacher,
of Milton, Rebecca Crehore, of that place.   Lived
at Dorchester and thence removed to Stoughton,
Mass., where he sold 60 acres of land to John Johnson, February 21, 1739, and bought it back for £700,
September 26 following.   He was a bricklayer and
farmer, and died, (Town Rec. of Stoughton), September 3, 1745, aged 70.   His widow Rebecca died
February 2, 1747, aged 73.   Children, born in Stoughton:
        I Timothy, born in 1699; baptized Dec. 15,
            1699; died in infancy.

* Mr. John Pelton, as shown by Dorchester records, must have been an
invalid for some years before his death.

II John, born in 1700; died Mar. 6, 1727;
   probably unmarried.
III Timothy, born about 1703; baptized Dec.
   5, 1703; died Mar. 20, 1727.
IV Susannah, born in 1705; baptized May 4,
   1712; married Richard Sticknie, former
   husband of her sister Mary.
V Mary, born about 1707; married Richard
   Sticknie. She had at least four children:
   Mary, d. Feb. 12, 1736; Bethiah, d. Feb.
   13, 1736; Solomon, d. Mar. 1, 1736;
   Jonas, d. Oct. 14, 1758, æ. 18 years.
   Mary, "wife of Richard Stickney," died
   Nov. 20, 1745, after which Mr. Stickney married her sister, Susannah, as
   above, as appears by a deed mentioned
   below.
VI Hepzibah, born in 1709; baptized Mar. 4,
   1712; died Feb. 25, 1727.
VII Christien, born in 1713; baptized Oct. 13,
   1713; married Jonathan Warren, and
   lived until after 1751.

NOTE.—April 15, 1751, Richard Sticknie and wife
Susannah, and Jonathan Warren and wife Christien,
executed a deed of partition of 45 acres of land in
Stoughton, the wives being heirs of Robert Pelton,
deceased. (Town Records of Stoughton, Mass)
And here ends the male line in descent from John
Pelton², oldest son of John¹ of Dorchester.


**27. Samuel Pelton²**, second son of John¹, born at
Dorchester, Mass., about 1647; married (Mo. 5) May
16, 1673, by Mr. Stoughton, to Mary Smith, daugh-

ter of *John Smith, Quartermaster, of Dorchester; mariner. He lived in Dorchester down to about 1687 when, as appears by Bristol, R. I. (then Mass.), records, he lived there on the Mount Hope farm.† After the birth of three or more children, he went to Seekonk, Mass., and probably died there about 1713.

NOTE.—Much effort has been made, by searching family, church, town and county records of Seekonk, Rehoboth and Taunton, Massachusetts, to find the place and time of death of Samuel Pelton and his wife Mary all in vain, but as his name appears

---

* "John Smith, Quartermaster," as he was known in Dorchester, in 1630-35 was living at Foxteth Park, near Liverpool, England, under the ministry of Rev. Richard Mather. Mary, only child of John Smith and his first wife, Mary Ryder, was there born July 20, 1630. In April, 1635, the Smith and Mather families together journeyed to Bristol, whence they sailed May 23, 1635, for America. On the way to Bristol, young Nathaniel Mather, son of Rev. Richard, and Mary Smith, were borne by the same horse, each in a panier. They settled at Dorchester, where Smith soon lost his wife, and then married (2d) Mary ———, by whom he had several children, among them another Mary, who married Samuel Pelton, as above. (3) He married Widow Katherine Pelton, whose relationship to John Pelton[1] is unknown, and who survived him and died in Boston, July 17, 1710, æ. 92. Smith's will is dated December 30, 1676, and was proved July 25, 1678. He died September 17, 1676. (N. E. Gen'l Reg.) Extract from will mentions: "Wife Katherine and sons John and other children." "Whereas it is said my daughter Mary Smith hath received part of her portion, it is to be understood of my daughter Mary Pelton, who has received about twenty pounds or more, as by my books will appear, pg 166." "Lastly, as far as my daughter, Mrs. Mary Hinckley is concerned, she is paid what I promised her upon her marriage with Nathaniel Glover, as will appear by a writing under her hand and seal, bearing date, 1, 6, 1660. Therefore I do not give her anything in this my Will." Mary Smith (1) oldest daughter of John Smith, had married Nathaniel (born Prescott, Eng., 1630-31), son of Mr. John Glover. He died young (May 21, 1657), leaving three children, Nathaniel, John and Anna. Her hand was afterward sought by Gov. Thomas Hinckley, of Barnstable, Plymouth Colony. His suit was opposed by the Glovers on account of the difference in their ages, Mary 27, and he much older, the children of Mrs. Glover, three, and eight of his; with the added fact that she must remove to another colony. But after waiting some months and the signing by him of papers giving up all claim to her property they were married. Highly honored through life, she died at Barnstable, greatly regretted, July 29, 1703, æ. 73 years. (See Glover Memorial, p. 165.)

† This farm of 550 acres, sold in 1770, was described " as the farm on which Samuel Pelton lived."

in the land records of Suffolk county (Boston), Mass.,
in a deed of 1699, as of "Bristol, New England,"
and in a deed of 1713 as "of Seekonk, New England,'
and then disappears from those records, and is re-
placed by that of his son "Samuel and Sarah his
wife," of Nassau (Long Island), in the Province of
New York, in a deed dated May 24, 1714, it is
probable that Samuel, Sen., died in 1713 or 1714, in
the town of Rehoboth, or in Seekonk, Mass.

NOTE.— By Church Records of Dorchester Mary
Smith, "Samuel Pelton's wife, owned the covenant,"
Oct. 22, 1682.

Children, the first five born in Dorchester, Mass.,
the remaining three, (Bristol Records), in Bristol,
R. I.:

34      I Samuel, b. Jan. 26, 1675; m. Sarah ——;
          date unknown; d. date unknown.

      II Mary, born May 29, 1678; married, (Ded-
          ham Records), Dec. 12–24, 1712, Na-
          thaniel Colburn.  He seems to have
          removed soon after from the town and
          nothing is known of their fate.

      III Deliverance, born July 31, 1680; nothing
          further known.

55      IV John, b. Jan. 9, 1682; m. about 1705,
          Jemima ——; d. July 15, 1735.

161     V Ithamar, b. (probably May), 1686; m.
          unknown; d. previous to Apr. 25,
          1749.

162     VI Henry, b. Bristol, R. I., Dec. 10, 1690;
          m. Apr. 29, 1712, Mary Rose; d. 1763.

      VII Sarah, born Mar. 23, 1693, Bristol. R. I.,
          "Thursday, 10 o'clock, A. M.;" no other
          record.

513 VIII Benjamin, b. Bristol, Sept. 3, 1698; m.

5

—— Keziah ——; d. Hopewell, N. J.,
1775; wife in 1780.

NOTE.— Bristol Church Records give Robert "a
youth," baptized Apr. 30, 1687, and Susannah, Sept. 6,
1702. These were evidently children of his brother
John.


**21. Samuel Pelton**[4], first son of Samuel[3], John[1],
born at Dorchester, Mass., January 26, 1675 (erro-
neously registered as son of John); married Sarah
——; place, date and name unknown. Our knowledge of his life is, unfortunately, very meagre. It is,
however, known from the land records of Suffolk Co.,
Boston, Mass., that he lived for some time on Long
Island, N. Y., then called Nassau, where he and his
wife, Sarah, signed a deed of certain parcels of land
in Suffolk Co., Mass., May 24, 1714. Nothing is
known of the place or time of his death, which last
was probably at middle age. It is said that he lived
in or near Huntington, L. I., which is probable, his
youngest brother, Benjamin, having bought a house
and land there, in 1723. The maiden name of his
wife tradition says was Whiting, which is also probable, as relatives of that name, it is known, visited
her descendants in Connecticut. Diligent search
among the defective town records of Long Island
has brought no knowledge on these points or as to
the death of his wife Sarah.   Children :

35       1 Robert, born Feb. 13, 1716; married ——,
              1739, Martha Beachgood ; died May
              26, 1760.

NOTE.—As Samuel was probably married by 1700,
or soon after, it is more than probable that he had
several children before the birth of Robert.   This
opinion is confirmed by " An account of money laid

out for provisions for my Aunt Mary Pelton," running for some length of time, and found on the last page of an account book of his grandson, Samuel, now in possession of Wm. H. Pelton, of Warwick, N. Y., now 1892, living in Passaic, N. J.

1691981

**84. Robert Pelton**, only known son of Samuel³, Samuel², John¹, born near Huntington, Long Island, N. Y., February 13, 1716, whence he crossed over to Stamford, Conn., by or before 1739, as he, early in that year, there married Martha, daughter of John and Hannah Beachgood, of that place. Occupation, farmer and carpenter and joiner. Residence, Stamford, Conn., in that part of the township once known as Middlesex, now the township of Darien. He died May 26, 1760, as we find recorded in the account book, previously mentioned, of his son Samuel. Martha, his widow, previous to 1774 (at some time unknown), had married Joshua Lounsbury, and lived in North Castle, Westchester county, N. Y., where she died about 1820 or 1821, or later, at a great age; reputed by tradition to have been more than 100 years old. Children, born at Darien:

86 　I Samuel, b. Dec. 21, 1739; m. Feb. 7, 1763, Rebecca Holmes; d. Dec. 20, 1801.

　II Sarah, born Sept. 3, 1742, died in infancy.

　III Sarah, born June 19, 1744; married John Bell, of Darien; date of death unknown.

54 　IV William, b. last day of Feb., 1746-7; m. July 20, 1766, Catherine Smith; d. New York city, summer of 1810.

　V Richard, born, date unknown; living Sept. 1, 1774; died previous to May 4, 1786; said to have been named after Richard Lettridge, a friend of his father.

6

VI Hannah, born, date unknown; died before
Nov. 19, 1774.
VII Deborah, born April 4, 1759; died before
Aug. 20, 1766.

NOTE. — From the Land Records of Stamford we
find that Robert bought land, March 20, 1745--6, of
Thomas Youngs for £56, s. 13, d. 4 ; of Jas Scofield,
August 22, 1746, for £105 ; of Thomas Youngs, Oct.
3, 1746, for £200, 7, 6; of Daniel Lowden, Feb. 20,
1748 9, for £59 ; of Jonathan Selleck, May 13, 1749,
for £28 ; of Ezra Waterbury, Sept. 3, 1754, for £78 ;
and of the same, March 4, 1755, for £32, all of Stamford, Conn. His homestead descended to his son
Samuel and grand son Robert, who sold it to Samuel
Gorham, whence it passed to Mr. John T. Hecker, of
the milling firm of the Hecker Bros., New York, who
made it his summer residence until his death. Now,
1892, owned by his son, John V. Hecker.

The Pelton family burying-ground is near the barn.
It contains an expensive vault built by Mr. Hecker.


**85. Samuel Pelton**, first son of Robert⁴, Samuel³,
Samuel², John¹, born Stamford, now Darien, Conn.,
December 21, 1739; married there February 7, 1763,
Rebecca Holmes (born January 29, 1738--9), daughter of John and Rebecca (Bell) Holmes, of that place.
He was a carpenter and joiner and farmer. He lived
in Darien, and there died, December 20, 1801. He
was probably an Episcopalian, as his son John was
baptized in that church in Stamford. His wife Rebecca, in April, 1805, removed with her oldest living
son, John, to Warwick, N. Y., and there died, December 23, 1822, a favorite with all and an earnest
Christian woman. Children, born in Darien, Conn.:

    I Robert, born Jan. 4, 1764; died Aug. 28,
        1766, æ. 2 years, 7 months, 24 days.
28  II John, b. Feb. 28, 1766; m. (1) Nov. 7,
        1790, Deborah Fancher; (2) May 4,
        1831, widow Mary (Board) Denton; d.
        Warwick, N. Y., May 4, 1856.
    III Hannah, born July 1, 1768; died when
        about nine years old.
45  IV Robert, b. March 15, 1771; m. Oct. 28,
        1797, Mary Slauson; d. Jan. 18, 1869,
        æ. nearly 98 years.
    V Rebecca, born about 1773; died when
        about 15 years of age.
50  VI Samuel, b. Oct. 11, 1776; m. (1) Dec.
        23, 1797, Rachel Bates; (2) widow
        Hannah Woodruff, about 1839 or 1840;
        d. June 24, 1857.
    VII Richard, born May 24, 1779; died at
        home, Sept. 13, 1798, of yellow fever,
        contracted in New York city.

NOTE.— Samuel Pelton, his son Richard, and probably his two daughters, Hannah and Rebecca, as well as his father, Robert, and brother Richard, and, perhaps, a sister or two of Robert, lie buried in the "Pelton burying-ground," on the homestead in Darien now owned by John V. Hecker, of New York city and Darien. It contains a costly family vault built by Mr. John T. Hecker, deceased.

From an account-book of Samuel Pelton, owned by his grandson, William H. Pelton, now, 1892, of Passaic, N. J., and from the cover of a "Sum-book," used by his grandson, Henry Pelton, now owned by Samuel Pelton, of Warwick, N. Y., many of these names, facts and dates have been obtained. Not a person bearing the name of Pelton now lives in

Darien, Conn., neither a person of the name who
was born there.

**36. John Pelton[6]**, second son of Samuel[5], Robert[4],
Samuel[3], Samuel[2], John[1], born at Darien, township
of Stamford, Conn., February 28, 1766; married (1)
at Darien, November, 7, 1790, Deborah Fancher (b.
Dec. 12, 1763), daughter of Sylvanus Fancher and
his wife Priscilla Smith. She died, Warwick, N. Y.,
January 30, 1829. (2) In the church at Blooming
Grove, Orange Co., N. Y., May 4, 1831, Widow
Mary (Board) Denton (b. Aug. 5, 1768), daughter
of Joseph Board, of Boardville, Pompton, N. J., who
died November 12, 1853. Occupation in Connecticut a carpenter and joiner. April 10–13, 1805, he
removed with his family to Warwick, Orange Co.,
N. Y., sailing around through Long Island Sound
and up the Hudson river to New Windsor, in a sloop
owned and commanded by David Fancher. Here
he had bought a farm of Mr. Cornelius Lazear,
known as the "Vance farm" formerly owned by
John Vance, succeeded by his son, James Vance,
now occupied, 1892, by his grandson, William W.
Pelton. Here he was a prosperous farmer, an active
Christian elder for many years in the Dutch Reformed Church, a man highly respected for honor
and integrity in matters both of church and State.
And here he died May 4, 1856, over ninety years old.
Children, born in Darien, Conn., excepting the
youngest:

40        I Henry, b. Oct. 7, 1791; m. (1) Jan. 14,
           1815, Elizabeth Morehouse; (2) Apr.
           20, 1820, Elizabeth Johnson; d. July
           26, 1873.

II James, born May 17, 1794; served a term
in the War of 1812 with Great Britain,
and died at home in Warwick, N. Y.,
Dec. 13, 1814.

**45** III John, b. Jan. 2, 1797; m. Apr. 12, 1831,
Emeline Wright; d. June, 3, 1875.

IV Richard, born Dec. 23, 1798.   Grew up a
young man of ability, a general favorite,
and died in Warwick, N. Y., unmarried.
He was killed on his father's farm on an
island in Wawayanda Creek, Jan. 28,
1830, by the fall of a tree that he and
his brother John were felling.

V Hannah, born Feb. 11, 1801; married at
home, Nov. 3, 1830, John Kieran; lived
at New Milford, Orange Co., N.Y.   One
child, John P. Kieran, b. Jan. 24, 1832;
now, 1892, living in Newark, N. J.
Died at New Milford, N. Y., March
28, 1868; buried in Warwick cemetery.

VI Rebecca, born Jan. 19, 1803; married at
home, Warwick, N. Y., Jan. 6, 1825,
George Morehouse (b. Aug. 11, 1801; d.
June 14, 1873), son of Jeremiah and
Magdelene (Dill) Morehouse, of that
place; lived in Warwick; had 2 children,
Charles L., b. Oct. 9, 1825; m. Dec. 22,
1852, Julia A. Sanford; now, 1890,
living at Warwick, and Deborah Rebecca, b. Jan. 14, 1829; m. at Warwick,
Nov. 29, 1864, Charles R. Van Duzer;
d. there, Oct. 3, 1874.   Three children.
Rebecca died Jan. 18, 1829.

VII Polly (Mary), born Warwick, N. Y., July
8, 1805; married there, June 17, 1835, to

Charles Jackson (b. May 5, 1798), son of Michael Jackson, of Florida, Orange Co., N. Y., where she lived a well-known Christian woman, liked by all and there died Dec. 6, 1884, and was there buried Dec. 9, 1884. Mr. Jackson died Jan. 11, 1878.

NOTE.— Mrs. Jackson had no children, but adopted Deborah R., daughter of her sister Rebecca. She was remarkable for ardent, steadfast piety, a woman of great tact, and like her mother, a general favorite to the last with old and young, and like her father retained her interest in affairs of church and State as long as she lived.

**88. Henry Pelton**, oldest son of John[6], Samuel[5], Robert[4], Samuel[3], Samuel[2], John[1], born in Darien, Conn., October 7, 1791; removed with his father and family to Warwick, Orange Co., N. Y., he, with the hired man and cattle, crossing the Hudson at Fishkill, the remainder of the family coming around by water to New Windsor; reaching Warwick, Saturday, April 13, 1805. He there married (1) January 14, 1815, a near neighbor, Elizabeth Morehouse, daughter of Jeremiah and Magdalene (Dill) Morehouse, born November 8, 1792; died August 1, 1818. (2) At Warwick April 20, 1820, Elizabeth, daughter of Richard and Susannah (Sayre) Johnson of that place, born December 27, 1891; died there January 2, 1874. Occupations, teacher, carpenter and joiner, and after marriage a farmer. Lived in Warwick, N. Y., on the farm now (1892) owned by a Mr. Mabee. He was a prosperous farmer, an intelligent public-spirited man respected by all, a devoted Christian, long an officer, deacon and elder, and leader of the

choir in the Reformed Dutch Church in Warwick, a
pioneer in the temperance reform and active in every
good word and work as long as he lived. His
"Recollections of the Early Days, Religious and
Secular, of Warwick" are quoted in the last history
of Orange county, and are considered a standard
authority. He saw three churches stand on the site
of the Reformed Dutch Church, and helped to build
two of them. He lived on and attended to his farm
down to within a few weeks of his death, which
occurred July 26, 1873. Buried in Warwick cemetery. Children, born in Warwick, N. Y.:

    I Still born.

42    II Samuel, b. July 18, 1818; m. Dec. 25, 1844;
        Hannah B. Demarest.

42    III Jeremiah M., b. Sept. 1, 1821; m. May 5,
        1857, Sophia Amelia McEwen.

    IV Elizabeth Ann, born Feb. 9, 1824; married
        at Warwick, N. Y., Cornelius Henry
        Demarest, b. ——; d. Dec. 10, 1889,
        son of Cornelius C. and *Polly (Mary)
        Christie Demarest of Warwick. Mr.
        Demarest, a farmer, was long President
        of the Warwick Nat. Bank, an excellent
        upright Christian who served for years
        as an officer of the Reformed Dutch
        Church of Warwick. Children: (1)
        James, b. Aug. 29, 1846; d. Dec. 19,
        1846. (2) Charles M., b. Feb. 5, 1848;
        m. Oct. 5, 1870, Annie E. Armstrong;
        4 children. (3) Frederick, b. Jan. 19,
        1850; d. May 11, 1851. (4) DeWitt

---

* Mrs. Demarest was sister to Rev. John I. Christie, who for years was
pastor of the Reformed Dutch Church, Warwick, and belonged to the
Christies of near Fort Lee, N. J.

C., b. Feb. 18, 1852; m. Sept. 8, 1881, Hattie Hudson; 1 child. (5) Mary E., b. Apr. 29, 1854; m. Oct. 29, 1879, Christie Romaine; 4 children. (6) Henry P., b. Oct. 25, 1856; m. June 13, 1883, Ella J. Toland; 2 children. (7) Julia, b. May 29, 1858. (8) David, b. Feb. 27, 1860. (9) Annie, b. Apr. 24, 1862.

**40. Samuel Pelton**, oldest son of Henry⁷, John⁶, Samuel⁵, Robert⁴, Samuel³, Samuel², John¹, born July 18, 1818; married at Warwick, N. Y., December 25, 1844, Hannah B. Demarest, b. May 19, 1822, daughter of Frederic and Jemima (Brinkerhoff) Demarest of that place. Occupation, teaching (temporarily) and farming. Residence, 1890, Warwick, Orange Co., N. Y. Children, born at Warwick, N. Y.:

> I Anna, born Aug. 14, 1848.
> II Henry, born Feb. 12, 1864. In 1892, a farmer and surveyor at Warwick, N. Y.

**40. Jeremiah M. Pelton**, second son of Henry⁷, John⁶, Samuel⁵, Robert⁴, Samuel³, Samuel², John¹, born at Warwick, N. Y., Sept. 1, 1821; m. there May 5, 1857, Sophia Amelia McEwen, b. Dec. 5, 1835, in Ulster county, N. Y., daughter of Thomas Colden and Jane (Clark) McEwen of Warwick. Lived in Warwick, N. Y. Farmer, land surveyor and music teacher until December 31, 1856, when he removed to New York city, where he had had business interests during previous years. Occupation there a dealer in pianos and organs up to June 1, 1866, when he joined the organ manufacturing firm of Peloubet, Pelton & Co., of New York and Bloomfield, N. J., with which he

JEREMIAH M. PELTON.

J. M. Pelton

continued up to January 1, 1880, when he sold his interest in the firm to the remaining members thereof and resumed his old business, continuing it up to May, 1885. He has some reputation as a composer of music, principally vocal, sacred and secular.* In 1892 still living in New York city. Author of this work. Children, born in New York:

    I Julia Wisner, born north-east corner of Second avenue and East Nineteenth street, Mar. 22, 1860; married Nov. 12, 1886, to J. William Daniels, son of William Daniels of Brooklyn, N. Y. Two sons: (1) Frederic Knowlton, b. 4043 Sansom street, Philadelphia, Pa., Jan. 4, 1890. (2) Lester Clearman, b. Philadelphia, Pa., Nov. 17, 1891; d. June 22, 1892. Residence, 1892, Philadelphia, Pa.

    II Henry Colden, born north-east corner of Second avenue and East Nineteenth street, N. Y., Oct. 18, 1868. Graduate of Grammar School No. 70, of Columbia Grammar School, and of Columbia University School of Mines; Architectural division Class of 1889, stroke oar on University crew of '89; architect, living 1890, at 328 West Twenty-third street, New York city, place of business, 111 Broadway, Trinity building.

**38. John Felton**[6], third son of John[6], Samuel[5], Robert[4], Samuel[3], Samuel[2], John[1], born Darien, Conn., Jan. 2, 1797, removed to Warwick, N. Y., 1805; mar-

---

* Was one of the founders of the Orange County Musical Association, and an officer thereof until he left the county.

ried there, April 12, 1831, Emeline Wright, daughter
of William Wright and Jane (Blain) Wright, daughter of John Blain, of Warwick, and Ovid, N. Y.
Lived on his father's homestead, Warwick, N. Y.,
from 1805, to his death, June 3, 1875, respected by
all. Mrs. Pelton, born Ovid, N. Y., June 13, 1806;
died at Warwick, N. Y., July 24, 1885. Children,
born in Warwick, N. Y.:

> I James, born Feb. 8, 1832, lived with his
> father excepting for a short time in New
> York city; died at his father's, Warwick,
> N. Y., of consumption, Sept. 22, 1856.

**44** II Richard, b. March 27, 1834; m. Nov. 6,
1856, Margaret C. Rynus, of New York,
who d. Oct. 29, 1871, from an explosion
of naphtha. Living, in 1892, at Warwick, N. Y.; a farmer. No children.

**43** III William W., b. Dec. 15, 1837; m. Dec. 16,
1867, Almeda Knapp.

**44. William W. Pelton**, third son of John[7], John[6],
Samuel[5], Robert[4], Samuel[3], Samuel[2], John[1], born War-
wick, Orange Co., N. Y., Dec. 15, 1837; married at
Sugar Loaf, township of Chester, Orange Co., N. Y.,
Almeda Knapp, daughter of John and Maria
(Holbert) Knapp, of that place. Farmer. Residing,
in 1890, on the John Pelton homestead, Warwick,
N. Y. Children, born in Warwick:

> I John, born Sept. 11, 1868.
> II Grace, born April 24, 1870; married at
> home, Dec. 17, 1890, to Frank Holbert,
> son of Albert R., and wife Mary
> (Wisner) Holbert, of Warwick, N. Y.
> Residence, 1891, Brooklyn, N. Y.; one
> child, Remsen Wisner Holbert, b. Oct.
> 26, 1891.

III  Almeda, born July 9, 1875.
IV  Geraldine Hammond, born Sept. 17, 1877.

**86. Robert Pelton**[6], third son of Samuel[5], Robert[4], Samuel[3], Samuel[2], John[1], born Darien, Conn., March 15, 1771; married there, Oct. 28, 1797, Mary Slason or Slausen, daughter of Nathaniel Slason and his wife Lydia (Bates) Slason, of that place.  They were said at the time to have been the handsomest couple ever married in Darien.  Shoemaker and farmer.  He lived for a short time with his father and mother on the Pelton homestead in Darien, but finally sold it, and with his brother John and their families, removed to Warwick, Orange Co., N. Y., coming by sloop owned by David Fancher, in April, 1805, around by New York, from Darien on the Sound to New Windsor on the Hudson, and thence to Warwick, about twenty-eight miles.  He bought a farm of John Blain, and afterward lands of Nathaniel Blain and others, now, 1892, owned by the heirs of William M. Sanford, and there died, January 18, 1869, aged 97 years, 10 months and 3 days.  He was for many years an elder in the Reformed Dutch Church in Warwick, and an earnest supporter thereof.  His wife Mary, born May 27, 1778; died July 12, 1865.  Children, all but the first, born in Warwick, N. Y.:

    I Elias, born Darien, Conn., June 1, 1804; unmarried; a farmer; lived with his father in Warwick, N. Y., and there died, March 9, 1865.

**46**    II Nathaniel, b. May 11, 1807; m. (1) Nov. 24, 1831, Clarissa Strong ; (2) Jan. 26, 1836, Sarah Baird ; d. June 19, 1880.

    III Lewis, born June 1, 1810, millwright; died unmarried at his father's house, July 10, 1833.

     IV Sarah Ann, born Sept. 4, 1812; married at home, March 3, 1858, to David Fancher, of Brooklyn, E. D., N. Y., (died Sept. 21, 1867), son of Sylvanus Fancher, of Darien, Conn., and Warwick, N. Y.; died Brooklyn, E. D., March 19, 1881.

**47**    V James, b. Jan. 8, 1815; m. (1) Sep. 16, 1835, Ann A. Lobdell; (2) Abbie M. Hinsdale, widow, Sept. 5, 1855.

**48**    VI William Henry, b. Jan. 2, 1817; m. Jan. 22, 1840, Sarah Louise Hoyt.

     VII Elizabeth, born Jan. 7, 1820; married Warwick, N. Y., Oct. 18, 1838. William H. Anway, son of David Anway (sometimes called Nanny), of Amity, Warwick, N. Y. Lived for some time at Amity. He deserted her, and died unknown; afterward she lived respected in New York city for a long time, but died in Warwick village, Wednesday morning, June 13, 1888.

**50** VIII Francis, b. Jan. 28, 1823; m. Apr. 3, 1856, Elizabeth Jones.

**45. Nathaniel Pelton**, second son of Robert[6], Samuel[5], Robert[4], Samuel[3], Samuel[2], John[1], born Warwick, Orange Co., N. Y., May 11, 1807; married (1), Steuben Co., N. Y., November 24, 1831, Clarissa Strong, (born October 27, 1812; died November 12, 1832), daughter of Benjamin and Ann (Burt) Strong of Steuben Co., N. Y.; (2) January 26, 1836, at Warwick, N. Y., Sarah Baird. Lived in New York city and in Warwick, N. Y. Miller and farmer. Long an officer in the Reformed Dutch Church in Warwick. Died, Warwick, N. Y., June 19, 1880; his wife, Sarah Baird, died April 1, 1886.

**46. James Henry Pelton**, only child of Nathaniel⁷, Robert⁶, Samuel⁵, Robert⁴, Samuel³, Samuel², John¹,
born Warwick, N. Y., October 12, 1832; married (1)
New York, May 13, 1858, Sarah E. Ketchum, daughter of Ezra C. and Jerusha Ketchum, of New York,
who died, ——; (2) at Waterloo, N. Y., June 1,
1871, Mrs. Sarah P. (Fancher) Pomeroy, daughter
of William Henry Fancher (died March 29, 1887),
and his wife, Adelia (Crosby) Fancher (died December 27, 1885), of Waterloo, N. Y.  Occupation, the
clothing business.  Residence, 1892, Brooklyn, E.
D., N. Y.  Children, born in Brooklyn, E. D., N. Y.:

    I Sadie A., born Aug. 6, 1873.
    II James F., born Jan. 10, 1878.
**47** III William F. (adopted), b. Jan. 13, 1864;
       m. Sept. 29, 1886, Mamie G. Genung.

**47. William F. Pelton**, adopted son of James
H.⁸, Nathaniel⁷, Robert⁶, Samuel⁵, Robert⁴, Samuel³,
Samuel², John¹, born at Waterloo, N. Y., January 13,
1864; married at Waterloo, N. Y., September 29,
1886, Mamie G., daughter of Seth P. and Sarah Ge-
nung, of Waterloo, N. Y.  Child:

    I William Genung, born July 21, 1888.

**45. James Pelton**, fourth son of Robert⁴, Samuel³,
Robert⁴, Samuel³, Samuel², John¹, born at Warwick,
N. Y., January 8, 1815; married (1) at Sherburne,
Chenango Co., N. Y., September 16, 1835, Ann
A. Lobdell, daughter of John Lobdell, of that place,
(died April 18, 1853); (2) at Norwich, N. Y., Sep-
tember 5, 1855, Mrs. Abbie M. Hinsdale, daugh-
ter of Dr. Harvey Harris, of Norwich, N. Y.  Occu-
pation, farmer, livery-stable, horse dealer.  Lived in
New York, then in Sherburne, N. Y., and again in
New York; in 1892 in Brooklyn, E. D.  Child:

**47. Robert Hinsdale Pelton**, born New York,
June 7, 1857; married at Whitestone, Long Island,
N. Y., March 31, 1886, Irene Merritt, daughter of
Capt. I. J. Merritt, of that place, who died July 5,
1887, after an illness of one day; (2) in Brooklyn,
N. Y., Oct. 16, 1889, Miss Lillie L. Hazeldine,
daughter of Harvey Hazeldine, of New York city.
Occupation, bookkeeper and secretary.  Child:

> I Guy R., born at Whitestone, N. Y., Aug.
> 29, 1890.  Residence, 1892, White-
> stone, N. Y.

**45. William Henry Pelton**, fifth son of Robert[6],
Samuel[5], Robert[4], Samuel[3], Samuel[2], John[1], born
Warwick, N. Y., January 2, 1817; married Warwick,
N. Y., January 22, 1840, Sarah Louisa Hoyt (died
May 20, 1879), daughter of James and Lydia (Leeds)
Hoyt, of that place.  Farmer in Michigan and in
Warwick, bookseller and stationer, and long time
postmaster in Warwick.  In 1892, living in Passaic,
N. J.  Children, born in Warwick, N. Y.:

> 49   I Gideon H., b. Nov. 20, 1840; m. Aug. 23,
> 1865, Fannie Petty; d. Aug. 23, 1865.
> II Lydia L., born July 22, 1842; teacher; died
> Warwick, N. Y., Aug. 11, 1863.
> III Theodore F., born Aug. 27, 1844; died
> Apr. 24, 1845.
> IV Mary E., born Oct. 22, 1846; died at
> home, Sept. 24, 1865.
> 49   V Maurice Hoyt, b. Feb. 6, 1848; m. Jan.
> 15, 1873, Alvaretta Ogden.
> 50   VI Joseph H., b. Oct. 22, 1849; m. Mar. 29,
> 1877, Elizabeth Guthrie; d. Dec. 9,
> 1885.

VII Emily, born Mar. 28; 1855; married War-
       wick, N. Y., to Joseph H. Wright, son
       of James and Mary Wright, of Passaic,
       N. J.   Children: Wm. Pelton, b. Nov.
       14, 1883; Marie Louise, b. Apr. 14, 1886.
       Residence, 1892, Passaic, N. J.   Mr.
       Wright is manager in a large print
       works.

**48. Gideon H. Pelton**, first son of William H.[1],
Robert[6], Samuel[5], Robert[4], Samuel[3], Samuel[2], John[1],
born Warwick, N. Y., November 20, 1840; married
Moriches, Long Island, N. Y., August 23, 1865,
Fannie, daughter of John Pettie, of Moriches.   He enlisted August 21, 1862, and served in the 124th Regiment of New York Volunteer Infantry, from its
organization, July and August, 1862, in the Third
and Second Corps, to the time of its discharge at
the end of the war.   After his marriage he lived in
New York city until his death, September 28, 1867.
He was wounded at Gettysburg, July 2, 1863.   The
hardships of the service probably hastened his death.
Child:
       I Charles Gideon, born New York, Aug.
          7, 1867.
Mrs. Pelton married (2) January 31, 1877, Alanson Edwards, and in 1886, lived in Moriches, Long
Island, N. Y.

**48. Maurice Hoyt Pelton**, third son of William
H.[1], Robert[6], Samuel[5], Robert[4], Samuel[3], Samuel[2], John[1],
born at Warwick, N. Y., February 6, 1848; married
there, January 15, 1873, Alvaretta Ogden, daughter
of William L. Ogden, of Warwick.   Occupation,
hardware merchant.   Residence, 1892, Warwick,
Orange Co., N. Y.   Child:

I Louisa May, born Warwick, N. Y., May
21, 1875.

**48. Joseph E. Pelton**[7], fourth son of William H.[6],
Robert[5], Samuel[4], Robert[3], Samuel[2], Samuel[2], John[1],
born Warwick, N. Y., October 22, 1849; married
at Newburgh, N. Y., March 29, 1877, Elizabeth,
daughter of John Guthrie, of that place. Occupation, baggage-master on the railroad. Residence,
Newburgh, N. Y., where he died, December 9, 1885.
Children, none.

**45. Francis Pelton**[6], sixth son of Robert[5], Samuel[4], Robert[3], Samuel[2], Samuel[2], John[1], born Warwick,
Orange Co., N. Y., January 28, 1823; married
New York city, April 3, 1856, Elizabeth Jones,
daughter of Amos Jones, of that city. Residence, for
some years, Brooklyn, E. D. In 1892, Keyport, N. J.
Children, born in Brooklyn, E. D., N. Y.:

    I Mary E., born May 9, 1858.
    II Sarah E., } born Nov. 15, 1860; died Jan.
                30, 1861.
    III Lewis, } born Nov. 15, 1860; died Feb.
                25, 1861.
    IV Edwin H., } born Jan. 27, 1863.
    V George S., } born Jan. 27, 1863; died Jan.
                20, 1864.
    VI William J., } born Mar. 31, 1864; died
    VII Anna R., }
    VIII Amelia G., } Apr. 1, 1864.
    IX Clarence A., born May 27, 1865; died
        Nov. 1, 1866.

**46. Samuel Pelton**[5], fourth son of Samuel[4],
Robert[3], Samuel[2], Samuel[2], John[1], born Darien, Conn.,
October 11, 1776; married (1) Darien, Conn.,

December 23, 1797, Rachel Bates (b. May 3, 1775;
d. July 21, 1837), daughter of Charles Bates, of that
place; (2) about 1839 or 1840, Widow Hannah
Woodruff, of West Milford, N. J., at Penn Yan, N.
Y. Tailor; farmer. Lived at Sharon, Conn., thence
removed, first, to Penn Yan, N. Y., where he bought
a farm and lived for years; and, second, to New
Straitsville, Perry Co., O., where he died, June 24,
1857. Children:

      I Sons,  } born Feb. 5, 1799; died Feb. 5,
      II Twins, }    1799.
**51**  III Alfred, b. Oct. 11, 1802; m. Sept. 9, 1829,
          Eliza A. Lines; d. Mar. 28, 1875.
      IV Julia Ann, born Sharon, Conn., Sept. 9,
          1808; married Penn Yan, N. Y., ——,
          1838, to Alexander Cole; died Dec.
          10, 1867. Left 2 sons, George and
          Oscar, who lived at Prattsburgh, N. Y.
**52**  \ Linus Bates, b. Oct. 5, 1814; m. Sept. 23,
          1838, Hettie Maria Woodruff; d. Oct.
          15, 1877.


**56. Alfred Pelton**[7], third son of Samuel[6], Samuel[5],
Robert[4], Samuel[3], Samuel[2], John[1], born at Sharon,
Conn., October 11, 1802; married there, Sept. 9,
1829, Eliza A., daughter of Benjamin Lines, of
that place. Removed to Penn Yan, N. Y., thence to
Naples, N. Y., thence returned to Penn Yan, and removed to Green Bay, Wis., and finally to Omro, Wis.,
where he died, March 28, 1875. Occupation at Penn
Yan, Green Bay and Omro, a merchant; at Naples,
N. Y., a tanner. His family, in 1885, were still living at Omro, Wis. Mrs. Pelton died March 28,
1884. Children:

8

I Harriet, born Penn Yan, N. Y., Feb. 28,
1833; married Green Bay, Wis., Dec.
21, 1858, Capt. M. J. Meade.   One
child, John F., b. July 13, 1860.   Residence, 1892, Kaukauna, Wis.

II Julia, born Naples, N. Y., Feb. 3, 1835;
married Green Bay, Wis., July 21, 1853,
J. G. Beaumont, son of Dr. William
Beaumont (of physiological renown as
to digestion), of the U. S. army.   Children: 1. May, b. May 20, 1855; 2. William, b.July 14, 1857; 3. Douglass Irwin,
b. Sept. 2, 1859; 4. Ethan Allen, b. May
7, 1861; 5. Sophia, b. Nov. 18, 1863; 6.
Julia, b. Oct. 19, 1871. Residence, 1890,
Green Bay, Wis.

III Sophia, born Dec. 23, 1838; died July
22, 1857.

52   IV Charles, b. Mar. 24, 1844; m. Apr. 24,
1872, Maggie E. Sheppard.


**51. Charles Pelton**, only son of Alfred[7], Samuel[6],
Samuel[5], Robert[4], Samuel[3], Samuel[2], John[1], born
Penn Yan, N. Y., March 24. 1844; married. April
24, 1872, Maggie E. Sheppard.   Merchant, living,
1892, at Omro, Wis.   Children, none.


**50. Linus Bates Pelton**, second son of Samuel[6].
Samuel, Robert[4], Samuel[3], Samuel[2], John[1], born
Sharon, Conn., October 5, 1814; married Penn
Yan, N. Y., September 23. 1838, Hetty Maria (b.
May 23, 1814), daughter of Daniel Woodruff and his
wife Hannah (Tichenor), of West Milford, Passaic
Co., N. J.   He removed with his father's family to
Penn Yan, Yates Co., N. Y., thence to New Straits-
ville, Perry Co., O., where he died, October 15, 1877.

Farmer.  Children, the first three born in Penn Yan,
N. Y., the fourth in Uniontown, O.:

> I  Charlotte Louisa, born Sept. 1, 1839; mar-
> ried Logan Co., O., Nov. 21, 1869, John
> Mason, son of James Mason, of Waynes-
> burg, Pa.  One child, Hetty Maria, b.
> Sept. 24, 1870, m. Nov. 6, 1888, Silas
> C. Campbell.  Children: Mary L. and
> Wm. Mason.  Residence, 1878, Nelson
> Valley, O.
>
> II  Julia Ann, born Aug. 16, 1841; married
> Feb. 4, 1864, Benjamin F. Mark, who
> died at Rome, Ga., July 22, 1864; a mem-
> ber of the Veteran Corps of the 27th
> O. Vol. Inf'y.  In 1878, a widow, living
> with her mother at New Straitsville, O.;
> m. (2) Feb. 9, 1882, George Fluhart.
> Children: Maggie, b. July 11, 1884;
> Ellis, b. Apr. 21, 1886.  Residence,
> 1891, Pleasant Hill, Cass Co., Mo.
>
> III  Rachel Eliza, born Oct. 22, 1843; married
> in Logan Co., O., Nov. 27, 1866, John
> Deacon (d. at New Straitsville, O., Aug.
> 27, 1866), son of Nathan Deacon, of
> Gore, O.  One child, Mary Jane, b.
> Aug. 11, 1867.
>
> IV  Mary Ann, born July 28, 1846; married
> Uniontown, O., Sept. 20, 1866, Wm. H.
> Moore, son of Rob't Moore, of Lou-
> don Co., Va.  Residence, 1878 Fulton-
> ham, O.; 8 children: Daughter, d. day of
> birth;  Linus R.; Oscar W.; Frank H.;
> Lula E.; Fred. B.; Lillie Josephine, b.
> Feb. 21, 1883; Harrison Delmore, b.
> Feb. 10, 1885; d. Mar. 17, 1889.

**25. William Pelton**, second son of Robert[4], Samuel[3], Samuel[2], John[1], born Darien, Conn., "last day of February," February 28, O. S., 1746–7; married, New York, July 20, 1766, Catharine, daughter of Richard and Catharine Smith, of New York city. Shoemaker, and lived the latter part of his life in New York, and there died in the summer of 1810, having been a paralytic for sometime before his death. His wife Catharine, born October 4, 1747, O. S.; died August 23, 1806. Children, probably born in New York city:

    I Deborah, born Dec. 30, 1767; married Jacob Simonson, of New York city.

    II Catharine, born Mar. 20, 1768; died July 21, 1772.

    III Richard, born May 15, 1772; died Aug. 10, 1773.

    IV ——; still born.

    V Catharine, born July 28, 1776; died Sept. 14, 1777.

    VI ——; lived one month.

    VII Catharine, born June 15, 1779; married John Gilmore, of New York; died ——.

    VIII Martha, born Dec. 27, 1781; died June 27, 1788.

    IX Hannah, born Dec. 24, 1784; married New York, May 29, 1800, Peter* Chappel (died Oct. 8, 1828). Children: 1. William Pelton, b. Apr. 13, 1801; 2. Catharine, b. Nov. 28, 1807; d. July 5, 1841.

    X Martha, born Dec. 24, 1786; no further record.

---

* Peter Chappel married Frances Hutchinson, June 22, 1765. Made freeman of New York 1767. Is this the same Peter? Probably his father.

XI  Naomi, born Nov. 15, 1792; died Apr. 30, 1793.

NOTE.—William Pelton Chappell, son of Peter and Hannah (Pelton) Chappell, m. August 3, 1822, Maria Louise Howes, daughter of Kimball and Elizabeth Howes, of New York. Children: Eliza Jane, b. July 29, 1823; d. May 3, 1850; William Pelton, b. Sept. 6, 1825; d. Nov. 30, 1850; Alonzo, b. Mar. 1, 1828; artist, specialty, book illustrating. Residence, Middle Island, Suffolk Co., N. Y.; George, b. Jan. 1, 1830; John, b. Mar. 29, 1832; Still born; Jefferson, b. Aug. 20, 1840, lived a few months; Theodore, b. Sept. 1, 1842; Angelo, b. Dec. 9, 1845; d. in infancy.

**81. John Pelton**, second son of Samuel², John¹, born in Dorchester, Mass., January 9, 1682; married, probably, in the fall of 1705, Jemima, place, exact date of marriage and maiden name of wife unknown (though it was probably Johnson). He was probably married in or near Dorchester, as in Miss Larned's "History of Windham Co., Conn.," we find it recorded "that in 1706 John Pelton, Jeremiah Plymton and Charles and Paul Davenport, of Dorchester, Mass., bought lands and fences of Jeremiah Fitch in the southern part of CANTERBURY in that county." In 1708 John Leffingwell also sold them land. At what time he left Windham Co. is unknown, but he probably kept his interest there down to 1715, for on January 19 of that year (notwithstanding he had bought land and built a house in Haddam, Conn.), as we also learn from Miss Larned, he with Jeremiah Plymton and others of Canterbury and the sheriff, met at the house of Jabez Utter, to dispossess him of lands claimed by Capt. Jonathan Belcher, attorney

sale of his Haddam property, as above stated, he probably returned to Lyme, for on the day of that sale he in Lyme, March 28, 1719. bought land of Ebenezer Coleman.  He had previously, March 9, 1717-18, bought land in Lyme of Isaac Willey, being in this deed designated as of Groton, Conn.  Again, June 25, 1722, he bought land in Lyme, of Rich'd Ely; also of him, June 25, 1722, and of him, again, May 7, 1725, and February 7, 1728-29; in the last deed being designated as of Saybrook, Conn.

SAYBROOK.——On May 21, 1725, William Pratt sold several parcels of land for £250, to John Pelton, of Lyme, Conn.  February 2, 1725-6, Philip Shattuck and Margaret his wife, Quit-Claim the above lands to John Pelton, of Saybrook, Conn.; showing that he had removed to Saybrook.  The same day Pratt, Shattuck and wife convey land to John Pelton, of Saybrook.  March 16, 1727, "John Clark, Nathan Pratt, Hezekiah Buckingham and Samuel Willard laid to John Pelton, three pieces of land in *Pautopouge quarter."  Again in 1730, and in 1730-31, land was laid out to him.  In February 23, 1730-31, John Clarke and Thomas Starkey conveyed land to him.

MIDDLETOWN, Conn., in that part now Chatham and Portland.  The exact date of his removal to Middletown is unknown.  The land records show that on March 6, 1734, he bought of George Beck-with, 378 acres of land for £450; of the estate of Nathaniel Woodward, September 16, 1735, 200 acres for £236.  This last conveyance is a release by the School Commissioner to the heirs of John Pelton, of a mortgage on "School Lands" that he had bought; he having died July 15, 1735, as appears by the fol-

---

*Sometimes spelled Pautipaug.

lowing inscription on his tombstone, now standing in
the old graveyard in Essex, Conn. :

   "Here lieth ye body
  of Mr. John Pelton who
  departed this life July ye  .
   15, 1735 in ye 52 year
    of his age."

He died in the midst of a very active life, and in
the mature vigor of his mental powers. Careful
search has been made through his many land conveyances to find any mention of his occupation, but in
vain. It is probable that he was a carpenter and
joiner; a builder. Children, the first three born in
Canterbury, Conn., the birthplace of the others not
known with certainty:

  I Mary, born Oct. 21, 1706 ; married Middletown, Conn., Dec. 11, 1735, Thomas
   McCleve. Children: Robert, b. Aug.
   23, 1736; Thomas, b. Feb. 15, 1737–8;
   Josiah, b. Dec. 5, 1740. She d. Dec.
   12, 1740.

59  II John, b. Feb. 29, 1708; m. (1) Dec. 9,
   1731, Elizabeth Champion ; (2) March
   25, 1756, Martha Shipman; d. Jan. 29,
   1786.

227  III James, b. July 21, 1710; m. Jan. 14, 1735–6,
   Elizabeth Burr, d. ——, ——.

282  IV Phineas, b. probably about 1712; m. (1)
   May 22, 1740, Mary McKay; (2) unknown ; d. May 24, 1799.

307  V Johnson, b. ——, 1714; m. March 3, 1748,
   Keziah Freeman ; d. Dec. 13, 1804, æ.
   90. (Tombstone.)

   Was not *Johnson* named after his
  maternal grandfather?

330   VI Josiah, b. ——, 1714; m. about 1750, Hannah Churchill; d. Feb. 2, 1792, æ. 78. (Tombstone.)

      VII Jemima, born about 1715 or '16; married Jan., 1733, Gideon Buckingham (b. Feb. 22, 1708), son of Hezekiah and Sarah (Lay or Leigh) Buckingham, of Saybrook, Conn.; time of death unknown.

      VIII Sarah, born about 1717 or '18; married Jan. 18, 1738–39, Daniel Comstock, of Saybrook, Conn. Children: 1. Daniel S., b. Sept. 1, 1739; 2. Daniel, b. Sept. 30, 1740; 3. Asa, b. Mar. 6, 1742–43; 4. Sarah, b. Sept. 8, 1745; d. Saybrook, Conn., Sept. 20, 1745.

      IX Elizabeth, born about 1720. No other record.

      X Keturah, born about 1721. No other record.

352   XI Joseph, b. Apr. 15, 1722; m. Sept. 27, 1744, Anna Penfield; d. Dec. 31, 1804, æ. 83 years.

**55. John Pelton[5]**, first son of John[4], Samuel[2], John[1], born in Canterbury, Windham Co., Conn., February 29, 1708; married (1) Elizabeth Champion at Saybrook, Conn., December 9, 1731, who died December 5, 1755; (2) March 25, 1756, Martha Shipman, daughter of John Shipman, of Chester, Conn. He lived on his father's homestead at Saybrook (now, by division of Saybrook, in Essex), and there died, January 29, 1786, and was buried near his father in the old burying-ground at Essex, Conn., where his head-stone still stands, bearing the following inscription, viz.:

"In Memory of
Mr. John Pelton who died
Jan^y 29^th 1786
In his 81^st year."

His family record is in the possession of Tensard
D. Pelton, of Gustavus, Trumbull Co., Ohio.   Children, born at Saybrook, Conn.:

By the first wife :

        I  "Our first son was born Sept. 15, 1732;"
           died in infancy.

      II  Elizabeth, born Oct. 7, 1735;  died (Town
           Record) Feb. 2, 1750.

62  III  John, b. Nov. 27, 1735; m. about 1758,
           Abigail Miller; d. Apr. 17, 1819.

75  IV  Nathan, b. May 2, 1738; m. (1) Nov. 23,
           1763, Ruth Thompson; (2) Sept. 30,
           1790, widow Mary Waters; d. May 16,
           1813.

94    V  Ithamar, b. Nov. 22, 1740; m. Asenath
           Pratt, about 1764; d. Mar. 16, 1826.

      VI  Lucy, born Mar. 5, 1743; died (Town
           Record), May 2, 1748.

158  VII  Josiah, b. Aug. 15, 1745; m. (1) Dec. 10,
           1767, Mary Griswold; (2) Aug. 20,
           1811, widow Chloe Gilder; d. Sept. 3,
           1818.

164  VIII  William, b. Dec. 2, 1747; m. about 1790,
           Lois Harvey; d. May 25, 1825.

     IX  Eliza, born Feb. 26, 1749; no further
           record; probably married Robert Den-
           nison, of Essex, Conn.

      X  Lucy, born Sept. 11, 1752; married (1)
           Oct. 7, 1779, William Miller, Jr., who

died Nov. 2, 1795; children, six; (2) date, and name unknown.

XI Sarah, born Jan. 2, 1755; died in infancy.

By the second wife:

188 XII Joseph, b. Nov. 25, 1756; m. about Nov., 1778, Prudence Pelton; d. June 15, 1837.

XIII Ruth, born Jan. 17, 1758; married Chatham, Conn., Theophilus Lord, of Lyme, Conn. In 1876, a daughter, Mrs. Lucy Luther, over 90 years old, lived in Hadlyme. One of Mrs. L.'s daughters married a Mr. Morgan, and their son, Dr. Morgan, in 1876, lived in Middletown, Conn.

XIV Martha, born Aug. 24, 1759; married about 1784, John Pelton, her cousin, son of Josiah Pelton, of Chatham, Conn.; died at Springwater, Livingston Co., N. Y., Feb. 16, 1846.

XV Priscilla, born Sept. 10, 1761; married Middletown, Conn., Mar. 27, 1782 (Middletown Records), Timothy Butler. Children, five. Lived in New Hartford or Harwinton, Conn.

203 XVI Phineas, b. Dec. 5, 1763; m. May 6, 1784, Margaret Tucker; d. Mar. 5, 1847.

XVII Sarah, born Jan. 1, 1766; married Middletown, Conn., Mar. 3, 1785, Samuel Simmons, Jr., and removed to Lyme, N. H.; died Monroe, N. H., Aug. 21, 1862. A daughter, Mrs. Polly Ward, lived Hanover, N. H., in 1875. Mrs. S. used to say that she had two troubles and a half: her Joseph was lame, the old grey goose was dead, and she was out of snuff.

**213** XVIII Jonathan, b. May 21, 1768; m. about 1789,
　　　　　Elizabeth Baker; d. Dec. 3, 1850.
　　　XIX Elizabeth, born Oct. 5. 1771; married
　　　　　——— Benjamin Tucker, an able farmer,
　　　　　of New Hartford, Litchfield Co., Conn.,
　　　　　and there lived and there died.  Her
　　　　　descendants still live in New Hartford.
**220** XX David, b. Dec. 30, 1773; m. June 15.
　　　　　1796, Lucy Stone; d. Aug. 22, 1821.
**226** XXI Israel, b. Apr. 1, 1775; m. about 1807,
　　　　　Lois Wright; d. Mar. 20, 1830.
　　　XXII Jemima, born Aug. 3, 1779; married
　　　　　Essex, Conn., Sept. 24, 1801, Russell
　　　　　Post, of that place (who was born there,
　　　　　Sept. 13, 1778).  Lived in Essex, and
　　　　　there Mr. Post died Nov. 8–13. 1876;
　　　　　his wife, Jemima, having died in 1852.

NOTE.— April 24, 1733, Ebenezer Brockway conveyed lands in Essex. to John Pelton, Jr. January 16,
1733-4. Abraham Andrews conveyed land to the
same. Dec. 17, 1736, he bought land of Hezekiah
Buckingham.  Again Nov. 18, 1737, of William
Parker, and April 25, 1738, of John Clarke. June 17,
1731. he records the marks that shall designate his
cattle, and again January 6, 1747–8.  On September
12, 1749. he was admitted a freeman, etc., etc.

After John Pelton's death, his widow married Dr.
Jos. Bishop, of Saybrook, whose first wife was widow
Keturah (Mott) Parker, widow of Captain Abner
Parker, of Saybrook. Mrs. Bishop, second, died sud-
denly; date unknown.


**53. John Pelton**. second son of John[4], John[3],
Samuel[2], John[1]. born Saybrook, now Essex, Conn.,
Nov. 27, 1735; married about 1758, Abigail Miller, of

Rocky Hill, Hartford Co., Conn. Removed to Chatham, now Portland, Conn., where he lived, and there died, April 17, 1819. His wife, as appears from public records, died April 3, 1812. Occupation shipbuilding, at the yard lately owned by Sylvester Gildersleeve. He was short and stout, and of florid complexion. Children, probably born at Portland:

63  I John, b. 1765; m. (1) Jerusha Sage; (2) widow Chapman; (3) Sally (Warner) Pelton, widow of his brother William; d. Nov. 8, 1826, æ. 61.

  II Elizabeth, born April 3, 1767; married Luther Matson, of Glastonbury, Conn.; lived at Eastbury, Conn., and there died, Oct. 8, 1813.

  III Lucy, born ——; married May 14, 1801 (Ch. Rec.), Edmund Matson, of Glastonbury, Conn. No children. Died in the house where she was born, Portland, Conn.

73  IV William, b. ——, 1775 (bapt. March 19, 1775); m. Sally Warner; d. Oct. 8, 1813.

  V Jonathan, born ——; died June 8, 1790. (Ch. Rec.)

  VI Nathan, born ——, 1771; baptized June 2, 1771 (Rec. 1st Cong. Ch., Portland); probably died young, as we find no further record of him.

NOTE.—The records of this family are quite fragmentary and uncertain as to the order of births. It is probable that other children were born and died in infancy, the records of which have not been found.

63. **John Pelton**, first son of John⁵, John⁴, John³, Samuel², John¹, born Chatham, now Portland, Conn.,

about 1765; married (1) Jerusha Sage, about 1785 or 1786 (died April 3, 1812). sister of Mrs. Marshall Pelton, of Portland, and daughter of Lemuel Sage, of Middletown, Conn.: (2) widow Chapman; (3) Sally (Warner) Pelton, widow of his brother William. Lived at Portland, Conn., and there died, "Nov. 8 1826, aged 61." Children, born at Portland:

By his first wife:

      I Clarissa, born Sept. 19, 1787; married Aug. 27, 1815, Jeremiah Button, son of William Button, of Norwich, Conn. (b. Oct. 2, 1791; d. June 2, 1861.) Children: Lorinda, Egbert O., Cleveland and Jeremiah P., the last living, 1878, in Portland, Conn. Lived in Portland, and there died, June 5, 1861.

      II Betsey, born Oct. 16, 1790; married Alvin Brainard, son of Asa Brainard. of Haddam, Conn. Lived at Haddam, and there died, May 12. 1834. Children, 7. A son, Asa Atwood Brainard, lived at Higganum, Conn., in 1878.

      III Philena, born Sept. 15, 1789; married Aug. 10, 1812, Buckley Goodrich, son of Fredc Goodrich, of Glastonbury. Conn. Lived at Glastonbury and at Hunter, N. Y., where she died Jan., 1875–6; 7 children, 3 sons and 4 daughters.

65    IV Jonathan, b. July 30, 1794; m. Amy Goodrich. Nov. 17, 1812; d. Apr. 1, 1836.

68    V Orin, b. Apr. 24, 1797; m. (1) Sarah Fuller; (2) Elizabeth Matson, Aug. 12, 1830; d. Nov. 1, 1854.

70    VI Halsey, b. Oct. 14, 1800; m. (1) Jan. 22,

1827, Adeline Tracey; (2) Apr. 5, 1831, Julia Curtis; d. June 30, 1878.

**71** VII Samuel S., b. Dec. 9, 1805; m. July 10, 1830, Lydia Norton; d. 1857.

VIII Jerusha, born 1808; married Dec. 23, 1827, Wm. P. Button. Lived at South Glastonbury, Conn., and there died, Sept. 28, 1859. Children: Lucy A., Lavinia M., William W., and two that died in infancy.

**71** IX Roderick, b. Oct. 10, 1808; m. (1) Feb. 9, 1835, Nancy A. Wilcox; (2) Laura M. Wilcox, July 6, 1843; d. Oct. 11, 1871.

Children of Sally Warner Pelton, the second wife having had none.

X Catharine, born about 1817. Lived with Mr. Warner.

XI Lucy Ann, born about 1819; married June 19, 1838, Joseph Curtiss, of Berlin, Conn. Lived in Syracuse, N. Y., when last heard from.

XII Frances Mary, born about 1821; unmarried. Lived at New Haven, Conn.; died about 1860, at the house of her brother, Halsey Pelton, in Pewaukee, Wis.

Catherine, Lucy Ann and Frances Mary were baptized Oct. 20, 1822. (Ch. Rec.)

**62. Jonathan Pelton**, first son of John, John, John, John, Samuel John, born at Portland, Conn., July 30, 1794; married November 17, 1812, Amy Goodrich, who died January 1, 1838. He lived at Portland and here died, April 1, 1836. Children, born at Portland:

I Samantha, born Aug. 8, 1813; married
Portland, Dec. 30, 1830, Daniel Potter.
II Clarissa Matilda, born Feb. 28, 1815;
married Portland, Herman Hough, of
Meriden, Conn., July 4, 1839.
III Emily Elizabeth, born May 29, 1817;
married Aug. 21, 1842, Alexander
Houston, of Hartford, Conn.; died Feb.
22, 1855.
66   IV Charles, b. July 20, 1819; m. Feb. 14, 1843,
Sarah Goodrich.
67   V Reuben G., b. Aug. 17, 1822; m. May 23,
1850, E. A. Woodbridge.
VI Maria, born Aug. 25, 1825; married Jan.
18, 1854, Hayneth Porter Hansom.
Lived in Covington, Ky., where she
died, Jan. 29, 1876; left a daughter.
VII Amy Ann, born Oct. 25, 1828; married
Sept. 1, 1846, F. B. Moss.

**65. Charles Pelton**, first son of Jonathan[7], John[6],
John[5], John[4], John[3], Samuel[2], John[1], born Portland,
Conn., July 20, 1819; married Salem, Pa., Feb. 14,
1843, Sarah Goodrich. Living, in 1890, in Salem,
Wayne Co., Pa. Mrs. Sarah Pelton died December
9, 1889. Children:
67   I Franklin, b. Sept. 9, 1844; m. May 31,
1866, Mary Adelaide Walker.
67   II Florence, b. July 13, 1848; m. Oct. 28,
1869, Jane E. Walker.
67   III Leroy J., b. Sept. 12, 1852; m. Oct. 1,
1879, Olive J. Nash.

**66. Franklin Pelton**, first son of Charles[8], Jonathan[7], John[6], John[5], John[4], John[3], Samuel[2], John[1], born at Salem (Hamlinton P. O.), Wayne Co., Pa., September 9, 1844; married there, May 31, 1866, Mary Adelaide Walker (b. April 12, 1846), daughter of William J. Walker, of Binghamton, N. Y. Occupation, merchant. Residence, in 1890, at Moscow, Luzerne Co., Pa. Children, none.

**66. Florence Pelton**, second son of Charles[8], Jonathan[7], John[6], John[5], John[4], John[3], Samuel[2], John[1], born at Salem (Hamlinton P. O.), Wayne Co., Pa., July 13, 1848; married there, October 28, 1869, Jane E. Walker, born November 25, 1850, daughter of Sabrinus Walker, of Hamlinton, Pa. Residence, in 1890, Moscow, Pa. Occupation, merchant. Children:
    I Ella M., born Aug. 18, 1870.
    II Clair W., born May 18, 1884.

**66. Leroy J. Pelton**, third son of Charles[8], Jonathan[7], John[6], John[5], John[4], John[3], Samuel[2], John[1], born at Salem (Hamlinton P. O.), Wayne Co., Pa., September 12, 1852; married, Bethany, Pa., October 1, 1879, Miss Olive J. Nash, daughter of John Nash, of Hamlinton, Wayne Co., Pa. Residence, 1890, Hamlinton P. O., Pa. Child:
    I Homer, born June 29, 1883.

**65. Reuben G. Pelton**, second son of Jonathan[7], John[6], John[5], John[4], John[3], Samuel[2], John[1], born Portland, Conn., Aug. 17, 1822; married, Salem, Pa., May 23, 1850, Miss E. A. Woodbridge, daughter of William Woodbridge, of that place. Living, 1890, at Portland, Conn. Farmer. Child:

I Mary Augusta, born July 1, 1853; married
Portland, Conn., July 2, 1882, Edward
F. Bigelow, publisher and printer, b.
Colchester. Conn., Jan. 14, 1860, son of
Wm. S. Bigelow, of that place. Chil-
dren: Nellie P., b. Mar. 12, 1883; Wood-
bridge Fuller, b. Sept. 2, 1885; Flora,
b. May 22, 1890. Residence, in 1890,
Portland, Conn.


**68. Orin Pelton**[6], second son of John[6], John[5],
John[4], John[3], Samuel[2], John[1], born Portland, Conn.,
April 24, 1797; married (1) September 9, 1818, Sarah
Fuller; (2) August 12, 1830, Elizabeth Matson,
daughter of John Matson, of Thetford, Vt. Stone
mason; died, Glastonbury, Conn., November 1,
1854. Children :
          I Harriet, born July 13, 1819; married Dec.
               30, 1838, Reuben Tryon. Lived, 1876,
               Glastonbury, Conn. One child then
               living, Elizabeth A., b. July 13, 1848; m.
               to James Carter.
         II Jerusha S., by 1st wife, born Oct. 9,
               1827; died Oct. 18, 1827.
        III Daughter of 2d wife, born Feb. 13, 1832;
               died Feb. 15, 1832.
68   IV Leroy Delos, b. July 14, 1833; m. (1)
               Nov. 11, 1856, Isabel S. Hilliard; (2)
               Aug. 19, 1867, Mary H. Kenyon.


**68. Le Roy Delos Pelton**[7], only son of Orin[6],
John[6], John[5], John[4], John[3], Samuel[2], John[1], born South
Glastonbury, Conn., July 14, 1833; married (1)
Evanston, Ill., November 11, 1856, Isabel S., daughter

of James Otis Hilliard, of Middletown, Conn.; (2) August 19, 1867, at Hartford, Conn., Mary H. Kenyon, daughter of Sprague Kenyon, of that place. Dentist at Hartford, Conn., removing in April, 1880, to Oakland, Cal., and there died, April 24, 1891. Children :

> I Louis Courtland, b. June 23, 1859; m. Dec. 24, 1890, Agnes Stewart.
> II Jennie Theresa, born Oct. 8, 1861; married about 1882, Harry J. Armstrong; one daughter, Dorothy P. (b. July 12, 1889; died Dec., 1889); died May 15, 1890.
> III Ward Leroy, b. June 3, 1863 ; m. Mar., 1889, Mamie King.

**68. Louis Courtland Pelton**[9], first son of Leroy D.[8], Orin[7], John[6], John[5], John[4], John[3], Samuel[2], John[1], born South Glastonbury, Conn., June 23, 1859. Lived in Hartford, Conn., until nineteen years of age, then in Chicago, Ill., for some years, and in 1891 in New York city, where he married December 24, 1890, Miss Agnes Stewart, daughter of Robert D. Stewart, of Scotland. Printer. Residence, 1891, New York. As an athlete, middle-weight wrestler he won six matches, was never defeated, and stood ready to meet any middle-class wrestler in the State of New York.

**68. Ward Le Roy Pelton**[9], second son of Leroy D.[8], Orin[7], John[6], John[5], John[4], John[3], Samuel[2], John[1], born, Hartford, Conn., June 3, 1863. Lived in Hartford, removed to Oakland, Cal., in April, 1880; married there, March 5, 1889, Miss Mamie King, of Oakland. Occupation, the boot and shoe trade. Residence, in 1891, Oakland, Cal.; address, 1005 Broadway. Child:

I Edith Theresa, born at Oakland, Cal.,
Nov. 30, 1889.

**69. Halsey Pelton**, third son of John⁶, John⁵,
John⁴, John³, Samuel², John¹, born Portland, Conn.,
October 14, 1800; married (1), January 22, 1827,
Adeline Tracey, who lived only about eight months;
(2) April 5, 1831, Julia Curtiss, daughter of Jeptha
Curtiss, of Erie, Pa. Lived in Cleveland, Ohio,
and removed to Pewaukie, Wis., where he lived,
and there died, June 30, 1878. Occupation in Wisconsin, a manufacturer of lime. Children:

  **70**   I Edgar R., b. Jan. 10, 1832; m. Kate Peffer,
      Mar. 5, 1857.

  **70**   II William Halsey, b. Sept. 2, 1840; m. Nov.
      11, 1868, Eliza M. Brown.

  **71**   III Milo C., b. June 10, 1845; m. Aug. 29,
      1872, Helen L. Payne.

     IV Julia A., b. Apr. 16, 1847; at home, 1876.
     V and VI died in infancy.

**70. Edgar R. Pelton⁷**, first son of Halsey⁶, John⁵,
John⁴, John³, John², Samuel², John¹, born in Cleveland,
Ohio, January 10, 1832; married March 5, 1857, Kate
Peffer, daughter of George P. Peffer. Engineer.
Residence, 1876, Cincinnati, Ohio. Children:

     I Edgar H., born Oct. 21, 1858.
     II Ida E., born Cincinnati, O., Oct. 5, 1860.

**70. William Halsey Pelton⁷**, second son of Halsey⁶, John⁵, John⁴, John³, John², Samuel², John¹, born
September 2, 1840; married November 11, 1868, Eliza
M., daughter of Thomas Brown. Manufacturer of
lime. Residence, 1876, Pewaukee, Wis. Children:

     I Minnie J., born Oct. 13, 1869.
     II Annie J., born Dec. 11, 1872.

**76. Milo C. Pelton**, third son of Halsey[7], John[6], John[5], John[4], John[3], Samuel[2], John[1], born June 10, 1845; married August 29, 1872, Helen Payne, daughter of George Payne. Residence, 1876, Pewaukee, Wis. Manufacturer of lime. Children:

    I Helen M., born Oct., 1873.
    II Infant son, born and died Mar., 1875.

**62. Samuel R. Pelton**, fourth son of John[6], John[5], John[4], John[3], Samuel[2], John[1], born Hartford, Conn., December 9, 1805; married, Cleveland, Ohio, July 10, 1830, Lydia Norton Clothier. Died, Elyria, Ohio, 1857. Children:

    I Adeline J., born Sept. 4, 1832; died Nov. 20, 1834.
    II John B., born July 28, 1834; died 1853.
    III Charlotte, born Dec. 7, 1835; married Elyria, Ohio, June 10, 1852, Peter De Vries. Children of Mr. De Vries in 1876, lived in East Toledo, Ohio. 1. Mary, b. Apr. 28, 1853; m. Gale Ozier, Oct. 13, 1875; 2. John W., b. Dec. 20, 1859.

**63. Roderick Pelton**, fifth son of John[6], John[5], John[4], John[3], Samuel[2], John[1], born Portland, Conn., Oct. 10, 1808; married (1) Nancy A. Willcox, February 9, 1835, at Girard, Pa.; (2) July 6, 1843, Laura M. Willcox at Manchester, Pa., daughters of Perley I. Willcox, of Girard, Pa. Lived at Erie, Pa., and there died, October 11, 1871. Marble cutter. Children:

**73**    I Edward Livingston, b. Feb. 10, 1836; m. Apr. 21, 1864, Henrietta Ferguson.

**72**    II Roderick Jarius, b. Manchester, Pa., Aug.
31, 1837; m. Sept. 26, 1876, Frances
Louisa Kerr.

III Lucy Ann, born Aug. 27, 1839; married
Apr., 1864, Philip Honecker.  Residence, Erie, Pa.   Children: Charles A.,
b. May 19, 1865; Harrison H., b. Nov.
21, 1866; Laura May, b. June 12, 1869.

IV Charles Edwin, born at Erie, Pa., May 8,
1844; served in the War of the Great
Rebellion, in Company I, 83d Regiment of Pennsylvania Volunteers.

**71. Edward Livingston Pelton**[7], first son of
Roderick[6], John[6], John[5], John[4], John[3], Samuel[2], John[1],
born at Manchester, Erie Co., Pa., February 10, 1836;
married at Erie, Pa., April 21, 1864, Henrietta Ferguson, daughter of John Ferguson.   Occupation, dealer
in marble and granite.   Residence, in 1891, at Erie,
Pa.   Children, born at Erie, Pa.:

I Frank Edward, born Feb. 20, 1865.
II Joe Livingston, born Nov. 4, 1867.
III George, born Mar. 25, 1870; died Apr. 17,
1871.
IV Jay Roderick, born Sept. 20, 1872.
V Roy Ramsay, born May 22, 1876.
VI Ruth Maria, born Aug. 16, 1878.
VII Scott Blinn, born July 21, 1881.
VIII Grant, born Apr. 1, 1885.
IX Ward Cleveland, born Aug. 27, 1888.

**71. Roderick Jarius Pelton**[7], second son of
Roderick[6], John[6], John[5], John[4], John[3], Samuel[2], John[1],
born at Manchester, Erie Co., Pa., August 31, 1837;
married at St. Thomas, Ont., September 26, 1876,

Frances Louisa Kerr, of that place. Occupation, accountant, assistant auditor for the Michigan Central Railroad Co. at St. Thomas, Ont. Residence at St. Thomas, Ont. Children:

    I Frank Kerr, born July 26, 1877.

    II Harry Lee, born Oct. 22, 1883; died Dec. 11, 1884.

**62. William Pelton**, second son of John⁵, John⁴, John³, Samuel², John¹, born Portland, Conn., March, 1775 (baptized March 19, 1775, Ch. Rec.); married Sally Warner at Portland; shipbuilder. Lived at Portland, and there died suddenly, October 8, 1813 (October 6, 1813, by Ch. Rec.) Children, born at Portland:

**72**    I Nathan W., b. Sept. 18, 1799; m. Dec., 1818, Abigail Coleman.

    II Sarah, born ——, 1801; died May ——, 1823.

NOTE.— Mrs. William Pelton, above, married (2) her husband's brother John, as his third wife. (See page 64).

**72. Nathan W. Pelton**, only son of William⁶, John⁵, John⁴, John³, Samuel², John¹, born, Portland, Conn., September 18, 1799; married December 2, 1818, at Wethersfield, Conn., Abigail Coleman, daughter of Elisha Coleman; cabinet-maker. Lived at Wethersfield, Conn.; died there, February 4, 1884. Children, born in Wethersfield:

    I Hannah C., born Apr. 7, 1820; married Sept. 21, 1847, Daniel P. Bunce, of Waterbury, Conn. No children.

    II Elizabeth A., born Aug. 13, 1822; married Dec. 1, 1841, Philo S. Newton.

Residence, 1876, Hartford, Conn. Children: Annie Coleman, who married Dr. G. F. Hawley, Hartford, Conn., and Philo Woodhouse. Mr. Philo S. Newton died May 2, 1891.

III Sarah Maria, born Apr. 21, 1824; married Mar. 5, 1847, Isaac Sheals. Children: Charles D. and Ida E. In 1876, a widow, living at Wethersfield.

74    IV William H., b. Dec. 31, 1826; m. Apr. 24, 1851, Nancy A. Holden.

V Harriet D., born Oct. 20, 1828; married Jan. 25, 1856, Stephen Willard. Children: Stephen, Hattie, Mary, Eliza, Martha. Living, 1876, at Forestport, N. Y.

VI Mary F., born Dec. 24, 1840; married Wethersfield, Nov. 12, 1879, John G. Belden, son of Lathrop Belden, of that place. Residence, 1880, at Wethersfield.

**73. William H. Pelton**, only son of Nathan W.[7], William[6], John[5], John[4], John[3], Samuel[2], John[1], born Wethersfield, Conn., December 31, 1826; married April 24, 1851, Nancy A. Holden, daughter of Eber Holden, of Rocky Hill, Conn.; cabinet-maker. Residence, 1878, Rocky Hill, Conn. Children, born at Rocky Hill:

75    I William A., b. Apr. 20, 1853; m. Sept. 12, 1877, Miss Harriet A. Lyne.

II Fannie L., born Feb. 25, 1855; married at Brooklyn, N. Y., July 3, 1881, George F. Gill, son of George Gill, of Worcester, Mass. Residence, 1891, Philadelphia, Pa.

III Chauncey, born May 19, 1859.
75   IV Henry F., b. July 16, 1862; m. Oct. 24,
       1889, Anna M. Fischer.


**73. William A. Pelton**, first son of William H.[7],
Nathan W.[6], William[5], John[4], John[3], John[2], Samuel[2],
John[1], born at Rocky Hill, Conn., April 20, 1853 ;
married at Clinton, Conn., September 12, 1877, Miss
Harriet A. Lyne, daughter of Henry A. Lyne, of that
place.   Occupation, superintendent for Wilcox Silver
Plate Co., Meriden, Conn., where he resides, in 1891.
Children :
        1 Clifford Lyne, born Dec. 28, 1878.
        II Albert Lewis, born Feb. 1, 1881.


**74. Henry F. Pelton**, third son of William H.[7],
Nathan W.[6], William[5], John[4], John[3], John[2], Samuel[2],
John[1], born July 16, 1862, at Rocky Hill, Conn.; mar-
ried October 24, 1889, at Fort Douglass, Utah, Miss
Anna M. Fischer, daughter of Francis Fischer, of Salt
Lake City, Utah.   Address, 1891, Fort Douglass,
Utah.   Children :
        I William Henry, born March 4, 1891, in
          Utah.


**59. Nathan Pelton**, third son of John[4], John[3],
Samuel[2], John[1], born at Saybrook, Conn., May 2, 1738;
married (1) Nov. 23, 1763, at East Windsor, Conn.,
Ruth Thompson, daughter of James and Janet (Scott)
Thompson, of that place (b. June 1, 1740; d. June 21,
1789); (2) September 30, 1790, widow Mary Waters,
of Chatham, Conn (b. January 1, 1760).   His occupation was that of a shipsmith and farmer.   He is said
to have removed to E. Windsor about 1768, he having
bought land of Ebenezer Watson, April 28, of that
11

year. He and his brother Ithamar went up the Connecticut river together. Each built a house in E. Windsor. Both still stand. He again bought land in E. Windsor in 1771, and frequently afterward, both bought and sold. He died there, May 16, 1813.

Nathan was a sturdy scion from a sturdy puritan stock, both in mind and in body, and was honored in Church and in State. He ruled his house sternly, as the following anecdotes, told by his great-granddaughter, Mrs. Emily P. Miller, whose father and mother were both grandchildren of Nathan, will show:

"One evening his children, or grandchildren, had for visitors their cousins Phelps, and making more noise in their fun than the old gentleman thought proper, he left his bed and severely reprimanded them.

"On another occasion a dance being in progress in the neighborhood, he suspected that a son and daughter had gone there. He went to see, and finding them, took them home for the night as he thought, but they having inherited a fair share of their father's spirit, after all was quiet, returned to the dance and saw it out."

He attended church with utmost regularity, regardless of wind or weather, and from Saturday night to Sunday night, the New England Sabbath, scarcely allowed a word above a whisper in his house. He was not a favorite with the young, but was always a thoroughly reliable man.

He was of light complexion with light hair, and was short of stature, with broad shoulders and short neck and legs; characteristics of the early New England Peltons. Many stories are told of their great strength. This of Nathan, of East Windsor: That an anchor was to be moved, and men with oxen and a cart were gathered to do the work. He told them that if they would place the anchor on his shoulder he would carry it to the required place. They did so, and he carried it without difficulty, but the pressure burst his good cow-hide shoes.

The Peltons, both in England and America, are patriotic citizens and good fighters, both by land and sea, as is shown by the records of the various wars of this country and England.

At the beginning of the campaign of 1759, of the "Old French war," Nathan and his brother Ithamar were members of Capt. Peleg Redfield's Co. (1st Lt. George Nettleton; 2d, Abraham Pyler; Ensign, Edward Shipman), who joined the forces of Gen. Amherst, and served through the campaign. In 1760, Captain Redfield again served with his company. (Redfield Fam. History.)

The Family Bible of Nathan is in the possession of his grandson, Enoch Pelton, South Windsor, Conn.

It is said that in early life, Nathan Pelton, in Middletown, Conn., was connected in business with John Harper, a man of Scotch-Irish descent, who had married Miriam Thompson, daughter of James Thompson, of Windsor, Conn., another Scotchman; that Miriam's sister Ruth, while visiting her, met Mr. Pelton, who afterward married her. They, in time, removed to Windsor, where they became permanent residents, while John Harper went to New York State, bought 250 acres of land and founded Harpersfield in Delaware county. He was an associate of Sir William Johnson and Jos. Brant. In the Revolutionary War, Col. John Harper, commanding at Fort Schoharie, was warned by Brant of coming danger in time to save the lives of himself and family, even though his house was burned and the village destroyed. (See Jay Gould's History of Delaware Co., and also Stiles' History of Windsor, Conn.)

Children, probably all, or all but the first, born in East Windsor, Conn.:

**70** I *Nathan, b. Oct. 16, 1764; m. about 1789, Hannah Pease; d. June 7, 1856.

II Elizabeth, born Aug. 20, 1766, East Windsor, Conn.; married Nov., 1788, Daniel Phelps (d. March 21, 1854, in his 91st year), son of Noah Phelps, of Enfield, Conn. Lived East Windsor, Conn., and there died, Jan. 30, 1890. Children: Ruth, Noah, Hannah, Betsey, Daniel, Mary, James, Charlotte, William.

III Ruth, born Sept. 19, 1768; married Dec. 30, 1812, Daniel Phelps (widower of her sister, Elizabeth). Residence, East Windsor ; died Apr. 9, 1850. No children.

**85** IV Enoch, b. Aug. 7, 1770; m. Dec. 23, 1803, Sarah Matilda Buchanan; d. in 1829.

**86** V John, b. July 29, 1772; m. Jan. 1, 1797, Eunice Beebe; d. Mar. 31, 1864.

VI Lucy, born Nov. 7, 1774; married Dec. 12, 1797, Obadiah (b. Feb. 24, 1767), son of Noah Phelps, of Enfield. Children: Lucy, Diah, Charlotte, Elihu, Noah, Julia, Emily, William. Lived at Turin, Lewis Co., N. Y., and there died, Oct. 13, 1863.

VII James, 1, born Aug. 9, 1776; died July 19, 1778.

*Chatham Ch. Rec. says Aug. 24, 1766, but this is probably the date of his baptism.

     VIII James, 2, b Oct. 20, 1778; m. (1) Apr. 20, 1806, Clarissa Watson; (2) July 7. 9, 1812, Sophia Gaylord; (3) Feb. 16, 1834, Betsey Wolcott; d. Feb. 4, 1870.

     IX Sarah, born Oct. 12, 1780; married about 1798, Levi Terry (b. May 12, 1770; d. Mar. 19, 1836, at Floyd, Oneida Co., N. Y.), son of Ebenezer Terry, of Enfield, Conn. Children, nine: Sally, Julia, Nancy (m. Jason Ellsworth, whose first wife was Mary, dau. of Daniel and Elizabeth [Pelton] Phelps), Levi, Diantha, Hiram, Henry, Emily, Samuel. Lived Floyd, Oneida Co., N. Y. Died at Gerry, Chautauqua Co., N. Y., Aug. 27, 1869.

     X Joseph, born June 30, 1782; died Apr. 11, 1787.

**75. Nathan Pelton**[6], first son of Nathan[5], John[4], John[3], Samuel[2], John[1], born October 16, 1764, probably at Chatham, Conn.; married about 1789, Hannah Pease, daughter of Robert Pease, of Somers, Conn. Blacksmith and farmer. Lived at East Windsor and Somers, Conn., Whittingham, Vt., and about 1800 went to the "Black River Country," to West Leyden, Lewis Co., N. Y., where he was one of the first settlers, and where he lived and there died, June 7, 1856. His wife, Hannah, died of cancer, in Lee, Oneida Co., March 22, 1831; buried at West Leyden. He was a good man and, before a church was built in the neighborhood, held religious services in his own house. Children:

     I Sophronia, born E. Windsor, Conn., Feb.

8, 1791; married Sept. 7, 1812, Enos
Kent, son (probably) of Benjamin Kent
of Leyden, N. Y.  Lived there and
died Jan. 10, 1871.  Mr. Kent died
Sept., 1841.  Children, eight.

II Abiah, daughter, born Somers, Conn.,
June 14, 1792; married Feb. 20, 1811,
Solomon, son of Jeduthan Higbee, of
Turin, Lewis Co., N. Y.  Lived there
in 1879.

80  III Joseph, b. Nov. 20, 1793; m. May 1, 1816,
Mary Pelton; d. Spring of 1887, æ. 94.

82  IV Nathan, b. May 3, 1796; m. about 1820,
Amanda Barnes; d. Jan. 7, 1870.

V Hannah, born Whittingham, Vt., Aug. 15,
1798; married about 1816, David, son
of Heman Merwin, of Turin, N. Y.
Lived in Genesee Co., N. Y., and there
died, June, 1833.  Children, seven.

82  VI James, b. Mar. 2, 1801; m. Aug. 27, 1826,
Elizabeth Markham; d. Feb. 17, 1878.

VII Erastus, 1, born Dec. 24, 1806; died when
about 8 months old.

VIII Lucy, born Apr. 22, 1810; unmarried and
lived, 1879, at W. Leyden, N. Y.

83  IX Erastus, 2, b. Sept. 2, 1811; m. Oct. 20,
1832, Elmira P. Hunt.

X Sally, born Jan. 26, 1815; died Jan. 29,
1815.


**79. Joseph Pelton**, first son of Nathan, Nathan,
John, John, Samuel, John, born Somers, Conn.,
November 20, 1793; married East Windsor, Conn.,
May 1, 1816, Mary (his cousin), daughter of John
Pelton (p. 78), of that place.  Lived after marriage

about ten years in Lewis Co., N. Y., on a farm adjoining his father's, then in Connecticut, in Lancaster, Pa., in Tennessee, in Ohio, in Lansing, Mich., and in 1879 at Spring Mills, White Co., Tenn. Farmer. Died, Sparta, White Co., Tenn, in the Spring of 1887, aged 94.    Children:

> 1 Emily, born at E. Windsor, Conn., in the house of her grandfather, Nathan Pelton, Jan. 18, 1817; married Oct. 18, 1842, at Philadelphia, after having taught four years in Schaefferstown, Lebanon Co., Pa., to Geo. F. Miller, merchant, of that place (son of Frederick and Catherine Miller), who died Jan. 14, 1877. After marriage, at the general request, she taught a long time at Schaefferstown successfully, and was in every way an able and excellent woman. She died there, May 14, 1887. Children: 1. Thomas V., b. Oct. 3, 1843; 2. George Frederic, b. Feb. 28, 1845; d. Aug. 23, 1850.
>
> II Mary, born W. Leyden, Lewis Co., N. Y., Oct. 3, 1823; married (1) Schaefferstown, Pa., Sept., 1841, Wm. G. Renner, of that place; three children; (2) Mr. Walker. Lived, 1879, Spring Mills, White Co., Tenn., where Mr. Walker died. Supposed to have gone with her mother to live with her aunt, Mrs. Drake, her mother's sister, at Pittsford, Monroe Co., N. Y., 1889.
>
> 82 III Joseph Henry, b. Dec. 25, 1826; m. Dec. 23, 1853, Elizabeth Jane Cook.

**76. Joseph Henry Pelton**, only son of Joseph⁷, Nathan⁶, Nathan⁵, John⁴, John³, Samuel², John¹, born West Leyden, Lewis Co., N. Y., December 25, 1826, married Polk Co., Tenn., December 23, 1853, Elizabeth Jane, daughter of Joseph Cook, of Madisonville, Monroe Co., Tenn. Occupation, market gardener. Residence, 1889, Nashville, Tenn. Children:

    I Emily Effie, born Sept. 30, 1854.
    II James Oliver, born Feb. 28, 1858; died Feb. 4, 1864.
    III John Watson Beebe, born May 1, 1863.
    IV Alice Raines, born Dec. 14, 1864.
    V Maud, born Oct. 28, 1866.
    VI Ida, born Mar. 5, 1869; died Apr. 10, 1869.
    VII William McMurray, born Dec. 3, 1874.

**78. Nathan Pelton**, second son of Nathan⁶, Nathan⁵, John⁴, John³, Samuel², John¹, born Whittingham, Vt., May 3, 1796; married West Leyden, N. Y., about 1820, Amanda, daughter of Col. John Barnes, of that place. Carpenter and builder. Lived at Somerset, Hillsdale Co., Mich., and there died, Jan. 7, 1870. Mrs. Pelton born Jan. 17, 1799; died Oct. 4, 1872. Children:

    I Fidelia, born about 1821; married Stephen Giddings. Was living Mar., 1879.
    II Philena, born 1826; married Mr. Westcott. Living Mar., 1879.
    III Eleanor, born 1842; died Aug. 17, 1876, at Wheatland Centre, Hillsdale Co., Mich.

**79. James Pelton**, third son of Nathan⁶, Nathan⁵, John⁴, John³, Samuel², John¹, born West Leyden, Lewis Co., N. Y., March 2, 1801; married Turin,

N. Y., August 27, 1826, Eliza, daughter of Ebenezer Markham, of Turin. Shoemaker. Lived at Turin until 1861, when he removed to Holland, Ottawa Co., Mich., where he died February 17, 1878. Mrs. Pelton in 1884 married (2) Mr. L. M. Wilson, and lived, 1891, at Belleview, Mich. Children:

      I Abraham, born about 1828 or 1830, Turin, N. Y.; unmarried 1879; farmer in Holland, Mich. In 1891 still unmarried at Holland, Mich.

**79. Erastus Pelton**, fifth son of Nathan[6], Nathan[5], John[4], John[3], Samuel[2], John[1], born West Leyden, Lewis Co., N. Y., Sept. 2, 1811; married there, October 21, 1832, Elmira P. Hunt, daughter of Darius Hunt, of that place. Farmer. Mrs. Pelton died March, 1863. Residence, 1879, West Leyden, N. Y. Children:

82    I William, b. Oct. 4, 1833; m. Phœbe Money.
      II James, 1, born 1836; died 1839.
83    III James, 2, b. 1839; m. Miss Webb.
      IV George, born Feb., 1841. No return. Supposed to live in Michigan.

**82. William Pelton**, first son of Erastus[7], Nathan[6], Nathan[5], John[4], John[3], Samuel[2], John[1], born West Leyden, N. Y., Oct. 4, 1833; married about 1858–9, Phœbe, daughter of Solomon Money, of Rome, N. Y. Farmer. Residence, in 1879, Lee, Oneida Co., N. Y. Children:

      I Herbert, born Aug., 1860.
      II Charles, born July 28, 1866.

**83. James Pelton**, third son of Erastus[7], Nathan[6], Nathan[5], John[4], John[3], Samuel[2], John[1], born West

12

Leyden, N. Y., ——, 1839; married ——, Miss ——
Webb, but separated from her.　No report; supposed
to live, 1879, in Michigan.

**75. Enoch Pelton**, second son of Nathan[5], John[4],
John[3], Samuel[2], John[1], born East Windsor, Conn.,
August 7, 1770; married at Alexandria, Va., Dec. 23,
1803, Sarah Matilda Buchanan, daughter of a sea
captain, who died at sea.　Cabinet-maker at Alexandria, Va., where he died of cancer in the throat in
1829.　His widow died in Pittsburgh, Pa., July 15,
1852.　Mr. Pelton made the coffin for Gen. George
Washington.　A piece of the wood from which it was
made is still preserved in the family.　He was a very
quiet, benevolent man.　A French refugee was sup-
ported by Mr. Pelton for some years until his death
occurred.　Children, born Alexandria, Va.:

> I William, born Nov. 22, 1805; died at sea
> 1825, and was buried at Hampton
> Roads, Va.
>
> II Mary, born Oct. 10, 1807; married Oct.
> 10, 1825, Thomas G. Prettyman,* of
> Lewistown, Del. (b. Mar. 25, 1787; d.
> Washington, D. C., Dec. 11, 1857).
> Children, seven, three sons and four
> daughters.　Lived, 1875, Washington,
> D. C., with her daughter, Mrs. Dr. Jas.
> B. Moore.
>
> III Enoch, 1, born Jan. 29, 1808; died Dec.
> 15, 1808.
>
> IV Ruth Ann, born Oct. 15, 1809; died 1824.
>
> V James, born Aug. 5, 1811; died Washing-
> ton, D. C., 1831.
>
> VI Adaline, born Aug. 23, 1813; in 1875 un-

---

* Upholsterer for Baltimore & Ohio RR. Co.; claimed inventor of the
American swinging railroad truck.

married and lived in Whitehall, Greene
Co., Ill.

VII Enoch, 2, born Nov. 26, 1815.   He was
a saddle-and-harness-maker; went to
Texas and returned home; started again
in 1837 for Texas; was last seen in St.
Louis, Mo., and is supposed to have
died about 1843.

VIII Elizabeth, born Nov. 19, 1817; unmarried.
In 1875 she was living, Washington,
D. C., in the family of Geo. W. Riggs,
banker.

85   IX Lorenzo, b. Aug. 25, 1819; m. Oct. 17,
1844, Mary Ashcome.

X Joseph, born Mar. 11, 1822; died from
lock-jaw, produced by the kick of a
horse, in 1833.

XI Sarah, born Mar., 1824; died 1826.

XII, XIII Two others, that died in infancy;
no record.


**84. Lorenzo Felton**, sixth son of Enoch[6], Nathan[5], John[4], John[3], Samuel[2], John[1], born Alexandria,
Va., August 25, 1819; married Pittsburgh, Pa., Oct.
17, 1844, Mary Ashcome, daughter of James Ashcome, of St. Mary's Co., Md.   Shoe manufacturer,
1892, Louisville, Ky.   Children:

I Sarah, born Dec. 10, 1845; died Dec. 14,
1847.

II Lorenzo, born Feb. 8, 1848.

III Joseph, born July 17, 1850; died Oct., 1853.

IV Rebecca Adeline, born Apr. 27, 1853;
died Sept. 18, 1872.

86   V William Alfred, b. Aug. 31, 1855; m. Oct.
2, 1877, Mattie A. Bray.

VI Stella, born Aug. 26, 1859; married at
home, Feb. 8, 1876, to Henry A.
Mooney, farmer, Bardstown Junction,
Ky.

VII Cora, born Mar. 14, 1862.

VIII Carrie May, born Feb. 27, 1865; married
Mar. 15, 1888, to William V. Wolf, son
of Andrew Wolf of Elsas, Germany.
One child, William Cecil, born Nov.
11, 1889. Residence, in 1892, Louisville, Ky.

IX Virginia Lee, born Sept. 18, 1867; married Sept. 15, 1886, to Thomas E. Buck.
son of Ervin O. Buck, of Pine Bluff,
Ark., where she resides, in 1892. Children: 1. Cora Lee Buck, born Nov. 7,
1887; 2. Mildred Aline, born Apr. 19,
1891.

X Jesse Clay, born Oct. 24, 1870.

**85. William Alfred Pelton**, third son of Lorenzo, Enoch, Nathan, John, John, Samuel, John,
born Pittsburgh, Pa., August 31, 1855; married
October 2, 1877, Mattie A. Bray, daughter of John
and Elizabeth Bray, of Lebanon, Marion Co., Ky.
Children, none reported.

**75. John Pelton**, third son of Nathan, John,
John, Samuel, John, born East Windsor, Conn.,
July 29, 1772; married there, January 1, 1797, Eunice
Beebe (born December 12, 1777), daughter of Chris-
topher Beebe (who served seven years in the Revo-
lutionary war, and died two years after its close), of
New London, Conn. Farmer. Lived at Bissell's
Ferry, East Windsor, Conn., and died March 31,
1864, at Pittsford, Monroe Co., N. Y. He removed

from Connecticut in 1852 and to Pittsford, N. Y., in 1857.   Children:

  I Mary, born E. Windsor, Conn., Dec. 15, 1797; married there, 1816, Joseph Pelton, son of Nathan, of W. Leyden, N. Y.  Children, three.  (See Joseph Pelton, p. 80.)  Resided, 1879, with her daughter, Mrs. Miller, Schaefferstown, Pa.; in 1889, went to her sister, Mrs. Susan Drake, Pittsford, Monroe Co., N. Y.

87  II Austin, b. Dec. 2, 1801; m. (1) Jan. 21, 1822, Charlotte Pelton; (2) Lucy (Roberts) Williams.

  III Susan, born at her grandfather's, Nathan Pelton, E. Windsor, May 25, 1807; married there, Apr. 9, 1828, Elihu A. Drake (b. E. Windsor, Apr. 10, 1804; d. Pittsford, Monroe Co., N. Y., May 10, 1888), son of Gideon and Annie (Allen) Drake of E. Windsor.  One child, Elihu A. Drake.  Residence, 1889, Pittsford, Monroe Co., N. Y.


**86. Austin Pelton**, only son of John[6], Nathan[5], John[4], John[3], Samuel[2], John[1], born East Windsor, Conn., December 2, 1801; married (1) January 1, 1822, his cousin, Charlotte Pelton, daughter of Ithamar Pelton, his father's brother, of Middlefield, Mass., who died August 27, 1834; (2) Lucy (Roberts) Williams, widow, of Hartford, Conn.  Farmer.  Living, 1889, East Windsor Hill, Conn.  Children, born East Windsor Hill, Conn.:

88  I Christopher B., b. May 14, 1822; m. Feb., 1845, Mary J. Rockwell; d. Jan. 15, 1891.

89    II John Thompson, b. Sept. 9, 1824; m. Jan.
           24, 1847, Mary Bulkley.
90    III Rufus Austin, b. Oct. 14, 1826; m. (1)
           Nov. 30, 1848, Elmina Manley; (2)
           Aug. 25. 1850, Julia A. Edson; (3) Mary
           Beebe; (4) Hattie E. (Gibbs) Pierce;
           d. Mar. 8, 1873.
       IV Eunice, 1, born June 26, 1828; died Apr.
           26, 1829.
        V Eunice, 2, born July 22. 1830; married
           Aug. 27, 1850, E. Windsor, Henry
           Frost (b. Oct., 1830), son of Salmon
           Frost, of E. Windsor. Farmer. Chil-
           dren: Williard M., Angeline, Ada E.
       VI Abigail C., born Aug. 27, 1832; married
           at Windsor, Aug., 1855, Allen Blodgett
           (b. Jan. 17, 1816). son of Elihu Blod-
           gett of E. Windsor. Farmer, 1879,
           Windsor Hill, Conn.   Children: Arthur
           A., Annie W., Jennie A.
   By second wife:
      VII Hudson N., born ———.   Clerk, 1890,
           Ayslum street;   residence,   Francis
           street, Hartford Conn.   No report.
     VIII Alice, born ———.   No report.
       IX Benjamin F., born ———.   No report.


**87. Christopher E. Pelton**[8], first son of Austin[7],
John[6], Nathan[5], John[4], John[3], Samuel[2], John[1], born
East Windsor, Conn., May 14, 1822; married there,
February, 1845, Mary J. (born in 1826), daughter of
Samuel Rockwell and Harriet Hitchcock, of East
Windsor. Conn.   Farmer, living, in 1876, in East
Windsor, Conn.   Died at Enfield. Conn., January
15, 1891.   Children, born in East Windsor, Conn.:

89      I George S., b. Nov. 18, 1845; m. Oct.
            20, 1879, Jennie Grant.
       II Edward B., b. Mar. 16, 18, 1847; m. in
            Rochester, N. Y.
      III Elvira H., born May 5, 1852; married
            Richard A. Alexander, Jan. 29. 1870.
       IV Ernestine M., born Aug. 7, 1856; married
            Lewis C. Jacobs, Feb. 20, 1884.

86. Rev. George S. Pelton[5], first son of Christopher B.[4], Austin[3], John[6], Nathan[5], John[4], John[3], Samuel[2], John[1], born East Windsor, Conn., November 18, 1845; graduate of Amherst College 1872, of Hartford Theological Seminary 1877; married East Saginaw, Mich., Oct. 20, 1879, Jennie Grant, daughter of Eugene and Charlotte Grant, of Glyndon, Minn.   Has preached in Glyndon, Minn., 1877–1880; Deadwood, So. Dak., 1880–1883; Omaha, Neb., 1883–1886; Worcester, Mass., 1886–1889; in Higganum, 1889 to date, 1890.   Children, none.

87. John Thompson Pelton[6], second son of Austin[5], John[6], Nathan[5], John[4], John[3], Samuel[2], John[1], born East Windsor, Conn., September 9, 1824; married there, January 24, 1847, Mary (b. Jan. 12, 1825), daughter of Chauncey Bulkley, of Manchester, Conn. Carpenter.   Residence, 1879, Hazardville, Conn. Children:

            I Charlotte Starr, born Nov. 12, 1848; married Apr. 5, 1872, Charles Leonard Thompson (b. Aug. 5, 1848), son of Rev. Charles T. Thompson (Baptist minister), of Maidstone, Kent, Eng. Residence, 1879, Hazardville, Conn. Children: Leonard Charles, b. Feb. 1, 1874; Grace Elizabeth, b. Oct. 1, 1877.

II Olive Mary, born Mar. 19, 1854; married
Aug. 12, 1876, John C. Stephens. Tool-
maker, 1879. One child.

III Grace Greenwood, born July 8, 1856;
married Nov. 7, 1875, Jonathan M.,
son of Jonathan Reed, of Higganum,
Conn. In 1879 lived at Higganum.
Children: George, b. Apr. 19, 1877;
Clarence, b. Aug. 16, 1878.

**57. Rufus Austin Pelton**[7], third son of Austin[6],
John[6], Nathan[5], John[4], John[3], Samuel[2], John[1], born
East Windsor Hill, Conn., October 14, 1826; married
(1) at Stafford, Conn., November 30, 1848, Elmina
Manley; (2) August 25, 1850, at Stafford, Julia A.
Edson; (3) ——, Mary Beebe, daughter of Elias
Beebe, of Waterbury, Conn.: (4) November 26, 1868,
Mrs. Hattie E. (Gibbs) Pierce (b. Nov. 15, 1826),
daughter of Hiram B. Gibbs, of Goshen, Conn. A
painter. Died Waterbury, Conn., March 8, 1873.
He was about 5 feet 4 inches high, thick set, with
brown hair and blue eyes. Children:

By first wife, none.

By second wife:

I A son, that died in infancy.

II A son, that died young.

By third wife:

III Estelle, born Oct. 20, 1854.

IV Myron C., born at Hartford, Conn., Sept.
8, 1856; married at East Hampton,
Mass., Sept. 27, 1878, Mattie Alice
Bush, daughter of Joseph Bush, of
Florence, Mass. Farmer. Lived, in
1879, at Westhampton, Mass.

V Cora, born ——; no record.

     VI Carrie, born ——; no record.

    VII, VIII Twins, born ——; died in infancy.

    IX Frank, born —— ; no record.

By fourth wife:

       X Arthur Burton, born May 1, 1871; died Jan. 22, 1872.

**75. James Pelton**, fifth son of Nathan[5], John[4], John[3], Samuel[2], John[1], born East Windsor, Conn., October 20, 1778; married there, (1) April 20, 1806, Clarissa Watson, daughter of Robert Watson, of East Windsor, born ——, 1786; died March 27, 1807; (2) July 7, 9, 1812, Sophia Gaylord, daughter of Abiel and Mehitabel (Prior) Gaylord, of South Windsor, born July 22, 1793; died November 16, 1824; (3) February 16, 1834, Widow Betsey (Wolcott) Bissell, daughter of Ephraim Wolcott, who died August, 1851. Residence at East Windsor and South Windsor, Conn. Died at the latter place, February 4, 1870.

NOTE.—The family Bible of Nathan and James is in the possession of Mrs. S. W. Rockwell, of East Windsor Hill, Conn. Children:

By first wife:

       I Clarissa, born Feb. 27, 1807; married (1) in Vermont, Jas. Trumbull, Jr., son of Jas. Trumbull, of East Windsor, Conn. Lived in Vermont and in South Windsor, Conn.; removed to Joliet, Ill., and to St. Charles, Mo.: six children, one of them, a son, John Trumbull; (2) —— Brown; (3) —— Brown; died Feb. 11, 1873.

By second wife:

93    II Enoch Watson, b. Feb. 7, 1813; m. Apr. 21, 1856, Harriet Ellsworth King.

13

III  Harriet Frances, born Oct. 20, 1814; married East Windsor, Conn., Mar. 30, 1834, Daniel G. Sperry (b. July 4, 1807), son of Alfred Sperry, of Bethany (now Woodbridge), Conn.  Residence, 1889, E. Windsor Hill, Conn.  Children: 1. Harriet Sophia, b. Jan. 30, 1837; m. Nov., 1875, Edward P. Trumbull, son of James Trumbull and Clarissa Pelton; 2. Sarah Frances, b. Feb. 9, 1839; d. May 1, 1852; 3. Gilbert Daniel, b. Mar. 15, 1841; served in a regiment of Illinois cavalry; d. in the service in Forsyth, Mo., May 12, 1862; 4. Edla Elizabeth, b. June 5, 1843; graduated from the Woman's Med. Coll., Philadelphia, Pa., 1871; served there in hospital, 1871-2; then in the maternity in Paris, France; practiced in Pittsburgh, Pa., 1872-80; d. E. Windsor Hill, Conn., Oct. 5, 1880; 5. Martha Amelia, b. July 24, 1845; 6. Lewis Parsons, b. Jan. 23, 1848; graduated from Amherst Coll. 1873; admitted to Hartford Co. bar 1875; member Legislature 1876; first coroner, Hartford, 1885; m. Nov. 7, 1878, Elizabeth Ellsworth Wood, dau. Dr. Wm. Wood, of E. Windsor Hill, Conn.; 7. Cornelia Bradley, b. Mar. 18, 1851; 8. Ruth Thompson, b. July 4, 1854.

94  IV  Henry Thompson, b. Dec. 4, 1816; m. May 27, 1845, Susan Buckley.

V  James Bennett, born Dec. 13, 1819; died Sept. 7, 1821.

VI Martha Sophia, born Nov. 20, 1823; married Aug. 26, 1847, East Windsor Hill, Conn., Dr. Sidney Williams Rockwell, son of Nathaniel Rockwell, of that place, where they lived in 1889. Children: 1. James Pelton, b. May 11, 1848; 2. Sarah Charlton, b. Mar. 12, 1855; d. Aug. 24, 1855; 3. Anna Gaylord, b. Dec. 24, 1857.

By third wife:

VII James Bennett, born Dec. 4, 1834; in 1879 unmarried.

81 VIII Charles Nathan, b. Mar. 6, 1836; m. Oct. 29, 1862, Harriet Merrill Chandler.


**81. Enoch Watson Pelton**, first son of James⁴, Nathan³, John₃, John₂, Samuel², John₁, born East Windsor, Conn., February 7, 1813; married Hartford, Conn., Apr. 21, 1856, Harriet Ellsworth King, daughter of Roderick King, of South Windsor, Conn. Residence, 1879, South Windsor, Conn. Farmer. Children:

I Bayard, born Hartford, Conn., Apr. 15, 1858; in 1879 was clerk in the auditor's office of the In. & St. Louis R. R. Co.; died there, Apr. 5, 1880.

II Elizabeth Gaylord, born S. Windsor, Conn., Jan. 16, 1860.

III Roderick King, born S. Windsor, Jan. 24, 1862.

IV Oliver Newberry, b. S. Windsor, Jan. 16, 1865.

All living in 1879; none married at that date.

**91. Henry Thompson Pelton**[7], second son of James[6], Nathan[5], John[4], John[3], Samuel[2], John[1], born East Windsor, Conn., December 4, 1816; married at Manchester, Conn., May 27, 1845, Susan Bulkley (d. 1880 in Florida), daughter of Chauncey Bulkley, of Middle Haddam, Conn. Removed to Loda, Ill., and thence, in 1878, to Fairbanks, Alachua Co., Fla, and afterward to Lake Helen, Volusia Co., Fla., where he lived in 1889. Children:

>I Sophia, born Warehouse Point, Conn., Aug. 5, 1847; married Loda, Ill., Nov. 13, 1867, Volney Weaver, son of Henry Weaver, of Loda. Children: 1. Flora Bulkley, b. Dec. 22, 1869; 2. Gaylord, b. Apr. 29, 1872.
>
>II Jennie, born Sept. 19, 1850.
>
>III Arthur Henry, born Sept. 29, 1854, at East Windsor, Conn.
>
>IV Charles Bulkley, born Loda, Ill., June 27, 1858.

**91. Charles Nathan Pelton**[7], fourth son of James[6], Nathan[5], John[4], John[3], Samuel[2], John[1], born South Windsor, Conn., March 6, 1838; married there, October 29, 1862, Harriet Merrill Chandler, daughter of Charles M. Chandler, of New Hampshire. Residence, 1879, South Windsor, Conn. Hotel-keeper. Children:

>I Leonidas Chandler, born Nov. 8, 1863.
>
>II Martha Mary, born Nov. 8, 1864.
>
>III Addie Louise, born Mar. 20, 1866.

**59. Ithamar Pelton**[5], fourth son of John[4], John[3], Samuel[2], John[1], born at Saybrook (now Essex), Conn., November 22, 1740; married, about 1764, Asenath

Pratt, of Haddam, Conn.    He was a fine mechanic and a famous builder of his time.    He is said to have built thirteen churches, including the Congregational church at Essex, Conn., besides many mills and houses.    By the church records of Chatham he lived there in 1765 and 1766, and in 1774, or earlier, perhaps in 1768, in East Windsor, Conn., he having, it is said, gone up the Connecticut Valley with his brother Nathan or about the same time.    He there bought land and built him a house, still standing, and lived there for some years.    About 1781 or 1782 he removed to Middlefield, Hampshire Co., Mass., where he died March 16, 1826, his wife, Asenath, having died the previous year, March 22, 1825.

NOTE.— Persons living in 1879 remembered his driving down from Middlefield to Saybrook with his wife Asenath in a wagon made by himself.    He, with his brother, Nathan, served in the "French war" under Gen. Amherst, in Capt. Peleg Redfield's Co. (1st Lt. Geo. Nettleton, 2d, Abraham Tyler, Ensign, Edward Shipman), through the campaign of 1759.    This company also served in the campaign of 1760.    (Redfield Family History.)    He probably also served in the War of the Revolution, as he was at the burning of New London, Conn., in 1781.    (Worthington Pelton, p. 128.)    Children:

96    I Tabor, b. May 8, 1765; m. about 1789, Roxanna Moore; d. Nov. 26, 1826.
102    II Ezra, b. Aug. 21, 1767; m. May 17, 1794, Chloe Wright; d. Mar. 18, 1838.
        III Anna, born Apr. 4, 1770; married (1) Elias Ware; (2) Maston Tinker; four children.
126    IV Ithamar, Jr., b. Aug. 14, 1772; m. June 7, 1798, Charlotte Starr; d. Jan. 2, 1861.

**182** V Asahel, b. Aug. 3, 1774; m. (1) Anna
Denio, Dec. 31, 1798; (2) Feb., 1821,
Hannah Benson; (3) Aug. 6, 1824,
Sarah Gillett Richards; d. Mar. 21,
1857.

**142** VI Hezekiah, b. Feb. 21, 1777; m. (1) Hannah H. Axtelle, Mar., 1803; (2) Feb.
20, 1831, Mary Baldwin; d. Feb. 12,
1853.

**143** VII Joel, b. Aug. 19, 1779; m. (1) Ruth Field;
(2) Rosetta Edwards; d. Mar. 20, 1865.

VIII John, born July 3, 1782; drowned in the
Connecticut river, June 7, 1794.

**143** IX Cyprian, b. Dec. 31, 1785; d. May 16,
1821; probably lived west of Utica,
N. Y.; no other record.

**95. Tabor Pelton**, first son of Ithamar⁵, John⁴,
John³, Samuel², John¹, born May 8, 1765, probably in
Chatham, Conn.; married, about 1789, Roxanna
Moore. He probably went with his parents to
Middlefield, Mass. He was a carpenter and joiner.
Lived after marriage at Whitestown, N. Y., and at
Perrysburg, Cattaraugus Co., N. Y., where he died,
November 26, 1826. Children:

**97** I Tabor, Jr., b. June 29, 1790; m. Mary
Miner; d. Aug. 26, 1825.

II Polly, born Mar. 11, 1792; married Amos
Partridge; lived in Erie Co., N. Y., and
there died, Jan. 3, 1851. Children, six
living — fourteen in all.

III Asenath, born Mar. 17, 1794; died Aug.
15, 1814.

IV Laura, born 1796; married Junius Allen;
five children.

      V Orpha, born Sept. 22, 1798; married Hins-
dale Sheppard; died Apr. 24, 1834.
Children, six.

97    VI Osmyn, b. June 26, 1799; m. Feb. 1, 1823,
Samantha Nichols; d. Nov. 8, 1873.

      VII Ithamar, 1, born Apr. 10, 1805; died Apr.
3, 1807.

99 VIII Ithamar, 2, b. Dec. 25, 1808; m. May 7,
1837, Perdides Ware.

100   IX William M., b. Mar. 11 (31?), 1810; m.
Sarah Ware; d. Oct. 22, 1847.

      X Sarah Ann, born Mar. 18, 1811; married
Asahel Phelps.   Lived in Canada; four
children.

     XI Elder, born Oct. 24, 1812; died Aug. 26,
1832.

    XII Betsey, born Mar. 8, 1814; married Jona-
than Sheppard; died Dec. 24, 1829.
No children.

**96. Tabor Pelton, Jr.,** first son of Tabor[5], Ithamar[5], John[4], John[3], Samuel[2], John[1], born June 29, 1790;
married, about 1821, Mary Miner, of Perrysburg,
Cattaraugus Co., N. Y., where he lived, and there
died, August 26, 1825.   Children:

      I Caleb Miner, born Perrysburg, May 30,
1823; married at Leon, Cattaraugus
Co., N. Y., June 28, 1846, Mercy A.,
daughter of Milton and Hannah Kil-
burn, of that place.   No further record.

**96. Osmyn Pelton[6],** second son of Tabor[5], Ithamar[5], John[4], John[3], Samuel[2], John[1], born June 26,
1799; married at Perrysburg, N. Y., February 1,
1823, Samantha, daughter of Peleg Nichols, of that

place. Farmer. Lived at Perrysburg, and there died, November 8, 1873. Children, born at Perrysburg, N. Y.:

      I Orretti L., born June 17, 1824; married Dec. 19, 1846, John Smith, of Hanover, N. Y. Lived at Fredonia, N. Y., and died Oct. 9, 1850. No children.

98    II Simon, b. Mar. 13, 1826; m July 13, 1848, Rebecca Briggs.

      III Marvin, born Aug. 14, 1828; died Aug. 22, 1828.

      IV Frinda, born July 23, 1829; in 1876 unmarried.

      V Maria, born Nov. 4, 1831; married at Perrysburg, N. Y., July 3, 1853, Geo. A. Sheldon. Lived, 1876, at Adrian, Mich. Children: Fannie A., b. Sept. 11, 1856; C. C., b. Apr. 20, 1858; Cad, b. Feb. 24, 1861; Lillian, b. Sept. 20, 1864; Effie, b. Dec. 18, 1866.

      VI Philetus M., born Mar. 8, 1834; killed on the Erie railroad, June 8, 1850.

      VII Egbert, born June 2, 1836; died July 22, 1843.

99 VIII Lemon N., b. Nov. 10, 1839; m. Dec. 16, 1860, Phœbe Ann Flowers.

      IX Tyler, born Nov. 10, 1839; died Nov. 10, 1839.

      X Orpha, born July 15, 1844; unmarried in 1876.

99    XI Nathan P., b. Sept. 30, 1846; m. Aug. 5, 1875, Ella M. Austin.


**97. Simon Pelton**, first son of Osmyn[6], Tabor[5], Ithamar[4], John[3], John[2], Samuel[2], John[1], born Perrys-

burg, N. Y., March 13, 1826; married July 13, 1848,
Rebecca Briggs, daughter of Russler Briggs, of
Perrysburg. Residence, 1879, Custer City, Pa.
Children, none.

**87. Lemon N. Pelton⁷**, fifth son of Osmyn⁷,
Tabor⁶, Ithamar⁵, John⁴, John³, Samuel², John¹, born
Perrysburg, N. Y., November 10, 1839; married there,
December 16, 1860, Phœbe Ann Flowers (b. Dayton,
N. Y., July 20, 1844), daughter of Bradford Flowers,
of Oneida Co., N. Y. Carpenter and joiner. Lived,
1879, at Perrysburg, N. Y. Child:

 I Effie K., born Apr. 16, 1864; died Dec.
  1, 1864.

**87. Nathan F. Pelton⁷**, seventh son of Osmyn⁷,
Tabor⁶, Ithamar⁵, John⁴, John³, Samuel², John¹, born
Perrysburg, N. Y., Sept. 30, 1846; married at Go-
wanda, N. Y., Aug. 5, 1875, Ella M. (d. Nov. 6, 1881),
daughter of Leander Austin, of Persia, Cattaraugus
Co., N. Y. Farmer. Lived, 1879, at Custer City,
Pa., and thence removed that year to Perrysburg,
N. Y. Child:

 I Lyall, born Oct. 2, 1877.

**96. Ithamar Pelton⁶**, fourth son of Tabor⁶, Itha-
mar⁵, John⁴, John³, Samuel², John¹, born in Massa-
chusetts (probably at Middlefield), December 25,
1808; married at Perrysburg, N. Y., May 7, 1837,
Perdides Ware (d. May 3, 1867), daughter of Asa
R. Ware, of that place. Removed to Sun Prairie,
Wis., and there lived in feeble health, July 1, 1882.
Children:

 I Herbert M., born Apr. 18, 1841; died
  Sept. 16, 1856.

14

II Francis I., born Apr. 22, 1860; died Sept.
22, 1860.

**96. William M. Pelton[6]**, fifth son of Tabor[5],
Ithamar[4], John[3], John[3], Samuel[2], John[1], born March
11 (31?), 1810, in Massachusetts; married Perrys-
burg, N. Y., ———, Sally Ware, daughter of Asa R.
Ware, of that place. Carpenter. Removed, 1846, to
York Township, Dane Co., Wis., and there died,
October 22, 1847. Mrs. Sally Ware Pelton died
October, 1848. Children:

I Roxanna (or Rosanna), born about 1829;
married Wm. H. Yaw; last heard of
at Paw Paw, Neb.

100 II Theodore Gwary, b. July 4, 1830; m. (1)
Maria H. Phillips, Mar. 20, 1851; (2)
Jan. 27, 1856, Anna M. Bliss.

102 III Martin Van Buren, b. 1832; m. Huldah
Glover; d. July, 1871.

IV Eudora, born about 1841; married York
Township, Dane Co., Wis., Frank Van
Gaasbeck. Lived there; probably re-
moved to Kansas, and there died.

102 V Perry, b. about 1843; m. Mrs. Minerva
Brown.

VI Redella, born about 1845; married Arthur
Clyde. P. O. Osage, Iowa. No further record.

**100. Theodore Gwary Pelton**, first son of Wil-
liam M.[6], Tabor[5], Ithamar[4], John[3], John[3], Samuel[2], John[1],
born Gowanda, Erie Co., N. Y., July 4, 1830; mar-
ried (1) at Rutledge, N. Y., March 20, 1851, Hannah
M. Phillips, daughter of Roswell and Eunice Phillips,
of that place; (2) at Marion, Iowa, January 27, 1856,

Anna M. Bliss, daughter of Jeremiah Bliss, of that place.   In 1889 machinist and inventor (proprietor), Lyons, Iowa.   Children:
Of first wife:
**101**　　I Myron Wm., b. Feb. 19, 1852; m. May 27, 1877, Phila J. Meritt.
II Marcus A., born Dunkirk, N. Y., Nov. 19, 1854; unmarried, 1889.  P. O. Gerry, Chautauqua Co., N. Y.
Of second wife:
III Wilhelmina M., born Dec., 1857; died Aug. 30, 1858.
**102**　　IV Jeremiah Martin, b. Sept. 30, 1859; m. Sept. 10, 1881, Emma E. Gay.
V Theodore A., born Mar. 17, 1863; died Oct. 26, 1871.
VI Charles H., born Nov. 12, 1868; machinist.


**100. Myron William Pelton**[9], first son of Theodore G.[8], William M.[7], Tabor[6], Ithamar[5], John[4], John[3], Samuel[2], John[1], born Randolph, Cattaraugus Co., N. Y., February 19, 1852; married Cold Spring, Cattaraugus Co., N. Y., May 27, 1877, Phila J. Merritt (b. Sept. 18, 1853), of that place.  Residence, 1889, Township of Gerry, Chautauqua Co., N. Y. Children:
I Minnie M., born June 10, 1878, at Red House, Cattaraugus Co., N. Y.
II Addie L., born Aug. 27, 1880, at Red House, N. Y.
III Irving M., born Oct. 12, 1885, at Gerry, Chautauqua Co., N. Y.
IV Gloster A., born Aug. 30, 1887, at Gerry, Chautauqua Co., N. Y.

**100.** Jeremiah Martin Pelton[8], third son of Theodore G.[7], William M.[6], Tabor[5], Ithamar[4], John[3], John[2], Samuel[2], John[1], born September 30, 1859; married at Lyons, Iowa, September 10, 1881, Emma E. Gay, daughter of John Gay, of New York city. Occupation, engineer.  Children:

    I William M., born Aug. 30, 1882.
    II Jeremiah Perry, born June 17, 1886.

**100.** Martin Van Buren Pelton[7], second son of William M.[6], Tabor[5], Ithamar[4], John[3], John[2], Samuel[2], John[1], born Cattaraugus Co., N. Y., about 1832; married at Marion, Iowa, ——, Huldah Glover, daughter of John (?) Glover.  Died at Stockton, Cal., July, 1871.  Children:

    I William E.
    II Clara M.

**100.** Perry Pelton[7], third son of William M.[6], Tabor[5], Ithamar[4], John[3], John[2], Samuel[2], John[1], born Cattaraugus Co., N. Y., about 1843; married ——, probably in Oregon, Mrs. Minerva Brown(?).  Lived, when last heard from, about 10 or 12 years ago, on a farm about 12 miles east of East Portland, Ore. No further record; supposed, 1890, to be dead.

**94.** Ezra Pelton[5], second son of Ithamar[4], John[3], John[2], Samuel[2], John[1], born (probably in Chatham, Conn.) August 21, 1767; married May 17, 1794, Chloe Wright, daughter of Edward Wright, of Chester, Mass.   He lived in Middlefield until marriage, then in Chester, Mass., whence he returned to Middlefield in 1829, and there died in the winter of 1837–1838. Mrs. Pelton went with her sons to Prairie du Chien, and there died, aged 85 years.   Mr. Pelton inherited

the mechanical genius of his father. He was first a
cabinet-maker, and afterward an architect and builder,
a good workman, as the old buildings of Chester and
Middlefield still bear witness. He was a man of
strict religious principles, happy in his faith and an
earnest Christian. Children:

I Nancy A., born at Chester, Hampden Co.,
Mass., Sept. 2, 1796; married there,
May 27, 1816, Jeremiah R. Whipple, a
school-mate and neighbor. Residence,
for many years, at Saegertown, Crawford Co., Pa. Died there. July 6, 1887.

Miss Pelton was remarkable for good
judgment and a high order of intellect
that would have made her a woman of
note in any community. Having only
the advantages afforded by the common
schools of her time in New England,
she made such good use of them that
at an early age she had a fair English
education which, supplemented by the
example and training of a devoted and
wise mother, well fitted her for the
coming duties of life.

After her marriage to Mr. Whipple,
as above stated, they spent the first
years of married life on a farm in their
native place. Mr. Whipple, fond of
fine cattle and sheep, longed for richer
fields and pastures. As many New
England farmers were then removing
to the Western Reserve, in Ohio, he
went there to view that promised
land, the result being that he selected
a place for a new home, not in Ohio,

but over its eastern border in Crawford Co., Pa. In the spring of 1832, taking his family and the best of their Devonshire cattle and merino sheep, they began the then tedious journey to Meadville, Pa., where they arrived early in July, with family, flock and herd safe and sound. There, amid the privations of a new country, they commenced to make a new home for their growing family. To this great undertaking they applied themselves so resolutely and industriously, they, in the short space of sixteen years, had cleared the dense forest from a large farm, built (for that day) a good house and good barns, and were surrounded by the increase of herds and flocks; a prosperous family, honored and respected.

At this time (1848) their joint labors came to a sad end by the sudden sickness and death of Mr. Whipple. To this new state of things Mrs. Whipple quickly adapted herself and wisely and serenely devoted her life to the care of her children. Of these, at that time, three were married and four were minors. Married or single, each found a wise, helpful and sympathetic counselor in their mother.

She was always a woman of prayer, but church privileges were so limited, she seldom could attend church services. However, she availed herself of the first opportunity to attend those that were to her liking, became a member of an orthodox church, and for forty years was active in church affairs, supporting the preaching of the gospel liberally according to her ability.

Her influence over her children was such that eight out of nine followed her in church relationship, and now that she has gone, let it here be recorded that as she abounded in love and benevolence, her best monument is in the esteem and regrets found in the memories of those she left behind. Children: 1. Albert, b. Sept. 7, 1817; m. at Saegertown, Pa., Mary Amidon; d. in Hayfield, Crawford Co., Pa., Mar. 24, 1850. He was an enterprising farmer and drover. Mrs. Whipple died about the same time, leaving children Arminda, Edna, Emily, Alberta; 2. Susanna, b. May 8, 1819; m. Rev. D. Bagley of the Methodist Protestant Church; went overland to Oregon in early days and was very active and useful in church work. He was one of the founders of Methodism in that new country. Both are still active and living in Seattle, Washington; one child living. Clarence B. Bagley; 3. Edna A., b. Nov. 3, 1820; d. in 1821; 4. Ann E., b. Mar. 21, 1822; went with her sister overland to Oregon, and there married Rev. S. H. Mann, of the Oregon Conference. They have both been very useful workers, she being one of the

first woman class leaders and stewards
in Oregon.  She is now a widow.  Address, in 1892, Mrs. Rev. A. E. Mann,
Olympia, Washington; children raised:
Champion B., Ann Eliza, Florence
and Lyman; 5. Andrew J., b. Mar. 9,
1824; 7. Ambro, b. Oct. 10, 1827; some-
what alike in tastes and inclined to
educational matters; they taught schools
in winters, came near being bachelors,
but were saved from that fate by finally
marrying two sisters, intelligent and
estimable daughters of a neighbor by
the name of Carr; and settled on their
father's old farm.  Having inherited
their father's liking for fine stock they
indulged their taste in that way, as the
premium lists of their county fairs will
show.  Then the oil business and milling interests engaging their attention
for years, the old farm was sold with
many regrets and passed into the owner-
ship of strangers.  During these years
they and their wives held the position
of honorable and useful members of
society.  Andrew J. and family now,
1892, live in Kansas City, Mo., where
their two oldest sons are in business.
His wife was H. Jane Carr; their children, Attis A., Bis T., Wayne, Alice
M., Jenny, Laura L. and Andrew Carr,
all of whom, but two in school, are intelligent and energetic men and women
and happily married.  Mr. Ambro
Whipple married Lydia M. Carr.  They

now, 1892, reside in Meadville, Pa., where they are active in good deeds and valuable members of society. They had three sons, but lost two in early life, leaving but one, Ernest A., now a young man, married, and just starting in life. Messrs. A. J. and Ambro Whipple are connected with The Whipple Loan and Trust Co. of Kansas City, Mo.; 6. Edna A., 2d, b. Apr. 9, 1826, also took to and obtained a fine education, teaching successfully. She also made the overland journey with her sisters to Oregon about 1851 or 1852, where she soon married Mr. Geo. F. Colbert, with whom she lived happily many years until his death. Her address is now, 1892, Mrs. E. A. Colbert, Crawfordsville, Ore., where she lives honored and respected. Children: Luella, Viola, Raymond and George; 8. Jane, b. Nov. 15, 1829, a dutiful daughter, took kindly to education, was known as an original thinker, taught school a few terms, early married Rev. W. F. West, made the journey overland with her older sisters to Oregon, where her husband settled on a farm and became a local preacher. The hardships of a new country proving too great, she lost her health and died, comparatively young, June 4, 1878, at Jefferson, Ore., lamented by all who knew her. Children, Fort Boire, William, Ebbie, Myra, Leon and Ossian; 9. Lucy L., b. Dec.

2, 1832, bright and intelligent; married
Mr. O. J. Carr, a brother of the wives
of A. J. and Ambro Whipple, her
brothers. About three years after
marriage they removed by water to
Oregon and settled in Seattle, Washington, where she was very active in
church work, and where he was postmaster for many years. They are now
retired from active life. Having no
children of their own, they adopted a
niece, daughter of Mrs. Carr's deceased
sister, Mrs. West, who grew up respected
and well educated, and is now well
married; 10. Margaret, b. July 10, 1836,
d. May 1, 1842; 11. Emily, b. Apr. 17,
1837; d. Sept. 26, 1841; 12. Elmira E.,
b. Dec. 4, 1840; m. S. T. Carr, making
the fourth Whipple-Carr pair from the
same two families. Only seven years
old when her father died, she came
more exclusively under her mother's
control and received a training which
in after life showed itself in good words
and works. Her address in 1892 is
Mrs. T. S. Carr, Moziertown, Pa.
Children: 11. Willis, Jennie, Bertha,
Anna, Albert. The now living descendants of Mr. J. A. and Mrs. Nancy
A. Whipple are: Children, 7; grandchildren, 32; great-grandchildren, 48;
great-great-grandchildren, 1; total, 88.

II Marietta, born Nov. 17, 1798; died Apr.
1, 1807.

III  Asenath Pratt, born at Middlefield. Mass.,
      Apr. 21, 1800; married in 1854 George
      Skinner, of Westford, Otsego Co., N. Y.
      Like her mother she was a person of
      well-balanced mind and with a remark-
      able memory.   Always a friend in need
      she abounded in good works; retained
      her youth and faculties and worked
      in the Sunday-school and Bible class
      down to her last sickness.   She died at
      Westford, N. Y., Jan. 9, 1880, aged
      nearly 90 years   No children reported.
IV  Ezra,* born at Middlefield. Mass., in Nov.,
      1801; died Oct. 18, 1805.
 V  Champion, born at Middlefield. Mass.,
      Mar. 14, 1803; died at Prairie du Chien,
      Ill., Sept. 15, 1846   He was pre-emi-
      nently the " Elder Beloved," and con-
      fided in by every member of the family.
      Energetic and quick of thought and
      comprehension, he began life as a
      teacher, but soon turned his attention
      to trade.   He went West in 1842 and
      with his brother, Edward W., at Prairie
      du Chien, Ill., established and built up
      a large mercantile business that ex-
      tended to adjoining counties, and largely
      among the French and Indians.   Later,
      the two, with the help of their brother,
      Alonzo, commanded the larger share
      of the business of Prairie du Chien.
      They built the first elevator and flour-
      mill on the river at that place (the
      builder having been their brother,
      Ezra, Jr.).   It is in active operation at

this time, 1892. Champion Pelton was remarkable for his social qualities. He was probably the first temperance reformer of any considerable influence in Prairie du Chien, then a frontier town, notorious for gambling and for every shade of inebriety. Indeed it may be said that all of the brothers were temperance men before going West, and all united in the endeavor to lessen the saloon curse in that border town. The year 1846 will remain memorable in the annals of the Peltons of Prairie du Chien as the year of death. Champion and his brother Ezra, Jr.'s wife were buried the same day; Ezra, Jr., followed a few days later. Not a relative was able to attend either funeral, six members of their families lying near death's door at the time. There were not enough well persons to care for the sick, and medical attendance was not to be had.

VI Lucy Pratt, born Chester, Mass., Sept. 26, 1804; married Alanson Hewitt, of Westford, Oswego Co., N. Y., in 1831, and died at Prairie du Chien, Wis., Apr. 12, 1869. Mr. Hewitt, a thrifty farmer at Westford, N. Y., by reverses lost his property there and spent his later years near Prairie du Chien, on the Grand Gré Dairie farm, where he carried on an extensive dairy business, and died there about 1860, leaving three young sons to be reared and educated. Children, four sons and two daughters. The eldest, Herbert N., became a distinguished physician in Denver, and was also interested in mining property. He was of a literary turn of mind, and stood high with his associates. Date of his death unknown to the compiler. Rocefa and Eliza were young women of fine abilities. Rocefa died suddenly in 1849 at the school of her Aunt Dwight; Eliza went to Denver for her health and there died. Byron Hewitt, third son, born at Westford, N. Y., is a traveling salesman, residing in 1892 at Rochester, Ill. In the War of the Rebellion he entered the Union army as a private in Co. F, 8th Wis. Vol. Inft., but was promoted to a colonelcy for merit. He is a successful business man, is married, and has one daughter. Ezra Hewitt, born at Westford, N. Y., also enlisted in the army at Prairie du Chien. He was killed in the four days' fighting during Gen. Pope's retreat through Virginia. Samuel Hewitt, sixth and youngest child, also joined the Union army in the War of the Rebellion. He marched with Gen. Sherman to the sea and returned home without a wound. Joining his brother in business in Prairie du Chien, he married Anna Wheeler, and there died in 1873, leaving a widow with two children. The children were adopted by relatives and the mother returned to her parents.  She has since married a physician in Chicago; name to the compiler unknown.

117 VII Ezra, Jr., 2, b. Jan. 6, 1807; m. Nancy M. (Woodbine) Howe, about 1832; d. in Sept., 1846.

118 VIII Edward Wright, b. July 20, 1808; m. (1) Feb. 4, 1844, Sarah Brunson; (2) Frances Newton, Jan. 3, 1856; d. Dec. 2, 1873.

IX Almira Marietta, born at Chester, Mass., Mar. 13, 1810; educated at Wesleyan Academy, Wilbraham, Mass.; went south with a corps of teachers; married Rev. Holden Dwight, A. M., at Baton Rouge, La., June 13, 1839 (son of Daniel and Susan Lippet Dwight, of Dudley, Mass.), who died in the midst of great usefulness at Berea, O., Nov. 24, 1846, much beloved and respected.  The children of this marriage were: 1. Edward Champion, b. at Clinton, Miss., Nov. 13, 1840; m. at Freeport, Ill., Sept. 4, 1866, Minnie Guitteau, of that place.  He died at Minneapolis, Minn., Apr. 28, 1869, of consumption, resulting from an attack of typhoid pneumonia, after the second battle at Corinth, Miss., in 1862.  He was a musician in 8th Wis. Vol. Inft.; was discharged for permanent disability, returned home and entered the jewelry business, which he continued to his death.  He left one child, a daughter, who died June 20, 1882; 2. William

Fiske, b. at Norwalk, O., Feb. 6, 1843;
d. Aug. 12, 1843; 3. Susan Eliza, b. at
Norwalk, O., Feb. 6, 1844; m. at Patch
Grove, Wis., Dec. 10, 1862, Francis
Baillet, son of Francis E. and Martha
(Horton) Baillet, of Bridgeport, Wis.
Two children were born to them; the
mother was fatally injured by the ex-
explosion of a kerosene lamp, and died
Mar. 6, 1866. The children were
adopted by Mr. Baillet's sisters, who
reared them with loving care. The
first child, Harvey Dwight Baillet, born
at Prairie du Chien, Aug. 13, 1863,
graduated with honor in 1882 from the
High School at Black River Falls, Wis.,
and is now in the banking business at
Bowdle, South Dakota. Hattie, the
second child, b. Jan. 26, 1865, at Bridgeport, Wis., adopted by her aunt, Mrs.
David Austin, graduated from the High
School, and after two years in the
Woman's College at Milwaukee, gave
up her studies from ill health and married Cicero D. Hill, Dec. 24, 1890, at
La Crosse, Wis. Mr. Hill is a civil
engineer, employed by the city of Chicago. They have one child, David
Dwight, b. Dec. 31, 1891, and reside,
1892, at 6502 Madison ave., Wood
Lawn Park, Chicago.

Miss Pelton was naturally a teacher,
and taught even before she passed
through Wesleyan Academy. After
her graduation she was called as Pre-

ceptress of Amenia Seminary at
Amenia, N. Y. Her next call was to
Baton Rouge, La., where, with her
sister Eliza, she took charge of a seminary for young women. After her
marriage to Mr. Dwight she joined
him as an educator, first at Clinton,
Miss., at a proposed centenary college,
and later, when the malaria of the
South had driven them North, they resumed their work at Norwalk, O., where
they were associated with Dr., afterward Bishop Thompson. Pecuniary
embarrassment of the institute at Norwalk led the conference to remove the
school to Berea, O., Rev. and Mrs.
Dwight being appointed to take charge
of it. Here, after four months of over-
work, Mr. Dwight died, Nov. 24, 1846,
leaving Mrs. Dwight to continue on
for two years of excessive labor, when
she was obliged to resign and retire for
rest, with her two remaining children,
to Prairie du Chien, where loving
brothers and kind friends gave her a
hearty welcome. Here the change of
scene, with lessened responsibilities,
bringing returning health she resumed
school duties, and in 1849 and 1850
undertook the reform and reconstruc-
tion of the school system of Prairie du
Chien, introducing new text-books,
discipline and the first black-board ever
seen in the city; which seed thus planted
has grown until Prairie du Chien is

now in the advance guard as to school matters.

Here Mrs. Dwight married (2) Samuel G. Bassett, Jan. 1, 1851, a pioneer farmer from Vermont, who settled in or near Prairie du Chien when it required six weeks or more to make the journey, and when the country abounded in savage men and savage beasts. Old Fort Crawford was then the only trading post near. Setting out with a strong will and a mammoth breaking plow, drawn by seven yokes of oxen, he turned over the prairie sod that had lain for centuries unvexed save by the buffalo and the Indian, subdued the wild land and was ready when the railroads came to sell new settlers horses, cattle and farm products of his own raising.

This marriage ended Mrs. Dwight's teaching. Excessive work proving too much for even Mr. Bassett's iron constitution, he yielded to nature's laws and died at Minneapolis in Dec., 1871. Mrs. Bassett, left alone in declining years, again resumed the position of bread-winner. In her young days she chose the profession of teaching not so much as a means of support as for the opportunities it afforded for influencing the young for good. Looking around for something congenial to her tastes she chose the book business, which she pursued in Minneapolis,

Minn., with such success as not only to win a support, but in addition a competence that it is hoped will carry her through. For the last seventeen years she has given much time and strength to the interests of The Women's Christian Temperance Union, and now, 1892, the only living representative of thirteen children, her present residence is at 510 63d street, Englewood, Ill.

X Eliza, born at Chester, Mass., Oct. 28, 1811. She was remarkable for a most retentive memory, was educated at Wesleyan Academy, Wilbraham, Mass., graduating there in 1836. In 1837 she went South with a corps of teachers and took charge of the department of music in the Seminary at Baton Rouge, La., in which her sister Almira M. was teaching. But at the end of four months she was taken ill, and notwithstanding all that warm southern hearts could do was done for her, she died Feb. 27, 1838, in Christian faith and hope. An immense funeral showed how in that short space of time she had become beloved and respected.

XI Jonathan, born at Chester, Mass., Oct. 16, 1813. He was a studious man of good intellect, but by his father, the "book-worm," was taught the carpenter's trade, notwithstanding entreaties of friends and neighbors. Joining his brothers in Prairie du Chien, Wis., he died there, unmarried, in Sept., 1840.

**118** XII Alonzo, b. at Chester, Mass., Mar. 26,
1816; m. Nov. 29, 1845, Adelia Emeline
Taintor; d Sept. 21, 1891.
**120**XIII Leander Grandison, b. Oct 31; 1821; m.
Aug. 21, 1848, Martha A. Hurd; d.
Nov. 29, 1861 (or 1862).

**102. Ezra Pelton[1], Jr. (2d)**, third son of Ezra[6],
Ithamar[5], John[4], John[3], Samuel[2], John[1], born at Chester, Hampden Co., Mass., January 6, 1807; married
about 1832, Nancy M. (Woodbine) Howe.    He was
a carpenter and builder, a natural mechanic.    He removed with his family, in 1844, to Prairie du Chien,
Wis., and established himself there as a builder.    But
malarial fever soon invaded his home, taking first a
part of his children and then both himself and wife
in 1846, leaving of a family of eight, only two little
girls to follow their parents to their graves.    Children:
I Helen Maria, born Apr. 11, 1833; died at
Prairie du Chien, Wis., Sept. 8, 1845.
II Ida Estelle, born Mar. 14, 1834.    On the
death of her parents was adopted by
her uncle, Edward W. Pelton, who gave
her not only a home but the best
educational advantages New England
schools afforded.    She died while attending school at Hartford, Conn., Oct.
7, 1854; a bright, beautiful life lost to
this world.
III Emily Ordelia, born Dec. 21, 1837; also,
on the death of her parents, was adopted
by her uncle Edward W., and well cared
for and well educated.    She became a
successful teacher in California, honored
by all who knew her, and remarkable

for tact and ready wit in the social
circle. She lived for sometime at
Brownsville, Yuba Co., Cal. Her marriage, Sept. 15, 1885, in Balinas, Cal.,
to Dr. —— Wilson, ended her work as
a teacher. They now, 1892, live in San
Francisco, Cal. His given name and
their address are unknown to the writer.

IV Milo Ruthven, born Feb. 21, 1840; died
Mar. 9, 1844.

V Edward Dwight, born July 1, 1841; died
Sept. 14, 1845.

VI Asenath Pratt, born Aug. 5, 1843; died
June 12, 1845.

· 103. Edward Wright Pelton[7], fourth son of
Ezra[6], Ithamar[5], John[4], John[3], Samuel[2], John[1], born at
Chester, Mass., July 20, 1808; married (1) Sarah
Brunson, February 4, 1844; (2) Frances Newton,
Jan. 3, 1856. He went early to Prairie du Chien,
Wis., where he was for years connected with his
brother Champion in large mercantile, elevator and
milling enterprises, and accumulated a competence.
Like his brother he also was always ready to con-
tribute liberally to the welfare of relatives and friends,
and to any worthy object. In his later years fortune
seemed adverse, and losses by failures swept away
much of his fortune. His last days were spent at
Freeport, Ill., with his ever-faithful brother, Alonzo,
where he died, December 2, 1873. Children: one
child only, by the first marriage, that died in infancy.

102. Alonzo Pelton[7], sixth son of Ezra[6], Ithamar[5], John[4], John[3], Samuel[2], John[1], born in Chester,
Hampden Co., Mass., March 26, 1816, and was

*Alonzo Pelton*

brought up on his father's farm.  He removed to Prairie du Chien, Wis., about 1840, and there entered into the mercantile business with his older brothers, who had preceded him several years, and continued with them until 1867, when he went to Freeport, Ill., where he entered into partnership with his nephew, under the title of E. C. Dwight & Co., and did a large business in jewelry, pianos and organs.  Mr. Dwight retiring on account of ill health in 1869, Mr. Pelton became the head of the house.  Sometime after he removed his business to Chicago, where, connected with a man who left Mr. Pelton's careful ways, losses followed, many of which were doubtless the results of the great shrinkage of values on the resumption of specie payments.  Mr. Pelton was in every respect a noble, excellent man, active in every good word and work.  Converted at an early age, he had, at his death, been a church member for over fifty years, and for more than forty years had served the church as class-leader and in other official capacities.  November 29, 1845, he married at Prairie du Chien, Emeline Adelia Taintor, daughter of Ezekiel W. Taintor, an early settler of Wisconsin. Mr. Pelton died at Englewood, Ill., September 21, 1891.  Mrs. Pelton still resides at Englewood, Chicago, in 1892.  Children:

> I Dwight Champion, born Feb. 3, 1847; died June 11, 1868.
>
> II Leonora Martha, born Mar. 30, 1851; died Dec. 24, 1853.
>
> III Jessie Eliza, born Dec. 6, 1855; married Jan. 31, 1889, Charles Harshberger, of Englewood, Ill.  Merchant.  Residence, 1891, Englewood, Ill.

IV Martha Ruth, born Mar. 17, 1858; married Oct. 8, 1885, Charles E. Hatfield, lawyer, of Boston, Mass. Residence, in 1891, in West Newton, Mass.

V Charles Hobart, born Dec. 20, 1859. In 1891, unmarried. Residence, Englewood, Ill.

VI Hattie Josephine, born July 6, 1864; married Oct. 20, 1887, E. S. Whiteley. Lumber merchant. Residence, 1891, in Englewood, Ill.

VII, VIII Frederick, and a twin brother, born July 24, 1868; died the same day.

**102. Leander Grandison Pelton**[7], seventh son of Ezra[6], Ithamar[5], John[4], John[3], Samuel[2], John[1], born at Chester, Mass., Oct. 31, 1821; married Aug. 21, 1848, Martha A. Hurd. He received an academic education, and eventually followed his older brothers to Prairie du Chien, Wis. Taken with the gold fever, then so prevalent, he left his recently-married bride and went to California to seek a fortune. While he was absent his wife died, April 8, 1851, and he, after returning, died at Prairie du Chien in 1861.

**91. Ithamar Pelton, Jr.**, third son of Ithamar[5], John[4], John[3], Samuel[2], John[1], born (probably) in East Windsor, Conn., Aug. 14, 1772; married June 7, 1798, Charlotte Starr, daughter of Richard Starr, of Hinsdale, Mass. Removed from his father's homestead in Middlefield, Mass., which he owned and sold at that time, in 1832, to Litchfield, Medina Co., O., where he lived and there died, January 2, 1861. Farmer. Children:

I Charlotte, born Mar. 15, 1799; married Jan. 1, 1822, Austin Pelton (see p. 87), of East Windsor, Conn.; died at E. Windsor, Aug. 28, 1835.

122  II Ithamar Pratt, b. Sept. 13, 1800; m. Jan. 21, 1823, Sabrina A. Pelton.

III Priscilla, born Aug. 19, 1802; married (1) Reuben Ellsworth; (2) Willis Morton; died at East Hartford, Conn. Left one son, who in 1876 lived in Hartford, Conn.

126  IV Dexter, b. June 17, 1804; m. Sept. 30, 1834, Elizabeth Halliday; d. June 24, 1855.

127  V Lyman, b. Apr. 5, 1806; m. Sept. 23, 1830, Mary W. Pelton; d. Aug. 2, 1869.

VI Worthington, 1, born Jan. 28, 1808; died in infancy.

VII Sarah, born Apr 11, 1810; married Oct. 19, 1837, William Hurlbert, Westfield, Medina Co., O. One child, died Oct., 1840.

128 VIII Worthington, 2, b. Dec. 7, 1811; m. Oct. 16, 1834, Mary Wheeler.

129  IX Joseph, b. Mar. 11, 1814; m. May 6, 1840, M. H. Shumway.

130  X Trowbridge, b. Aug. 12, 1816; m. (1) about Feb., 1843, Martha Melissa Strong; (2) ——.

132  XI Cyprian, b. Jan. 1, 1821; m. Jan. 27, 1856, Flora A. Strong; d. Aug. 29, 1877.

132 XII Philander, b. Apr. 9, 1823; m. Emily Finn; d. Feb. 18, 1863.

XIII Clarissa Ann, born Aug. 22, 1826; married Jan. 22, 1847, James W. Young,

Harrisonville, Medina Co., O. Lived there, and there died about 1856. Children: 1. Albert, b. July 31, 1849; 2. No record; 3. Clarissa Adelia, b. Sept. 8, 1855.

**120. Ithamar Pratt Pelton**, first son of Ithamar⁶, Ithamar⁵, John⁴, John³, Samuel², John¹, born Middlefield, Mass., September 13, 1800; married January 21, 1823, Sabrina A. Pelton, daughter of Asahel Pelton (see p. 133), of Dalton, Mass. Farmer. Lived at Athens and Saugerties, N. Y., Middlefield, Mass., and removed from Massachusetts, in 1832, to Litchfield, Medina Co., O. In 1878 was living in La Grange, Ohio.

NOTE. — As stated, Mr. Pelton and family removed to Ohio in 1832. They settled on a farm in the woods, two miles east of the center of Litchfield Township, Medina Co. They were accompanied by five other families, making on their arrival a total of twenty families in the township. In the previous spring each adult male inhabitant held an office. On arriving they found their money reduced to fifty cents, with a letter awaiting them at the post-office, on which the postage was twenty-five cents. Their first two or three years there were years of privation and unremitting toil, it being difficult at first to get food enough for the family. During the first fall of their pioneer life, while the men were clearing the land, the women of the family gathered one hundred and fifty bushels of hickory nuts, which brought fifty cents per bushel. They had to go thirty miles to mill and seven to the nearest place to trade. At Litchfield Center there was but one little log house, used also for a post-office. Their first Fourth of

July in Ohio was celebrated by the assembling of the inhabitants of Litchfield early in the morning and their building a "meeting-house" in the style of those days, it being also used as a school-house. They enjoyed their Fourth immensely. When the Baptist Church was organized, the names of Mr. and Mrs. Pelton were enrolled among its thirteen members.

The celebration of the fifty-fifth anniversary of the marriage of Mr. and Mrs. Pelton of La Grange, O., in 1878, was the occasion of a very pleasant gathering of some forty guests, of whom there were five daughters and their families, and the families of two sons, deceased. *Local Journal.* Children:

124    I John Wesley, b. Dec. 23, 1823; m. Dec. 21, 1847, Sophia Ann Finn; d. Apr. 4, 1868.

125    II Clinton Pratt, b. Aug. 31, 1825; m. Nov. 8, 1846, Maria Cordelia Strong; d. Mar. 12, 1851.

III Charlotte Ann, born Middlefield, Mass., Aug. 28, 1827; married Litchfield, O., Feb. 23, 1845, Benjamin H. Northrop (d. Feb. 29, 1876), son of Ephraim Northrop, of Smyrna, Chenango Co., N.Y. Children, six; three girls and two boys living, 1879, at Lansing, Mich.

IV Hannah L., born Middlefield, Mass., Feb. 11, 1829; married (1) Litchfield, O., Dec. 4, 1847, Abraham Kimmel, who died Medina, O., July 26, 1869; (2) Clyde, O., June 6, 1860, Alfred Davis, lawyer, who died at Royalton, O., Aug. 27, 1870; two children; (3) at La Grange, O., Jan. 27, 1875, Elizur Goodrich Hastings. Residence, 1878, La Grange, O.

V Martha J., born Middlefield, Mass., Apr.
24, 1831; married (1) May 1, 1851,
Edwin H. Maydole, of Litchfield, O.;
(2) July 14, 1870, Daniel R. Belden,
son of Bildad Belden, of Grafton, O.;
(3) Dec. 17, 1874, Dorastes, son of
Dorastes Waite, of Jefferson Co., N. Y.
Residence, 1878, La Grange, O.

VI Lidana Lorina, born Litchfield, O., Nov.
12, 1839; married in Litchfield, Oct.
26, 1856, Salmon A., son of Samuel
Powers, of Amherst, Lorain Co., O.,
who served in the Union army in the
war of the Great Rebellion. Carpenter
and joiner. Residence, 1878, Elyria,
O. Children, two daughters.

126 VII Russell Denio, b. Dec. 26, 1843; m. Dec.
25, 1869, Mary Kemp.

VIII Sarah Sabrina, born Litchfield, O., May
31, 1847; married Nov. 13, 1866, Litchfield, O., Nelson M. Maydole (b. May
5, 1840), son of John J. Maydole, of
Lucas Co., Iowa. Residence, 1878, La
Grange Center, O. Children: Nettie
Zidona, b. July 10, 1869; Vesta Charlotte, b. Jan. 26, 1873, Edwin Chester,
b. Mar. 11, 1876.


**122. John Wesley Pelton**[9], first son of Ithamar
Pratt[8], Ithamar[7], Ithamar[6], John[5], John[4], Samuel[2], John[1],
born Dalton, Mass., December 23, 1823; married at
York, Medina Co., O., December 21, 1847, Sophia
Ann, daughter of Philo Fenn, of Byron, Genesee
Co., N. Y. Shoemaker. Lived at Bowling Green,
O., and there died April 4, 1868. Children:

      I Addison M., born Dec. 22, 1849; died un-
married, Bowling Green, O., Nov. 22,
1873.

**125** II Philo Fenn, b. Jan. 12, 1856; m. Mar. 21
1877, Clarissa Jane Lance.

      III Mary S., born Bowling Green, O., Sept.
25, 1860.

      IV Carrie N., born Aug. 29, 1863.

      V J. W. (said to be his full first name), born
Mar. 12, 1885.

**121. Philo Fenn Pelton**[9], first son of John
Wesley[8], Ithamar P.[7], Ithamar[6], Ithamar[5], John[4], John[3],
Samuel[2], John[1], born Bowling Green, O., January
12, 1856; married there, March 21, 1877, Clarissa
Jane, daughter of Henry Lance. Farmer. Child:

      I Ethel May, born May 27, 1878.

**122. Clinton Pratt Pelton**[8], second son of Itha-
mar P.[7], Ithamar[6], Ithamar[5], John[4], John[3], Samuel[2],
John[1], born Saugerties, N. Y., Aug. 31, 1825; married
at Litchfield, O., November 8, 1846, Maria Cordelia
Strong (b. Warren, Litchfield Co., Conn., Jan. 2, 1827),
daughter of Lysander Strong, of Chatham, Medina
Co., O. Cooper. Died at Oakland, Wis., March
12, 1851. Mrs. Pelton married (2) Valentine Zeller,
October 16, 1853, and removed to Pioneer, Williams
Co., O., where she lived in 1878. Child:

**125**   I Eugene Decelo, b. Nov. 27, 1847; m. Feb.
26, 1868, Sarah Eliza Cutler; d. Aug.
18, 1873.

**125. Eugene Decelo Pelton**[9], only son of Clin-
ton Pratt[8], Ithamar P.[7], Ithamar[6], Ithamar[5], John[4], John[3],
Samuel[2], John[1], born November 27, 1847; married

Marathon, Lapeer Co., Mich., February 26, 1868, Sarah Eliza, daughter of James B. Cutler, of Cadillac, Mich. Engineer of a boat on the lake. Was killed by a falling tree at Clam Lake, now Cadillac, Mich., August 18, 1873. Mrs. Pelton married (2) January 1, 1877, William M. Reed, of Ludington, Mich., where she lived in 1878. Children:

> I Mary Emma, born Marathon, Mich., Dec. 5, 1868. Residence, 1878, Cadillac, Mich., with her Grandfather Cutler.

**122. Russell Eben Pelton**[7], third son of Ithamar P.[6], Ithamar[5], Ithamar[4], John[4], John[3], Samuel[2], John[1], born Litchfield, Medina Co., O., December 26, 1843; married at Ridgeville, Lorain Co., O., December 25, 1869, Mary, daughter of Henry Kemp, of that place. Enlisted, Litchfield, O., September 1, 1864, served in the War of the Rebellion in Co. C, 176th Regiment of Ohio Volunteer Infantry, Second Division, under Gen. Thomas, in the Army of the Cumberland, and was honorably discharged at Nashville, Tenn., June 14, 1865. Child:

> I One adopted daughter, Ida May.

**120. Dexter Pelton**[5], second son of Ithamar[4], Ithamar[4], John[4], John[2], Samuel[2], John[1], born Middlefield, Mass., June 17, 1804; married Litchfield, Medina Co., O., September 30, 1804, Elizabeth Halliday (b. May 6, 1804), of Montgomery, Hampden Co., Mass. Removed to Center Township, Porter Co., Ind., and there died, June 24, 1855. His wife died April 5, 1875. Children:

> I Cilicia Elizabeth, born Litchfield, O., July 12, 1835; married Apr. 14, 1852, at

Valparaiso, Ind., John P. Jones.   Died
Feb. 25, 1856, leaving one child, Frank
W. Jones, b. Mar. 18, 1853.
II William Wallace, born Litchfield, O., May
27, 1837; died Sept. 22, 1858.
**127** III Andrew J., b. Jan. 8, 1845; m. Sept. 27,
1871, Charlotte M. Armstrong.

**126. Andrew J. Pelton**[7], second son of Dexter[6],
Ithamar[5], Ithamar[4], John[3], John[3], Samuel[2], John[1], born
Litchfield, Medina Co., O., January 8, 1845; married
at La Porte, Ind., September 27, 1871, Charlotte M.
Armstrong, daughter of R. V. Armstrong, of that
place.   Residence, 1879, South Bend, Ind.   Children:
I Eva, born Jan. 4, 1876.
II A son ——— ———, born July 9, 1878; died
Feb. 22, 1879.

**126. Lyman Pelton**[7], third son of Ithamar[6], Itha-
mar[5], John[4], John[3], Samuel[2], John[1], born Middlefield,
Mass., April 5, 1806; married September 23, 1830,
Mary W. (b. July 29, 1810), daughter of Asahel Pelton,
of Middlefield, Mass., and Austerlitz, N. Y.   Died at
Allairedon, Ingham Co., Mich., August 12, 1869,
Children:
**128** I Richard S., b. Dec. 3, 1831; m. (1) ———;
(2) ———.
II Mary J., born Litchfield, O., Apr. 1, 1833;
married S. J. Lamb, son of Samuel
Lamb.  Children, two.  Residence, 1878,
Mason, Mich.
**128** III Asahel H., b. Mar. 19, 1840; m. Aug. 2,
1863, Adaline Williams.
IV Ithamar D., born Litchfield, O., Mar. 30,
1849; in 1878 unmarried.  Residence,
Lansing, Mich.

**127. Richard S. Pelton**, first son of Lyman[7], Ithamar[6], Ithamar[5], John[4], John[3], Samuel[2], John[1], born Litchfield, O., December 3, 1831; married (1) Medina Co., O. (name not reported); (2) (no report). Lived, 1878, Millbury, Wood Co., O. Children:

    I Edwin.
    II Ella.
    III Charles.   Record incomplete.


**127. Asahel E. Pelton**, second son of Lyman[7], Ithamar[6], Ithamar[5], John[4], John[3], Samuel[2], John[1], born Litchfield, O., March 19, 1840; married Bowling Green, Wood Co., O., August 2, 1863, Adaline, daughter of Valentine Williams, of Ionia, Mich. Carpenter. Living, in 1878, in Lansing, Mich. Children:

    I Orlin, born Bowling Green, O., June 8, 1864.
    II Clara O., born Allairedon, Ingham Co., Mich., Sept. 23, 1866.
    III Orie M., born Allairedon, Mich., Apr. 24, 1870.


**120. Worthington Pelton**, fifth son of Ithamar[6], Ithamar[5], John[4], John[3], Samuel[2], John[1], born Middlefield, Mass., December 7, 1811; married at Litchfield, Medina Co., O., October 16, 1834, Polly Wheeler, daughter of William Wheeler, of Montgomery, Hampden Co., Mass. Engineer. Residence, 1878, Litchfield, O. Children, born there:

**129**     I William Almeron, b. Apr. 16, 1840; m. July 5, 1867, Gertrude M. Willis.
    II Almena, born Sept. 24, 1842; married January 3, 1866, C. N., son of J. H.

Carpenter, of Litchfield, O. Children: Mary A., born May 14, 1868. Residence, 1878, Litchfield, O.

III Angelina, born July 10, 1844; married Mar. 14, 1873, A. D., son of A. D. Willis, of Rutland, Vt. Children: Clifford E., b. Nov. 18, 1869. Residence, 1878, Litchfield, O.

IV Josephine, born Nov. 26, 1846; married January 29, 1873, Miller Dennis, son of George Dennis, of England. Child: Franklin P., b. Nov. 11, 1874. Residence, 1878, La Grange, Lorain Co., O.

**128. William Almeron Pelton[6]**, only son of Worthington[5], Ithamar[6], Ithamar[4], John[4], John[3], Samuel[2], John[1], born at Litchfield, Medina Co., O., April 16, 1840; married at La Fayette, O., July 5, 1867, Gertrude M., daughter of A. A. Willis, of Rutland, Vt. Mechanic. Residence, 1878, Litchfield, O. Children, born there:

I Clarissa, born May 2, 1868.
II Hugh Edward, born Sept. 16, 1875.

**129. Joseph Pelton[5]**, sixth son of Ithamar[5], Ithamar[4], John[4], John[3], Samuel[2], John[1], born Middlefield, Mass., March 11, 1814; married Oxford, Mass., May 6, 1840, M. H. Shumway, daughter of Levens Shumway, of Munson, Mass. Manufacturer. Residence, 1878, North Brookfield, Worcester Co., Mass. Died there, February 26, 1879. Children:

I Ellen Elizabeth, born Jan. 28, 1842; married Dec. 7, 1873, S. H. Emery, of East Canaan, N. H. Residence, 1879, Bellows Falls, Vt. One son.

**130**    II Joseph Oscar, b. May 14, 1845; m. June
11, 1871, Elizabeth Dolan.
**130**    III Charles Edgar, b. June 11, 1850; m. Dec.
25, 1871, Martha A. Collamer.
IV Frank Edward, born Mar. 9. 1853.   Residence, 1876, with his father.

**129. Joseph Oscar Pelton[8]**, first son of Joseph[7], Ithamar[6], Ithamar[5], John[4], John[3], Samuel[2], John[1], born Oxford, Mass., May 14, 1845; married Peru, Ind., June 11, 1871, Elizabeth, daughter of Thomas Dolan, of Peru, Ind.   Wool grader.   Residence, 1878, Peru, Ind.   No children.

**130. Charles Edgar Pelton[8]**, second son of Joseph[7], Ithamar[6], Ithamar[5], John[4], John[3], Samuel[2], John[1], born at Oxford. Mass., June 17, 1850; married at Franklin. N. H., December 25, 1871, Martha A., daughter of Thomas Collamer, of Burlington, Vt. Died at Ludlow, Vt., March 26, 1872, where his widow continued to live in 1876.   Child:
I Charles Edgar, Jr., born Ludlow, Vt., Oct. 7, 1872.

**120. Trowbridge Pelton[7]**, seventh son of Ithamar[6], Ithamar[5], John[4], John[3], Samuel[2], John[1], born Middlefield, Mass., August 12, 1816; married (1) Litchfield. Medina Co.. O., about February, 1843, Martha Melissa (b. May 31, 1821), daughter of Lysander Strong, of Chatham, Medina Co., O. Farmer.   Residence, 1878, Hebron, Jefferson Co., Wis.   Children:
**131**    I Lysander, b. Dec. 2, 1844; m. June 21, 1868, Marilla Hurd.
**131**    II Leander, b. Dec. 2, 1844; m. Nov. 16, 1868, Sarah L. Pond.

III Harriet Althea, born Litchfield, O., Dec.
25, 1846; married (1) Jan. 9, 1870,
William Brown; one child, Anna; (2)
Rome, Wis., Jan. 25, 1874, Benj. Ham-
mond, son of Stephen Hammond, of
Rochester, Mass. Residence, 1878,
Hebron, Wis. Children: David, Har-
riet, Melvina.

**132** IV Harlan P., b. July 14, 1850; m. Aug. 22,
1872, Eliza Ann Pond.

V Zenas J., born Ithaca, Richland Co.,
Wis., Nov. 23, 1853. In 1865 went
west with his mother to Buffalo Grove,
Buchanan Co., Iowa, and there staid.

**136. Lysander Felton**, first son of Trowbridge[3],
Ithamar[4], Ithamar[3], John[4], John[3], Samuel[2], John[1], born
Litchfield, Medina Co., O., December 2, 1844; mar-
ried at Cortland Station, Ill., June 21, 1868, Marilla
E., daughter of Curtiss Hurd, of Kingston, Ill.
Farmer. Lived from November 8, 1868, to March
4, 1872, in Nebraska. Residence, 1878, Afton, De
Kalb Co., Ill. (Address, De Kalb Center, Ill.)
Children:

I Edith, born July 8, 1870.
II Lester L., born July 25, 1875.

**136. Leander Felton**, second son of Trow-
bridge[1], Ithamar[5], Ithamar[4], John[4], John[3], Samuel[2],
John[1], twin brother of Lysander above, born Litch-
field, O., December 2, 1844; married at De Kalb, Ill.,
November 16, 1868, Sarah L., daughter of Samuel
Pond, of Keene, N. H. Residence, 1878, Courtland,
De Kalb Co., Ill. Child:

I Clarence H., born Courtland, Ill., Mar.
24, 1871; died July 9, 1877.

**130. Harlan Page Pelton**[7], third son of Trowbridge[7], Ithamar[6], Ithamar[5], John[4], John[3], Samuel[2], John[1], born Litchfield, Medina Co., O., July 14, 1850; married at Sycamore, Ill., August 22, 1872, Eliza Ann Pond. Lumberman, Ewart, Mich. Address, 1878. Five Lakes, Lapeer Co., Mich. Wife Eliza Ann died March 5, 1875. Children:

 I Erberd Frederick, born Aug. 28, 1873.
 II Eliza Ann, born Mar. 4, 1875; died Mar. 11, 1875.

**126. Cyprian Pelton**[6], eighth son of Ithamar[6], Ithamar[5], John[4], John[3], Samuel[2], John[1], born Middlefield, Hampden Co., Mass., January 15, 1821; married Litchfield, O., January 27, 1856, Flora Amanda Strong (b. May 16, 1834), daughter of Lysander Strong, of Warren, Conn., and Chatham, Medina Co., O. Residence, 1876, Kent, Portage Co., O., where he died, August 29, 1877, from injuries received about three and a half years before. Carpenter and joiner; an excellent man and a good mechanic. Children, none.

**120. Philander Pelton**[6], ninth son of Ithamar[6], Ithamar[5], John[4], John[3], Samuel[2], John[1], born Middlefield, Mass., April 9, 1823; married Medina, O., September 9, 1848, Emily Finn, daughter of Edward Finn, of York, O. Carpenter and joiner, Litchfield, O., where he died, February 18, 1863. Children:

 I Matilda D., born Mar. 30, 1852.
 II Cora E., born Oct. 2, 1858.

**94. Asahel Pelton**[5], fourth son of Ithamar[5], John[4], John[3], Samuel[2], John[1], born at East Windsor, Conn., August 3, 1774; married (1) December 31, 1798, Anna Denio, daughter of David Denio, of

Deerfield, Mass. (b. Nov. 28, 1780; d. Dalton, Mass., Dec. 1. 1821); (2) February, 1821, Hannah Benson, of Hinsdale, Mass., who died in childbirth, Coxsackie, N. Y., in 1822; (3) August 6, 1824, Sarah Gillett, daughter of J. Richards, of Hinsdale, Mass., who died in Wisconsin.   Mr. Pelton lived in Windsor and Dalton, Mass., and removed from Dalton, Mass., to Athens, N. Y., February, 1820, and thence to Austerlitz, Columbia Co., N. Y., April 7, 1830, where he died, March 27, 1857.   Children:

135      I John, b. Aug. 9, 1800; m. Jan. 8, 1824, Sarah R. Hinckley; d. Jan. 28, 1867.

II Preston, born July 26, 1802; died at Dalton, Berkshire Co., Mass., Sept. 10, 1813.

138  III Hart Leverett, b. Mar. 26, 1804; m. (1) Feb. 22, 1834, Ruth Miller; (2) Nov. 27, 1844, Sylvia Etta Miller, sisters; d. Sept. 7, 1848.

IV Sabrina A., born Dec. 22–26, 1806; married Jan. 21, 1825, Ithamar Pratt Pelton, son of Ithamar Pelton, Jr. (see p. 122). Living, 1878, at La Grange, O.

V Horace M., born Apr. 26, 1808; died Aug. 6, 1815.

VI Mary W., born July 28, 1810; married Sept. 23, 1830, Lyman, son of Ithamar Pelton, Jr. (see p. 127), of Middlefield, Mass., and Litchfield, O.   Residence, 1879, Lansing, Mich.

138 VII Sumner Maynard, b. Jan. 26, 1812; married (1) Dec. 27, 1841, Phila Bedell; (2) Oct. 30, 1856, Sylvia Etta Miller; (3) Nov. 5, 1873, Jeannette C. Johnson; d. May 18, 1879.

140   VIII Lysander Preston, b. Sept. 27, 1813; m.
            (1) Nov. 9, 1837, Lucinda Reynolds
            Packard; (2) Feb. 22, 1844, Cornelia
            C. Evarts.
141   IX Horace Birt, b. Oct. 3, 1815; m. May 9,
            1837, Mary Corley.
      X Laura, born Dalton, Mass., Mar. 24, 1817;
            married (1) Claverack, N. Y., May 15,
            1841, Isaac Persons (b. May 6, 1810;
            d. July 31, 1856), son of Isaac Persons,
            of Dutchess Co., N. Y.; children, three;
            (2) Sodus, N. Y., Jan. 13, 1870, Wm.
            Becker (b. Dec. 13, 1812), son of Jos.
            Becker, of Hillsdale, N. Y.; no children.
            Residence, 1879, Sodus, N. Y.
      XI Asahel, Jr., born June 8, 1818; died un-
            married, at Austerlitz, Columbia Co.,
            N. Y., Aug. 11, 1842.
      XII Harriet Newell, born Mar. 8, 1820; mar-
            ried at Spencertown Columbia Co.,
            N. Y., Abner W. Hitchcock (b. Nov.
            22, 1819), son of Orlando Hitchcock,
            of Alford, Mass.  One child, Francis
            A., b. Apr. 13, 1847.  Residence, 1879,
            at Lansing, Mich.
      XIII Hannah, born Apr. 11, 1826; died Oct. 2,
            1827.


182. John Pelton[7], first son of Asahel[6], Ithamar[5], John[4], John[3], Samuel[2], John[1], born Windsor,
Berkshire Co., Mass., August 9, 1800; married at
Madison, N. Y., January 8, 1824, Sarah R. Hinckley
(b. May 6, 1870, Washington, Berkshire Co., Mass.),
daughter of Bezaleel Hinckley, of Lee, Oneida Co.,
N. Y.  Lived at Athens, N. Y.; removed to Reeds-

burg, Sauk Co., Wis., in 1850, and there died, January 28, 1867. Farmer. Mrs. Pelton died at the house of Mr. E. L. Montross, June 26, 1890, aged 83 years. Children:

**135**     I Hiram, b. Aug. 31, 1825; m. Jan. 30, 1849, Deborah Seaman.

       II Sarah Ann, born at Athens, N. Y., June 22, 1827; married at Four Miles Point light-house, Greene Co., N. Y., Feb. 5, 1851, to Enos L. Montross, of Athens, N. Y. Children: Frederic, b. Nov. 12, 1851; d. Aug. 23, 1854; Ivah, b. Nov. 7, 1855; d. Mar. 9, 1860.

**136**     III George, b. Feb. 9, 1830; m. Nov. 16, 1854, to Phœbe T. Montross.

**137**     IV Charles A., b. Apr. 9, 1831; m. (1) Jan. 11, 1857, Nancy Maria Oakes; (2) Jan. 24, 1870, Mrs. Emily (Temple) Wakefield.

       V Hannah, born May 3, 1836.

**137**     VI John Edgar, b. Dec. 15, 1842; m. Oct. 15, 1868, Olive A. Kellogg.

**138**     VII Jason M., b. about 1845. No report.

**135. Hiram Pelton**[8], first son of John[7], Asahel[6], Ithamar[5], John[4], John[3], Samuel[2], John[1], born at Saugerties, N. Y., Aug. 31, 1825; married at Athens, N. Y., January 30, 1849, Deborah Seaman, daughter of Samuel Seaman, of that place. Gardener. Living, in 1890, at Dallas, Barron Co., Wis. Served in the United States Navy in the War of the Southern Rebellion. Was mate on the steamboat "Connecticut" until she was sent by the government to Fortress Monroe for hospital purposes. Children:

    I Emma E., born June 15, 1851; died Aug.
20, 1854.
    II Ida E., born June 11, 1854; died Feb. 18,
1879.
    III Alva S., born Sept. 28, 1856.
    IV Maynard, born Dec. 13, 1858.
    V Marion, born July 8, 1861; died Sept. 3,
1864.
    VI Ernest A., born July 11, 1867.
    VII Fanny B., born Oct. 22, 1882.

**134. George Pelton**, second son of John, Asahel, Ithamar, John, John, Samuel, John, born at Austerlitz, Columbia Co., N. Y., February 9, 1830; married at Reedsburg, Wis., November 16, 1854, to Phœbe T. Montross, daughter of Samuel Montross, of that place. Farmer. Living, in 1890, at Reedsburg, Sauk Co., Wis. Children:

**136**    I S. Aylmer, b. June 1, 1856; m. Dec. 30,
1882, Frankie M. Battles.
**137**    II Montross, b. Dec. 13, 1859; m. Nov. 21,
1888, Mary J. Nye.
    III George Meredith, born May 1, 1863; died
Oct. 4, 1865.

**136. S. Aylmer Pelton**, first son of George, John, Asahel, Ithamar, John, John, Samuel, John, born at Reedsburg, Sauk Co., Wis., June 1, 1856; married there, December 30, 1882, Frankie M. Battles. Farmer. Living, in 1890, at Reedsburg, Wis. Children:

    I Guy, born Apr. 16, 1884.
    II Glen E., born Sept. 28, 1885.
    III Clara, born Jan. 17, 1888.

**136. Montross Pelton**, second son of George⁸, John⁷, Asahel⁶, Ithamar⁵, John⁴, John³, Samuel², John¹, born at Reedsburg, Wis., December 13, 1859; married there, November 21, 1888, Mary J. Nye. Farmer. Residence at Reedsburg, Wis., in 1890. Children, none.

**184. Charles A. Pelton**, third son of John⁷, Asahel⁶, Ithamar⁵, John⁴, John³, Samuel², John¹, born at Greenbush, Penobscot Co., Me., April 9, 1831; married (1) at Portage, Columbia Co., Wis., January 11, 1857, Nancy Maria Oakes, daughter of Edward and Nancy Oakes (d. Mar. 2, 1868); (2) at Hilbourn City, Wis., January 24, 1870, Mrs. Emily (Temple) Wakefield (b. at Reading, Mass., Mar. 30, 1833), daughter of Timothy and Sophronia Temple. Farmer. Lived, in 1890, at Reedsburg, Wis. Children:

 I Olive Wheeler, born Feb. 11, 1859; married at Reedsburg, Wis., Charles Powell. Residence, 1890, at Reedsburg, Wis.
 II May, born Dec. 2, 1860; died Sept. 2, 1862.
 III Charles, born Jan. 17, 1868.
 IV Willis T., born Oct. 7, 1872.

**185. John Edgar Pelton**, fourth son of John⁷, Asahel⁶, Ithamar⁵, John⁴, John³, Samuel², John¹, born at Athens, N. Y., December 15, 1842; married at Baraboo, Wis., Oct. 15, 1868, Olive A. Kellogg, daughter of George and Hannah Kellogg, of Prairie du Sac, Wis. Farmer. Residence, in 1890, at Reedsburg, Sauk Co., Wis. Children:
 I Bertha E., born Apr. 16, 1871.
 II Maude Genevieve, born Nov. 29, 1875.

**181. Jason M. Pelton**, fifth son of John, Asahel, Ithamar, John, John, Samuel, John. Address, 1891, Dallas, Wis.; written repeatedly, no reply.

**182. Hart Leverett Pelton**, third son of Asahel, Ithamar, John, John, Samuel, John, born Austerlitz, Columbia Co., N. Y., March 26, 1804; married (1) February 22, 1834, Ruth Miller; (2) November 27, 1844, Sylvia Etta Miller, daughters of John Miller, of Greenfield, Saratoga Co., N. Y. (Ruth, b. July 8, 1813; d. June 21, 1844; Sylvia Etta, b. Mar. 23, 1820; d. Mar. 28, 1872). Lived in Schenectady, N. Y.; died Albany, N. Y., September 7, 1848. Children, of wife Ruth:

    I Harriet Amelia, born 1838; died 1840.
    II Ruth Harriet, born June 7, 1844; married
        Syracuse, N. Y., Mar. 20, 1873, Edward
        J. Van Epps, of Schenectady, N. Y.
        (b. Mar. 28, 1847). Occupation, shoe-
        dealer. Children, none.

Children of wife Sylvia Etta, four, who all died in infancy.

**183. Sumner Maynard Pelton**, fifth son of Asahel, Ithamar, John, John, Samuel, John, born Windsor, Berkshire Co., Mass., January 26, 1812; married (1) Philac Bedell, December 27, 1841, New Baltimore, N. Y. (b. July 31, 1817; d. Hillsdale, Columbia Co., N. Y., Dec. 4, 1854); (2) Schenectady, N. Y., October 30, 1856, Sylvia Etta, widow of Hart Leverett Pelton, daughter of John Miller, of Greenfield, Saratoga Co., N. Y. (d. Mar. 28, 1872); (3) Jeannette C. Johnson, at Johnstown, N. Y., November 5, 1873. Carpenter and builder. Died suddenly from

paralysis and congestion of the brain, Schenectady,
N. Y., at 3 A. M., Sunday, May 18, 1879.  Children:

**126**    I Adelbert, b. Jan. 21, 1843; m. —— Morrison; d. June 22, 1879.

II Emma Jane, born June 24, 1849, New Baltimore, N. Y.; married Geo. E. Beide, June 3, 1872, Brooklyn, N. Y. Residence, 1879, Brooklyn.  Children, three.

III Benjamin Case, born Oct. 13, 1853, at New Baltimore, N. Y.

IV Archie T., born May 7, 1857; died July 27, 1859.

V Edith Althea, born July 4, 1860.

VI Sarah Elizabeth, born July 9, 1863; died Aug. 12, 1863.

**126. Adelbert Felton**, first son of Sumner Maynard', Asahel', Ithamar', John', John', Samuel', John', born January 21, 1843, Hillsdale, N. Y.; married Jersey City, N. J., ——, —— Morrison, daughter of James D. Morrison, 374 Communipaw avenue, of that city.  Lived in New York city and there died, Sunday, June 22, 1879.  Children, none living.

**127. Lysander Preston Felton**, sixth son of Asahel', Ithamar', John', John', Samuel', John', born Dalton, Mass., September 27, 1813; married (1) November 9, 1837, Lucinda Reynolds Packard (b. Aug. 2, 1817); (2) Cornelia Catherine Evarts (b. July 8, 1819), February 22, 1844, Hillsdale, N. Y. (d. May 10, 1874).  Blacksmith.  Living, 1875, Austerlitz, Columbia Co., N. Y., and in 1879 at Richmond, Berkshire Co., Mass.  Children:

**140**     I Harlan Page, b. Sept. 18, 1838; m. Feb.
21, 1864. Louisa Winklepleck; killed
in battle at Atlanta, Ga., Aug. 3, 1864.

**111**     II Charles E., b. Mar. 24. 1845; m. Oct. 17,
1876, Amanda E. Sprague.

III Mary L., born Nov. 6, 1846: married May
1, 1871, Alfred O. Harvey (b. Feb. 12,
1847).  In 1891 lived at Austerlitz,
N. Y.; one child, Willis Harvey.

**141**     IV Homer L., b. July 16, 1848; m. Sept. 15,
1875, Sarah Gage.

V Laura Anna, born Apr. 15, 1850; married
May 1, 1871, Hiram Cole (b. Aug. 10,
1850).   Children: 1. A son, that died
in infancy; 2. Clarence, and two others;
died Jan. 9, 1884.

VI A son, born and died Dec. 23, 1851.

**141**  VII David Martin, b. July 8, 1853; m. Oct.
14, 1877, Alice Spencer.

VIII Harriet Almeda, born Mar. 15, 1861.

IX Infant son, born Sept. 14, 1868; died the
same day.


**139. Harlan Page Pelton**, first son of Lysander
Preston[7], Asahel[6], Ithamar[5], John[4], John[3], Samuel[2],
John[1], born September 18, 1838; married in Wood
Co., O., February 21, 1864, Louisa Winklepleck; killed
in battle at Atlanta, Ga., August 3, 1864.   One
child, Armilda, daughter, born November 16, 1864;
married at Bozeman, Mont., June 13, 1891, A. S.
Trescott, of that place, and there lived November
6, 1891.

Mrs. Pelton married (2) March 3, 1867, at Spiker,
Neb., Mr. John B. Porter, of that place.

**189. Charles E. Pelton**, second son of Lysander P., Asahel, Ithamar, John, John, Samuel, John, born March 24, 1845; married October 17, 1876, Amanda E. Sprague, of Alford, Mass. Lived, in 1879, at Spencertown, Columbia Co., N. Y.; in 1891 a merchant at East Chatham, N. Y. Children, none.

**190. Homer B. Pelton**, third son of Lysander P., Asahel, Ithamar, John, John, Samuel, John, born July 16, 1848; married September 15, 1875, Sarah Gage. Farmer. Living, 1879, at Penn Yan, N. Y. Children:

    I Carrie C., born June 12, 1876.
    II Charles E., born Oct. 15, 1878.
    III George B., born June 27, 1880.
    IV John, born Mar. 13, 1882; died Aug. 15, 1882.

**191. David Martin Pelton**, fifth son of Lysander P., Asahel, Ithamar, John, John, Samuel, John, born July 8, 1853; married at West Stockbridge, Mass., October 14, 1877, Alice Spencer, daughter of Robert Spencer. In 1879 lived at Housatonic, and in 1891 at Dalton, Mass. A manufacturer of chemicals for paper mills. Children:

    I Walter A., born Sept. 5, 1878.
    II Howard M., born July 11, 1880.
    III Cora L., born at Dalton, Mass., Feb. 11, 1883.

**192. Horace Birt Pelton**, seventh son of Asahel, Ithamar, John, John, Samuel, John, born Dalton, Mass., October 3, 1815; married at Athens, N. Y., May 9, 1837, Mary Corley, daughter of John Corley, of that place. Living, 1876, at Corona, Long Island, N. Y. Carpenter and sailor. Children:

> I Charlotte A., born July 13, 1838; married
> Athens, N. Y., Feb. 25, 1862, Malachi
> Garrison; died Sept. 30, 1862.
> II Lysander, born August 27, 1839.
> III Miranda P., born Dec. 7, 1842; married
> at Catskill, N. Y., July 4, 1860, Wm.
> Henry Edwards, who was killed, Chi-
> cago, Ill., June 28, 1870.
> IV George Judson, born Mar. 4, 1846.
> V James P., born Nov. 15, 1847.
> VI Horace O., born June 22, 1853.
> VII Elizabeth, born Feb. 7, 1855.

**94. Hezekiah Pelton**, fifth son of Ithamar[5], John[4], John[3], Samuel[2], John[1], born East Windsor, Conn., February 21, 1777; married (1) Peru, Berkshire Co., Mass., March, 1803, Hannah Hathaway Axtelle, daughter of Ebenezer Axtelle; (2) February 20, 1831, at Sidney, Delaware Co., N. Y., Mary Baldwin, daughter of Simon Baldwin, of Cornwall, Conn. Carpenter and joiner. About 1781 went with his father's family to Middlefield, Mass., and lived there and in adjoining towns until 1826, when he removed to Franklin, Delaware Co., N. Y., thence to Saugerties, N. Y., where he lost his wife, thence returned to Franklin, and there died, February 12, 1853. Buried in North Walton, Delaware Co., N. Y. Children:

> I Abigail A., born Sept. 20, 1804; married
> at Franklin, N. Y., Dec. 25, 1825,
> Hezron Benedict. Lived in North
> Walton, Delaware Co., N. Y., and there
> died, Aug. 8, 1864.
> II Mariette, born Feb. 3, 1806; married Col.
> Nathan Beckwith, of Red Hook,

Dutchess Co., N. Y., where he died, Feb., 1857.

III Hannah M., born Nov. 25, 1810; married North Walton, Delaware Co., N. Y., Apr. 15, 1838, George L. Hodge. In 1890 lived at Rainbow, Hartford Co., Conn. Children, five.

IV Asenath E., born Mar., 1818; died unmarried, June, 1827.

V Harriet C., born Mar. 11, 1820; married Kingston, N. Y., Feb. 9, 1837, John W. Leonard. Lived, 1890, at Rainbow, Hartford Co., Conn.

VI Elizabeth, born Aug. 22, 1822; died unmarried.

142 VII Hezekiah P., b. Sept. 26, 1832; m. Feb. 22, 1858, Adeline A. Beardsley.

144 VIII Salmon S., b. Mar. 7, 1834; m. Jan. 11, 1859, Jane Bennett.

IX Mary A., born Feb. 28, 1836; married Sept. 5, 1861, Theron Saterlee, son of Jos. Saterlee, of Franklin, Delaware Co., N. Y. Residing there in 1878.

**142. Hezekiah P. Felton**, first son of Hezekiah[6], Ithamar[5], John[4], John[3], Samuel[2], John[1], born Sidney, Delaware Co., N. Y., September 26, 1832; married February 22, 1858, Adeline A. Beardsley, daughter of Benj. Beardsley, of Franklin, Delaware Co., N. Y., where he resided in 1875. Farmer. Children:

I Deliaette, born June 6, 1860.

II Edward F., born Nov. 5, 1862.

III Salmon B., b. Apr. 23, 1867.

IV Charles A., born Jan. 20, 1871.

V Arthur M., born Aug. 26, 1873.

VI Minnie M., born Oct. 5, 1875.

**142. Salmon S. Pelton**[7], second son of Hezekiah[6], Ithamar[5], John[4], John[3], Samuel[2], John[1], born Delaware Co., N. Y., March 7, 1834; married January 11, 1859, Franklin, Delaware Co., N. Y., Jane Bennett, daughter of Abijah Bennett. Lived, 1878, at Woodbine, Harrison Co., Iowa. Children:

    I Elijah E., born Nov. 5, 1862; died Sept. 25, 1863.
    II Merritt H., born Dec. 30, 1865.
    III Nora M., born June 25, 1869.
    IV Ira B., born Nov. 1, 1871.
    V Burton L., born Sept. 24, 1874.

**94. Joel Pelton**[6], sixth son of Ithamar[5], John[4], John[3], Samuel[2], John[1], born East Windsor, Conn., August 19, 1779; married Middlefield, Mass., about 1803, Ruth Fields, daughter of Deacon Zachariah Fields, of that place, who died March, 1822. Wife Ruth died about 1819; (2) about 1823 Rosetta Edwards, of Cairo, N. Y., daughter of Stephen Edwards, of Athens, N. Y. Farmer. Lived Middlefield, Mass., Cairo and Coeymans and Coeymans Hollow, Albany Co., N. Y., where he died, March 20, 1865. His wife, Rosetta, died March 20, 1870. He served as constable, justice of the peace and as sheriff.

NOTE.— It is said he had 21 living children; if so this record lacks a number of names, probably of those dying in infancy, the first wife having borne 11 children. Children:

    I Joel F., born Middlefield, Mass., Aug. 23, 1805; died unmarried at Mantua, Portage Co., O., June 1, 1831-4.
146    II Ira C., b. June 22, 1807; m. (1) July 4, 1831, Charlotte G. Rowe; (2) Oct. 20, 1867, Mary A. Wentz.

**148** III Hiram S., b. June 7, 1809; m. (1) Oct. 17,
1839, Mehitable E. Sawyer; (2) Eliza
Hackley; d. May 26, 1847.

**149** IV Alson Homer, b. May 23, 1811; m. Nov.
11, 1839, Laura Thomson.

V Thankful, b. (probably) about 1813; lived
nine years.

**150** VI Milo Sandford, b. Feb. 14, 1815; m. Nov.
21, 1844. Louisa Maria Harrington; d.
May 12, 1849.

VII Mary, born Savoy, Mass., May, 1819;
married there, May 12. 1839, Milton
Nash, son of Rev. Jonathan Nash, of
that place (Cong'l minister); died Middlefield. Mass., May 9, 1847, leaving
three sons,(five children died in infancy).

VIII, IX, X, XI No record.

Children of the second wife:

**150** XII Aaron, b. Aug. 24, 1824; m. (1) Nov. 5,
1845, Eleanor Wickham; (2) Catharine
Green.

**152** XIII James, b. Sept. 1, 1828; m. (1) Jan. 13,
1855, Gertrude Rarick; (2) Apr. 11,
1866, Rhoda Cornelius.

XIV Moses E., born ——, 1830; unmarried.
Living, 1878, Indian Fields, Albany
Co., N. Y.

XV Joel, Jr., born ——; written, no return.

XVI Ruth Ann, born Coxsackie, N. Y., Nov.
17, 1835; married Albany, N. Y., Aug.
30, 1853, Bernard Ward (d. Sept. 11,
1874). son of Peter Ward. of Newburgh, N. Y. Children, eight. Residence, 1879. Matawan, Monmouth
Co., N. J.

XVII Rebecca Jane, born Coxsackie, N. Y., Apr.
9, 1840; married Sept. 10, 1853, Justin
Felt, son of John Felt, of Holyoke,
Mass.; died West Troy, N. Y., June
27, 1856. Her husband died, leaving a
son, Charles H., b. June 27, 1855, who
married, had two children and lived,
1879, at Greenbush, N. Y.
XVIII, XIX, XX, XXI No record.


**148. Ira C. Pelton**, second son of Joel[6], Ithamar[5],
John[4], John[3], Samuel[2], John[1], born Middlefield, Mass.,
January 22, 1807; married (1) at Sand Lake, Rensselaer Co., N. Y., July 4, 1831, Charlotte G. Rowe,
daughter of Chauncey Rowe, of Nassau, N. Y.; (2)
at Prairie du Chien, Wis., October 20, 1867, Mrs.
Mary A. Wentz, daughter of Richard Valentine, of
Mount Sterling, Wis. Farmer. Removed to Pennsylvania in 1836; to Prairie du Chien, Wis., in 1860;
thence to DeWitt, Saline Co., Neb., where he died
February 10, 1879.
NOTE.—He stated that two brothers of John[3], first
of Essex, Conn., went to Long Island, N. Y.; one of
the very few traditions preserved. Samuel, the
oldest, and Benjamin, the youngest, of John[3]'s brothers
went to Huntington, Long Island, N. Y. (See pp.
33 and 34.) Children:
147      I Edwin C., b. Mar. 25, 1833; m. May 23,
1858, Ruth A. Palmer.
II Albert H., born Jan. 20, 1835. Served in
Co. D, 11th Regt., Ill. Vol., and died
Oct. 30, 1861, at Camp Lyon, Bird's
Point. Mo.
III Chauncey R., born Feb. 2, 1837; died Mar.
14, 1837.

IV Mary Olivia, born July 21, 1838; married
   at Greene, Erie Co., Pa., Aug. 27, 1859,
   Frank (b. Mar. 27, 1840, at Smarden,
   Co. Kent, Eng.), son of James Home-
   wood, of Westfield, N. Y.  Farmer.
   Children, six.  Lived, 1878, at Witts-
   burg, Cross Co., Ark.
147   V Milo Sandford, b. Nov. 12, 1841; m. Sept.
   24, 1866, Mary E. Potter.
147   VI Daniel R., b. May 19, 1844; m. Feb. 24,
   1864, Catharine A. Valentine.
   VII Ida May, born Oct. 2, 1868.


**146. Edwin C. Pelton**, first son of Ira C.[7], Joel[6],
Ithamar[5], John[4], John[3], Samuel[2], John[1], born at Sand
Lake, Rensselaer Co., N. Y., March 25, 1833; mar-
ried Durand, Winnebago Co., Ill., May 23, 1858, Ruth
A. Palmer, daughter of Randall Palmer, of Rhode
Island.  Farmer.  Living, 1878, Deerfield, Chicka-
saw Co., Iowa.  Children:
   I Albert Enos, born Jan. 24, 1865.
   II Alura K., born Feb. 5, 1873; died Mar. 3,
   1873.


**146. Milo Sandford Pelton**, fourth son of Ira
C.[7], Joel[6], Ithamar[5], John[4], John[3], Samuel[2], John[1], born
at Greene, Erie Co., Pa., November 12, 1844; mar-
ried at Staceyville, Mitchell Co., Iowa, September 24,
1866, Mary E., daughter of Stillman Potter, of that
place.  Farmer.  Living in 1878 at Riceville, Mitchell
Co., Iowa.  Children, none in 1878.


**146. Daniel R. Pelton**, fifth son of Ira C.[7], Joel[6],
Ithamar[5], John[4], John[3], Samuel[2], John[1], born at Greene,
Erie Co., Pa., May 19, 1844; married at Plattsville,

Grant Co., Wis., February 24, 1864, Catharine A., daughter of Richard Valentine, of Mount Sterling, Wis. Physician and surgeon. Residence, 1878, De Witt, Saline Co., Neb., 1892, Topeka, Kans. Children:

    I Frank, born Nov. 8, 1869.
    II George Herbert, born June 16, 1873.
    III Amy, born July 14, 1878.

**144. Hiram S. Pelton**, third son of Joel⁶, Ithamar⁵, John⁴, John³, Samuel², John¹, born Middlefield, Mass., June 7, 1809; married (1) at Crown Point, Ind., October 17, 1839, Mehitable E. Sawyer (d. Apr. 1, 1842, aged 26), of Deep River, Lake Co., Ind.; (2) April 12, 1844, Eliza Hackley. Merchant. Died Crown Point, Ind., May 26, 1847. Children:

148    I Milo S., b. Sept. 29, 1840; m. (1) Dec. 15, 1868, Agatha Williams; (2) Apr. 4, 1873, Eliza A. Erb.

    II Mary E., born Feb. 9, 1845, at Crown Point, Ind.; married May 18, 1870, Thomas J. Wood, lawyer, son of Darius C. Wood, of Terre Haute, Ind. Residence, 1878, Crown Point, Ind. Children: Charles Harvey, 7 years old; Flora May, 6 years; Alice P., 2 years; Ora Eliza, 9 months.

**148. Milo S. Pelton**, first son of Hiram S.⁷, Joel⁶, Ithamar⁵, John⁴, John³, Samuel², John¹, born Crown Point, Lake Co., Ind., September 29, 1840; married there (1) December 15, 1868, Agatha Williams (d. May 9, 1872), daughter of William R. Williams, of that place; (2) April 4, 1873, Eliza A. Erb, of Canada. Farmer. Residence, 1878, at Crown Point, Ind. Children:

I Mary C., born Oct. 1, 1869; died June 6, 1871.

II Hiram S., born Oct. 23, 1874.

**144. Alson Homer Pelton**, fourth son of Joel[6], Ithamar[5], John[4], John[3], Samuel[2], John[1], born at Middlefield, Mass., May 23, 1811; married Peru, Berkshire Co., Mass., November 11, 1839, Laura Thomson (d. Oct. 11, 1866), daughter of Elias Thomson, of Peru, Mass. Residence, 1879, Peru, Mass. Children, born at Peru:

I Armonella, } born Oct. 9, 1840; at home, unmarried 1879.

II Armarilla, } born Oct. 9, 1840; married May 7, 1863, Thomas F. Barker, son of Asahel Barker, of Hinsdale, Mass., where she lived in 1879. Children, four.

III Sandford H., born Jan. 1, 1843. In 1879 at home, unmarried.

148 IV Grafton S., b. Nov. 24, 1844; m. Mar. 1, 1876, Ada E. Matoon.

V Mary J., born June 8, 1847; married Mar. 27, 1877, Everett O. Foss, of Pelham, N. H., where she lived in 1879. No children.

**148. Grafton S. Pelton**, second son of Alson Homer[7], Joel[6], Ithamar[5], John[4], John[3], Samuel[2], John[1], born at Peru, Berkshire Co., Mass., November 24, 1844; married Lenox, Mass., March 1, 1876, Ada E. (b. Aug. 27, 1853), daughter of James F. Mattoon, of Lenox. Farmer. Residence, 1879, Lenox, Mass. Children:

I Minnie Alice, born June 23, 1877.

**144. Milo Sandford Pelton**[7], fifth son of Joel[6], Ithamar[5], John[4], John[3], Samuel[2], John[1], born Middlefield, Mass., February 14, 1815; married Boston, Mass., November 21, 1844, Louisa Maria, daughter of Daniel Harrington, of Cornwallis and Antigonish, Nova Scotia. In New York city 1842-3, a wholesale stationer and paper dealer; afterward, till 1847, with Good, Pelton & Noble, in the same business; thence removed to Ware, Mass., and engaged in the clothing business, and there died, May 12, 1849. Height, 5 feet 10 inches; florid complexion, blue eyes, hair dark. Children:

  **156**    I Sandford Harrington, b. Sept. 28, 1845; m. Nov. 16, 1869, Mary Georgiana Darby.

          II George McElwain, born Sept. 10, 1847; died Aug. 12, 1848.

          III Mary Louisa, born Oct. 10, 1848.

**156. Sandford Harrington Pelton**[8], first son of Milo S.[7], Joel[6], Ithamar[5], John[4], John[3], Samuel[2], John[1], born at New York city, September 28, 1845; removed with his parents to Ware, Mass., and, after his father's death, with his mother to Nova Scotia. Married at Yarmouth, N. S., November 16, 1869, Mary Georgiana Darby, daughter of Capt. Joseph William Edward Darby, of Halifax, N. S. Residence, 1892, Yarmouth, N. S. Barrister and attorney-at-law. Children:

          I Charles Sandford, born Apr. 30, 1870.

          II Eva St. Clare, born Dec. 2, 1872.

          III Arthur Edward Waldemar, born Apr. 16, 1878.

**145. Aaron Pelton**[7], sixth son of Joel[6], Ithamar[5], John[4], John[3], Samuel[2], John[1], born at Athens, N. Y., August 24, 1824; married (1) Coeymans, N. Y.,

November 5, 1845, Eleanor, daughter of Eccal Wickham, of that place; (2) Catharine Green, daughter of William Green, of Coeymans, N. Y.  Residence, 1878, Bethlehem, Albany Co., N. Y.  P. O. Becker's Corners, N. Y.  Children:

    I Helen L., born Sept. 6, 1846.

    II Eleanor, born Sept. 5, 1847, Bethlehem, N. Y.; married there, Aug. 1, 1864, John Van Alstyne.  Children: Mary L., b. Dec. 13, 1865; Peter S., b. Nov. 25, 1868; Hattie L., b. Sept. 5, 1870; Charles H., b. Apr. 20, 1872; Chatie J., b. Feb. 1, 1874; d. Feb. 9, 1874; Henry B., b. Jan. 4, 1877; William G., b. Aug. 7, 1879.  Residence, 1879, Bethlehem, Albany Co., N. Y.

    III Joel Pratt, b. Dec. 14, 1851; m. ———. P. O. Callanan's Corners, Albany Co., N. Y.; written, no reply.

    **151**  IV Eccal, b. May 29, 1853; m. Jan. 23, 1873, Elizabeth Shadow.

    V Hannah, born Aug. 24, 1856.

    VI Aaron B., b. Dec. 23, 1857.

    VII Ruth Ann, born June 13, 1859; married Coeymans, N. Y., Oct. 27, 1872, Wonderful E. Shuter (b. Mar. 11, 1852).  Children: Ada, b. July 8, 1874.  Residence, 1879, Becker's Corners, N. Y.

    VIII Carrie, born June 26, 1861.

    IX Mary Catharine, born Nov. 16, 1863.


**150. Eccal Pelton**, second son of Aaron[7], Joel[6], Ithamar[5], John[4], John[3], Samuel[2], John[1], born Bethlehem, Albany Co., N. Y., May 29, 1853; married there, January 23, 1873, Elizabeth Shadow, daughter of

Peter Shadow, of that place. Farmer. Residence, 1879, Becker's Corners, Albany Co., N. Y. Children:

    I Charles C., born Apr. 24, 1876.
    II Eccal E., born May 10, 1878.
    III Peter C., born July 10, 1879.

**111. James Pelton**, seventh son of Joel[6], Ithamar[5], John[4], John[3], Samuel[2], John[1], born Coxsackie, N. Y., September 1, 1828; married (1) Bethlehem Church. Albany Co., N. Y., January 13, 1855, Gertrude Rarick, daughter of Peter Rarick, of Coeymans, N. Y. (d. Feb. 2, 1864); married (2) at the same place, April 11, 1866, Rhoda Cornelius, daughter of Peter Cornelius, of Coeymans. Mason. Residence, 1878, South Bethlehem, N. Y. Enlisted July or August, 1862, in the 41st N. Y. Vols. for three years. Discharged for disability after about four months' service. Enlisted again April 3, 1865, in the 91st N. Y. Vols. for one year, and served to the end of the war. Children:

    I Rebecca Jane, born Dec. 19, 1856; married September 17, 1873, Benjamin Wickham. Residence, 1878, Coeymans Hollow, N. Y. Children: Mary Jane, b. May 22, 1874; Edward, b. June 4, 1876; John Henry, b. April 14, 1878.
    II Rachel, born Jan. 3, 1858; died Jan. 17, 1858.
    III James Henry, born Feb. 14, 1859.
    IV Moses, born May 21, 1861; died Sept. 27, 1864.
    V Infant, born Jan. 15, 1864; died Jan. 16, 1864.

Children of the second wife:

    VI Margaret Ellen, born Jan. 6, 1865.

**48. Cyprian Pelton[8]**, eighth son of Ithamar[7],
John[6], John[5], Samuel[4], John[3], born Middlefield, Mass.,
December 31, 1785; married ——— ———; died Whites-
boro, N. Y., and is said to have had five children,
two sons and three daughters; one son named Lysander, and one daughter, Angeline.   Nothing more
known.

**59. Josiah Pelton[5]**, fifth son of John[4], John[3],
Samuel[2], John[1], born Essex, Conn., August 15, 1745;
married (1) December 10, 1767, Mary Griswold,
daughter of (supposed) Giles Griswold, of East
Guilford, Conn. (d. Mar. 7, 1811, aged 64); (2) August 20, 1811, Widow Chloe Gilder, formerly of Hartford, Conn. (b. July 22, 1768; d. July 27, 1838).
Ship-carpenter and farmer.   Lived at Killingworth,
Conn., but in the spring of 1800 went with his son
Jesse to Ohio to survey the north half of the Township of Gustavus, Trumbull Co., O., which he had
bought.   In the spring of 1802 he removed his
family to Ohio, stopping first at Vernon, while prepa-
rations were being made in Gustavus for a home; and
in the summer passed through the wilderness to
Gustavus were he and they settled on new lands,
forming, with his sons, quite a colony of Peltons,
and where he died September 3, 1818.   Children:
 **155**     I Ithamar, b. Oct. 26, 1769; m. Mercy
             Griffin; d. Mar. 16, 1832.
         II Lydia, born Mar. 7, 1772; married John
             Lane.
 **161**   III Elias, b. Feb. 3, 1774; m. Mary Folsom;
             d. Feb., 1823.

IV  Zilpha, born Feb. 23, 1776; married Apr.
6, 1804, Eliphaz Perkins, the first marriage in Gustavus.   No children.
174  V  Jesse, b. June 7, 1778; m. Sept. 12, 1802,
Ruhama DeWolf; d. Oct. 1, 1862.
175  VI  Zenas, b. Feb. 15, 1780; m. Nov. 7, 1811,
Margaret Reid; d. Nov. 8, 1871.
176  VII  Julius, b. May 4, 1786; m. Feb. 12, 1810,
Hannah Folsom; d. June 12, 1862.
181  VIII  Harvey, b. Mar. 20, 1790; m. Oct. 24,
1816, Mary Bailey.

Six other children died in infancy.   Their places
in the register are unknown; probably two belong
between Zenas and Julius, two after Julius, and two
after Harvey.

NOTE.--Josiah Pelton, on his brother William's
refusal to act as executor for his father's will, took
his, William's, place, and settled up the affairs of the
estate of John Pelton, 2d, of Saybrook, Conn.   In
this way the account book of his father, containing
his father's family record, now in the possession of
Tensard D. Pelton, of Gustavus, O., came into his
hands.   On Mr. Pelton's return from his first visit to
Ohio he offered one hundred acres of land as a present to the first woman that would make her home in
the new settlement.   His son Jesse, after consulta-
tion with her, accepted the offer for Miss Ruhama
DeWolf, of Granby, who went with them to Ohio
and there married Jesse in 1802.   On the journey
west they passed through New Haven and New York
to Philadelphia, thence by "arks" (large six-horse
wagons) to the Ohio river; down that river on a flat-
boat to Beaver, and by ox teams sixty-five miles to
Vernon, Trumbull Co., O.   After a log cabin had
been built at Gustavus the family was taken there, fol-

lowing a "blazed" track through the wilderness. Still Mr. Pelton had to make frequent visits to Vernon for provisions. On one of these trips he saw a panther in a tree nearly over his head. Tying his hat and coat to a bush, and leaving his dog on guard, he returned to his cabin, a distance of three miles, for his rifle, came back and shot the panther, which measured nearly seven feet from tip to tip.

Game at that time was plentiful, and so tame that animals and birds scarcely feared man, deer feeding near at hand and wild turkeys flying down and feeding on the corn given to the domestic fowls and pigs.

At that time the nearest grist-mill was at Beaver, Pa., ninety miles away; stores were distant, and neighbors on the north were eighteen and on the west fifteen miles off.

**153. Ithamar Pelton**[6], first son of Josiah[5], John[4], John[3], Samuel[2], John[1], born Essex, Conn., October 26, 1769; married, summer of 1791, Mercy Griffin. He lived in Essex, Vt., from about 1794 to 1805, in the fall of which latter year he removed to Gustavus, O., where he settled on a farm and there died, March 16, 1832. His wife Mercy (b. Feb. 25, 1774) died September 14, 1844. Children:

    I Eunice Loraine (shortened to Laura), born May 4, 1792; married Gustavus, O., July 10, 1808, Roger Perkins; farmer (b. in Connecticut); d. in Illinois, July 11, 1855.

    II Flora, born in Connecticut, Sept., 1793 (as given by Mrs. Elizabeth Mowry); died June, 1797.

    III Oritta, born in Essex, Vt., Feb. 9, 1795; married (1) Feb. 14, 1813, Jasper Partridge, who died July 6, 1831; (2) about 1839, John Williams. Lived Gustavus, O., until her second marriage, then in Coldbrook, Ashtabula Co., O., where she died, Mar. 22, 1845. Children, nine; by the first marriage.

IV Achsah, born in Essex, Vt., Aug. 6, 1797; married in 1814, Noah Folsom. Lived in Wayne, Ashtabula Co., O., and in Baconsburg, O. Removing to Illinois in 1833 he disappeared on the way and was never heard of. She died in Illinois in 1844.

157 V Josiah, b. Feb. 18, 1799; m. Sept. 26, 1824, Mary (Polly) Wakeman; d. 1837.

157 VI Lester, b. July 7, 1801; m. Sept. 7, 1833, Mary (Polly) Rood.

VII Elizabeth, born Essex, Vt., Aug. 21, 1803; married Feb. 11, 1824, Isaac Mowry. Living, 1876, at Johnstonville, O. Children, 10; grandchildren, 18.

158 VIII Samuel G., b. June 11, 1805; m. Aug. 1, 1827, Matilda Kelly; d. June 5, 1857.

161 IX Hiram, b. Gustavus, O., Feb. 3, 1807; m. ——, Hannah Ballard; d. Apr., 1851.

162 X Albert, b. Mar. 26, 1809; m. (1) Lucina Rood; (2) Mary L. Jones; d. about 1849.

XI Lucius, born Gustavus, O., Apr., 1812; died Jan., 1813.

163 XII Ithamar, Jr., b. Mar. 26, 1816; m. (1) Nov. 3, 1836, Susannah Ann Jones; (2) Mar. 12, 1856, Lucina Almira Jones.

164 XIII Charles Wesley, b. Oct. 6, 1818; m. Jan. 2, 1839, Demis Isham.

**155. Josiah Pelton[7]**, first son of Ithamar[6], Josiah[5], John[4], John[3], Samuel[2], John[1], born Essex, Chittenden Co., Vt., February 18, 1799; married Wayne Co., O., February 26, 1824, Mary Wakeman. Lived at Wayne, Ashtabula Co., O., and there died in 1837. Children:

> I Jonathan, born about 1826; residence and record unknown.
>
> II Orvilla, born 1828; residence and record unknown.
>
> III Samuel, born 1830; residence and record unknown.
>
> IV Frederick, born 1832; residence and record unknown.

**156. Lester Pelton[7]**, second son of Ithamar[6], Josiah[5], John[4], John[3], Samuel[2], John[1], born at Essex, Vt., July 7, 1801; married September 7, 1833, Gustavus, O., Mary Rood, daughter of David Rood, of that place. In 1877 a farmer at Gustavus, O. Children:

> 157   I James W., b. Feb. 24, 1834; m. Nov. 7, 1857, Corintha A. Snyder; d. Feb. 15, 1862.
>
> 158   II William Jason, b. July 31, 1835; m. July 26, 1865, Mrs. Mary J. Morse.
>
> III Cordelia, born Aug. 5, 1838; married Aug. 23, 1864, Stephen D. Mallett. Children: Alice E., b. Sept. 4, 1865, and Benjamin F., b. June 1, 1870. Residence, 1878, Wayne, Ashtabula Co., O.
>
> IV Emma, born June 30, 1846; married Sept. 15, 1863, William Wakeman. In 1877 lived at White Bluffs, Dickinson Co., Tenn. Children, four.

V George F., born Nov. 30, 1847. Lived, 1878, with his father.

**157. James W. Pelton⁷**, first son of Lester⁶, Ithamar⁵, Josiah⁴, John⁴, John³, Samuel², John¹, born Gustavus, Trumbull Co., O., February 24, 1834; married Turnersville, Crawford Co., Pa., November 7, 1857, Corintha A. Snyder (b. May 1, 1841), daughter of John Snyder, of Hartford, O. Lived at Hartford, O. Enlisted August 16, 1861, for three years; served in Co. A, Emerson Opdyke, Captain, 41st O. Vols. Died of typhus fever, Louisville, Ky., February 15, 1862. Children:

 I Franklin G., born Apr. 15, 1859, at Hartford, O.; died Oct. 22, 1859.
 II Clara O., born Nov. 11, 1860.

Widow Corintha married (2) at Mount Pleasant, Ia., February 15, 1865, Emerson J. Badger, and lived, 1878, in Westchester Co., Ia.

**157. William Jason Pelton⁷**, second son of Lester⁶, Ithamar⁵, Josiah⁴, John⁴, John³, Samuel², John¹, born at Gustavus, O., July 31, 1835; married at Beaver, Crawford Co., Pa., July 26, 1865, Mrs. Mary J. (Hoyt) Morse, daughter of Christopher Hoyt, of Newville, DeKalb Co., Ind. Gardener and fruit dealer at Paris, Kent Co., Mich. P. O. Grand Rapids, Mich., 1878. Children:

 I George Wildes, born Oct. 19, 1869, at Concord, DeKalb Co., Ind.
 II Mary Etta, born Apr. 14, 1871, Newville, DeKalb Co., Ind.

**155. Samuel G. Pelton⁶**, third son of Ithamar⁵, Josiah⁴, John⁴, John³, Samuel², John¹, born Essex, Vt., June 11, 1805; married Gustavus, O., August 1, 1827,

to Matilda Kelly, of Connecticut.   Removed to Fon
du Lac, Wis., and there died, June 5, 1857.   Carpenter and farmer.   Children:

**159**    I Walter K., b. Apr. 29, 1828; m. July 20,
             1854, Philinda Breed.
**160**    II Francis Wilson, b. Aug. 28, 1829; m. June
             11, 1850, Amanda Breed.
         III Lester, born Jan., 1831; died Sept. 21,
             1832.
          IV Philena, born Feb. 22, 1833; married at
             Fon du Lac, Wis., Jan. 20, 1856, Bezaleel
             Spencer, of Washington Co., N. Y.
             Lived, 1876, at Byron, Fon du Lac Co.,
             Wis.   Children, four.
           V Malvina A., born Oct. 4, 1834; married
             Nov. 8, 1851, J. H. Gilbert, and died
             at Fon du Lac, Wis., Sept. 23, 1857;
             left two children.
**160**   VI Edwin, b. Dec. 31, 1837; m. 1857, Delia
             Robertson; d. July 30, 1867.
**161**  VII Griffin S., b. July 14, 1840; m. Mar. 29,
             1866, Harriet Steenburg; d. Jan. 18,
             1869.
        VIII Henry, born Jan. 13, 1843; died Mar. 18,
             1861.
          IX Milford A., born Feb. 13, 1850.   Lived,
             1876, at Edgerton, Rock Co., Wis.


**158. Walter K. Pelton**[6], first son of Samuel G.[7],
Ithamar[6], Josiah[5], John[4], John[3], Samuel[2], John[1], born
Gustavus, O., August 29, 1828; married July 20, 1854,
Philinda Breed.   He served five months in the War
of the Great Rebellion, and was honorably discharged.
Lived, 1876, at Dorchester, Clark Co., Wis.   No
children.

**158. Francis Wilson Pelton⁸**, second son of Samuel G.⁷, Ithamar⁶, Josiah⁵, John⁴, John³, Samuel², John¹, born Gustavus, O., August 28, 1829; married at Byron, Wis., June 16, 1850, Amanda M. Breed, of that place. Farmer. Lived, 1876, at Fon du Lac, Wis. Children:

160     I Wells Stacey, b. May 3, 1851; m. Nov. 3, 1875, Fanny Jones.

    II Emma S., born Sept. 15, 1854.

    III Nina M., born May 18, 1858.

    IV Eva Josephine, born Feb. 21, 1860.

**160. Wells Stacey Pelton⁹**, first son of Francis W.⁸, Samuel G.⁷, Ithamar⁶, Josiah⁵, John⁴, John³, Samuel², John¹, born May 3, 1851; married November 3, 1875, Fanny Jones. Children, none in 1876.

**158. Edwin Pelton⁸**, fourth son of Samuel G.⁷, Ithamar⁶, Josiah⁵, John⁴, John³, Samuel², John¹, born December 31, 1837; married in 1857, Delia Robertson. Served in the Great Rebellion, and died at Fon du Lac, Wis., July 30, 1867, from disease contracted in the army. His widow died in March, 1873. Children:

160     I Henry G., b. Oct. 18, 1857; m. Ada F. Avery, Apr. 10, 1883.

    II Philinda, born 1859; died New London, Wis., Mar. 20, 1873.

    III Truman, born 1860; died May 1, 1875.

    IV Edna, born July, 1862.

    V Eddie (Edwin?), born in the spring of 1866.

**160. Henry G. Pelton⁹**, first son of Edwin⁸, Samuel G.⁷, Ithamar⁶, Josiah⁵, John⁴, John³, Samuel², John¹, born at Janesville, Wis., October 18, 1857; married at Manchester, N. H., April 10, 1883, Ada F. Avery, daughter of Charles H. Avery, of that place. Occupation, restaurateur. Residence, 1891, at Oshkosh, Wis. Children, born at Oshkosh:

 I Edna L., born Jan. 30, 1884.
 II Mary M., born Nov. 9, 1887.
 III George A., born Mar. 18, 1889.

**158. Griffin S. Pelton**, fifth son of Samuel G.[1], Ithamar[6], Josiah[5], John[4], John[3], Samuel[2], John[1], born July 14, 1840; married March 29, 1866, Harriet Steenburg. Lived at Fon du Lac, Wis. Served in the army of the Great Rebellion, and died January 18, 1869, from disease there contracted. In 1876 his widow still lived in Fon du Lac. Children, none.

**135. Hiram Pelton**, fourth son of Ithamar[6], Josiah[5], John[4], John[3], Samuel[2], John[1], born in Gustavus, O., February 3, 1807; married Trumbull Co., O., Hannah Ballard. Farmer. Removed to Byron, Fon du Lac Co., Wis., and there died, April, 1851. His wife died about the same time. Children:

 I Burton, born ——; died unmarried, near
  Youngstown, O.
 II Sanford, born ——; died unmarried in
  1844.
**161**  III Newcomb, b. Nov. 18, 1836; m. Oct. 18,
  1863, Gertrude E. Palmer.
 IV Lydia M., born ——; married Charles
  Prentiss, and went to California.
 V Andrew J., born ——; died July 21, 1864.

**161. Newcomb Pelton**, third son of Hiram[7], Ithamar[6], Josiah[5], John[4], John[3], Samuel[2], John[1], born Gustavus, O., November 18, 1836; married Byron,

Fon du Lac Co., Wis., October 18, 1863, Gertrude E. Palmer, daughter of N. H. Palmer, of Adrian, Mich. Farmer. Lived, 1876, at Sparta, Wis. Children:

 I Irving, born July 21, 1864.
 II Elmer, born Oct. 25, 1866.
 III Myrtre, born Nov. 29, 1868.
 IV Lester, born Mar. 5, 1871.
 V Marian, born May 23, 1875.

**157.** Albert Pelton⁷, fifth son of Ithamar⁶, Josiah⁵, John⁴, John³, Samuel², John¹, born Gustavus, O., March 26, 1809; married (1) Lucina Rood, daughter of David Rood, of Wayne, O.; (2) at Gustavus, O., October 16, 1837, Mary L. Jones, daughter of Luther Jones, of Gustavus (born in Avon, N. Y., March 4, 1818). Lived, 1878, with her daughter, Mary L. Kearns, in Marengo, Iowa Co., Ia. Mr. Pelton served in the Mexican war, and died on the way home, at Memphis, Tean. Children, by first wife:

 I Oshea.
 II Elvira L.
 III Edgar.
 IV Martha, married Joshua Middleton; died Gustavus, O.

Children by second wife:

**163** V Salmon S., b. Oct. 12, 1839: m. Oct. 12, 1864, Melissa Bowman.
 VI Angeline S., born Feb. 2, 1842; married Oct. 30, 1859, Theodore Kearns. Lived, 1878, Iowa Co., Ia. Children, three, all living in 1878.
 VII Mary L., born June 22, 1844: married (1) June 16, 1865, Oliver W. Dorwin; (2) Mar. 23, 1878, James H. Kearns.

Lived, 1878, Marengo, Iowa Co., Ia.
One child, by the first marriage.

VIII Charles H., born Feb. 14, 1847; married but no report returned. Lived, 1878, at Painesville, O. Wife and child died.

**102. Salmon S. Pelton**, fourth son of Albert[6], Ithamar[5], Josiah[4], John[3], John[2], Samuel[1], John[1], born Fremont, O., October 12, 1839; married Painesville, O., October 12, 1864, Melissa Bowman, daughter of John Bowman, of Warren, O. In 1878 a merchant in Warren, O. Children:

I Henry B., born Nov. 15, 1865; died Dec. 3, 1865.

II Albert B., born Apr. 15, 1867.

**155. Ithamar Pelton, Jr.**, seventh son of Ithamar[5], Josiah[4], John[3], John[2], Samuel[1], John[1], born Gustavus, O., March 26, 1816; married (1) at Gustavus, November 13, 1836, Susannah Ann Jones (b. July 16, 1816; d. Apr. 6, 1855); (2) Lucina Ann Jones, Berea, O., July 24, 1828, daughter of Benoni Jones. In 1876 a Free Will Baptist minister at Pierpont, O. Children, by first wife:

I Angelina Mahala, born June 4, 1838, Gustavus, O.; died May 25, 1841.

II Mahlon Josiah, born in Gustavus, O., Oct. 23, 1844; died Pierpont, O., Dec. 3, 1865.

By the second wife:

III Lelia Estella, born Dec. 14, 1862, at Pierpont, O.

IV Mary Bell, born Feb. 23, 1866, Pierpont, O.

**145. Charles Wesley Pelton**, eighth son of Ithamar⁶, Josiah⁵, John⁴, John³, Samuel², John¹, born at Gustavus, O., October 6, 1818; married January 2, 1839, Demis Isham (b. June 29, 1821), daughter of Ansel Isham. Veterinary surgeon. Lived, 1876, at Fon du Lac, Wis. Children:

> I Martha M., born Aug. 1, 1840; married — —, Albert Hodge.
> II Lydia L., born Apr. 10, 1843.
> III Richard R., born July 8, 1846; died Sept. 8, 1846.
> IV Vandalia A., daughter, born Apr. 20, 1849; died Feb. 9, 1860.
> V Ida V., born Feb. 24, 1850; married Feb. 24, 1871, to Frank Ewers.

**168. Elias Pelton**, second son of Josiah⁵, John⁴, John³, Samuel², John¹, born at Killingworth, Conn., February 3, 1774; removed to Essex, Chittenden Co., Vt., and there, in 1799, married Mary (Polly) Folsom, daughter of Thomas Folsom. He returned from Vermont to Connecticut by flat boat down the Connecticut river, and then removed to Gustavus, O., being the second man who, with his family, made this township his home. He was a carpenter and joiner, and farmer. He lost his life by being frozen to death on the way home from the lake shore, February 4, 1823. Mrs. Pelton died about 1843. Children:

> I Zilpha, born Nov. 15, 1801; married 1821, Benoni Jones. Lived at Bedford, Cuyahoga Co., O. Died at Kinsman, O., in 1877. Children, Almira, Orvilla. Lusina.

II Barbara, born July 15, 1803, the first white child born in the Township of Gustavus; married Mar. 22, 1822, Hezekiah Barnes.  Lived in 1878 at Gustavus, O.  Children, nine—seven living at that time: Juliett, Almira, Rosetta, Addison, Upson, Maryetta, Philemon, Salmon, Hezekiah.

**165** III Gustavus Storrs, b. May 22, 1805; m. Mar. 22, 1829, Lydia Bailey.

IV Sarah (Sally), born Oct. 9, 1807; unmarried; lived and died at Bedford, Cuyahoga Co., O.

**167** V Thomas, b. Aug. 4, 1809; m. (1) Apr. 18, 1832, Jane Dyer; (2) Mrs. Stiles.

VI Lucina, born July 9, 1811; married at Gustavus, Joseph Kelly.  Lived there, thence removed to Milwaukee, Wis., and there died.  Children, six.

VII Mary (Polly) M., born Mar. 13, 1813; married Lyman Roberts.  Lived in Gustavus; removed to California and there died.  Children, none.

**168** VIII Elias, Jr., b Dec. 13, 1816; m. Oct. 10, 1839, Almira Imas; d. Mar. 13, 1855.

**170** IX Elsander, b. May 19, 1819; m. Nov. 4, 1842, Philotha M. Sparks; d. Mar. 20, 1850.

X Alcinda, born Apr. 3, 1821; married Charles Van Horn; six children.

**171** XI Alonzo D., b. July 17, 1823; m. June 10, 1850, Mary J. Bell.


**161. Gustavus Storrs Pelton**, first son of Elias⁶, Josiah⁵, John⁴, John³, Samuel², John¹, born at Gustavus,

Trumbull Co., O., May 22, 1805, the first white boy
born in the township. Married there, March 22,
1829, Lydia Bailey, daughter of Iddo Bailey, of
Haddam, Conn. Carpenter and farmer. Lived, in
1876, at Russell, Geauga Co., O. Children:

**167** 1 Flavel B., b. Feb. 1, 1830; m. Mar. 17,
1852, Orvilla Robinson.

II Jane D., born Nov. 14, 1831; married Jan.
7, 1867, Mr. Harmon, who died Feb. 8,
1869; no children. Living, in 1876, at
Russell, Geauga Co., O.

**167** III Emory A., b. June 24, 1833; m. Dec. 18,
1857, Sarah M. Gates.

IV Mary (Polly), born Jan. 25, 1835; married
Sept. 3, 1855, John Hall. In 1876 was
living in Kansas. Children, ten; nine
then living.

V Sarah (Sally), born Jan. 4, 1839; no other
record.

VI Ervilla, born Jan. 26, 1841; married Orson
Sweet, July 17, 1859; one daughter.
Lived, 1876, at Prairie Home, Shelby
Co., Ill.

VII Lucinda, born Nov. 23, 1842; married (1)
Jan. 25, 1862, William Babcock, who
died Dec. 18, 1862; (2) Dec. 25, 1867,
Vivalda Mansfield. Children: Ellen
Augusta, born Nov. 5, 1869; Vivern
Shirley, b. Nov. 8, 1874.

VIII Philena, born Mar. 1, 1845. In 1876
living at her father's home.

IX Thomas, born May 16, 1848; died Aug.
6, 1848.

X Amaretta M., born Dec. 30, 1852; married Oct. 1, 1874, Hermon Green.
Farmer. Living, 1876, at Russell, O.

**165. Flavel E. Pelton**, first son of Gustavus Storrs[7], Elias[6], Josiah[5], John[4], John[3], Samuel[2], John[1], born February 1, 1830; married March 17, 1852, to Orvilla Robinson, daughter of Samuel Robinson, of Russell, O., where he lived in 1876.   Children:

I   Arthur E., born Dec. 31, 1852.
II   Willie A., born Oct. 29, 1854.
III   Dewey B., born Jan. 25, 1857.
IV   Herbert E., born Mar. 21, 1859.
V   Ernest C., born Jan. 19, 1861.
VI   Cora M., born Dec. 26, 1862.
VII   Ida C., born Feb. 8, 1865.
VIII   Rosa Estelle, born Mar. 14, 1867.
IX   Nora E., born Feb. 18, 1869.
X   Guy S., born Mar. 28, 1874.

**165. Emory A. Pelton**, second son of Gustavus S.[7], Elias[6], Josiah[5], John[4], John[3], Samuel[2], John[1], born Gustavus, O., June 24, 1833; married (1) at Chester, Geauga Co., O., December 18, 1857, Sarah M. Gates, daughter of Luther Gates, of that place.   Residence, in 1876, Russell, Geauga Co., O.   Farmer.   Wife Sarah M. died December 14, 1875; (2) ——— ———. Children:

By first wife:

I   Ira C., born May 29, 1858.
II   Elmer S., born Aug. 3, 1860.
III   Adelbert, born Feb. 27, 1865.
IV   Homer, born Apr. 28, 1868.

By second wife:

V   Anna S., born Dec. 14, 1879.

**164. Thomas Pelton**, second son of Elias[6], Josiah[5], John[4], John[3], Samuel[2], John[1], born Gustavus, Trumbull Co., O., August 4, 1809; married (1) Trumbull Co., O., April 18, 1832, Jane Dyer, daughter of Norman Dyer, of that county. In 1876 a farmer living at Berlinville, Erie Co., O.; (2) Elizabeth Ann Rowland, of Huron Co., O. Children:

**168**  I Omar H., b. Mar. 10, 1833; m. Dec. 23, 1855, Ella E. Alverson.

II Lorina, born July 2, 1834; married May 8, 1855, M. J. Daniels. Lived at Lansing, Mich.; died Feb. 13, 1870; one son, dead.

III Parintha, born Aug. 3, 1836; married Dec. 29, 1859, Orson E. Turner. Living, in 1876, at Norwalk, O.; one son.

IV Manilla, born Mar. 13, 1839; married Mar. 15, 1864, J. W. Edmonds. Lived, in 1876, at Lansing, Mich.; two sons.

V William Henry, born Dec. 16, 1840; died in the army, July 31, 1862.

VI Frederic D., born May 9, 1851; unmarried in 1876.

VII Stella, born Apr. 5, 1856; at home in 1876.

**167. Omar H. Pelton**[7], first son of Thomas[6], Elias[5], Josiah[4], John[3], John[2], Samuel[2], John[1], born March 10, 1833; married December 23, 1855, Ella E. Alverson. In 1876 lived at Norwalk, O. Child:
I Edah, a daughter.

**161. Elias Pelton, Jr.**[6], third son of Elias[5], Josiah[4], John[3], John[2], Samuel[2], John[1], born at Gustavus, O., Dec. 13, 1816; married October 10, 1839, Almira Imas. Lived at Gustavus, but died at Toledo, O., March 13, 1855. Children:

**168**    I Giles H., b. Nov. 14, 1840; m. July 12,
              1879, Emma Pright.
**169**    II Delmar A., b. Feb. 4, 1842; m. July 14,
              1874, Mary Johnson.
**170**   III Elias C., b. Aug. 14, 1843; m. Dec. 25,
              1868, Maria Clegg.
           IV Louisa M., born Sept. 26, 1846; married
              Jan. 16, 1865, Linus Osgood, son of
              Theophilus Osgood. Children, two.
              Living, in 1879, in Erie, Monroe Co.,
              Mich.
            V Amaretta A., born Jan. 1, 1848; married
              Feb. 23, 1869, William Powlesland, son
              of John Powlesland; no children. In
              1879 lived in Toledo, O.
           VI Melissa A., born Nov. 14, 1849; married
              May 5, 1872, Edgar Albring, son of
              Ira Albring. Children, four. Resi-
              dence, 1879, in Sylvania, Lucas Co., O.
          VII Mary M., born June 13, 1852. In 1879
              unmarried and lived in West Toledo, O.

**168. Giles H. Pelton**, first son of Elias[8], Elias[6],
Josiah[5], John[4], John[3], Samuel[2], John[1], born Gustavus,
Trumbull Co., O., November 14, 1840; married Bedford, Monroe Co., Mich., July 12, 1879, Emma,
daughter of David Pright, of that place. In 1880 a
farmer, living in West Toledo, O. Children, none
reported.

**169. Delmar A. Pelton**, second son of Elias[7],
Elias[6], Josiah[5], John[4], John[3], Samuel[2], John[1], born at
Gustavus, O., February 4, 1842; married Bedford,
Mich., July 14, 1874, Mary Johnson, daughter of
James Johnson, of that place. In 1879 a farmer,
living in West Toledo, O. Children:

I Luie L., born Aug. 25, 1875.
II Davis B., born Feb. 28, 1877.
III James E., born Aug. 14, 1879.

**168. Elias C. Pelton**, third son of Elias⁷, Elias⁶, Josiah⁵, John⁴, John³, Samuel², John¹, born at Gustavus, O., August 14, 1843; married at Whitford, Monroe Co., Mich., December 25, 1868, Maria Clegg, daughter of Richard Clegg, of Lambertville, Mich. In 1879 a wagon-maker in West Toledo, O. Children:
I Charles, born Dec. 21, 1869.
II Richard, born Dec. 15, 1872; died Oct. 26, 1874.
III Minnie, born Sept. 2, 1875.

**161. Alexander Pelton⁷**, fourth son of Elias⁶, Josiah⁵, John⁴, John³, Samuel², John¹, born at Gustavus, Trumbull Co., O., May 19, 1819; married Warren Co., O., November 4, 1842, Philotha M. Sparks, daughter of Erastus Sparks, of Greene, Trumbull Co., O. Died at Florence, Erie Co., O., March 20, 1850. Farmer and innkeeper. Children:
I Alonzo E., born Sept. 9, 1843; died Florence, Erie Co., O., Mar. 4, 1849.
II Mina J., born May 29, 1847; married Warren, O., Apr. 29, 1863, Portland Hyde. Lived, 1878, at Garrettsville, O.
**171** III Francis, b. Apr. 22, 1849; m. Dec. 25, 1875, Lizzie Turner.
Note.— Mrs. Pelton married (2) October 28, 1851, Hiram Mowry, a son of Elizabeth, daughter of Ithamar, son of Josiah Pelton (p. 156), who committed suicide January 3, 1870, from loss of property. Children, by this marriage, two sons. In 1878 she lived in Warren, O.

170. **Francis Pelton**, second son of Elsander, Elias, Josiah, John, John, Samuel, John, born at Florence, Erie Co., O., April 22, 1849; married at Marion, Ind., December 25, 1875, Lizzie Turner, daughter of Robert Turner, of England, now of Niles, O. Farmer. Residence, in 1878, Alexandria, Madison Co., Ind. Child:

   I Charles Elsander, born Sept. 5, 1877.


171. **Alonzo Dwight Pelton**, fifth son of Elias, Josiah, John, John, Samuel, John, born Gustavus, O., July 17, 1823, after his father's death; married at New Haven, Allen Co., Ind., June 10, 1850, Mary J. Bell, daughter of Martin Bell. Publisher; former owner of the "Toledo Blade," of Toledo, O. Was also a manufacturer of agricultural machinery. At about the age of seventeen he went to Southern Iowa, among the Sacs and Fox Indians, Black Hawk then being chief, where he stayed three years, and then returned home on account of the sickness of his mother, who died soon after, about 1843. Residence, 1879, at Toledo. In 1892 printer and stationer in Toledo, O. Children:

   I Eva, born Aug. 5, 1851.
   II Ada, born Sept. 12, 1853; died Oct. 8, 1854.
   III Lillie Bell, born June 27, 1855; died July 28, 1855.
**172**  IV Dwight Alonzo, b. Sept. 10, 1856; m. Jan. 18, 1876, Kittie Eloise Arnold (who died Dec. 21, 1884); d. Apr. 13, 1886.
   V Mary Belle, born Feb. 7, 1863; married to Henry P. Tobey, Feb. 6, 1889.

**171. Dwight Alonzo Pelton**, first son of Alonzo
D.[7], Elias[6], Josiah[5], John[4], John[3], Samuel[2], John[1], born
September 10, 1856; married January 18, 1876, Kittie
Eloise Arnold, who died December 21, 1884.   Mr.
Pelton died April 13, 1886.   Children:

    I Florence Eloise, born Nov. 7, 1876.
    II Hugh B., born Aug. 8, 1881.
    III Cora Belle, born Nov. 27, 1884.


**158. Jesse Pelton[6]**, third son of Josiah[5], John[4],
John[3], Samuel[2], John[1], born at Killingworth, Conn.,
June 7, 1778; married, Vernon, Trumbull Co., O.,
September 12, 1802, Ruhama DeWolf, daughter of
Joseph DeWolf, of Granby, Connecticut.   He went
to Gustavus, O., with his father in 1800, to locate his
father's land, and there stayed till he, his father, returned in the spring of 1802.   His family formed the
third Pelton family in Gustavus.   Farmer.   Died in
South Shenango, Crawford Co., Pa., October 1,
1862.   He was of dark complexion, with black eyes,
5 feet 9 inches in height, weighing 165 pounds.
Children :

    I ——, born July 3, 1803; died at birth.
    II Mary S., born Sept. 21, 1805; married
        Gustavus, O., Apr. 8, 1830, Harry
        Lyman, son of Josiah Lyman, of New
        Hartford, Conn.   Lived, in 1878, at
        Florence, Benton Co., Ia.   Children:
        Amanda S., b. Jan. 29, 1831; d. May 1,
        1835; Silas H., b. Apr. 28, 1833; Sarah
        G., b. July 13, 1836; Ira N., b. Aug. 6,
        1838.
    III Ruhama C., born Sept. 20, 1809, at Gus-
        tavus, O.; married Jan. 9, 1839, Robert
        Hilton, son of John Hilton, of Cul-

pepper C. H., Va.; died Port Byron,
Ill., Oct. 13, 1867. Children: George,
b. Oct. 20, 1839; Electa M., b. Jan. 15,
1841; Annie E., b. Sept. 28, 1842;
Henry, b. Jan. 13, 1845.

IV Sarah D., born Dec. 22, 1811; married
Sept. 26, 1853, John W. Buckman.
Lived, in 1877, at Le Claire, Scott Co.,
Ia.; no children.

**173** V Joseph D., b. May 2, 1814; m. Sept. 12,
1839, Jane, daughter of Andrew Mc-
Quiston.

VI Electa M., born Apr. 5, 1816; died unmarried, Sept. 15, 1840.

**174** VII George K., b. Apr. 12, 1818; m. Oct. 6,
1847, Mary A. King.

VIII Cynthia L., born Nov. 13, 1820. Living
unmarried, 1878, at Gustavus, O.

**174** IX Sidney Rigdon, b. Jan. 2, 1823; m. May
11, 1854, Sarah Ann Breckenridge.

**175** X Tensard D., b. Mar. 18, 1825; m. Jan. 29,
1873, Sarah Nesbitt.

XI Eugene S., born June 10, 1828; died Apr.
24, 1837.

**172. Joseph D. Pelton**[6], first son of Jesse[6],
Josiah[5], John[4], John[3], Samuel[2], John[1], born Gustavus,
O., May 2, 1814; married South Shenango, Crawford
Co., Pa., September 12, 1839, Jane McQuiston,
daughter of Andrew McQuiston, of Hartstown,
Crawford Co., Pa. Farmer. Lived, in 1878, at
South Shenango, Pa. Complexion fair, height 5 feet
9 inches; weight 140 pounds. Children:

I Martha Isabel, born Sept. 28, 1840; married Oct. 5, 1869, John W. Marshall, of

South Shenango, Pa., where she lived in 1878. Children, two.

II Ruhama Elizabeth, born Oct. 14, 1842; married Sept. 12, 1874, William A. Blake, of Andover, Ashtabula Co., O., where she lived in 1878; one child.

III Sarah Electa, born May 9, 1846; died Feb. 22, 1858.

**172. George K. Pelton[7]**, second son of Jesse[6], Josiah[5], John[4], John[3], Samuel[2], John[1], born at Gustavus, O., April 12, 1818; married Kinsman, O., October 6, 1847, Mary A. King, daughter of William King, of that place. Farmer. Lived, in 1880, at Burg Hill, Trumbull Co, O. Children:

I Myra, born July 9, 1851.

174    II John Sanderson, b. May 21, 1859; m. Aug. 25, 1887, Emily O. Mason.

**174. John Sanderson Pelton[8]**, only son of George K.[7], Jesse[6], Josiah[5], John[4], John[3], Samuel[2], John[1], born at Burgh Hill, Trumbull Co., O., May 21, 1859; married at Hartford, O., August 25, 1887, Emily O. Mason, daughter of Ralph Mason, of that place. Occupation, farming. Residence, in 1892, Burgh Hill, O. Child:

I George Mason, born June 8, 1890.

**173. Sidney Rigdon Pelton[7]**, third son of Jesse[6], Josiah[5], John[4], John[3], Samuel[2], John[1], born Gustavus, O., January 2, 1823; married at North Liberty, Pa., May 11, 1854, Sarah Ann Breckenridge, of that place (b. Apr. 30, 1830). Physician, in 1878, living at Pine Grove, Mercer Co., Pa. Height, 5 feet 10 inches; complexion dark, eyes and hair black. Children:

I Charles A., born Aug. 20, 1856.
II Mary Ruhama, born Apr. 25, 1862.
III Fried? (Fred?), born Nov. 28, 1872.


**172. Tenward D. Pelton**, fourth son of Jesse⁶, Josiah⁵, John⁴, John³, Samuel², John¹, born at Gustavus, Trumbull Co., O., March 18, 1825; married there, January 29, 1873, Sarah Nesbitt, daughter of James Nesbitt, of Conningtown, County Cavan, Ireland. Children, none reported.


**158. Henry Pelton⁵**, fourth son of Josiah⁵, John⁴, John³, Samuel², John¹, born at Killingworth, Conn., February 15, 1780; married at Shenango, Pa., November 7, 1811, Margaret Reid, daughter of William Reid, of that place. Lived in Pennsylvania, in Paw Paw, Mich., and died in Lawton, Mich., November 8, 1871. Mrs. Pelton died in Paw Paw, July 19, 1862. Children:

        I Mary (Polly) R., born Sept. 5, 1812; married Oct. 13, 1831, William R. Sirrine. Lived, in 1876, at Paw Paw, Mich. Children, four.
        II William R., born Oct. 2, 1815; died Oct. 18, 1834.
        III John W., 1, born Sept. 17, 1818; died Oct. 6, 1819.
**175**    IV John W., 2, b. Nov. 8, 1820; m. June 2, 1842, Susanna Titus.
        V Lucinda, born Dec. 5, 1822; died in June, 1825.


**175. John W. Pelton⁶**, third son of Zenas⁵, Josiah⁵, John⁴, John³, Samuel², John¹, born in Gustavus, Trumbull Co., O., November 8, 1820; married in Shenango,

Pa., June 2, 1842, Susanna Titus, daughter of William Titus, of Gustavus, O. Lived, in 1876, in Lawton, Mich.; dealer in grain and produce. Children:

    I Virginia, born Apr. 7, 1843; died Dec. 21, 1861.

    II Caroline, born Nov. 2, 1844; died Sept. 1, 1853.

    III William, born June 9, 1848; married Sept., 1875, Sarah Phillips. In 1876 living in Lawton, Mich. Cigarmaker.

    IV Ida, born Feb. 15, 1851.

    V John, Jr., born Oct. 16, 1855.

    VI Carrie, born Nov. 11, 1861.

**152. Julius Pelton**[6], fifth son of Josiah[5], John[4], John[3], Samuel[2], John[1], born at Killingworth, Conn., May 4, 1786; married at Gustavus, Trumbull Co., O., February 12, 1810, Hannah Folsom (sister of the wife of his brother Elias), daughter of Thomas Folsom, of that place. Removed with his father and family to Gustavus in the spring of 1802, and there lived a farmer, and there died, January 12, 1862. Children:

177    I Augustus G., b. Dec. 20, 1810; m. Aug. 22, 1834, Mary Wakefield.

    II Philena, born Apr. 27, 1812; married in Aug., 1830, Lyman Roberts. Lived at Gustavus, O., and there died, May 3, 1832; left two children, a son, Lucien R., b. Jan. 27, 1832; m. Nov. 12, 1853, Eliza A. Breed.

178    III Lysander J., b. Jan. 11, 1814; m. Feb. 1, 1836, Harriet Williams.

    IV Hannah Annis, born Apr. 3, 1816; married Jan. 8, 1834, Reuben Barber, son of Zenas Barber, of Gustavus, O.; eight children.  Lived, in 1878, at Gustavus, O.

**178**    V Winthrop F., b. June 30, 1818; m. Sept., 1846, Sophronia Beer.

**181**    VI Buel B., b. Apr. 28, 1821; m. (1) Jan. 30, 1850, Ruhama Bradley; (2) Amanda L. Beer.

**176. Augustus G. Pelton**, first son of Julius⁵, Josiah⁴, John⁴, John³, Samuel², John¹, born at Gustavus, Trumbull Co., O., December 20, 1810; married there, August 22, 1834, Mary Wakefield, daughter of Elijah Wakefield, of Kinsman, O.  Carpenter and farmer. Living, in 1878, at Greenburgh, Trumbull Co., O. Children:

I Hannah, born Apr. 1, 1835; died in infancy.

II Winthrop, born Mar. 22, 1836; died in infancy.

III Desta, born Feb. 22, 1838; married Feb. 3, 1863, W. W. See.  Children: One son and four daughters.  Living. 1878, at Cortland. Trumbull Co., O.

IV William S., born Feb. 5, 1844; died in the U. S. service, Sept. 18, 1864, in the recruiting camp at Cleveland, O.

**177**    V Reuben L., b. Nov. 8, 1848; m. Dec. 22, 1870, Mary Hillman.

**177. Reuben L. Pelton**, third son of Augustus G.⁶, Julius⁵, Josiah⁴, John⁴, John³, Samuel², John¹, born at Gustavus, Trumbull Co., O., November 8, 1848; married at Cortland, O., December 22, 1870, Mary Hillman, daughter of Charles Hillman, of Greensburg. O.  Residence, 1890, at Greensburg, O.  Farmer. Children:

    I Lillie, born Oct. 15, 1873.
    II Minnie, born Mar. 5, 1876; died Mar. 15, 1876.

**176. Lysander F. Pelton[7]**, second son of Julius[6], Josiah[5], John[4], John[3], Samuel[2], John[1], born at Gustavus, O., January 11, 1814; married there, February 1, 1836, Harriet Williams, daughter of Israel Williams, of that place. Horse trainer, 1877. Children:

    I De Etta, born June 24, 1837; married Apr. 7, 1870, C. Macham. Living, in 1878, in Gustavus, O.; no children.
    II Aurelia, born Apr. 25, 1840; married Dec. 24, 1868, J. Watrous. Residence, 1878, Gustavus, O.; no children.
    III Mina, born Mar. 8, 1846; married Feb. 2, 1865, G. Cowden. Living, 1878, at Gustavus, O. Children, two.
    IV Ella, born Feb. 29, 1852; married Oct. 25, 1874, G. Murphy. Living, 1878, at Payson, Adams Co., Ill. Children, two.

**176. Winthrop F. Pelton[7]**, third son of Julius[6], Josiah[5], John[4], John[3], Samuel[2], John[1], born Gustavus, Trumbull Co., O., June 30, 1818; married there, September, 1846, Sophronia Beer, of Brookfield, O. Farmer and auctioneer. Living, 1878, in Wayne Co., O. Children:

**178**    I Cushman W., b. June 7, 1847; m. (1) Mar. 26, 1870, Coralinn M. Gifford; (2) Jan. 5, 1881, Rhoda C. Boughton.
**179**    II Chapin B., b. Apr. 18, 1849; m. Jan. 10, 1869, Lizzie Griffith.
**180**    III Judd, born July 17, 1852; m. Dec. 17, 1885, Amanda E. Winch.

180     IV Arvine W., b. Oct. 3, 1858; m. Mar. 15,
              1886, Eva Rowe.
180     V Ellsworth, b. Mar. 28, 1861; m. Mar. 28,
              1890, Sadie Reed.
180     VI John R., b. Sept. 2, 1862; m. Jan. 4, 1887,
              Philinda Phillips.


**178. Cushman W. Pelton**, first son of Winthrop
F.¹, Julius⁶, Josiah⁵, John⁴, John³, Samuel², John¹, born
at Johnson, O., June 7, 1847; married (1) at Monroe,
O., March 26, 1870, to Coralinn M. Gifford, daughter
of David S. and Mary J. Gifford, of Conneaut, O.,
who died December 4, 1878; (2) January 5, 1881, to
Rhoda C. Boughton, daughter of Seymour and Charlotte Boughton, of Conneaut, O.   In 1878 lived in
Cleveland, O.; business, mercantile.   In August,
1881, removed to Conneaut, O., and began business
for himself, where he has since built up the largest
mercantile business in the county.   He is still, in
1892, actively engaged therein.   Children:
       I Barbara B., born Nov. 23, 1872.
       II Julius S., born Nov. 3, 1878.
       III Albert G., born Oct. 4, 1881.
       IV Charlotte I., born Mar. 28, 1883.
    Mr. Pelton in February, 1864, enlisted in 2d Ohio
Volunteer Cavalry, was taken prisoner at Ream's
Station, Va., on June 27, 1864; confined for two
months in Libby Prison, Richmond, Va., then paroled
and soon exchanged, and was mustered out of service
in June, 1865.


**178. Chapin E. Pelton**, second son of Winthrop
F.¹, Julius⁶, Josiah⁵, John⁴, John³, Samuel², John¹, born
at Johnsonville, O., April 8, 1849; married there,

January 10, 1869, Lizzie Griffin, daughter of
———, of ———. In 1892 living in Belmont, La
Fayette Co., Wis. Occupation, ———.

**178. Judd Pelton**, third son of Winthrop F.¹,
Julius⁶, Josiah⁵, John⁴, John³, Samuel², John¹, born at
Johnstonville, Trumbull Co., O., July 17, 1852; married at Homestead, Alleghany Co., Pa., December 17,
1885, Amanda E. Winch, daughter of Henry F.
Winch, of that place. Shoemaker. Residence, in
1892, at Auburn, N. Y. Children:

      I Amelia H., born Mar. 4, 1887; died Sept.
        7, 1887.
      II Adeline, ⎫
              ⎬ born Dec. 23, 1888.
      III Alice, ⎭

**178. Arvine W. Pelton**, fourth son of Winthrop
F.⁷, Julius⁶, Josiah⁵, John⁴, John³, Samuel², John¹, born
at Kinsman, October 3, 1858; married at Chagrin
Falls, O., March 15, 1886, to Eva Rowe, of that place.
Merchant. Residence, in 1892, at Conneaut, O.
Children, none.

**178. Ellsworth Pelton**, fifth son of Winthrop
F.⁷, Julius⁶, Josiah⁵, John⁴, John³, Samuel², John¹, born
at Kinsman, O., March 28, 1861; married at Columbus, O., May 28, 1890, to Sadie Reed, daughter of
——— Reed, of that place. Book-keeper. Residence,
in 1892, at Conneaut, O. Child:

      I Robert R., born June 8, 1891.

**178. John E. Pelton**, sixth son of Winthrop F.⁷,
Julius⁶, Josiah⁵, John⁴, John³, Samuel², John¹, born at
Johnston, Trumbull Co., O., September 2, 1862;
married January 4, 1887, at Conneaut, O., Philinda

Phillips, daughter of Belle and Devogar Phillips, of that place. Occupation, salesman. Residence, in 1892, in Conneaut, O. Children:

  I Sophronia Belle, born July 11, 1890.
  II Delphine Philinda, born July 16, 1891.


**176. Buell B. Pelton[6]**, fourth son of Julius[5], Josiah[4], John[3], John[2], Samuel[2], John[1], born at Gustavus, O., April 28, 1821; married (1) January 30, 1850, at Johnston, O., Ruhama Bradley, daughter of Dr. Ariel Bradley, of that place; (2) at Gustavus, O., September 2, 1858, Amanda L. Beer, daughter of John Beer. In 1878 a farmer and merchant at Gustavus, O. In 1891 a resident of Cortland, O. Children:

  I Emma A., born June 4, 1851.
  II Ruhama, born Nov. 29, 1853; married July 4, 1875, to Avery Love, of Mecca, O.


**153. Harvey Pelton[6]**, sixth son of Josiah[5], John[4], John[3], Samuel[2], John[1], born Killingworth, Conn., March 20, 1790; married at Gustavus, O., October 24, 1816, Mary Bailey, daughter of Iddo Bailey, from Connecticut, who died July 22, 1859, in the 60th year of her age, in Cascade, Sheboygan Co., Wis., and was buried in Wildwood Cemetery, Sheboygan City. Farmer. Lived in Gustavus and Russell, O.; died May 10, 1838, at Russell, Geauga Co., O., and there buried. Children:

182  I Seth, b. Feb 26, 1818; m Sept. 25, 1843, Harriet Scott.
183  II Alvin, b. Dec. 1, 1819; m. Apr. 3, 1851, Caroline M. McFarland.

**183** III Russell, b. Jan. 20, 1822; m. Oct. 3, 1847,
Eliza Thompson.

IV Miranda, born Aug. 20, 1824, at Gustavus,
O.; married Aug. 7, 1854, William F.
Lawrence, of Chagrin Falls, O. Living,
1876, at Clayton, Faribault Co., Minn.
Children, five.

V Mary B., born Nov. 3, 1826, at Gustavus,
O. Living, 1876, at Clayton, Minn.;
unmarried.

**184** VI Samuel Newell, b. July 5, 1829; m. July
1, 1863, Elizabeth J. Phillips; (2) Mrs.
Louise Victoria Meyers.

VII Abigail Elizabeth, born July 25, 1832, at
Gustavus, O.; married at Chagrin Falls,
O., Jos. H. Wilbur (b. Mar. 3, 1824).
Died in Michigan, Aug. 25. 1865. Chil-
dren: Ella Dulcina, b. Aug. 7, 1856,
and William Henry, b. Sept. 10, 1859.

VIII Martha Eliza, born Sept. 2, 1835, at Gustavus, O.; married Jerome B. Legg, of
St. Louis, Mo., where they lived in
1876.

IX Lydia Ann, born July 11, 1838; died Cas-
cade, Wis., Oct. 2, 1858; buried in
Wildwood cemetery, in Sheboygan
City, Wis.

**181. Seth Pelton[7]**, first son of Harvey[6], Josiah[5],
John[4], John[3], Samuel[2], John[1], born Gustavus, O., Febru-
ary 26, 1818; married September 25, 1843, at Russell,
O., Harriet Scott, daughter of Justin Scott, of New
Burgh, O. Mechanic. Living, in 1876 and in 1892,
at Sheboygan, Wis. Children:

    I Alzina, born at Russell, Geauga Co., O.,
Mar. 15, 1845; married September 16,
1866, Thomas Shiel, of Illinois. In
1876 lived at Chenoa, Ill. Children:
Hattie May, b. Nov. 3, 1867; Ella
Louise, b. July 1, 1869; Arthur, b.
Mar. 11, 1872.

    II Mary Camden, born at Lyndon, Wis.,
Dec. 14, 1847; married Sept. 27, 1871,
Otis Parker Wheeler.

    III Arthur Scott, born at Lyndon, Wis., Oct.
1, 1849.

    IV Elmore Massena, born Lyndon, Wis.,
May 28, 1853.

    V George Walter, born Lyndon, Wis., Dec.
5, 1854.

    VI Harriet Augusta, born Sheboygan City,
Wis., Nov. 18, 1857; died Feb. 26,
1858.

    VII Ida Lydia, born Sheboygan City, Wis.,
May 18, 1860.

**181. Alvin Pelton[6]**, second son of Harvey[5],
Josiah[5], John[4], John[3], Samuel[2], John[1], born Gustavus,
O., December 1, 1819; married at Bainbridge, O.,
April 3, 1851, Caroline M. McFarland. Farmer.
Lived, 1876, at Oberlin, O. Children:

    I Clarence Newe, born at Russell, O., Oct.
24, 1852.

    II Flora L., born Oberlin, O., Sept. 4, 1856,
married there, Millard F. Franks, Nov.
24, 1875.

    III Carrie, born Oberlin, O., Mar. 15, 1860.

**181. Russell Pelton[6]**, third son of Harvey[5],
Josiah[5], John[4], John[3], Samuel[2], John[1], born Gustavus,

O., January 20, 1822; married Lyndon, Wis., October 3, 1847, Eliza Thompson, daughter of Levi Thompson, of Genesee Co., N. Y. Farmer. Removed to Lyndon, Juneau Co., Wis., in 1846, and was living there in 1876. Children:

**184**    I Levi Harvey, b. July 10, 1848; m. July 23, 1873, to Kate Ellen Brown.

     II Martha Margaret, born June 1, 1854.

**183. Levi Harvey Pelton**, first son of Russell[7], Harvey[6], Josiah[5], John[4], John[3], Samuel[2], John[1], born Lyndon, Wis., July 10, 1848; married July 23, 1873, to Kate Ellen Brown. Residence, in 1876, at Fon du Lac, Wis. Children:

     I Martha Margaret, born June 1, 1874.

     II Alice Martha, born Fon du Lac, Wis., Jan. 4, 1876.

**184. Samuel Newell Pelton**, fourth son of Harvey[6], Josiah[5], John[4], John[3], Samuel[2], John[1], born Gustavus, Trumbull Co., O., July 5, 1829; married (1) Bainbridge, O., July 1, 1863, Elizabeth J. Phillips (d. May 4, 1874), daughter of D. S. Phillips, of North Adams, Mass: (2) at Cleveland, O., December 18, 1878, Mrs. Louise Victoria Meyers (b. Feb. 14, 1842, Sutton, St. James, Lincolnshire, Eng.), daughter of Isaac Boardman. Residence, 1876, at Chagrin Falls, Cuyahoga Co., O. Harness-maker. Children, born at Chagrin Falls, O.:

     I Daniel Alvin, born Sept. 20, 1865.

     II George Newell, born May 23, 1867.

     III Myra Betsey, born Dec. 25, 1872.

**59. William Pelton**, sixth son of John[4], John[3], Samuel[2], John[1], born at Saybrook (Essex), Conn, December 2, 1747; married about 1769, Lois Harvey, of East Haddam, Conn.    In early life was a sea captain.    Removed about 1807 or 1808 to Pultney, Steuben Co., N. Y., where he occupied a farm, and there died, May 25, 1825.    He was the last Pelton that owned his father's home at Essex, Conn. Children:

185      I William, b. Feb. 9, 1771; m. Dec. 22, 1789, Ruth Clark; d. Nov. 27, 1839.

         II Lois, born about 1773; married (1) Mr. Gaylord: (2) Mr. Whitaker; died ——.

186    III John, b. about 1775; m. about 1797, Prudence Pratt; d. Mar., 1813; dates uncertain.

         IV Anna, born about 1777; married a Mr. Ball.    Lived and died at Watertown, N. Y.

         V Lucy, born about 1779; died young.

187     VI Ezra, b. Apr. 28, 1781; m. (1) Asenath Clark; (2) June 29, 1836, Mrs. Esther Paulding Pinkerton; d. Aug. 15, 1877.

        VII Elizabeth, born 1783; married Mr. Burden.    Lived and died near Towlesville, Steuben Co., N. Y.

       VIII Lucinda, born 1785; married Nathan Bell.    In 1876 both were dead.

**184. William Pelton[6], Jr.,** first son of William[5], John[4], John[3], Samuel[2], John[1], born in or near Saybrook, Conn., February 9, 1771; married December 22, 1789, Ruth Clark.    He was a cabinet-maker in early life; a sea captain through the War of 1812, and afterward a farmer.    He died at Cohocton, Steuben Co., N. Y., Nov. 27, 1839.    His wife born August 19, 1872; died July 12, 1846.    They removed from Hartford, Conn., to Utica, N. Y., thence to Yates Co., N. Y., and finally to Cohocton.    Children:

**186**   I Alfred, b. Nov. 26, 1790; m. (1) Anna
Thoms; (2) Abby Ingraham; d. Oct.
22, 1861–2.

II Phœbe, born Sept. 25, 1792; married Pultney, N. Y., Dec. 4, 1810, John Nickerson; died Cohocton, Steuben Co., N. Y.,
Aug. 4, 1846; seven children.

III Sarah, born Sept. 22, 1795; married James
White, and both died in Virginia.

IV Roxana, born Oct. 1, 1797; married (1)
Abram Gillet; (2) Charles Erwin.
Lived, in 1875, at West Union, Pa.

**188**   V Hiram, b. Sept. 30, 1800; m. (1) Betsey
Arnold, Danville, N. Y.; (2) Lavinia
Winslow.

**190**   VI Sterling, b. Oct. 22, 1802; m. Feb. 6, 1821,
Sarah Brown.

VII Clarissa, born Sept. 3, 1804; married (1)
Oct. 2, 1822, Dr. Philo Andrews; seven
children; (2) John Nickerson, former
husband of her sister Phœbe; no
children.

**191** VIII Clark, b. May 21, 1810; m. 1829, Julia
Sager; d. Nov. 21, 1834.


**185. Alfred Pelton**, first son of William[6], Wil-
liam[5], John[4], John[3], Samuel[2], John[1], born in Connecticut,
November 26, 1790; married (1) Anna Thoms, daugh-
ter of Stephen Thoms, of Sangerfield or Winfield,
Herkimer Co., N. Y. (whom he left); (2) January
15, at Pultney, N. Y., Abbey Ingraham. Shoemaker.
Said to have played well on the violin. Died at
Canastota or at Rathboneville, Steuben Co., N. Y.,
October 22, 1861–2. Children of the first wife:

187     I Collins, b. Pultney, N. Y., Dec. 26, 1810;
          m. Nov. 21, 1838, Nancy A. (Ingraham)
          Harris.

187     II Grove Alfred, b. 1814; m. 1842, Mary
          Miller.

  Children of second wife:

186    III William A., born about 1816 or '18; no
          record.

      IV Sarah, born May 19, 1822; married John
          W. Torrance.  Lived, 1875, at Clyde, O.

      V Jane E., born May 3, 1824; married Ben-
          jamin Roselle.  Lived at Spring Mills,
          Oakland Co., Mich., and died Apr. 13,
          1860.

188    VI James A., b. Sept. 26, 1826; m. Apr. 3,
          1847, Matilda Hiler.


**186. Collins Pelton[1]**, first son of Alfred[1], William[6], William[5], John[4], John[3], Samuel[2], John[1], born at
Pultney, Steuben Co., N. Y., December 26, 1810;
married Branchport, N. Y., November 21, 1838, Mrs.
Nancy A. (Ingraham) Harris, daughter of Ebenezer
Ingraham, of Connecticut.  Farmer.  Lived, in 1875,
at Rathboneville, Steuben Co., N. Y.  Children, none.


**186. Grove Alfred Pelton[1]**, second son of Alfred[1],
William[6], William[5], John[4], John[3], Samuel[2], John[1], born
Winfield, Herkimer Co., N. Y., 1814; married at
West Winfield, N. Y., 1842, Mary Miller, daughter
of James Miller.  Merchant.  In 1875 living at
Jacksonville, Fla.  Children:

      I Mary, born 1845; living 1875.

      II Grove A., Jr., born 1847; died 1848.

     III Rose, born 1859; living 1875.

**186.** WILLIAM A. PELTON*, third son of Alfred*, William*, William*, John*, John*, Samuel*, John*, born (no record). Residence, 1875, variously given as at Sabinsville and Ridgebury, Tioga Co., Pa., and Collins Station, Huron Co., O. Children; no record.

**186.** JAMES A. PELTON*, fourth son of Alfred*, William*, William*, John*, John*, Samuel*, John*, born at Palmyra, N. Y., September 26, 1826; married at Pultney, Steuben Co., N. Y., September 3, 1847, Matilda Hiler, daughter of Jacob Hiler. Lived, in 1876, at Branchport, N. Y. Children:

    I Myron E., born Mar. 28, 1849.
    II Ellen, born Apr. 3, 1850; married July 4, 1875, William Race.
    III Avilla, born Sept. 13 1853.

**186.** HIRAM PELTON*, second son of William*, William*, John*, John*, Samuel*, John*, born September 30, 1800; married (1) September 30, 1823, Elizabeth Arnold, of Dansville, Livingston Co., N. Y., who died July 23, 1853; (2) Cleveland, O., Lavinia Winslow. Shoemaker. Lived, 1876, at Collins, Huron Co., O. Children:

**189**    I James Clark, b. Oct. 5, 1824; m. Sept. 19, 1844, Elizabeth Barnes.
    II Helen Ann, b. — —; married (1) Antioch O., 1845, Joel Serverus; (2) Thomas Gallagher; (3) James Gailland; died Apr. 5, 1865.
**189** III William, b. — —; m. Chloe Huntley; d. Jan. 31, 1873.
**189** IV David Maxwell, b. Nov. 17, 1826; m. Jan. 23, 1853, Alsenia Whitney.
    V Nancy; no record returned.
    VI, VII, VIII Died in infancy.

**186. James Clark Pelton**, first son of Hiram', William⁶, William⁵, John⁴, John³, Samuel², John¹, born Wayne Co., N. Y., October 5, 1824; married, February 14, 1846, Elizabeth Barnes, daughter of William Barnes, of Barnesville, Monroe Co., N. Y.  Boot and shoemaker.  Has lived South and West and in California; in 1876 in Dallas Centre, Dallas Co., Ia.; 1879 in Burlington, Coffey Co., Kan.; in 1886 lived in La Grande, Union Co., Ore.  Children:
189      I Theodore R., b. Aug. 17, 1847; m. Mar. 3, 1874, Ellen Jane Bellis.
        II William Clark, born Nov. 22, 1856.
        III George R., born Aug. 4, 1858.
        IV Hiram Scott, born Sept. 1, 1861.
        V Ida Laura, born Dec. 27, 1866.

**189. Theodore R. Pelton**, first son of James Clark⁸, Hiram⁷, William⁶, William⁵, John⁴, John³, Samuel², John¹, born Zanesville, O., August 17, 1847; married Indianapolis, Ind., Mar. 3, 1874, Ellen Jane (b. Richmond, Ind., July 4, 1852), daughter of William Bellis, of Indianapolis, formerly of Northumberland Co., Eng.  Machinist.  In 1879 living in Indianapolis, Ind.  Children:
        I William, born Dec. 25, 1874.
        II Lulu May, born Apr. 11, 1877.

**188. William Pelton**, second son of Hiram', William⁶, William⁵, John⁴, John³, Samuel², John¹, born ——; married ——, Chloe Huntley.  Died in Oregon, January 31, 1873.  Children, none.

**188. David Maxwell Pelton**, third son of Hiram⁷, William⁶, William⁵, John⁴, John³, Samuel², John¹, born November 17, 1826, at Geneva, N. Y.;

married at Middleburgh, Cuyahoga Co., O., December 9, 1853, Alsenia Whitney, daughter of Daniel Whitney, of that place. Pumpmaker. Residence, 1878, at Mount Morris, N. Y. Killed by a circular saw, Cleveland, O., April 24, 1886. He was at that time President of the Cleveland Pump Manufacturing Co. Children:

    I Jenny M., born at Cleveland, O., Nov. 28, 1854.

    II Willis, born Cleveland, O., Feb. 27, 1868.

**185. Sterling Pelton**[6], third son of William[6], William[5], John[4], John[3], Samuel[2], John[1], born —— ——, Conn., October 22, 1802; married Pultney, Steuben Co., N. Y., February 6, 1821, Sarah Brown, daughter of Ezekiel Brown, of that place. Lived, in 1875, at Kanona, Steuben Co., N. Y. A great hunter and a hotel-keeper. Children:

    I Ruth, born Dec. 2, 1823; married Cohocton, Steuben Co., N. Y., Aug. 4, 1840. Henry Reynolds. Living, 1876, Italy Hill, Yates Co., N. Y.; seven children.

    II Mary, born Oct. 25, 1825; married Russell Gray.

    III Nancy, born Mar. 11, 1828; married Lewis Brooks.

    IV Roxana, born Oct. 10, 1830; died May, 1873.

    V Phœbe, born Mar. 15, 1833; married Washington Graham.

**190**  VI Charles, b. Mar. 26, 1840; m. Sept 11, 1862, Maggie Van Riper.

**196. Charles Pelton**[7], only son of Sterling[6], William[6], William[5], John[4], John[3], Samuel[2], John[1], born

March 26, 1840; married September 11, 1862, at Italy Hollow, N. Y., Maggie Van Riper, daughter of Jeremiah Van Riper, of that place. Lived, 1876, at Wheeler Centre, Steuben Co., N. Y. Farmer. Children:

        I Sarah, born Jan. 7, 1864.
        II Clara, born Feb. 18, 1866.

**185. Clark Pelton**, fourth son of William, William, John, John, Samuel, John, born May 21, 1810; married ——, 1826- 9, Julia A. Sager; died November 21, 1834. Wife Julia A. died 1865. Children:

        I Henrietta, born about 1829; married Tyler Cogswell. Lived, in 1876, at Prattsburgh, Steuben Co., N. Y.
191    II Samuel C., b. 1831; m. 1855, Emma Winslow.
        III Caroline, born about 1833; married Peter Van Ness.

**191. Samuel C. Pelton**, only son of Clark, William, William, John, John, Samuel, John, born in Steuben Co., N. Y., 1831; married 1855, Emma (Emily Jane, of Holton's Winslow Geny.) Winslow, daughter of Jonathan Winslow, of Henrietta, Monroe Co., N. Y. Occupation, in 1876, produce dealer, Collins, Huron Co., O. Child:

        I Clark, born ——, 1857; horse trainer, Cleveland, O.

**184. John Pelton**, second son of William, John, John, Samuel, John, born probably at or near Essex, Conn., about 1774; married there, about 1795, Prudence Pratt (b. Dec. 28, 1768). Lived at Whitestown and Pultney, N. Y. Died at Pultney, March 3, 1813. Shoemaker. Children:

**190**    I Nathan Harvey, b. June 6, 1796; m. Oct.
14, 1819, Pamelia A. Balcom.

**191**    II Rufus, b. Mar. 30, 1798; m. (1) Apr. 12,
1821, Lucy Sturdevant; (2) Apr. 14,
1864, Elvira Webster.

**195** III Calvin, b. 1803; m. ——, Mary Ann Van
Doran; d. Jan. 12, 1843.

IV Almira, born 1806; married Russell
Brown.

**191. Nathan Harvey Pelton**, first son of John⁶,
William⁵, John⁴, John³, Samuel², John¹, born Whites-
town, N. Y., June 6, 1796; married Perrysburgh,
Cattaraugus Co., N. Y., October 14, 1819, Pamelia
A. Balcom. Lived, 1876, at Viola, Richland Co.,
Wis., to which place he removed in 1842. Children:

I Pamelia A., born Aug. 5, 1823; died Feb.
18, 1833.

**192**    II Orville A., b. Mar. 7, 1825; m. Dec. 31,
1843, Allette Woodward.

**193** III John I., b. Nov. 10, 1827; m. May 28,
1854, Joanna Pine.

IV Sarah, born May 11, 1830; married May
11, 1850, Aaron Hawley. Lived, 1876,
at Forest, Richland Co., Wis.; four
children.

**193**    V Ezra O., b. July 16, 1832; m. July 4, 1865,
Emily Thomas.

VI Francis C., born at Prattsburgh, N. Y.,
July 15, 1834; died in the U. S. army
at Columbus, Tenn., Aug. 26, 1862;
not married.

**194** VII Lewis F., b. Mar. 10, 1842; m. Oct. 30,
1875, Ella I. Smith.

VIII Jane A., born Genesee, Waukesha Co.,
      Wis., May 8, 1845; married July 4,
      1867, Austin Emory.    Lived, 1876,
      in Sauk Co., Wis.
IX Anna B., born at Genesee, Waukesha Co.,
      Wis., July 13, 1848; died Sept. 6, 1851.


**188. Orville A. Pelton**, first son of Nathan H.,
John⁶, William⁵, John⁴, John³, Samuel², John¹, born
March 7, 1825; married December 31, 1843, Allette
Woodward.   Lived, 1876, at Touchet P. O., Walla
Walla Co., Washington Territory.   Children, said
to be five; no report of them.


**189. John E. Pelton**, second son of Nathan H.,
John⁶, William⁵, John⁴, John³, Samuel², John¹, born at
Perrysburgh, N. Y., November 10, 1827; married
Buffalo, N. Y., May 28, 1854, Joanna Pine, daughter
of Samuel Pine.   Lived, 1876, at Wauwatosa, Mil-
waukee Co., Wis.   Contractor and builder.   Children:
   I Ovelia J., born Mar. 8, 1855.
  II Hiram S., 1, born Oct., 1856; died July
     18, 1857.
 III Hiram S., 2, born Jan. 7, 1858.
 IV Julia A., born July 20, 1859.
  V Andrew E., born Dec. 10, 1864.
 VI Lillie M., born May 23, 1874.


**190. Ezra O. Pelton**, third son of Nathan H.,
John⁶, William⁵, John⁴, John³, Samuel², John¹, born
July 16, 1832; married July 4, 1865, Emily Thomas.
Lived, 1876, in Sauk Co., Wis.   Child:
   I Francis D., born May 27, 1866.

**190. Lewis F. Pelton⁸**, fifth son of Nathan H.⁷, John⁶, William⁵, John⁴, John³, Samuel², John¹, born Prattsburgh, Steuben Co., N. Y., March 10, 1842; married October 30, 1875, Ella I. Smith. Lived, 1876, at Forest, Richland Co., Wis. Children; none reported.

**191. Rufus Pelton⁷**, second son of John⁶, William⁵, John⁴, John³, Samuel², John¹, born Frankford, Herkimer Co., N. Y., March 30, 1798; married (1) Pultney, Steuben Co., N. Y., April 12, 1821, Lucy Sturdevant, daughter of James Sturdevant, of Norfolk, Conn.; (2) Elvira Webster, April 14, 1864. Lived, in 1876, at Jefferson, Ashtabula Co., O. Removed to Ohio about 1837 or 1838.    Children:

> I Harriet N., born Jan. 7, 1822; married Sept. 15, 1839, *Joshua Giddings. Children, three. Lived, 1876, at Cherry Valley, Ashtabula Co., O.
>
> II Martha A., born Feb. 23, 1826; married (1) July 2, 1846, Ezra Pelton, son of Ansel Pelton, by whom she had a daughter, Emma H.; (2) James Loveland. Children, three. Lived, 1876, at Cherry Valley, Ashtabula Co., O.
>
> 192 III John Clinton, b. Nov. 14, 1832; m. May 17, 1855, Sarah J. Graham.

**192. John Clinton Pelton⁸**, only son of Rufus⁷, John⁶, William⁵, John⁴, John³, Samuel², John¹, born November 14, 1832; married May 17, 1855, at Crawford, Pa., Sarah J. Graham, daughter of John Graham. Lived, 1876, at Castle Grove, Ia.; P. O., Monticello, Jones Co., Ia.    Children:

---

* Another report says married Alfred, son of John Williams, of Cherry Valley.

    I Ezra Luther, born June 11, 1856; died
       Feb. 3, 1857.
    II Alvaro Ashley, born May 31, 1858.
    III Truman Leland, born Dec. 13, 1863.
    IV Ulysses S. Grant, born Nov 25, 1865.
    V Rufus Clinton, born Sept. 26, 1872.
    VI Marshall Oliver, born Dec. 15, 1874; died
       Feb. 5, 1876.

**191. Calvin Pelton**, third son of John[6], William[5],
John[4], John[3], Samuel[2], John[1], born 1803; married
about 1828, Mary Ann Van Doran, daughter of Wil-
liam Van Doran, of Chester, N. J. Shoemaker.
Lived at Pultney, Italy Hill and Glade's Corners,
Steuben Co., N. Y. Died Prattsburgh, N. Y., Jan-
uary 12, 1843. His wife died January 3, 1873, at
Syracuse, N. Y. Children:

    I Mary Elizabeth, born June 7, 1830; mar-
      ried William H. Stryker. In 1879 lived
      in Syracuse, N. Y.
**195**    II Nathan Terry (now Terry W.), b. Jan.
      6, 1832; m. Sept. 4, 1855, Ada Beeman.
**196**    III Rufus Harvey, b. Jan. 13, 1834; m. Dec.
      29, 1856, Mary Ann, daughter of Cor-
      nelius Laughlin.

**195. Terry W. Pelton** (changed from Nathan
Terry), first son of Calvin[7], John[6], William[5], John[4],
John[3], Samuel[2], John[1], born Pultney, Steuben Co.,
N. Y., January 6, 1832; married at Italy Hill, Yates
Co., N. Y., September 4, 1855, Ada Beeman, daugh-
ter of Chauncey W. Beeman, of Cayuga, N. Y. Has
lived in Three Rivers, Paw Paw and Grand Rapids,
Mich., and was living in 1878, in Bloomington, Ill.
Wood carver. Children:

    I Chauncey W., born July 14, 1856.
   II Charles E., born June 6, 1858.
  III Henry A., born Mar. 17, 1860; died July
       12, 1863.
  IV L. D., born June 21, 1863.
   V Herbert L., born Nov. 24, 1865.
  VI Henry C., born Mar. 8, 1867.
 VII Cora Ada, born Apr. 8, 1869.
VIII Frederic, born Feb. 5, 1872.
  XI Pearl Garnet, born Apr. 13, 1875.

**105. Rufus Harvey Pelton**, second son of Calvin[7], John[6], William[5], John[4], John[3], Samuel[2], John[1], born Pultney, Steuben Co., N. Y., January 13, 1834; married Ann Arbor, Mich., December 29, 1856, Mary Ann Laughlin, daughter of Cornelius Laughlin, of Northfield, Washtenaw Co., Mich. Lived, in 1879, at Howell, Livingston Co., Mich. Cooper. Children:

    I Calvin Terry, born Ann Arbor, Mich.,
       Nov. 14, 1857.
   II William Henry, born Bloomington, Ill.,
       Feb. 17, 1860.
  III Frederic, born Bloomington, Ill., July 21,
       1862.
  IV Francis Vane, born Tremont, Ill., Mar.
       19, 1865.
   V Mary, born Ann Arbor, Mich., Dec. 28,
       1867.
  VI Edward, born Ann Arbor, Mich., Sept.
       11, 1870.
 VII Katharine, born Howell, Mich., Oct. 14,
       1873.
VIII Grace, born Howell, Mich., Nov. 19,
       1876.

**181. Ezra Pelton**, third son of William⁵, John⁴, John³, Samuel², John¹, born at Essex (Saybrook), Conn., April 28, 1781; married (1) about 1803, Asenath Clark, who died October 30, 1835; (2) June 29, 1836, Mrs. Esther (Paulding) Pinkerton, niece of one of the captors of Major Andre in the Revolutionary War. Farmer. Lived at North Urbana, Steuben Co., N. Y., to which county he came with his father about 1809, after having lived at Whitestown, N. Y., for some years. He was an excellent man. He and his wife were many years members of the Baptist church. He died at North Urbana, N. Y., August 15, 1877; his wife Esther February 27, 1882. Children, by first wife:

    I Lucina, born Dec. 18, 1804; married Mr. Osborn, whose son Samuel Osborn is a dealer in pianos, etc., in Brooklyn, N. Y.

    II Lewis E., born Sept. 9, 1810; died Apr. 14, 1832.

**197** III Clinton, b. Sept. 14, 1816; m. (1) Dec. 18, 1839, Laura Gillet; (2) Mar. 14, 1855, Elizabeth McCullough.

By second wife:

    IV Joseph, born May 1, 1837; died July 10, 1837.

    V Asenath, born Nov. 14, 1839; died Mar. 16, 1843.

    VI Carrie, born Nov. 13, 1843; married Aug. 10, 1862, Jas. S. Deane. Children, three. Left North Urbana, N. Y., in 1877; in 1886 lived at Brown Valley, Traverse Co., Minn.

**197. Clinton Pelton**, second son of Ezra⁶, William⁵, John⁴, John³, Samuel², John¹, born at Pultney,

Steuben Co., N. Y., September 14, 1816; married (1) there, December 18, 1839, Laura Gillet, daughter of Abraham Gillet, of Pultney; (2) at Jerusalem, Yates Co., N. Y., Elizabeth McCullough, of that place. Lived, 1875, at Pultney, on the Pelton homestead; P. O. address, Prattsburgh, Steuben Co., N. Y. Farmer. No further record.

59. Joseph⁵ Pelton, seventh son of John⁴, John³, Samuel², John¹, born at Saybrook (Essex), Conn., November 25, 1756; married Chatham, Conn., November, 1778, his cousin, Prudence, daughter of Josiah and Hannah (Churchill) Pelton, of that place. Farmer. Removed to Lyme, N. H., and there lived. Died June 15, 1837, at Fairley, Vt., his wife Prudence having died at Lyme, N. H., May 2, 1822. Children:

      I Jemima Archer, born Apr. 21, 1780; married Nov., 1805, Matthew Atherton. Children, five daughters; died Royalton, Vt., May 6, 1861.

      II Prudence, born July 14, 1782; died unmarried, Aug. 1, 1836.

199    III John Baldwin, b. Jan. 29, 1784; m. 1809, Anna Baldwin; d. Sept., 1864.

      IV James, 1, born May 12, 1785; died Oct. 12, 1786.

      V A son, born May 25, 1787; died May 26, 1787.

200    VI James, 2, b. Apr. 29, 1788; m. Sept. 6, 1829, Lucy Trumbull; d. Oct. 14, 1873.

      VII Mary, born Sept. 27, 1789. Lived, 1876, unmarried, at Lyme, N. H.

201 VIII Josiah, b. July 25, 1791; m. 1814, Persis Pelton; d. Oct. 14, 1872.

**202**  IX David, b. Dec. 23, 1792; m. (1) Mary
         Gaylord; (2) Mar. 1, 1820, Mary Trum-
         bull; (3) Oct. 14, 1824, Judith Bailey; d.
         Oct. 31, 1870.

    X Joseph, born Oct. 14, 1795; died Dec. 12,
         1796.

    XI Phœbe, born Dec. 26, 1799; died Mar. 5,
         1801.


**198. John Baldwin Pelton**, first son of Joseph⁵, John⁴, John³, Samuel², John¹, born Essex, Conn., January 29, 1874; removed to Lyme, N. H., thence to Chester, Conn., about 1819 or 1820, where he, about 1809, had married a cousin, Anna Baldwin, daughter of James Baldwin, of that place. Occupation, a quarryman, in which business he was a partner with Russell Pelton, who removed later to Brooklyn, adjoining Cleveland, O. He died Essex, Conn., September 20, 1864. Children:

    I Lucy Ann, born Lyme, N. H., June 10,
         1811; married George Hill, of Guilford,
         Conn.; died Dec. 28, 1862; no children.

    II Lavinia B., born Lyme, N. H., July 25,
         1814; married Middletown, Conn., May
         29, 1836, Richard L. Spencer, of Guil-
         ford, Conn.; five children; died Dec.
         12, 1862.

**200** III Joseph, b. Apr. 17, 1816; m. June 12,
         1842, Jerusha Griffing.

    IV Ruth Shipman, born Lyme, N. H., Mar.
         14, 1818; unmarried. Lived, 1876, at
         Elmwood, Cass Co., Neb.

    V Lydia, born Chester, Conn., June 7, 1820;
         died Nov. 30, 1822.

**200**   VI James Baldwin, b. Aug. 22, 1822; m.
(1) Aug. 15, 1847, Nancy Melissa
Brooks; (2) Oct. 6, 1875, Fanny E.
Bliss.

VII  Lydia Sophronia, born May 4, 1828; married Aug. 22, 1847, Sheldon G. Stannard, of Westbrook, Conn.   Lived, in
1876, at Greentop, Mo.


**199. Joseph Pelton**, first son of John Baldwin,
Joseph², John⁴, John³, Samuel², John¹, born at Lyme,
N. H., April 17, 1816; married at Madison, Conn.,
June 12, 1842, Jerusha Griffing, daughter of Samuel
Griffing, of that place.   Farmer.   In 1876 lived at
East River, Madison, Conn.   Children, none.


**199. James Baldwin Pelton**, second son of
John Baldwin⁵, Joseph⁴, John⁴, John³, Samuel², John¹,
born August 22, 1822, at Chester, Conn.; married
(1) August 15, 1847, Melissa Brooks, daughter of
Enos Brooks, of Waterbury, Conn.; (2) October 6,
1875, Mrs. Fanny E. Bliss, daughter of Eliphalet
Barker, of Branford, Conn.   Engineer and miller.
Residence, 1876, at Branford, New Haven Co., Conn.
Children, none.


**198. James Pelton**, third son of Joseph⁴, John⁴,
John³, Samuel², John¹, born probably at Essex, Conn.,
April 29, 1788; married September 6, 1829, Lucy
Trumbull.   Died October 14, 1873.   He was an excellent citizen, a great reader, an intelligent and
genial man.   He was born, lived and died in Lyme,
N. H.   Children, none.

**198. Josiah Pelton**, fourth son of Joseph[6], John[5], John[4], Samuel[2], John[1], born Lyme, N. H., July 25, 1791; married in 1814, at Plymouth, Vt., Persis Pelton, daughter of Freeman Pelton, of Chatham, Conn., and Plymouth, Vt. (p. 310). Farmer. Lived at Lyme, N. H., and there died, October 14, 1872. Children:

201    I Sylvester Augustin, b. Sept., 1823; m. ——; d. Sept. 10, 1866.

      II Prudence, born Oct. 11, 1827; died, unmarried, Aug. 15, 1865.

201    III Josiah Churchill, b. Oct. 5, 1831; m. May 7, 1857, Mary Ann Roycroft.


**201. Sylvester Augustin Pelton**, first son of Josiah[6], Joseph[5], John[4], John[3], Samuel[2], John[1], born Lyme, N. H., September, 1823; married ——, ——; died September 10, 1866. Children, two. No record given.


**201. Josiah Churchill Pelton**, second son of Josiah[6], Joseph[5], John[4], John[3], Samuel[2], John[1], born Plymouth, Vt., October 5, 1831; married at Philadelphia, Pa., May 7, 1857, Mary Ann Roycroft, daughter of Samuel Roycroft, of Scotland. Served in the Union army in the War of the Great Rebellion. A farmer. Lived, in 1885, at Lyme, N. H. Children, born at Lyme:

      I Samuel Josiah, born Aug. 2, 1859.

      II Mary Jane, born July 4, 1861.

      III Delsina A., born May 15, 1863.

      IV Prudence, born Mar. 4, 1865.

      V Ella M., born Feb. 21, 1867.

      VI Miriam Frances, born Apr. 4, 1869.

**198. David Pelton⁶**, sixth son of Joseph⁵, John⁴, John³, Samuel², John¹, born at Lyme, N. H., December 23, 1792; married (1) Mary Gaylord, of East Windsor, Conn.; (2) Mary Trumbull, Lyme, N. H., March 1, 1820; (3) October 14, 1824, Judith Bailey (b. Sept. 15, 1789), daughter of Major Asa Bailey and Abigail (Abbot) Bailey (b. Jan. 27, 1746), of Bath, N. H. Carpenter. Lived at Lyme, N. H., and Hanover, N. H., and there died, October 31, 1870. Children (by first wife none):

By second wife:

    I Zerviah Gaylord, born Aug. 9, 1821; died Aug. 23, 1821.

By third wife:

    II Mary Trumbull, born Mar. 24, 1824, Lyme, N. H.; married July 9, 1848, Anthony Rock (b. Jan. 14, 1845).

    III Ann Sutherland, born July 2, 1825; died Oct. 14, 1845.

    VI Patience Bailey, born Jan. 23, 1827. Lived, 1876, at Hanover, N. H. In 1891 still living in Hanover.

**202**   V James Harris, b. Mar. 10, 1829; m. (1) July 3, 1856, Cordelia Emma Wheeler; (2) Feb. 23, 1858, Julia M. Bird.

**203**   VI David Brewster, b. Apr. 30, 1833; m. Mar. 12, 1864, Mary Moore Bailey.

**202. James Harris Pelton⁷**, first son of David⁶, Joseph⁵, John⁴, John³, Samuel², John¹, born at Lyme, N. H., March 10, 1829; married (1) Lebanon, N. H., July 3, 1856, Cordelia Emma Wheeler, daughter of Silas Wheeler; (2) at New Haven, Vt., February 23, 1858, Julia Maria Bird, daughter of Caulfield Bird. Residence, 1876, Hanover, N. H. Boarding-house. Children:

By first wife:

**203**    I George Edwin, born May 6, 1857; m. June 27, 1881, Alice M. House, of Lebanon, N. H.

By second wife:

    II Walter Elijah, born Sept. 19, 1863. Residence, 1876, at Hanover, N. H.

    III Anna Leighton, born Feb. 21, 1866; died May 15, 1869.

**203. George Edwin Pelton**[7], first son of James Harris[6], David[5], Joseph[4], John[4], John[3], Samuel[2], John[1], born Hanover, N. H., May 6, 1857; m. June 27, 1881, Alice M. House, of Lebanon, N. H. Printer. Living, in 1887, at Rutland, Vt. Children, none.

**202. David Brewster Pelton**[7], second son of David[5], Joseph[4], John[4], John[3], Samuel[2], John[1], born Lyme, N. H., April 30, 1833; married at Lyme, N. H., March 12, 1864, Mary Moore Bailey, daughter of Amos Bailey, of that place. Carpenter. Living, 1876, at Hanover, N. H. Wife, Mary M., died August 2, 1875. Children:

    I Frank Brewster, born Aug. 18, 1865; died Sept. 4, 1865.

    II Mary Emma, born July 31, 1866.

    III Frank Bailey, born April 23, 1872.

**59. Phineas Pelton**[4], eighth son of John[4], John[3], Samuel[2], John[1], born at Saybrook (Essex), Conn., December 5, 1763; married at Chatham, Conn., May 6, 1784, Margaret Tucker, daughter of Noah Tucker, of Saybrook, Conn. Lived at Essex, Branford and Chatham, Conn., and in 1804 removed with ox teams from Essex to Lyme, N. H.; thence to Bridgewater,

Oneida Co., N. Y., and thence, in 1819, to Pultney, Steuben Co., N. Y., where he died, March 5, 1847. Farmer. His wife, Margaret, born April 5, 1764, died July, 1850. His complexion and hair were dark, his eyes blue. The last years of their lives were spent with their son Israel. Children:

> I Hannah (or Anna), born Dec. 25, 1784; married at Saybrook, Conn., Aug. 12, 1809, Samuel Bushnell. Lived at Saybrook, Conn., and there died, Sept. 1, 1845. Had two sons and perhaps other children.
>
> II Priscilla (twin with Martha), born Oct. 27, 1786; married ——, Adolphus Dimock. Removed to Sutton, Ontario, and died at Broome, Ontario, July 15, 1863. Children, nine.
>
> III Martha (twin), born Oct. 27, 1786; married Dec. 29, 1808, Abnon Grant (b. Apr. 21, 1783). Lived at Lyme, N. H., where she died, May 21, 1862. Children, eleven. Of these, Mrs. Eunice Harrington lived, in 1876, at East Alsted, N. H.; another daughter, Mrs. L. P. Litchfield, in 1883, lived in Bath, Me., and a son, Noah Grant, in 1884, lived at Harrison, Ind. Mr. Grant died Sept. 8, 1831.
>
> IV Margaret, born Jan. 1, 1789; married Cyrus Hewes (or Hughes). Lived in Lyme, N. H., and there died, Apr. 22, 1826, and was buried in her garden. Children, eight, of whom, in 1876, only George Hewes, of New Orleans, was living.

V  Rhoda, born Mar. 23, 1791; married Mar. 9, 1814, Ahimaz Gilbert (b. Brookfield, Mass., Mar. 12, 1787; d. Mar. 28, 1874). Lived at Lyme, N. H., and died Mar. 25, 1865.  Children, nine; one daughter, Mrs. Rhoda R. Chandler, in 1890, lived at Lunenburgh, Essex Co., Vt.

**207**  VI  Phineas, Jr., b. Dec. 7, 1793; m. Julia Stebbins.

**207**  VII  Ansel, b. July 25, 1796; m. Jan. 1, 1823, Betsey Thomas; d. Apr. 23, 1865.

VIII  Ruth Lord, born Dec. 8, 1798; married at Bridgewater, Oneida Co., N. Y., in 1819, Philo Roberts (b. Apr. 28, 1798; died at Cuba, N. Y., Sept. 8, 1885), son of Nathaniel Roberts, of Norfolk, Conn., Paris and Bridgewater, N. Y., and Azubah, daughter of Joseph' Pelton, of Chatham, Conn. (p. 352), and sister of Reuel Pelton, of Oneida and Chautauqua Co., N. Y.  Lived, 1880, at Cuba, N. Y., and there died, Apr. 7, 1886, in a ripe old age, and in Christian hope to join her husband where parting shall be no more.  Children: (1) Lucy Eliza, born Sept. 13, 1820; married Massena M. Langdon; died Aug. 7, 1855.  (2) Israel Pelton, born Sept. 25, 1822; married Oct. 11, 1849, Electa Richardson; children, William Philo, Franklin Eugene, Ruth Augusta, Electa Seville, Sedocia Adell, Effie Vercilla, Myrtie Eliza.  (3) Oren Philo, born Dec. 7, 1824; married Nov. 22, 1824, Huldah M. Hastings, who died

May 8, 1890; children, Dora Eliza,
William Bion, Emma Eloise, Frank L.,
Jennie Louise.  (4) Lyman Augustus,
born Jan. 28, 1827; married Jan. 1, 1849,
Jemima Randolph; died May 30, 1890;
children, Lucy Elizabeth, Mary Emma,
Ruth Eloise, Carrie May, Herman.
(5) Luman Erastus, born June 22, 1829.
(6) Emma Statira, born June 26, 1831;
married June 26, 1861, Jerome B. Bigelow.  (7) William Marcy, born Oct. 5,
1833; married Dec. 22, 1864, Cornelia
Keller; children, George Keller, William Alfred, Carlton Bradley, Anna
May, James Douglass.  (8) Ansel
Bacchus; born Mar. 21, 1836; married
Jan. 8, 1864, Margaret McDermott;
children, Richard W., Ella M., Edwin
B., Maggie, Onia, Lizzie, Grace, Nellie,
Martha, Charles Paul, Wallace, Willis,
Twins.  (9) Orpha Eloise, born June
18, 1838; married Oct. 29, 1872, Wil-
liam H. Bartholomew.*  Residence, in
1891, Cuba, N. Y.  (10) Margaret
Azubah, born Sept. 24, 1841; married
Aug. 24, 1863, Robert B. Way, who
died Oct. 10, 1874; one child, Cecilia
Eloise, born July 5, 1868.  Soprano in
1892 in Holy Trinity W. 21st St., New
York.

**209** IX William M., b. Feb. 1, 1801; m. 1820,
Sarah Wheeler; died Oct., 3, 1872.

X Lucy M., born Lyme, Conn., May 31,
1803; married Prattsburgh, N. Y., Mar.
7, 1823, John B. Curtis, son of Ephraim

---

* Who died from apoplexy, at home, Sept. 1, 1892.

Curtis, of Long Island, N. Y.   Children,
six.   In 1876 a widow living at Prattsburgh, N. Y.

**211**   XI Israel, b. Oct. 4, 1806; m. Dec. 20, 1833,
Lucinda Early; d. Sept. 15, 1869.

NOTE.— A partial family record in a Bible is in
care of W. Curtis, Hammondsport, N. Y., son of
Mrs. Lucy M. Curtis above.   Phineas' Bible is in the
possession of Mrs. Lucy M. Curtis at Prattsburgh,
N. Y.


**208. Phineas Pelton, Jr.,** first son of Phineas⁵,
John⁴, John³, Samuel², John¹, born at Essex or Chat-
ham, Conn., December 7, 1793; married ——, at
Bridgewater, Oneida Co., N. Y., Julia Stebbins, of
Paris, Oneida Co., N. Y.   He is said to have lived
in Paris, N. Y., and in Lamar, Clinton Co., Pa., and
some accounts say that he died there or at Towanda,
Pa., about 1833.   Others say that he went to Gusta-
vus, Trumbull Co., O.   Children, as given by his
sister, Mrs. Curtis: Miles, William and Margaret.
As given by Mrs. Louisa Daily, of Penn Yan, N. Y.:
William, Elizabeth and Rhoda.


**203. Ansel Pelton⁶,** second son of Phineas⁵, John⁴,
John³, Samuel², John¹, born Branford, Conn., July 25,
1796; married at Pultney, Steuben Co., N. Y., Jan-
uary 1, 1823, Betsey Thomas, daughter of Sylvanus
Thomas.   Lived at Pultney, N. Y., until about 1837,
when he removed to Cherry Valley, O., in September
of that year, and thence, in April, 1848, to Gustavus,
Trumbull Co., O., where he died, April 3–23, 1865.
His wife, Betsey, died March 27, 1868.   Farmer.
Children:

**208**   I Amos, b. Dec. 8, 1823; m. Dec. 15, 1844,
Rebecca Lafferty; d. Nov. 29, 1855-6.

**208**    II Ezra, b. Mar. 20, 1825; m. July 2, 1846,
            Martha A. Pelton; d. Jan. 14, 1848.
**209**    III Elias, b. May 13, 1828; m. July, 1853,
            Clara Heriott.
           IV Rhoda M., born at Pultney, N. Y., Apr.
            28, 1829; married Dec. 30, 1871, at
            Cherry Valley, O., Levi Knapp, son of
            David Knapp, of that place.  Living
            in 1878; no children.
**209**    V Lewis, b. Mar. 25, 1832; m. Nov. 2, 1854,
            Jerusha Lindsley.
           VI Elizabeth, born Pultney, N. Y., Mar. 14,
            1837; married at Gustavus, O., Oct. 31,
            1860, Selvin B. Fobes, farmer, son of
            Artemas K. Fobes, of Dover, Lyons
            Co., Ia.  Lived, 1878, at Cherry Valley,
            Ashtabula Co., O.


**207. Amos Pelton[7]**, first son of Ansel[6], Phineas[5],
John[4], John[3], Samuel[2], John[1], born at Pultney, N. Y.,
December 8, 1823; married at Brookfield, Trumbull
Co., O., December 15, 1844, Rebecca Lafferty, daugh-
ter of James Lafferty, of that place.  Carpenter.
Died Gustavus, Trumbull Co., O., November 29,
1855.  Children:
           I Sylvanus T., born Jan. 14, 1847; died
            Oct. 14, 1847.
           II Ezra, born Aug. 20, 1848; died Sept., 1849.
           III Eugene, born Jan. 11, 1851; died Mar.
            24, 1869.
           IV Libbie C., born Feb. 21, 1852; died Oct.
            22, 1865.


**207. Ezra Pelton[7]**, second son of Ansel[6], Phineas[5],
John[4], John[3], Samuel[2], John[1], born at Pultney, N. Y.,

March 20, 1825; married Cherry Valley, Ashtabula Co., O., July 2, 1846, Martha A. Pelton, daughter of Rufus Pelton, of that place. Farmer. Died at Cherry Valley, O., January 14, 1848. His widow married (2) James Loveland. Lived, 1876, at Cherry Valley, O. Child:

> I Emma H., born July 8, 1848; married Nov. 19, 1870, Mitchell Warren, of Bloomfield, Trumbull Co., O. Children: Clyde J., b. Aug. 26, 1872; Alton, b. Mar. 11, 1874; Bertha, b. Mar. 3, 1877.

**207. Elias Pelton**, third son of Ansel⁷, Phineas⁶, John⁵, John⁴, Samuel², John¹, born Pultney, Steuben Co., N. Y., May 13, 1828; married July 8, 1853, at Espeyville, Crawford Co., Pa., Clara Heriott, daughter of Aaron Heriott. Shoe trade. Lived, in 1876, at Union City, Erie Co., Pa.; has removed since to some Western State. Children:

> I Ansel, born Dec. 4, 1855.
> II Howe, born Jan. 4, 1863.
> III Lena, born Sept. 8, 1866.

**207. Lewis Pelton**, fourth son of Ansel⁶, Phineas⁵, John⁴, John³, Samuel², John¹, born at Pultney, Steuben Co., N. Y., March 25, 1832; married at Gustavus, O., November 2, 1854, Jerusha Lindsley, daughter of Jesse Lindsley, of that place. Farmer. Residence, in 1878, at Gustavus, O. Children, none.

**203. William M. Pelton**, third son of Phineas⁵, John⁴, John³, Samuel², John¹, born in Connecticut, probably at Saybrook or Chatham, February 1, 1801; married in Pultney, N. Y., in 1820, Sarah Wheeler

(b. Aug. 12, 1806), daughter of Elias Wheeler, from New Hampshire. Married by Rev. James Hotchkin. Died at Penn Yan, Yates Co., N. Y., October 3, 1872. Children:

I Elvira, born Apr. 12, 1826; married Shadrach Norris, Sept. 12, 1847. In 1876 lived in Pultney, Steuben Co., N. Y.; one child, Esquire Norris.

II Sarah, born Nov. 19, 1828; married Sept. 13, 1846, Ira Loundsbury. Lived, in 1876, at Angelica, N. Y. Children, five.

III Louisa A., born Aug. 17, 1830; married May 11, 1851, Joseph Daily. Lived, in 1876, at Penn Yan, Yates Co., N. Y. Children, six.

IV John W., born June 10, 1833; died Sept. 23, 1833.

V Ruth R., born Apr. 10, 1831; married May 4, 1851, Willis Redon; five children; died Nov. 22, 1862.

VI Nancy O., born Aug. 10, 1835; married Oct. 12, 1854, John House. In 1876 a widow, living in Penn Yan, N. Y.

VII Lucinda, born Dec. 28, 1836; died unmarried, June 27, 1852.

VIII Belinda P., born Mar. 21, 1839; married Dec. 29, 1864, Wm. M. Barrow. In 1876 lived at Jerusalem, Yates Co., N. Y.; two children.

IX Wesley M., born Mar. 23, 1841; died in the army, July 22, 1862.

X Mary F., born Mar. 25, 1843; married (1) —— ——; (2) Dec. 24, 1872, William Tate. In 1876 lived at Canandaigua, N. Y.; one child.

**211**    XI James H., b. May 16, 1846; m. Dec. 17,
                1867, Margaret Norton.
        XII Caroline R., born June 4, 1848; married
                Sept. 1, 1867, Wm. Barber.   Lived, in
                1876, in Yates Co., N. Y.   Children,
                four.


**260. James W. Pelton**, second son of William
M.[6], Phineas[5], John[4], John[3], Samuel[2], John[1], born May
16, 1846; married December 17, 1867, Margaret
Norton.   Lived, in 1876, at Grand Rapids, Mich.
Child:
        I Name unknown.


**203. Israel Pelton**, fourth son of Phineas[5], John[4],
John[3], Samuel[2], John[1], born at Lyme, N. H., October
4, 1805 or 6; married at Wheeler, Steuben Co., N. Y.,
December 20, 1833, Lucinda Earley, daughter of
James Earley, of Delaware Co., N. Y.   Farmer.
Lived at Pultney, N. Y.; removed October 17 to 28,
1854 (some say 1851), to Chickasaw, Chickasaw Co.,
Ia., and died September 15, 1869, in Floyd Co., Ia.
His widow, in 1876, lived in Charles City, Floyd Co.,
Ia.   Children:
        I Margaret, born Dec. 18, 1834, Pultney,
                N. Y.; married July 30, 1859, at Brad-
                ford, Ia., by Elder Bryant, to Daniel
                Moore.   In 1876 they lived in Bassett,
                Chickasaw Co., Ia.; eight children.
        II Sarah, born June 5, 1836; married at
                Chickasaw, Ia., Oct. 12, 1856, John
                Cox; seven children.   Farmer.   Lived,
                1877, at Bassett, Ia.
        III Harriet, born June 11, 1838; married at
                Charles City, Ia., Feb. 1, 1856, Henry

28

Hunn, son of Clermont Hunn. Children, three. Lived, in 1877, in Floyd Co., Ia.

**212**  IV Oliver, b. Sept. 1, 1840; m. Mar. 18, 1864, Ellen Hunn.

V Ansel, born Oct. 1, 1842; served in the army in the Great Rebellion, in Co. H, 4th Iowa Cavalry, about one year, and was then discharged for disability, and died May 5, 1866, unmarried.

**213** VI Phineas, b. Feb. 4, 1844; m. Feb. 16, 1876, Melissa M. Huckins.

VII Thomas, born July 18, 1847; unmarried in 1877. A farmer, living at Charles City, Floyd Co., Ia.

**213**VIII Justus, b. June 11, 1850 (twin); m. Nov. 18, 1872, Mary Ann Knapp.

IX Naomi, born June 11, 1850 (twin); married at Charles City, Ia., Jan., 1877, Hugh Phillips. Children, two. Lived, in 1877, at Chickasaw, Ia.


**211. Oliver Pelton**[7], first son of Israel[6], Phineas[5], John[4], John[3], Samuel[2], John[1], born September 1, 1840; married at Charles City, Ia., March 18, 1864, Ellen Hunn, daughter of William Hunn. Farmer. Served about four years in the army, in Co. H, 4th Iowa Cavalry. Lived, in 1877, in Floyd Co., Ia. Children:

I Arthur, born Mar. 12, 1867.

II Etta, born Oct. 1, 1869; died June 5, 1873.

III James Ephraim, born June 12, 1873 (May 16, 1872 ?).

IV Israel, born Nov. 5, 1876.

**211. Phineas Pelton**, third son of Israel, Phineas, John, John, Samuel, John, born February 4, 1844; married Charles City, Ia., February 16, 1876, Melissa Maud Huckins, daughter of Joseph Huckins, of Floyd Co., Ia. Farmer. Lived, in 1877, at Charles City, Ia. Child:

I Maud, born Nov. 22, 1876.

**211. Justus Pelton**, fifth son of Israel, Phineas, John, John, Samuel, John, born June 11, 1850; married Mossville, Ia., November 18, 1872, Mary Ann Knapp, daughter of Hiram Knapp, of Charles City, Ia. Child:

I Israel, born 1874; died June 10, 1874.

**59. Jonathan Pelton**, ninth son of John, John, Samuel, John, born at Saybrook (Essex), Conn., May 21, 1768; married about 1789, Elizabeth Baker (b. Jan., 1771; died June 2, 1859). Blacksmith. Died at Leonardsville, Madison Co., N. Y., December 3, 1850. Family record said to be in possession of Mrs. Harriet Babcock, daughter of William B. Pelton, Leonardsville, N. Y. Children:

**214** I William Baker, b. Nov. 5, 1790; m. Nov. 23, 1815, Lucy Webster; d. Jan. 20, 1839.

II Timothy, born June 21, 1792; died Feb. 2, 1814.

**215** III Homer, b. Dec. 1, 1793; m. May 18, 1814, Mary Cheney; d. Mar., 1868.

IV Temperance, born Oct. 5, 1795; married Mr. Andrews, brother of the husband of Martha.

**218** V Jonathan, Jr., b. Sept. 7, 1797; m. about 1820, Caroline E. Seymour; d. Sept. 16, 1867.

IV Elizabeth, born Oct., 1799, at Sangerfield,
Oneida Co., N. Y.; married there, Jan.
1. 1823, Isaac Stevens; twelve children.
Lived, in 1876, at Kalamazoo, Mich.;
died Dec. 19, 1878.

VII Martha, born Aug. 11, 1802 (twin); married Isaac Andrews. Lived in Connecticut and died in 1872. Children, four;
one son, John Andrews, in 1876, lived
at W. Winsted, Conn.

VIII Mary, twin, born Aug. 11, 1802; no further record.

IX Lucy M., born Sept. 22, 1804; married
Warren Cheney. Lived, 1876, at Good-
richville, Genesee Co., Mich. Children,
seven.

**219** X Edward Shipman, b. Dec. 7, 1807; m.
Elizabeth Maria——; d. Sept. 26, 1848.

XI Delia, born July 24, 1810, Sangerfield,
N. Y.; married Oct. 14, 1827, Rudolph-
son B. Loring. Lived, 1876, at Oshtemo,
Mich.; five children; removed to Michigan in 1837.

**219** XII Timothy Jewett, b. Oct. 20, 1813; m. Dec.
25, 1834, Caroline Copernoll.


**213. William Baker Pelton**, first son of Jona-
than, John, John, Samuel, John, born at Saybrook,
Conn., November 5, 1790; married at Burlington,
Otsego Co., N. Y., November 23, 1815, to Lucy
Webster, daughter of Stephen Webster. Blacksmith.
Died at Marshall, Oneida Co., N. Y., January 20,
1839; frozen to death.. Children:

I Charles C., born Oct. 18, 1816; unmarried;
master machinist; went, it is said, from

Newark or Paterson. N. J. (probably Paterson), to take the first locomotive engines to Cuba, and on his return from his second trip there was taken ill and died in a hospital in Philadelphia about Apr. 11, 1850.

II Francis, born Feb. 28, 1819; married Oct. 18, 1842, Mary Skinner; died Oct. 20, 1842; farmer; no children.

III William Harrison, born Waterville, Oneida Co., N. Y., Feb. 22, 1822; married Attleboro, Mass., Nov. 5, 1845, Eliza A. Claflin; died Nov. 17, 1887; no children; contractor. His widow, in 1887, lived at Dodgeville, Bristol Co., Mass.

IV Harriet, born Feb. 22, 1822; married Sept. 9, 1846, William A. Babcock, of Pharsalia, N. Y. Lived, in 1876 and in 1888, at Leonardsville, N. Y. Children, Mary L., Charles and Harriet.

**213. Homer Pelton[4]**, third son of Jonathan[5], John[4], John[3], Samuel[2], John[1], born in Connecticut, probably at or near Saybrook, December 1, 1793. Shoemaker. Removed to Auburn, N. Y., and there married, May 18, 1814, Mary Cheney, daughter of Joseph Cheney, of that place. He settled in his business in Marcellus, Onondaga Co., N. Y., thence removed to Michigan and bought a farm; dying at Hadley, Lapeer Co., Mich., in March, 1868. Children:

1 Julia A., born Mar. 27, 1815; married Nov. 17, 1847, Horatio N. Richards. Lived, 1875, at Armada, Macomb Co., Mich. Children, Irene and Homer.

**216**     II Joseph W., b. Apr. 12, 1817; m. Mar. 5,
            1840, Mary F. Cowdin.

**217**     III George H., born Feb. 19, 1819; m. June
            15, 1854, Laura Carl.

            IV Elizabeth C., born Feb. 23, 1821; married
            Nov. 28, 1844, Edward Cady.   Lived,
            1875, at Rochelle, Ogle Co., Ill.   Chil-
            dren, Martha, Don, Mary and Ella.

**217**     V Gilbert Motier, b. Apr. 20, 1824; m. Feb.,
            1857, Jane Angell.

            VI Mary A., born Nov. 20, 1826; married at
            Lapeer, Mich., Jan. 20, 1847, Henry
            Gibson.   Children, two.   Died Dec. 3,
            1868.

**217**     VII Richard W., b. Nov. 23, 1829; m. Clarinda
            Butler, Sept. 28, 1851.


**215. Joseph W. Pelton[7]**, first son of Homer[6],
Jonathan[5], John[4], John[3], Samuel[2], John[1], born at Mar-
cellus, Onondaga Co., N. Y., April 12, 1817.   Farmer.
Married at Brandon, Mich., March 5, 1840, Mary F.
Cowdin.   Lived, in 1876, at Hadley, Lapeer Co.,
Mich.   Children:

            I Julia E., born May 3, 1843; died May 13,
            1865.

            II Mary E., born Feb. 14, 1845; married
            Nov. 11, 1869, to Frederic G. Bullock.
            Living in 1876.

**217**     III Herbert F., b. Nov. 2, 1847; m. Apr. 15,
            1871, Adelma L. Bullock.

            IV Homer, born July 1, 1851.

            V Helen J., born June 21, 1857; died Feb.
            18, 1871.

**216. Herbert F. Felton**[8], first son of Joseph W.[7], Homer[6], Jonathan[5], John[4], John[3], Samuel[2], John[1], born November 2, 1847; married April 15, 1871, Adelina L. Bullock.   No further record.

**215. George H. Felton**[7], second son of Homer[6], Jonathan[5], John[4], John[3], Samuel[2], John[1], born at Marcellus, N. Y., February 19–21, 1819.  Book-keeper. Married at Romeo, Macomb Co., Mich., June 13, 1854, Laura Carl, daughter of Eben Carl, of Lenox, Macomb Co., Mich.  Residence, 1875, at Mount Clemens, Macomb Co., Mich.  Children, none.

**215. Gilbert Matier Felton**[7], third son of Homer[6], Jonathan[5], John[4], John[3], Samuel[2], John[1], born at Marcellus, N. Y., April 20, 1824; married February, 1857, Jane Angell.  Died at Adrian, Mich., November 7, 1858.  Children:
> I Elnora, born May, 1858; said in 1876 to have been then living nine miles south of Adrian, Mich.   P. O., Adrian, care of Gardner Davis.

Some say there was another child, name unknown.

**215. Richard W. Felton**[7], fourth son of Homer[6], Jonathan[5], John[4], John[3], Samuel[2], John[1], born at Marcellus, N. Y., November 23, 1829; married about 1852 Clarinda Butler, daughter of J. H. Butler, of Brandon, Mich.  Farmer.  Living, in 1876, at Hadley, Mich.  Children:
> I Melvin, born Feb. 23, 1854.
> II Infant son, born 1856; died when two weeks old.
> III Ella L., born July 30, 1859; died Jan. 15, 1860.

IV Letta J., born Dec. 20, 1861; died Jan.
21, 1862.
V Mary E., born Nov. 18, 1863.
VI Gilbert M., born Sept. 24, 1865.
VII Orlando J., born Dec. 25, 1867.
VIII George H., born June 3, 1870.
IX Charles E., born May 6, 1873.

**212. Jonathan Pelton⁶, Jr.,** fourth son of Jonathan⁵, John⁴, John³, Samuel², John¹, born probably in
Connecticut, September 7, 1797; married about 1822,
Caroline E. Seymour, daughter of Josiah Seymour,
of New Hartford, N. Y. Butcher. Died in Utica,
N. Y., September 16, 1868. Removed from Connecticut to Paris Hill, Oneida Co., N. Y., thence to
Sangerfield Centre, and to Oriskany Falls, N. Y.,
where he lived in 1848; afterward to Utica, N. Y.
Children:
218     I Henry S., b. July 27, 1824; m. Nov. 23,
1849, Sarah Hopkins.
II Julia, born ——, 1834.
III Lucy J., born, 1846.

**218. Henry S. Pelton⁷,** first son of Jonathan⁶,
Jonathan⁵, John⁴, John³, Samuel², John¹, born July 27,
1824, at New Hartford, Oneida Co., N. Y.; married
at Depere, Wis., November 13, 1849, to Sarah Hopkins. Physician, Ypsilanti, Mich., in 1876. Children:
I Caroline E., born Jan. 22, 1851.
II Charles J., born Sept. 20, 1853.
III Mary M., born Aug. 17, 1856.
IV Ella F., born Oct. 6, 1858.
V Wesley M., born Apr. 18, 1863.
VI William J., born Jan. 12, 1866.
VII Della A., born Nov. 4, 1867.

VIII Homer J., born Apr. 5, 1870.
IX Nelly E., born Feb. 4, 1872.
X Herbert H., born Sept. 19, 1873.
XI Grant A., born Aug. 14, 1875; died Sept. 7, 1876.

**212. Edward Shipman Pelton⁶**, fifth son of Jonathan⁵, John⁴, John³, Samuel², John¹, born Oneida Co., N. Y., December 7, 1807; married about 1838, Eliza Maria ——. Shoemaker. Died September 26, 1848, at Forge Hollow, near Waterville, Oneida Co., N. Y.  Child:

**219**    I William Baker, b. Oct. 20, 1839; m. May 26, 1863, Jane Small.

**219. William Baker Pelton⁷**, only son of Edward S.⁶, Jonathan⁵, John⁴, John³, Samuel², John¹, born at Forge Hollow, Oneida Co, N. Y., October 20, 1839; married at Troy, N. Y., May 26, 1863, Jane Small, daughter of Samuel Small, of England. Spinner of wool. Lived, in 1876, at Utica, N. Y. Children:

I Eliza Maria, born Utica, N. Y., Nov. 19, 1864.
II William Samuel, born Apr. 28, 1867.

**213. Timothy Jewett Pelton⁶**, sixth son of Jonathan⁵, John⁴, John³, Samuel², John¹, born at Sangerfield, Oneida Co., N. Y., October 20, 1813; married at Exeter, Otsego Co., N. Y., December 25, 1834, Caroline Copernoll, daughter of Peter Copernoll, of Otsego Co., N. Y.  Lived, in 1876, at Exeter, Monroe Co., Mich. Blacksmith.  Removed to Michigan, November 5, 1845.  Children:

29

  I Mary M., born Oct. 4, 1835; married Apr.
    20, 1855, to S. C. Goodall. Lived,
    1875, in Chesaning, Mich.
  II Jacob M., born Oct. 4, 1835; died Jan.
    18, 1843.
**220** III Edward J., b. Sept. 11, 1840; m. Mar. 7,
    1865, Kate Bovee.
  IV. Caroline E., born Apr. 20, 1843; married
    Jan. 1, 1860, Gilbert Darling. Died
    Nov., 1872, at London, Monroe Co.,
    Mich.
  V Martha D., born Feb. 17, 1846; married
    Mar., 1869, Gersham Palmer. In 1875
    lived at Dundee, Mich.
  VI Margaret, born May 27, 1851; married
    Mar., 1867, Delos Lambkins. Lived,
    1875, at London, Monroe Co., Mich.
  VII Ellen, born Dec., 1853; married Dec. 21,
    1872, Perry Lambkins. Lived, 1875,
    at London, Mich.
  VIII Menzo, born Aug. 5, 1859.

**220. Edward J. Pelton**, second son of Timothy
Jewett[7], Jonathan[5], John[4], John[3], Samuel[2], John[1], born
September 11, 1840, in Oneida Co., N. Y.; married
March 7, 1865, Kate Bovee. Lived, in 1875, at
Grass Lake, Jackson Co., Mich. Children:
  I William, born Nov. 27, 1865.
  II Hattie, born July 4, 1868.

**59. David Pelton[5]**, tenth son of John[4], John[3],
Samuel[2], John[1], born at Saybrook (now Essex), Conn.,
December 30, 1773; married at Lyme, N. H., June
15, 1796, Lucy Stone (b. Apr. 17, 1777), daughter of
Abner Stone, of Fitz William, N. H. He was an

excellent, well-known, Christian gentleman. He died suddenly, falling from his horse in a fit of apoplexy, at Bradford, Vt., August 22, 1821. His widow married (2) Simeon Fillmore, uncle of President Millard Fillmore, of Clarence, Erie Co., N. Y. She died, Clarence, N. Y., April 30, 1848. Mr. Pelton was successful in business, accumulated property, and left his family well off at his death. Children, born at Lyme, N. H.:

  I, II Twin sons, born in Aug., 1797; lived but a few hours.

  Reuben Chamberlain; adopted June 12, 1797.

  III Abner Mellen, born Mar. 22, 1799; died Sept. 3, 1800.

222 IV Brewster, b. Mar. 18, 1801; m. (1) Mar. 27, 1827, Thirza Skinner; (2) Feb. 23, 1854, Mrs. Jenette May Wickham; d. Aug. 30, 1872 (or July 30? as given by his sister Mrs. Barber.)

  Caroline Pierce; adopted Jan. 25, 1802.

  V Lucy, born Lyme, N. H., Jan. 19, 1803; married May 23, 1826, at Lyme, N. H., to Col. Josiah Barber, of Canaan, N. H. Lived in Canaan, Franklin, Andover, Bradford, Warner and Nashua, N. H.; in the last place from 1842 up to his death, July 30, 1875. Mrs. Barber, in 1876, was a manufacturer of knit goods at Nashua, N. H., and still lived there in 1889. Children: David Pelton, b. Apr. 24, 1827; Eliza Pelton, b. Nov. 11, 1828, and Lucy R., b. July 20, 1834.

223 VI David Mellen, b. Nov. 26, 1804; m. Sally Ross, Nov. 26, 1831; d. Apr. 3, 1872.

**225** VII Ahira, b. Dec. 25, 1806; m. June 1, 1830,
Mary M. Alexander; d. Oct. 2, 1837.

VIII Nancy, born July 25, 1809; married Sept.
12, 1832, Thos. J. Stevens, merchant,
of Clarence, Erie Co., N. Y. Children,
four. Died Feb. 2, 1840, while on the
way to Michigan.

IX Lambert, born May 26, 1811; learned tanning and died at Canaan, N. H., Mar.
5, 1832.

X Eliza, born Nov. 6, 1813; died Oct. 3,
1834, at Lyme, N. H.

**226. Brewster Pelton**, fourth son of David,
John[4], John[3], Samuel[2], John[1], born at Lyme, N. H.,
March 18, 1801; married (1) at Lyme, N. H., March
27, 1827, Thirza Skinner, daughter of Capt. Cyrus
Skinner, of Lyme. She had no children; died Oberlin, O., February 9, 1853; (2) at Cleveland, O., February 23, 1854, Mrs. Jenette May (Arnold) Wickham
(born Sept. 1, 1811, at Haddam, Conn.), daughter
of Simon Arnold. He was a man of enterprise and
of sterling integrity and piety. In early manhood he
was a dealer in cattle, afterward a merchant. In
1834 he removed to Oberlin, O.; one of fifty families
who there settled. He built the second house in
Oberlin, and there established himself as the leading
merchant of the place. Looked up to and trusted by
all, he became by common consent their banker.
From its beginning the college in Oberlin found in
him a staunch friend and liberal supporter. At his
death he was still a member of its Board of Trustees
— an office held by him for many years. He remembered the college at that time by a gift of $25,000.
In 1850 (or 1852 as stated by another) he removed

BREWSTER PELTON.

to Cleveland, O., where he purchased property on
the west side of that city.   With President Mahan,
General Merchant and George Slade, he endeavored
to establish a university in that part of the city, since
known as University Heights—their aim having
been to give an education both classical and scientific.
An effort was also made to establish on the Heights
a school for young ladies similar to that of Mount
Holyoke in Massachusetts.

Both of these enterprises failed from causes beyond
the control of Mr. Pelton and his associates, much to
their regret.   Identified with all movements for the
improvement of Cleveland, and especially of his own
ward, it may be said that he was the founder of the
Congregational Church upon the Heights, contribut-
ing one-fifth of its entire cost when it was built, and
giving liberally to its support so long as he lived.
Simple and unobtrusive in his habits in life, he died
in Christian hope and peace, at Cleveland, O., August
30, 1872.   Child (by his first wife none); by his
second wife:

> I Thirza Jennette, born at Cleveland, O.,
> Mar. 29, 1856; married there June 28,
> 1876, George William Kinney (b. Ober-
> lin, O., Oct. 4, 1852), of Oberlin, O.,
> son of Geo. Kinney, deceased.   Chil-
> dren: 1. Brewster Pelton, b. Sept. 26,
> 1877; 2. Ralph Parsons, b. Sept. 30,
> 1880; 3. Jeannette, born Jan. 16, 1891.
> Mrs. Pelton and daughter were living
> in Cleveland, O., in 1892.

**226. David Mellen Pelton**, fifth son of David[4],
John[3], John[2], Samuel, John[1], born at Lyme, N. H.,
November 26, 1804; married at Hanover, N. H.,

November 26, 1831, Sally Ross, daughter of Deacon
Thomas Ross, of that place. Tanner and shoemaker,
and afterward a farmer. Lived at Hanover, N. H.,
until December, 1854, when he removed to London,
Madison Co., O., where he died, April 3, 1872.
Children, all born in Hanover, N. H.:

> I Lucy B., born May 2, 1834; married Han-
> over, N. H., Jan. 19, 1853, J. C. Bridg-
> man. Lived, 1876, at 43 E. High
> street, London, O.; six children.
>
> II Isabel F., born Aug. 30, 1840; married
> (1) July 17, 1859, J. Fritts, who died
> 1862; one son, Fred C. Fritts, b. Mar.
> 26, 1860; (2) Jan. 27, 1867, Edward C.
> McClemens, who died Oct. 10, 1869;
> one child; (3) Oct. 7, 1871, Dr. B. F.
> Welsh, of California, Hamilton Co.,
> O.; one child. Died May 4, 1875, at
> California, O.
>
> 221 III David C., b. June 22, 1843; m. June 4,
> 1864, Jennie E. Cannon.
>
> IV Brewster, born Aug. 23, 1848; died un-
> married, Nov. 7, 1871; telegraph oper-
> ator.
>
> V Franklin R., born Aug. 20, 1852; died
> Mar. 2, 1857.

**223. David C. Pelton,** first son of David Mellen⁶,
David⁵, John⁴, John³, Samuel², John¹, born at Hanover, N. H., June 22, 1843; married at London, O.,
June 1, 1864, Jennie E. Cannon, daughter of Matthew
W. Cannon, of Mount Sterling, O. In 1876 was
dispatcher of trains and assistant railroad superintendent at Corsicana, Tex., whither he removed in

1873 and left in 1886.  In 1891 Mr. Pelton resided in Lordsburgh, New Mexico; his family in Gainesville, Tex.  Children:

 I Jesse Elmon, born London, O., Jan. 21, 1866.
 II Brewster David, born Mattoon, Ill., Jan. 17, 1872.
 III Flora Amy, born Corsicana, Tex., Oct. 19, 1873.
 IV Maud Cannon, twin, born Corsicana, Tex., Nov. 22, 1877.
 V Myrtle Brown, twin, born Corsicana, Tex., Nov. 22, 1877; died Nov. 19, 1878.

**220. Alvin Pelton**[6], sixth son of David[5], John[4], John[3], Samuel[2], John[1], born at Lyme, N. H., December 25, 1806.  He learned tanning with Lyman Wright, of Troy, N. H., and married June, 1830, Mary M. Alexander, daughter of Phineas and Ada Alexander, of that place.  Removing to Sterling, Mass., he worked at pottery, and there died, October 21, 1837.  His widow, Mary M., married (2) February 26, 1839, Edmund Maynard, of Sterling, and in 1875 lived at Leominster, Mass.  Children, born at Sterling:

 I Lucy Anlowra, born Dec. 20, 1831; died Apr. 24, 1832.
 II Mary Eliza, born May 6, 1833; married Nov. 28, 1855, Horace N. Hammond, son of Nathaniel and Orpha Hammond, of Avon, Me.  Residence, 1875, Ayer, Mass.  One child, Lizzie Imogene, b. Aug. 29, 1856.
 III Nathaniel Lambert, born Dec. 3, 1834; died Jan. 5, 1836.

IV  Albert Ahira, born Nov. 13, 1836; learned
shoemaking at Pepperell, Mass.; enlisted in Co. A, 15th Regt. of Mass.
Vols., July 10, 1861; was taken prisoner
at Ball's Bluff, Va., Oct. 22, 1861; was
released May 31, 1862, and honorably
discharged at Alexandria, Va., Nov. 29,
1862.   He married Dec. 14, 1863, Anna
M. Blood, daughter of Nathan and
Mindwell Blood, of Pepperell, Mass.
Mrs. Pelton died June 10, 1866.   In
1875 Mr. Pelton still lived in Pepperell.
Occupation, shoemaker.   No further
record.

**58. Israel Pelton**[5], eleventh son of John[4], John[3],
Samuel[2], John[1], born at Saybrook (Essex), Conn.,
April 1, 1775; married there, about 1807, Lois Wright,
daughter of Cornelius Wright, of that place.   Blacksmith.   He lived at Essex and at Durham, Conn.,
dying at Durham, March 20, 1830, of lung fever,
after a short sickness.   Children:

I  Eliza M., born Apr. 20, 1808; married
Jan. 19, 1828, Asa W. Penfield, of
Glastenbury, Conn.; six children.  She
died Jan. 9, 1875, of apoplexy.
II  Electa, born May 2, 1813; married at
Centre Brook, Conn., Jan. 18, 1853,
Alpheus R. Blake, merchant, from
North Guilford, Conn., who died June
25, 1859.  Mrs. Blake, in 1877, lived
at Clinton, Conn.; no children.

**65. James Pelton⁴**, second son of John³ (first of Saybrook, Conn.), Samuel², John¹, born in the township of Canterbury, Windham Co., Conn., July 21, 1710 (Town Record); married at Middletown, Conn., Jan. 14, 1735-6, Elizabeth Burr, (Town Record). Settled in Haddam, close to the line of Guilford, and there died about 1794, as his will was admitted to probate April 27,.1795. His wife died about 1798. Farmer. Children (as their order of birth is unknown the sons are placed together; the records of Haddam being very imperfect):

      I Elizabeth, born at Middletown, Conn., Aug. 5, 1738; married about 1760, Stephen Johnson (brother of Ruth Johnson, who married her brother James). Lived in Haddam, and died about 1830.

228    II James, b. Apr. 3, 1741; m. Nov. 19, 1767, Ruth Johnson; d. 1808.

244    III John, b. ——, 1745; m. (1) Huldah ——; (2) Widow Thankful ——; d. Aug. 12, 1803, æ. 58 years.

251    IV Benjamin, b. ——, 1753; m. Hannah Snow; d. Aug. 25, 1821.

      V Lucy, born ——; married (Haddam Rec.) Nov. 11, 1772, Samuel Stannard.

262    VI Phineas, b. 1758; m. Rebecca Johnson; d. Jan. 17, 1850.

      VII Sarah, born ——; married Francis Lewis, who died in 1814. They lived near Turkey Hill, in the eastern part of Haddam, Conn. Children, six.

    VIII Martha, born ——; no further record.

     IX Abigail, born ——; no further record.

      X Jemima, born ——; no further record.

30

NOTE.—Tradition says he had a very strong voice; that once on a time his corn fan having been lent and not returned, he climbed upon the roof of an out building and called aloud, "Bring home my corn fan." It came home, brought by a neighbor living a mile off.

The land records of Haddam show that James Pelton sold land January 30, 1753, for a consideration of £2,000.


**227. James Pelton⁵**, first son of James⁴, John³, Samuel², John¹, born at Middletown, Conn., April 3, 1741 (Town Records); married November 19, 1767, Ruth Johnson. Lived in Guilford, Conn., the most of his life. Farmer. He exchanged farms with David Hall, and in 1800 or 1801 removed to Essex, Chittenden Co., Vt., his sons Samuel and James going with him. He died August, 1808, at the house of one of his brothers* in Hartford, Washington Co., N. Y., while on his way from Vermont to Connecticut, from the effects of a malignant carbuncle or tumor. His wife, an excellent Christian woman, died in Vermont in 1829, over 93 years old. Children (the exact order of birth unknown):

      I Anna, born in Haddam, 1768; died unmarried.

**229**   II Josiah, b. Aug. 3, 1770; m. Nov., 1793, Eunice Doan; d. Aug. 12, 1819.

      III Sally, born in Haddam, Conn., 1772; married Francis Lewis.

**233**   IV Samuel, b. 1775; m. Hannah Hopkins Hall; d. Apr. 27, 1854.

**237**   V James, b. Oct. 30, 1777; m. Nov., 1799, Lois Stevens; died July 27, 1851.

---

* His brother John.

VI  Ruth, born about 1779, in Haddam, Conn.;
       became low spirited and finally in Ver-
       mont, deranged.

242  VII  Johnson, b. Nov. 30, 1782; m. Dolly Hall;
       d. Oct. 13, 1825.

     VIII  Jemima, born 1784, in Haddam, Conn.;
       married Elisha Youmans.

**226. Josiah Felton**, first son of James[6], James[5], John[4], Samuel[3], John[2], born in Haddam, Conn., August 3, 1770; married there, November, 1793, Eunice *Doan (b. July 16, 1770), daughter of Phineas Doan, of Haddam. Farmer. Lived in Haddam, about five miles west of Higganum and the Connecticut river. He died there, August 12, 1819, his wife having died September 11, 1817, aged 48. Both were good, industrious people and earnest Christians, and their good example was followed by all their children. Children, born in Haddam:

230   I  Ansel, b. Nov. 23, 1794; m. in 1823,
          Rebecca Gates; was living in 1876.

      II  Mary (Polly), born Oct. 13, 1796; mar-
          ried Dec. 3, 1854, Jacob Beam, who
          died Aug. 31, 1861. Lived for years
          at Fostoria, O. In 1876 was living at
          Cresco, Saunders Co., Neb. An excel-
          lent Christian woman.

      III  Betsey (Elizabeth), born Dec. 22, 1798;
          married Aug., 1823, Coleman Clark.
          Lived in Haddam, Conn., and there
          died, on the old place, Oct. 28, 1858.
          Children, seven. Mr. Clark was judge
          of the Probate Court for that district.

231   IV  Asahel, b. Apr. 8, 1801; m. July 17, 1836,
          Electa Burr; d. Dec. 31, 1873.

---
* Now Doane.

V Zervias, born Sept. 22, 1803; married
Apr. 7, 1825, Russell Andrews.   Lived,
in 1876, at Cresco, Neb.   Children,
nine.
VI Martha, born Apr. 8 (23?), 1806; married
Mar. 18, 1841, R. M. Finch.   Children,
two.   Lived, 1876, at Wioto, Cass
Co., Ia.
**232** VII Phineas D., b. Mar. 27, 1810; m. (1) June
26, 1839, Harriet Burr; (2) Aug. 10,
1842, Triphena Holmes; (3) Sept. 17,
1864, Hannah M. Munn.


**229. Ansel Pelton[7]**, first son of Josiah[6], James[5],
James[4], John[3], Samuel[2], John[1], born at Haddam, Conn.,
November 23, 1794; married there, Spring of 1823,
Rebecca, daughter of Jonathan Gates, of near Watertown, N. Y.   Removed to Covington, Wyoming Co.,
N. Y., October 9, 1823; thence to Spring Green,
Sauk Co., Wis., where he lived in 1876.   Farmer
and surveyor.   A religious man of the highest reputation.   Wife, Rebecca, died in 1862.   Children:
**230**    I Jonathan Gates, b. July 15, 1825; m. Apr.
23, 1846, Paulina E. Randall.


**230. Jonathan Gates Pelton[8]**, only son of Ansel[7],
Josiah[6], James[5], James[4], John[3], Samuel[2], John[1], born at
Covington, Genesee Co., N. Y., July 15, 1825; mar-
ried there, April 23, 1846, Paulina E. Randall, daughter of Aaron E. Randall, of Covington.   Removed
to Spring Green, Sauk Co., Wis., and there was
living in 1876.   Physician.   Children:
**231**    I Byron Randall, b. Mar. 27, 1847; m. Nov.,
1870, Helen Tunstall.
II Mary Helen, born Aug. 21, 1849.

III Ann Elizabeth, born July 27, 1851.
IV George Edward, born June 2, 1855; died
Feb. 22, 1863.
V Olive Rosette, born Oct. 15, 1857.
VI Ella Rebecca, born Feb. 22, 1860.
VII John Lewis, born Feb. 26, 1863; died
Dec. 23, 1863.

**220. Byron Randall Pelton⁹**, first son of Jonathan Gates⁸, Ansel⁷, Josiah⁶, James⁵, James⁴, John³, Samuel², John¹, born March 27, 1847; married November, 1870, Helen Tunstall, who died April 5, 1871. Children, none.

**221. Asahel Pelton⁷**, second son of Josiah⁶, James⁵, James⁴, John³, Samuel², John¹, born at Haddam, Conn., April 8, 1801; married there, July 17, 1836, Electa Burr, daughter of Jonathan Burr, of Haddam. Farmer. Removed to Central New York, October 9, 1823, and died December 31, 1873, at LaGrange, Wyoming Co., N. Y. Children:
I Harriet, born May 31, 1837; married
August 24, 1858, Edward R. Perkins.
Lived, in 1876, at Cleveland, O. Children, three.
II Anna M., born Nov. 4, 1838; married
Oct. 31, 1859, Hiram Crouch. Children, five. Residence, in 1876, at
Colorado Springs, El Paso Co., Col.
III Phineas D., born Mar. 17, 1840; died
Dec. 31, 1865.
IV Ellen A., born Aug. 18, 1841; died unmarried, Nov. 3, 1865.
V Hannah, born Jan. 18, 1843. Lived, unmarried, 1876, at LaGrange, N. Y.

**232**   VI Wallace J., b. Mar. 22, 1844; m. Nov.
25, 1868, Eliza C. Howard.
VII Orpha, born Apr. 28, 1846; died unmarried, July 19, 1870.
VIII Marvilla, born July 1, 1848; married Dec.
1, 1873, Benjamin H. Benedict.   Lived,
in 1876, at Red Creek, Wayne Co., N. Y.

**231. Wallace J. Pelton**, second son of Asahel[6],
Josiah[5], James[4], James[3], John[3], Samuel[2], John[1], born
LaGrange, Wyoming Co., N. Y., March 22, 1844;
married at Buffalo, N. Y., November 25, 1868, Eliza
C. Howard, daughter of Austin A. Howard, of that
place.   In 1876 lived at LaGrange, Wyoming Co.,
N. Y.   Farmer.   Children, born at LaGrange, N. Y.:
I Lettie H., born Oct. 12, 1869; died May
17, 1875.
II Austin H., born May 28, 1873.
III Walter C., born Feb. 13, 1875.

**229. Phineas Denn Pelton**, third son of Josiah[6],
James[4], James[3], John[3], Samuel[2], John[1], born at Had-
dam, Conn., March 27, 1810; married (1) Middletown,
Conn., June 26, 1839, Harriet Burr, daughter of
Jonathan Burr, of Haddam, Conn.   Removed to
Western New York, and thence to Kentucky.   His
wife Harriet died at LaGrange, Ky., May 29, 1840;
(2) August 10, 1842, Triphena Holmes, of Brockport,
N. Y., who died at Bardstown, Ky., August 11, 1844;
(3) September 17, 1846, Mrs. Hannah M. Munn, at
Brockport, N. Y.   Mr. Pelton was educated at the
Genesee Wesleyan Seminary in Western New York
in the years 1834, '35 and '36, usually teaching three
or four months each winter, and at the Wesleyan
University at Middletown, Conn., in 1837-8, after

which he taught thirteen years—eight of them in
Kentucky, two in Dayton, O., one in Miamis-
burgh, O., and two in Findlay, O.   He then entered
the ministry in the North Ohio Conference of the
M. E. Church, in which he served for six years, until
his health failed, since which, up to 1876, he was on
the superannuated list, and lived at that time at
Clyde, O.   Child:

> I Wilbur Fiske, born at Bardstown, Ky.,
> May 31, 1843.   In 1861, at the age of
> 18 years, he went from Madison, Wis.,
> as Captain of a Company, the Randall
> Zouaves, was taken prisoner, escaped
> from prison with a comrade, sickened,
> and died, Sept. 20, 1864, and was buried
> by his comrade near La Grange, Tex.

**220. Samuel Pelton[6]**, second son of James[5],
James[4], John[3], Samuel[2], John[1], born in Haddam (or in
Guilford, near the line of Haddam), Conn., in 1775;
married in or near Essex, Chittenden Co., Vt. (where
he had gone with his father), about 1796, Hannah Hopkins Hall, daughter of Dr. David Hall, formerly of
Connecticut, and granddaughter of Dr. Hopkins of
Goshen, Conn.   Lived in Essex, Vt., and thence in
1816, removed to Perry Centre, near Geneseo, N.
Y.; thence, in 1834 or '35, to Centreville, Allegany
Co., N. Y., where he died April 27, 1854, aged 79
years, according to the record on his tombstone.   His
wife, Hannah, died at the house of John Ingersoll, in
Centreville, N. Y., March 30, 1856.   Both are buried
at Centreville.   He was an earnest Christian, and an
excellent man, long an exemplary elder in the Presbyterian Church.   At the battle of Plattsburgh, N.
Y., in the War of 1812, he served as a volunteer, and

fought on a Sunday. His pastor, Rev. Mr. Morgan, in a sermon censured him for breaking the Sabbath.

In Vermont he was a farmer, and also carried on the tanning business and boot and shoe making. He also engaged in the lumber business. In the State of New York he was a farmer. He was an enterprising, thorough business man. Mrs. Pelton was a woman of superior and commanding intellect, in religion a Quakeress. They were among the early settlers of the Genesee Valley. Their family Bible is said to be in the possession of Mrs. Martha Parkis, who lived, in 1879, with her son, Newell Parkis, at Marshall, Mich. Children:

**235** I Edwin, b. about 1798; m. Hannah Gorham; d. 1836 to 1840.

II Maria, born in 1803, in Vermont, and died in infancy.

III Angelina, born about 1805, in Essex, Vt., married, about 1827, George Parkis, son of Jas. Parkis; died Dec. 5, 1873, at Rose, Oakland Co., Mich.; children, four. A daughter, Mrs. Warren Breed, lived, in 1879, at Rose, Mich.

IV Hannah Hopkins, born March 21, 1808, in Vermont; married Aug. 18, 1832, at Washington, Macomb Co., Mich., Abraham T. Powell, son of Archibald Powell of that place; lived there and there died, July 5, 1833; one child, Sarah C. Powell, who married Wesley Miller, and lived, in 1879, at Dryden, Lapeer Co., Mich.

V Lucy, born about 1811, in Essex, Vt., and there died when about three years of age.

285      VI Samuel, b. March 29, about 1817; m. (1)
            Tamzen C. Warner; (2) Agnes J. Moore.
            Lived, in 1876 and '77, in San Francisco,
            Cal., and in Salem, Ore.
        VII Lucy Adaline, born about 1819; died at
            the age of six years.

**232. Edwin Pelton**, first son of Samuel[6], James[5],
James[4], John[3], Samuel[2], John[1], born at Essex, Chittenden Co., Vt., about 1798; removed with his father
and family in 1816 to Perry Centre, Genesee Valley,
N. Y.; married there Hannah Gorham. Teacher and
farmer; a superior mathematician.  He lived at Perry,
Wyoming Co., N. Y., and there died of strangulated
hernia, 1836 to 1840.   Children:
        I  A daughter, living in Michigan in 1879.
        Not found.

**233. Samuel Pelton, Jr.[7]**, second son of Samuel[6],
James[5], James[4], John[3], Samuel[2], John[1], born at Perry
Centre, south-west of Geneseo, N. Y., March 29, 1817;
married (1) about 1836, Tamzen Clemenza Warner
(b. May 23, 1812; d. Nescatunga, Kans., spring of
1888) daughter of Strong Warner of Centreville, N. Y.;
(2) at St. Louis, Mo., Miss Agnes J. Moore of Cumberland Valley, Pa.   He was sent to college, but did
not complete his course ; is a farmer and inventor
and writer on these subjects.  When about fifteen
years old he invented the first revolving horse rake,
which was long in use, and has made since many
other useful inventions, especially those relating to
agricultural machinery, threshers, horse-powers, water
wheels, etc., which are famous in California.   He
has lived in Western New York, in Pennsylvania, in
Maryland, in Missouri, in Colorado, California and in
Oregon.   In 1876 lived in Salem, Or., a manufacturer

31

of threshers and horse-powers.  Residence, in 1892,
Dickinson, N. Da.  His wife, Agnes J., is a descend-
ant of an Irish nobleman; in religion, a Covenanter.
Children (all by the first wife):

    I Aaron B., born 1837; died 1840.

**236**  II James B., b. Feb. 11, 1839; m. March
       13, 1860, Margaret A. Stevens.

    III Mary C., born Centreville, N. Y., Dec. 2,
       1842; m. at Hopkins, Mich., Feb. 23,
       1875, Charles W. Sprague (b. in Ba-
       tavia, N. Y.).  Carpenter.  Residence,
       1879, Otsego, Allegan Co., Mich.; in
       1887, at Nescatunga, Kans.; in 1892, at
       Edmond, Oklahoma.  Child, Lena J.,
       b. June 8, 1876.

    IV Pauline E., born at Centreville, Alle-
       gany Co., N. Y., Dec. 17, 1846; married
       at Otsego, Allegan Co., Mich., Sept.
       7, 1870, Dr. William K. Darling, son of
       Samuel Darling, of Bush, Chautauqua
       Co., N. Y. Residence, 1879, at Hopkins,
       Allegan Co., Mich.  Died Apr. 8, 1891.
       No children.

    V Maria Elizabeth, born in 1843; died in
       infancy.

**237**  VI Edwin William, b. May 26, 1850; m. (1)
       Jan. 1, 1870, Gracie Castle (divorced);
       (2) Nov. 28, 1878, Inez E. Darling.

**235. James B. Pelton**, second son of Samuel⁶,
Samuel⁵, James⁴, James³, John³, Samuel², John¹, born
at Centreville, Allegany Co., N. Y., February 11, 1839;
married at Mount Pleasant, Md., March 13, 1860,
Margaret A. Stevens (b. Mount Pleasant 1836).*

---

* Died in Oklahoma October 9, 1890, after having lived in Kansas from
1887 to 1889, when they entered Oklahoma.

daughter of Rezon Stevens of that place. Machinist,
carriagemaker and inventor. Residence, in 1879,
Mount Pleasant, Frederick Co., Md. Children:

 I Willis E., born April 10, 1861.
 II Leuvern S., born June 4, 1863; died at
  Centreville, N. Y., Aug. 29, 1865.

**236. Edwin William Pelton**, third son of
Samuel[6], Samuel[5], James[4], James[3], John[3], Samuel[2],
John[1], born at Centreville, Allegany Co., N. Y., May
26, 1850; married (1) at Plainwell, Allegan Co., Mich.,
January 1, 1870, Gracie Castle, daughter of Peter
Castle, of Orangeville, Berry Co., Mich., (divorced);
(2) Plainwell, Mich., November 28, 1878, Inez E. Darling (b. Chautauqua Co., N. Y., May 17, 1861), daughter of William K. Darling, of Hopkins, Mich. Farmer.
Lived, in 1887, at Coldwater, Comanche Co., Kans.;
in 1892 in Frisco, Oklahoma. Children:

 I Leuvern Warner, by 1st wife, born Nov.
  27, 1871.
 II Charles W., born Dec. 9, 1880.
 III Claudius J., born Aug. 29, 1883.

**228. James Pelton**, third son of James[5], James[4],
John[3], Samuel[2], John[1], born at Haddam, Conn.,
October 30, 1777; married at Killingworth, Conn.,
November, 1799, Lois Stevens (b. January 14, 1781),
daughter of Lorin Stevens of Madison, Conn. Re-
moved to Essex, Chittenden Co., Vt., and on account
of his health returned to Killingworth, Conn., about
1803. Farmer, shipbuilder and sailor. Died at
Clinton, Conn., July 27, 1851. His wife, Lois, died
April 12, 1860.

 Note. — He showed the family trait — mechanical
ability — by building his own wagon at Essex, Vt.,
even to the casting of lead boxes for the wheels.

This wagon he drove down to Connecticut, on his
return with his family.   On arrival he offered himself
as a ship-carpenter but was rejected for alleged want
of experience.   He at once bought a large boat, cut
her in two and lengthened her.   Seeing the quality
of his work, the shipbuilder, who had refused him
employment, offered him a place in his yard at good
wages. This offer he refused, and rigging up his boat
he put to sea in it, his own master.   Children:

238    I Philander, b. July 1, 1802; m. Sarah
            Rossiter; d. March 1, 1878.

239    II Alfred, b. April 15, 1804; m. 1826, Hetty
            A. Wilcox; d. 1871.

240    III James, b. July 26, 1809; m. Jan. 13, 1834,
            Emily Kelsey.

241    IV Asa S., b. July 29, 1816; m. March 26,
            1840, Harriet Kelsey; d. Feb. 22, 1886.

242    V William Nelson, b. Sept. 6, 1825; m. Aug.
            13, 1848, Mrs. Maria Cable; d. June 23,
            1883.

238. **Philander Pelton**[6], first son of James[6],
James[5], James[4], John[3], Samuel[2], John[1], born at Essex,
Vt., July 1, 1802, removed to Haddam, and then to
Killingworth. Conn.; married Clinton, Conn., Miss
Sarah, daughter of David Rossiter, of that place,
A sailor.   His wife, Sarah, died April 10, 1867.   He
died Clinton, Conn., March 1, 1878.   Children:

            I Sarah Isabella, born at Clinton, Conn.,
                Sept. 23, 1840; married, May 10, 1882,
                at 41 Charlton street, N. Y., George
                S. Edwards, son of Beach Edwards, of
                Huntington, Conn. One child, George
                S. Edwards, Jr., b. Seymour, Conn.,
                Feb. 28, 1883.   Lived at Seymour,
                Conn., in 1888.

**237. Alfred Pelton**, second son of James⁴, James⁵, James⁴, John³, Samuel², John¹, born at Haddam, Conn., April 15, 1804 (April 16, 1805); married in 1826, Hetty A. Wilcox. Lived at Haddam and Killingworth, Conn.; died at Clinton, Conn., May 17, 1871. Sea captain. Children, born at Killingworth, Conn.:

> I Lois M., born in 1827; married (1) Richard H. Bushnell; children, Giles R., Russell H.; (2) Edward Goodwin; children, Mary A., Moses A., Sarah E.
>
> II Ellsworth, born in 1829; died in 1829.
>
> 238 III Ellsworth W., b. 1832; m. Sarah Stannard; d. 1875.
>
> IV Elizabeth M., born in 1835; married Richard Lane; children, Chas. Dwight, Jesse E., and Walter R. Lived at Clinton, Conn.
>
> V Hettie Anna, born in 1840; married Nathaniel Stevens; one child, Nathaniel K.
>
> 239 VI Alfred C., b. March 14, 1846; m. Dec. 21, 1871, Laura Parks.
>
> VII Grace Irene, born in 1848. In 1888, lived unmarried at Clinton, Conn.

**238. Ellsworth W. Pelton**, second son of Alfred⁵, James⁶, James⁵, James⁴, John³, Samuel², John¹, born Killingworth, Conn., in 1832; married Sarah Stannard. Lived at Clinton, Conn. Sea captain and held a commission in the U. S. Navy through the War of the Rebellion. Died ——, 1875. Children, none.

**239. Alfred C. Pelton**, third son of Alfred⁵, James⁶, James⁵, James⁴, John³, Samuel², John¹, born Killingworth, Conn., March 14, 1846; married (1) at

Clinton, Conn., Dec. 21, 1871, Laura Parks, daughter
of Edwin Parks of that place.  Sea captain; served
in the U. S. Navy through the War of the Rebellion.
Wife Laura died August 21, 1879; (2) at Clinton,
Conn., November 11, 1880, Augusta Dee, daughter of Russell Dee, of Clinton.  Residence in 1888
at New London, Conn., where he had lived since
1881.   Children:

> I Charles A., born Oct. 15, 1872.
> II Ralph E., born Dec. 20, 1874; died March
> 4, 1876.

**237. Capt. James Pelton**[6], third son of James[5],
James[4], James[3], John[2], Samuel[2], John[1], born at Killingworth, Conn., July 26, 1809; married there, January
13, 1834, Emily Kelsey, daughter of James Kelsey
of that place.  Occupation, pilot on the Sound steamboats running to New York, and sea captain.  He
was disabled by an accident on a steamer and laid
up from active service.  Lived, in 1877, at Clinton,
Conn.   Children, born in Killingworth, Conn.:

> I Harriet Elizabeth, born May 27, 1835;
> married March 29, 1860, to Joseph H.
> Merrills, of Clinton, Conn., where she
> lived in 1875.
> 211   II James Henry, b. July 7, 1837; m. Jan. 1,
> 1862, Sarah Harris.
> III Louis Foster, born Oct. 8, 1842.  Served
> through the whole time of the War of
> the Great Rebellion in the Army of the
> Potomac.  Lived, in 1875, at Clinton,
> Conn.
> IV Ellen Augusta, born Dec. 15, 1844; unmar-
> ried in 1875.

**250. James Henry Pelton**[8], first son of James[7], James[6], James[5], James[4], John[3], Samuel[2], John[1], born at Clinton, Conn., July 7, 1837; married January 1, 1862, to Sarah Harris, of Deep River, Conn. Sailor. Held a commission in the United States Navy throughout the War of the Rebellion. In 1875 he held the position of engineer of a steamboat sailing from New York city, his family living in Clinton, Conn.; died at Clinton, Conn. In 1888 his widow lived in Deep River, Conn. Children:

 I Carrie L., born Sept. 25, 1862; married at Deep River, Oct. 25, 1882, Frank H. Watrous, of Clinton, Conn.; one son, Leon H., b. Sept. 8, 1883. Res., 1890, at Deep River, Conn.

 II Eugene H., born Aug., 1865.

 III Frank L., born June, 1867.

**287. Asa S. Pelton**[7], fourth son of James[6], James[5], James[4], John[3], Samuel[2], John[1], born at Killingworth, Conn., July 29, 1816; married there, March 26, 1840, Harriet Kelsey, daughter of James Kelsey; physician, merchant and druggist. Residence at Clinton, Conn., where he died, February 22, 1886. He was a man of character and influence in church and state. Children:

 I Mary Elizabeth, born at Clinton, Conn., Nov. 30, 1848; died Dec. 4, 1848.

 II John Stevens, born Killingworth, Conn., Aug. 26, 1855.

**237. William Nelson Pelton**[7], fifth son of James[6], James[5], James[4], John[3], Samuel[2], John[1], born at Killingworth, Conn., September 6, 1825; married at Clinton, Conn., August 13, 1848, Mrs. Maria Cable,

daughter of Zebediah Austin Cobb, of that place.
Lived, in 1875, at New London, Conn. Sailor, pilot
on Sound steamboats sailing from New York city,
and captain. Died at New London, Conn., June 23,
1883. Children:

    I Virginia M., born July 24, 1850, at Clinton, Conn.; married at New London, April 1, 1875, James Young, of that place, formerly of Lynn, Mass.

    II Corrinna, born at Clinton, Conn., April 9, 1852; married at New London, July 28, 1870, John O'Brien, son of James O'Brien, of Keene, N. H.

**938. Johnson Pelton**[6], fourth son of James[5],
James[4], John[3], Samuel[2], John[1], born in Haddam, Conn.,
November 30, 1782; removed with his father to Essex,
Chittenden Co., Vt., and there married Dolly Hall,
sister to the wife of his brother, Samuel, daughter
of David Hall, whose wife was a Talmadge; thence
removed to Genoa, Delaware Co., O., where he died,
October 13, 1825. Occupation, shoemaker and
farmer. Children:

    I Fanny S., born Jan. 10, 1810; married Mr. Dickinson; died March 12, 1837; children, three, who all died young.

    II Alcina, born June 29, 1812; died, unmarried, June 1, 1841.

    III Ferdinand, b. April 12, 1813; m. July 4, 1839, Mary Blue.

    IV Minerva, born Genoa, O., April 5, 1816; married there, March, 1845, Charles Dean, son of Lebbeus Dean, of Columbus, O. Died May 1, 1873; five children, all living in 1877: 1. Charles A., b. Jan.

26, 1846; 2. Eliza C., b. April 5, 1848;
3. Edward P., b. Jan. 16, 1850; 4.
John A., b. Oct. 22, 1852; 5. Johnson
Talmage, b. Jan. 18, 1857.
V Edward, born Aug. 13, 1818; went to
California for his health, and there died,
Sept. 19, 1850.


**242. Ferdinand Pelton**[1], first son of Johnson[6],
James[5], James[4], John[3], Samuel[2], John[1], born at Genoa,
Delaware Co., O., April 12, 1813; married at Piqua,
O., July 4, 1839, Mary Blue, daughter of Uriah Blue,
of that place. Removed to Warsaw, Ind., and thence
to Seneca, Nemaha Co., Kan., where he lived in 1877.
Shoemaker and farmer. Children:
I Johnson, born Dec. 6, 1840; died Sept. 2,
1843.
II Rolando, born May 27, 1843; died March
4, 1844.
III Elizabeth W., born March 4, 1845; mar-
ried, Oct. 8, 1867, G. W. Johnson.
Lived, in 1877, at Seneca, Kan.; chil-
dren, Edward Perry, Nellie May, and
Jay.
**243** IV Edward Rolando, b. March 24, 1847; m.
May 23, 1870, Christina Nelson.
V Ada, born March 4, 1851; married Dec.
4, 1870, F. M. Newton. One daughter,
Lena. Lived, in 1877, at Seneca, Kan.


**243. Edward Rolando Pelton**[7], third son of
Ferdinand[7], Johnson[6], James[5], James[4], John[3], Samuel[2],
John[1], born Warsaw, Ind., March 24, 1847; married
May 23, 1870, at Hiawatha, Kan., Christina Nelson,
32

daughter of Ole Nelson, of Little Sand, Norway.
Lived, in 1877, in Robinson, Brown Co., Kans.
Farmer.  Children:

    I Alfred Ferdinand, } born Feb. 13, 1871.
    II Anna May,       } born Feb. 13, 1871.
    III Edward Owen, born Aug. 22, 1876.


**227. John Pelton**, second son of James⁴, John³,
Samuel², John¹, born in 1745 in Haddam or Guilford,
Conn.; married (1) about 1772, Huldah Graham (supposed) who died April 25, 1794, aged 45 years; (2)
Widow Thankful ———. Farmer.  Lived in Hartford,
Conn.; moved to Hartford, Washington Co., N. Y.,
about the last of the eighteenth century, and there
was injured by a heavy log of wood, and died August
12, 1803, aged 48 years.   Children:

    I Hannah, born 1774; married James Mc-
        Clenathan; removed to Madison, Madi-
        son Co., N. Y., and there died, Feb. 8,
        1841, æ. 67 years.  Children, five.  Mr.
        McC. died there, April 7, 1852.
**245**  II Stephen Edwin, b. Feb. 13, 1777; m. 1803,
        Susanna Eldredge, d. April 29, 1827.
**249**  III Joshua, b. March 17, 1779; m. 1836, Su-
        sanna Eldredge Pelton (widow of
        Stephen E.); d. Jan. 31, 1858.
    IV Lydia, born Hartford, Conn., Sept. 12,
        1781; married at Hartford, N. Y., Feb.
        14, 1801, Elisha Jackway; died there
        Sept. 17, 1842. Children, John, b. Nov.
        25, 1801, Polly, b. July 4, 1804. Jonathan,
        b. July 6, 1806, Almina, b. June 27, 1808
        (d. May 7, 1875), Asenath, b. June 9,
        1812 (d. March 23, 1833). Wells, b. July

24, 1814 (d. June 1, 1846), Stephen, b. May 10, 1810 (d. 1812), Susan, b. 1808 (d. 1810).

V Elizabeth, born 1783; unmarried, became insane and hung herself with a skein of thread, July 9, 1847.

VI Huldah, born in 1786; married a Mr. Johnson, and went to Canada, where she lived and died.

VII Chloe, born Aug. 13, 1788; married at Hartford, N. Y., about 1806, Phineas Holbrook, of that place. Removed to Virgil, Cortland Co., N. Y. Died at Harford, Cortland Co., March 27, 1863, aged 73 years, 6¼ months. Children, eleven. Her daughter, Chloe, Mrs. Wheeler, of Lapeer, Cortland Co., N. Y., has the family record.

**214. Stephen Edwin Pelton⁶**, first son of John⁵, James⁴, John³, Samuel², John¹, born at Hartford, Conn., February 13, 1777; married in 1803, at Hartford, Washington Co., N. Y., Susanna Eldredge, daughter of John Eldredge, of that place. Lived at Hartford, N. Y., and there died, April 29, 1827. He was a farmer, a good man, very quiet, and being ill was little known out of his neighborhood and church relations. He died in Christian peace. He was small in stature, with light complexion and blue eyes. His wife married (2) her husband's brother, Joshua. She was a very able, intelligent woman, and the whole family were much respected. Children, born Hartford, N. Y.:

**217** I John, b. Sept. 5, 1804; m. Fanny Jackway; d. Aug. 19, 1870.

II Huldah, born Jan. 29, 1806; married at
Hartford, N. Y., March 2, 1825, Gideon
Brayton; 1870 removed to Minnesota
and in 1877 lived at Kasson, Dodge Co.,
in that State. Children, Charles, b.
Sept. 16, 1827, Harrison, b. April 22,
1840, Hiram, b. Dec. 25, 1842.

III Horace, born Sept. 18, 1807; died Oct.
28, 1826.

249 IV Joshua, b. April 25, 1809; m. about 1831,
Esther Payne; d. Aug. 23, 1843.

250 V Thomas, b. April 27, 1811; m. Nov. 18,
1839, Lovilla Graves; d. Sept. 27, 1872.

VI Amanda, born Nov. 11, 1812; married at
Hartford, N. Y., Feb. 14, 1833, Nathaniel Bull; died in childbirth, the child
also dying March 6, 1834.

VII Minerva, born Oct. 24, 1814; married
Aug. 22, 1836, Arnon Archer (b. Oct. 1,
1814), of Granville, N. Y., who was, in
1877, a lawyer in Palmyra, N. Y. Children, Edward Percy, b. Oct. 26, 1849
(killed by lightning, June 10, 1871);
Mary A., b. Feb. 1, 1853.

VIII Sarah M., born Feb. 1, 1816; married at
Hartford, Sept. 14, 1837, Harley H.
Hawks, son of Moses Hawks, of that
place. Lived, in 1877, at Atlantic, Cass
Co., Ia. Children: Julia, b. June 14,
1838; Dexter F., b. March 20, 1841.

251 IX Rufus, b. June 13, 1818; m. (1) Dec. 8,
1843, Mary A. Hitchcock; (2) Oct. 9,
1853, Sarah E. Sunderlin; d. Nov. 7,
1881.

**252**  X Stephen E., Jr., b. April 26, 1820; m.
Jan. 15, 1850, Elizabeth Soper.

XI Warren, born April 15, 1822; died July
14, 1824.

XII Hannah Ann, born April 15, 1827; married at Halfday, Lake Co., Ill., Oliver
P. Gates, of Oberlin, O. Lived at St.
Paul, Minn.; died at Money Creek Valley, Minn., Nov. 25, 1858. Children,
three; left one son living.

**245. John Pelton**[6], first son of Stephen E.[5], John[4],
James[4], John[3], Samuel[2], John[1], born at Hartford, Washington Co., N. Y., September 5, 1804; married there,
about 1825, Fanny Jackway, daughter of George Jackway, of Hartford. Farmer. Removed to Warren
Co., N. Y., in 1837, and thence to Stirling, Cayuga
Co., N. Y., in 1849, and there died, August 19, 1870.
Children:

**247**  I Stephen, b. March 25, 1827; m. March
20, 1851, Violet Carter.

**248**  II George Warren, b. June 21, 1836; m.
Helen L. Savery, Aug. 10, 1862.

III Amanda Jane, born Hartford, N. Y., Sept.
29, 1837; married at Stirling, N. Y.,
Aug. 8, 1866, David W. Vine. Residence, 1877, at North Victory, Cayuga
Co., N. Y. Children, Francis, b. Oct.
27, 1871; Floyd, b. July 20, 1873; Carrie,
b. Oct. 27, 1874; David, b. Aug. 7, 1876.

**247. Stephen Pelton**[7], first son of John[6], Stephen
E.[5], John[4], James[4], John[3], Samuel[2], John[1], born at Hartford, Washington Co., N. Y., March 25, 1827; married, Stirling, N. Y., March 20, 1851, Violet Carter,

daughter of Charles Carter. Farmer. Lived, in 1877, at North Victory, Cayuga Co., N. Y. Children:

**248** I Charles, b. March 23, 1853; m. Nov. 15, 1876, Mary Murray.

**248** II John, b. Sept. 4, 1856; m. Jan. 17, 1875, Mary Howland.

III Amanda, born March 20, 1858; married, March 16, 1877, James Snyder, of Wayne Co., N. Y. Lived, 1878, at Stirling, Cayuga Co., N. Y.

IV Benjamin, born Aug. 20, 1861.

V Sarah Ann, born Jan. 9, 1863; married Nov. 15, 1877, Levi Stockwell. Lived, in 1878, at Stirling, N. Y.

VI Theodosia, born Aug. 6, 1869.

**247. Charles Pelton**[9], first son of Stephen[8], John[7], Stephen E.[6], John[5], James[4], John[3], Samuel[2], John[1], born at Stirling, Cayuga Co., N. Y., March 23, 1853; married at Stirling, November 15, 1876, Mary Murray, daughter of Charles Murray, of Fulton, N. Y. Residence, 1878, at Stirling. Child:

A son, born Nov. 20, 1877.

**247. John Pelton**[9], second son of Stephen[8], John[7], Stephen E.[6], John[5], James[4], John[3], Samuel[2], John[1], born at Stirling, N. Y., September 4, 1856; married there, January 17, 1875, Mary Howland, daughter of Fisher Howland, of Stirling. Laborer. Living, in 1876, at Murtville, N. Y. Child:

Altie, born Oct. 20, 1876.

**247. George Warren Pelton**[9], second son of John[8], Stephen E.[6], John[5], James[4], John[3], Samuel[2], John[1], born at Hartford, N. Y., June 21, 1836; married at Victory, Cayuga Co., N. Y., Aug. 10, 1862, Helen L. Savery, daughter of William Savery, of Devonshire, England. Lived, in 1877, at Stirling, N. Y. P. O., North Victory, N. Y. A miller. Children:

    I Mary S., born Oct. 23, 1863.
    II William H., born May 25, 1867.


**215. Joshua Pelton**[1], third son of Stephen E.[1], John[1], James[1], John[3], Samuel[1], John[1], born Hartford, Washington Co., N. Y., April 25, 1809; married there, about 1831, Esther Payne (born September 30, 1807), daughter of Peter Payne, of Hartford, Conn. Removed to Groton, Tompkins, Co., N. Y., in 1834 or '35, and thence, in September, 1840, or 1841, to Vernon, Lake Co., Ill., where he died, August 23, 1843. Children:

    I and II died in infancy; no record.
    III Mary Jane, born Jan., 1833; died Aug. 2, 1843.
    IV Hannah Ann, born Groton, N. Y., Aug. 21, 1837; married June 15, 1858, at Tremont, Lake Co., Ill., Salem Cruver. Lived, in 1878 at Lake Zurich, Lake Co., Ill. Children, eight: Mary J., b. Mar. 9, 1859 (d. Apr. 15, 1859); Sylvia C., b. May 11, 1860; Wallace B., b. Dec. 26, 1862, Francis P., b. Oct. 9, 1864 (d. Sept. 11, 1865); Curtis L., b. Nov. 26, 1869; Rodell S. and Rosewell E., b. Feb. 18, 1872 (d. July 13 and 14, 1872); Otis D., b. Nov. 15, 1873 (d. Jan. 29, 1877); Lulu M., b. Aug. 2, 1875 (d. Jan, 19, 1877).

V Horace, born in 1841; died Aug. 5, 1843.

Mrs. Pelton married (2) November 6, 1845, David Hawthorne and had children by him: Hiram, b. September 7, 1848; d. October, 1848; Samuel H., b. August 23, 1850; d. July 9, 1859. Mrs. Esther (Payne) Pelton died November 3, 1875.

**245. Thomas Pelton**[6], fourth son of Stephen E.[5], John[4], James[3], John[2], Samuel, John[1], born Hartford, Washington Co., N. Y., April 27, 1811; married at Groton, Tompkins Co., N. Y., November 18, 1839, Lovilla Graves, daughter of Charles Graves, of Vermont. He removed to Groton, N. Y., in 1834 or 1835, and thence in 1840 to Libertyville, Lake Co., Ill., and in April, 1858, to Cedar Township, Floyd Co., Iowa, where he died Sept. 27, 1872, and was buried at Howardville, Floyd Co., Iowa. Farmer. Mr. Pelton was an excellent man, a Christian, honored by all who knew him. Mrs. Pelton's address in 1878 was Cedar, Floyd Co., Iowa. Children:

> I Susan L., born in Lake Co., Ill., April 20, 1841; married there, Jan. 1, 1858, to Elisha J. Miner. Lived, in 1878, in Butler Co., Kans. Children, five.
>
> II Sarah A., born at Libertyville, Lake Co., Oct. 23, 1842; married, Floyd Co., Iowa, March 17, 1865, Walden E. Purdy. Lived, in 1878, in Sac Co., Iowa. Children, six.
>
> III Frank A., adopted son, b. Feb. 24, 1851; m. Dec. 6, 1876, Julia A. Haughey.

**250. Frank Adoniram Pelton**[7], adopted son of Thomas[6], Stephen E.[5], John[4], James[3], John[2], Samuel, John[1], born at Mechanic's Grove, Ill., February 24,

1851; married, Floyd Co., Iowa, December 6, 1876, Julia A. Haughey. His name was Frank Wheeler, and at the age of one year was adopted by Mr. and Mrs. Pelton. Farmer. Residence, in 1878, in Floyd Co., Iowa. Children, none given at that time.

**245. Rufus Pelton**[6], fifth son of Stephen E.[6], John[5], James[4], John[3], Samuel[2], John[1], born at Hartford, Washington Co., N. Y., June 13, 1818; married (1) December 8, 1843, at Libertyville, Lake Co., Ill., Mary A. Hitchcock, daughter of O. L. Hitchcock, of that place (who died April 12, 1853); (2) October 9, 1853, Sarah E. Sunderlin, daughter of Timothy Sunderlin, of Waukegan, Ill. He, in 1839 or 1840, removed with his stepfather, Joshua Pelton, and other members of his father's family to Libertyville, Lake Co., Ill. Farmer. Lived, in 1878, in Vernon, Lake Co., Ill. Post-office, Diamond Lake, Ill. Children, born at Vernon, Ill.:

**252**  I Warren B., b. Aug. 28, 1845; m Jan. 1, 1868, M. P. Hall.

II Frances C., born Jan. 31, 1847; married Oct. 18, 1866, to Homer D. Culver. In 1888, lived at Oberlin, Decatur Co., Kans. Children, three.

III Mary Ann, born Sept. 6, 1852; married Dec. 25, 1868, Henry Blows. In 1888, lived at Diamond Lake, Lake Co., Ill. One child.

IV Amanda M., born Dec. 18, 1854; married Loren E. Blunt. Residence, 1888, Evanston, Cook Co., Ill. Children, two.

V Emily J, born Oct. 2, 1856; died May 14, 1874.

33

**252**   VI  Frank H., b. Feb. 13, 1858; m. Dec. 31,
1880, Anna Davidson
**252**   VII  William H., b. Sept. 25, 1859; m. Sept. 10,
1886, Lillie Charlesworth.
      VIII  Walter R., born March 4, 1862.
      IX  Addie C., born May 4, 1863; married
George Davidson. Lived, in 1888, at
Compton, Lee Co., Ill.   One child.

**251. Warren D. Pelton**, first son of Rufus[7],
Stephen E.[6], John[5], James[4], John[3], Samuel[2], John[1], born
at Vernon, Ill., August 28, 1845; married January 1,
1868, M. P. Hall.   In 1888, lived at Osage, Mitchell
Co., Iowa.   Children, none reported.

**251. Frank H. Pelton[8]**, second son of Rufus[7],
Stephen E.[6], John[5], James[4], John[3], Samuel[2], John[1], born
at Vernon, Ill., February 13, 1858; married Decem-
ber 31, 1880, Anna Davidson, who died December
23, 1882.   Lived, in 1888, at Osage, Iowa.   Children,
two; names not given.

**251. William E. Pelton[8]**, third son of Rufus[7],
Stephen E.[6], John[5], James[4], John[3], Samuel[2], John[1], born
at Vernon, Ill., September 25, 1859; married September 10, 1886, Lillie Charlesworth. Lived, in 1888,
at Osage, Iowa.   One child; name not given.

**245. Stephen Edwin Pelton[7], Jr.**, sixth son of
Stephen E.[6], John[5], James[4], John[3], Samuel[2], John[1], born
at Hartford, Washington Co., N. Y., April 26, 1820;
married at Libertyville, Lake Co., Ill., January 15,
1850, Elizabeth C. Soper, daughter of Joseph Soper
and Electa (Mansfield) Soper, of Bombay, Franklin
Co., N. Y. (formerly of Milton, Vt.).   Lived, in 1877, at
Libertyville, Lake Co., Ill. Removed from Hartford,

N. Y., to Libertyville in 1839 or 1840, with his step-father and his family.   His height, 5 ft. 9 in.; complexion florid, hair brown.   Children:

> I George E. (adopted in 1853); born June 7, 1849.  Lived, in 1877, in Holton, Jackson Co., Kans.
>
> II Sarah S., born Sept. 20, 1853; died Aug. 11, 1863.

**244.  Joshua Pelton**, second son of John⁶, James⁵, John³, Samuel², John¹, born at Hartford, Conn., March 17, 1779; married in the spring of 1836, Susannah (Eldredge) Pelton, widow of his brother Stephen Edwin, having lived at Hartford, Washington Co., N. Y., unmarried up to this time.   He had managed his brother's estate and had cared for his children from the time of his brother's death, and after his marriage was a good father to them as they all testify. He was a farmer by occupation, and besides was Justice of the Peace and held other offices.   He was also prominent in church matters, a man looked up to and trusted generally.   About 1839 or 1840, he removed with his family to Libertyville, Lake Co., Ill., where he lived until he removed, late in 1857 or early in 1858, to Cedar, Floyd Co., Iowa, where he died at the house of his stepson, Thomas Pelton, January 31, 1858, and was buried at Howardville, Floyd Co., Iowa.

NOTE.—As shown above, Joshua married the widow of his brother Stephen Edwin, and became a good father to his children, making them his own and removing with them to Lake Co., Ill.   Here they were early settlers of a new country and paid the penalty of a removal from the high rolling lands of Washington Co., N. Y., to a prairie country, for in

their second or third year there they were all taken
ill with malarial complaints, fifteen at one time, all in
one house; three of them, Joshua, his stepson, and two
of his children dying in as many weeks.

For children, see those of Stephen Edwin, page
245; he had none of his own.


**227. Benjamin Pelton⁵**, third son of James⁴,
John³, Samuel², John¹, born Haddam or Guilford,
Conn., in 1753; married at Litchfield, Conn., about
1779, Hannah Snow.   Removed to Washington Co.,
N. Y., township of Hartford, and afterward to Pawlet, Vt.   He served in the Revolutionary Army, and
by reason of the great hardships there endured, he
became insane, and used to wander from his northern
home back to the old home in Connecticut, thus continuing for seventeen years, and finally died at the
house of his cousin, Marshall Pelton, son of Josiah
Pelton, at Portland, Conn., August 24 or 25, 1821.
In consequence of this sad state of affairs, his children became widely scattered; his wife, Hannah,
dying in Guilford, Medina Co., O., September or
October, 1844.   (Mrs. L. Griffiths, granddaughter of
Hannah Pelton Dickinson, daughter of Anna (Dickinson) Pimlot, of Sharon Centre, O.)

NOTE.--Pawlet, Vt., records show, vol. 2, p. 37, that
Benjamin Pelton sold land, Dec. 18, 1783, to Ethan
Cobb.   For services in the Revolution, Mr. Aaron
Pardee, of Wadsworth, O., obtained a pension of
above $800* for his widow.   Children:

255        I Benjamin, b. about 1781; m. Miss Belden;
         d. 1806.

---

*This was paid in silver, which was sent to Mr. Pardee from Pittsburgh,
Pa., in an axe box.

II Hannah, born at Pawlet, Rutland Co., Vt.,
Sept. 14, 1783; married (1) Jan. 1, 1800.
Silverton Dickson, by whom she had
seven children; (2) in Vermont, Oct.
11, 1814, Miles Culver; children, three;
died at Sharon, Medina Co., O., Aug.
14, 1874. at the house of her granddaughter. Mrs. L. J. Griffith, daughter
of Mrs. Anna Pimlot.

III Lucy, twin sister of Hannah, born Sept.
14, 1783; married Mr. Lounsbury.
Lived at Attica, N. Y.

256 IV Joseph, b. ——, 1785-7; m. (1) (2); d.
——.

257 V Charles, b. April 3, 1790 ; m. Dec., 1822,
Christina Ozman; d. Aug. 29, 1842.

258 VI David, b. March 17, 1793; m. 1816, Elizabeth Tabor; d. Jan. 24, 1879.

262 VII John, b. in 1800; m. July 4, 1831, Harriet
Cartter; d. about 1843.

**251. Benjamin Pelton**[4], first son of Benjamin[4],
James[4], John[4], Samuel[2], John[1], born (probably) at
Pawlet, Rutland Co., Vt., about 1781; married at
Benson, Vt., Miss Belden, probably about 1803 or
'4. Lived in Pawlet, Vt., and possibly at Essex, Vt.,
as he was killed at Essex by the fall of a tree in 1806.
His widow returned to her people in Benson, and
married (2) a Mr. Tucker, from which marriage four
daughters were born; all dead in 1879. Children:

256 I Daniel, b. June 14, 1805; m. Jan. 17, 1831,
Lovina Benson; d. April 21. 1838.

II Benjamin, born 1807 (after his father's
death). His nephews, Oscar A. and
Elbert A. Pelton, of Chicago, think he
went to Michigan.

**255. Daniel Pelton**, first son of Benjamin, Benjamin, James, John, Samuel, John, born in western Vermont, in Pawlet or Essex, June 14, 1805; married at Shelburne, Vt., January 17, 1831, Lovina Benson, daughter of Benoni Benson, of Massachusetts. Farmer. Died near Syracuse, N. Y., April 21, 1838. Children :

**256**    I Oscar Alonzo, b. Feb. 17, 1832; m.
    II James Riley, born July 3, 1834; died Aug. 5, 1835.
**253**    III Elbert Alexander, b. Nov. 21, 1836; m. Nov. 12, 1876, Anna Gates.
    IV Daniel Strong, born Nov. 1, 1838; died Aug. 1, 1839.

**256. Oscar Alonzo Pelton**, first son of Daniel, Benjamin, Benjamin, James, John, Samuel, John, born Syracuse, N. Y., February 17, 1832; married. No report. In 1891 said to have removed to near Syracuse, N. Y.

**256. Elbert Alexander Pelton**, third son of Daniel, Benjamin, Benjamin, James, John, Samuel, John, born at Syracuse, N. Y., November 21, 1836; married at Clinton, Rock Co., Wis., November 12, 1876, Anna Gates (b. June 26, 1847), daughter of Joseph Gates, of Clinton, Wis. Residence, 1879, Chicago, Ill. Milk dealer. In 1891 said to have removed to near Syracuse, N. Y. Child:
    I Jessie, born Oct. 31, 1877.

**254. Joseph Pelton**, second (some say the youngest) son of Benjamin, James, John, Samuel, John, born Pawlet, Vt., 1785–7, probably; married (1) (2) (no records). Lived and died in Cumberland, Md., it is said. Children, number unknown:

I Emory, was in Cleveland, O., the last
heard of.

II John.  No record known.


**251 Charles Pelton**[6], third son of Benjamin[5],
James[4], John[3], Samuel[2], John[1], born at Pawlet, Vt.,
April 3, 1790; married at Hudson, O., in December,
1822, Christiana Ozman (b. December 4, 1805),
daughter of Jacob Ozman, of Boston, O.  Farmer.
Lived at Chester Cross Roads, Geauga Co., O., and
there died, August 29, 1842.  Removed to Chester
in the spring of 1823.  Mrs. Pelton died August 12,
1862.  Children:

    I Althea, born Sept. 15, 1823; married in
        1846 at Chester, O., Othaniel Hoag, of
        Mayfield, Cuyahoga Co., O.  Children,
        four sons and one daughter.  Died at
        Breedsville, Van Buren Co., Mich.

    II Emeline, born Oct. 16, 1825; died un-
        married, May 10, 1855.

    III Hannah L., born July 21, 1827; married
        at Troy, O., by Elder F. Thompson,
        May 5, 1865, to Chester Lamb, of that
        place, a widower with eight children.
        She had none.  Residence, in 1880, Troy,
        O.  P. O., Welshfield, Geauga Co., O.

**258** IV Oliver O., b. July 13, 1829; m. Sept., 1854,
        Miranda Millard; d. April 20, 1863.

    V Lois A., born March 1, 1832; died, un-
        married, April 27, 1857.

**258** VI Thomas L., b. Feb 22, 1834; m. Dec. 10,
        1856, Susanna Happer.

    VII Mary L., born June 4, 1836; died May
        12, 1838.

VIII Nancy A., born Aug. 29, 1839; died Aug.
29, 1841.
IX Laura Ann, born Jan. 20, 1841; died Jan.
13, 1843.

**257. Oliver O. Pelton[6]**, first son of Charles[5],
Benjamin[5], James[4], John[3], Samuel[2], John[1], born at
Chester Cross Roads, Geauga Co., O., July 13, 1829;
married at Chardon, Geauga Co., Sept., 1854, Miranda
Millard, of Russell, O. Removed to Allegan Co.,
Mich., and there died April 20, 1863. Widow in 1879
said to live in the township of Dorr, Allegan Co.,
Mich.; was written and the letter returned "Not
found." Children, unknown.

**257. Thomas L. Pelton[6]**, second son of Charles[5],
Benjamin[5], James[4], John[3], Samuel[2], John[1], born at
Chester, Geauga Co., O., February 22, 1834; mar-
ried at Orange, Cuyahoga Co., O., December 10,
1856, Susanna Happer (b. March 12, 1835), daughter
of John Happer, of Cortland Co., N. Y. Farmer.
Lived in 1880 at Elm Hall, Gratiot Co., Mich. P.
O. Summer, Gratiot Co., Mich. Children:
I Nelson W., born March 13, 1858; died
Oct. 29, 1872.
II Charles O., born Aug. 11, 1861; died
Sept. 27, 1864.
III William H., born Oct. 14, 1865.
IV Newell, born July 15, 1873.
V Perry L., born April 9, 1876.

**251. David Pelton[6]**, fourth son of Benjamin[5],
James[4], John[3], Samuel[2], John[1], born at Pawlet, Vt.,
March 17, 1793; married in Summit Co., O., in 1816,
Elizabeth Falor, daughter of Adam Falor, of that
county. Farmer. Lived near New Portage, Sum-

mit Co., and at Wauseon, Fulton Co., O.; died
at Elm Hall, Gratiot Co., Mich., January 24, 1879.
Mrs. Pelton died at the house of her daughter, Mrs.
Veirs, at Wauseon, Fulton Co., O., August, 1878.

Note.— His father becoming deranged, he was
"bound out" to a Mr. Wooster in Rutland Co., Vt.
At 18 he entered the army as teamster in the War
of 1812. At the close he went to Ohio. He was
about five and one-half feet high, straight, well
built and broad shouldered, weighing 165 pounds.
Children:

   I Julia Ann, born 1819; died when about
    12 years old.

259 II Benjamin H., b. 1822; m. Mary D. Har-
    get; killed in battle, Aug. 6, 1864.

   III Elizabeth, born in Summit Co., O., Jan.
    13, 1824; married in Fulton Co., O.,
    Oct. 13, 1844, Jacob Gasche, son of
    Charles Gasche, of Prussia. Residence,
    1880, near Wauseon, Fulton Co., O.
    Farmer. Children, 1, Adeline; 2,
    Theresa; 3, Agnes; 4, Amarancy; 5,
    Wilfred B.

260 IV David J., b. Summit Co., O., Feb. 12,
    1826; m. June 2, 1850, Mary Alwood.

   V Hannah, born in 1827, died in 1844.

   VI George, born in 1829; died in infancy.

   VII Amarancy, born 1831; married Elisha
    Viers. Lived, in 1880, in Fulton Co.,
    O. P. O., Wauseon.

261 VIII William H., b. 1833; m. Mildred Thomas;
    d. about 1866.

261 IX Jesse L., b. Sept. 17, 1835; m. Sept. 11,
    1859, Cynthia Murray.

   X Talman, born 1837; died about 1839.

34

**258. Benjamin H. Pelton⁷**, first son of David⁶, Benjamin⁵, James⁴, John³, Samuel², John¹, born in Summit Co., O., in 1822; married Mary D. Harget. He served in the War of the Rebellion, in the 100th Regiment of Ohio Volunteer Infantry, and was killed August 6, 1864, shot through the breast in the battle of Eutaw Creek, before Atlanta, Ga. His widow married (2) David E. Austin, and removed to Indiana. Children, record incomplete:

      I Thomas, b. ——; killed on the cars while acting as brakeman.

      II Rachel, born ——; married George Wright.

      III Elizabeth, born ——; married, name unknown.

      IV Edward, born ——; no further record.

      VI Benjamin H., Jr., born ——; last heard of in the regular army.


**258. David J. Pelton⁷**, second son of David⁶, Benjamin⁵, James⁴, John³, Samuel², John¹, born in Summit Co., O., February 12, 1826; married, Fulton Co., O., June 2, 1850, Mary Allwood, daughter of E. K. Allwood, of that county. Lived in 1880 at Wauseon, Fulton Co., O. Farmer. Children:

      I Darius C., born May 21, 1852.

      II Clarissa, born Dec. 6, 1854.

      III Candace, born July 15, 1856.

      IV George, born Aug. 10, 1858; died Nov. 31, 1873.

      V Seth, born Sept. 15, 1860; died Nov. 31, 1873.

      VI Rosa, born June 2, 1862.

      VII Agnes, born June 4, 1864.

**258. William E. Pelton**, third son of David⁵, Benjamin⁴, James⁴, John³, Samuel², John¹, born in Summit Co., O., in 1833; married Mildred Thomas; died in Isabella Co., Mich., about 1866, aged 33 years.  His widow went to Knoxville, Tenn.  Children, none.

**258. Jesse L. Pelton**, fourth son of David⁵, Benjamin⁴, James⁴, John³, Samuel², John¹, born near New Portage, Summit Co., O., September 17, 1835; married in Fulton Co., O., September 11, 1859, Cynthia Murray, daughter of John Murray, of Holmes Co., O.  Teacher and farmer.  Lived in Elm Hall, Gratiot Co., Mich., from where he removed to Kansas in 1879.  P. O. in 1880, Medicine Lodge, Barbour Co., and in 1881, Sharon, Barbour Co., Kan.  Children:

<blockquote>

I Pericles, born June 29, 1860; died May 20, 1866.

II Vesta, born April 4, 1862; married Jan. 24, 1879, Demetrius Watkins, son of Joseph D. Watkins, of Gratiot Co., Mich.  Lived, in 1880, at Elm Hall, Gratiot Co., Mich.

III Leonard, born Mar. 3, 1864.  At home in 1880.

IV Agnes, born Feb. 23, 1866; died Jan. 26, 1873.

V William, born Jan. 10, 1868.  At home 1880.

VI Julia Ann, born April 18, 1870; died Oct. 16, 1872.

VII Elias, born June 1, 1873.

VIII Alice, born Feb. 11, 1875.

IX Albert, born May 13, 1877.

X Cynthia Hannah, born Sept. 17, 1879.

</blockquote>

**251. John Pelton[6]**, fifth son of Benjamin[5], James[4], John[3], Samuel[2], John[1], born at Pawlet, Vt., in 1800; married July 4, 1831, at Russell, Geauga Co., O., Harriet Cartter, daughter of Chandler and Anna Cartter, of Russell, Hampden Co., Mass. (Mrs. Pelton had a relative* who was long an honored judge in the District Court in Washington, D. C.) Farmer. Lived in Russell, Geauga Co., O., and there died about 1843. Mrs. Anna Cartter Pelton became deranged and died January 10, 1875. Children:

   I John Cartter, born Apr. 12, 1832. In 1880 lived, unmarried, at Chagrin Falls, Cuyahoga Co., O. Teamster.

   II Henry Clay, born June 19, 1833. Served in the war of the Great Rebellion and was drowned in Cumberland river while in the U. S. service.

   III Harriet Julia, born Oct. 22, 1834; married at Newbury, Geauga Co., O., Nov. 1, 1853, Wallace Chapman, son of Esquire Chapman of that county. Lived, in 1879, at Munson, O. Children: Alice, Orange, Martha, Hattie and Herbert. She died May 3, 1872.

   IV Harlow C., born Oct. 28, 1836. In 1880 he lived, unmarried, in Kingston, Tuscola Co., Mich.

   V William Harrison, born 1840; married Victoria Derthick. In 1880 was living in Canton, Lincoln Co., Dak. No further record.

**226. Phineas Pelton[5]**, fourth son of James[4], John[3], Samuel[2], John[1], born at Haddam or Guilford,

---

*Judge Cartter of the District Court.

Conn., in 1758; married, about 1778, probably in Hartford, Conn., Rebecca Johnson, daughter of Nathaniel Johnson of that place. Removed to Hartford, Washington Co., N. Y., about 1790, and thence to South Gower, Canada, in March, 1801, and there died January 17, 1850. Farmer. He was an upright, religious man, in earlier years a Presbyterian or Congregationalist, in later years a Baptist. He was strict in morality and integrity, a worthy descendant of Puritan lineage, never countenancing injustice or wrong of any kind. He was strong and convincing in argument and a ready and powerful debater. He took up a large tract of land in Canada and became well off. Was highly respected and maintained his business habits with his independence and ability to the last. His wife died some years before him. Her descendants claim that eight acres of land that came to Mrs. Pelton from her father, Nathaniel Johnson, of Hartford, lying in Hartford, and now covered by that city, belonged to her when she married Mr. Pelton and never was conveyed by her. Children:

26.1    I James, b. Aug. 22, 1779; m. Dec. 4, 1798, Harriet Clark; d. June 18, 1854.

II Polly, born about 1782; married John Luke. Lived at South Gower, Canada, and there died. No children.

III Phœbe, born about 1785; married Martin Walton. Lived and died at South Gower, Canada. No further record.

27.1    IV Phineas, Jr., b. in 1788; m. in 1816, Rachel Guernsey; d. Feb. 25, 1853. No further record.

V Ada, born about 1791; married about 1817, Jacob Fike; died at Park Hill.

Ontario, Aug. 9, 1874. Ten children;
six living in 1877.

VI Nabby, born about 1793; married Caleb
Johnston. Lived at Madrid, St. Lawrence Co., N. Y., and there died. Children: Phineas, Elijah, William, Lydia,
Lizzie, Adaline.

276 VII Elisha, b. Jan. 21, 1796; m. Feb. 23, 1819,
Mahala Brintnell; d. Feb. 2, 1868.

279 VIII Elijah, b. June 23, 1798; m. Jan. 1, 1823,
Peggy Brown.


262. **James Pelton**, first son of Phineas⁵, James⁴,
John³, Samuel², John¹, born at Haddam, Conn., August
22, 1779; married at Hartford, Conn., December 4,
1798, Harriet Clark, daughter of David Clark, of
Haddam. Farmer. Lived in Connecticut; thence,
soon after his marriage, removed to Hartford, Washington Co., N. Y.; thence possibly to Canada, and in
1806 to Champion, Jefferson Co., N. Y., and thence,
in 1824, to LaGrange, Lorain Co., O., where he died
June 18, 1854, and his wife, Harriet, on September 1,
1863. Children:

266 I David Clark, b. Feb. 4, 1800; m. (1) Dec.,
1823, Lydia Dodge; (2) Hannah Smith,
Dec. 6, 1833; (3) Jan. 3, 1853, Mrs.
Mary Burns.

II Sallie, born Oct. 7, 1802; married Jan. 7,
1822, Stanton Hopkins, of Champion,
N. Y. Lived in 1877, at La Grange,
Lorain Co., O. Four children.

III Prudence, born Aug. 21, 1804; died
Aug. 21, 1804.

IV Patience, born Aug. 21, 1804; married
(1) Jan. 6, 1822, at Champion, N. Y.,

Reuben Tiff; (2) April 25, 1825, Loammi Holcomb.    Removed to Wisconsin, and there died, April 16, 1864.

V  Lucy, born July 30, 1805; married Dec. 7, 1823, Stephen D. Cottrell, of Champion, N. Y.    Lived at Harrisonville, Medina Co., O., and there died, Aug. 16, 1844.

VI  Harriet, born Nov. 6, 1807; married (1) May 11, 1824, Jordan Tiff; (2) Jan. 1, 1858, Joseph Phelps. of Eaton, Lorain Co., O.    Lived, in 1878, at Pemberville, Wood Co., O.    Thirteen children.

270 VII  James Kelley, b. Feb. 4, 1810; m. Oct. 11, 1834, Sarah E. Loomis.

271 VIII  Phineas John, b. Sept. 16, 1812; m. Dec. 1, 1837, Electa Bentley.

272  IX  Eurotas Albert, b. Dec. 15, 1814; m. (1) Hattie Jackson, Aug. 18, 1836; (2) June 20, 1853, Mrs. Mary J. (Elvert) Smith.

X  Eliza, born at Champion, N. Y., March 5, 1817; married at La Grange, O., Aug. 10, 1840, William Rose, of that place. Three children.    Lived at La Grange, and there died, May 21, 1858.

273  XI  Daniel S., b. June 30, 1819; m. Dec. 4, 1839, Eleanor Helm; d. Nov. 24, 1873.

XII  Jane L., born at Champion, N. Y., Feb. 4, 1820; married at La Grange, O., May 23, 1840, Richard N. Loomis, of that place, where they lived, and where she died, Nov. 24, 1873.

XIII  Lydia Ann, born at Champion, N. Y., July 31, 1823; died unmarried, June 20, 1860.

NOTE.—Mr. Pelton was sent by some New York
land speculators to Lorain Co., Ohio, to examine and
report to them on the land there. He liked the
country so well he bought a half section for himself, and removed to it, being one of the earliest
settlers and founders of the county.

**264. David Clark Pelton**, first son of James⁶,
Phineas⁵, James⁴, John³, Samuel², John¹, born at Hartford, Washington Co., N. Y., February 4, 1800; married (1) at Champion, Jefferson Co., N. Y., December 6, 1823, Lydia Dodge, daughter of John
Dodge (died, 1832); (2) December 6, 1833, Hannah Smith, daughter of Jacobus Smith, of Canada
(d. June 30, 1852, aged 43); (3) January 3, 1853,
Mrs. Mary (Tippin) Burns, daughter of John Tippin, of London, England. Farmer. Lived in Champion, Jefferson Co., N. Y., and thence removed to
La Grange, Lorain Co., O., September 10, 1824,
and lived there in 1875. Children (by first wife):

    I Maria, born March 18, 1824; died Aug.
       19, 1825.

    II Martha, born Jan. 17, 1826; died Jan. 18, 1826.

    III Mary, born Nov. 10, 1827; died Nov. 11,
       1827.

    IV Clark, born June 14, 1829; died Dec. 19, 1830.

**268**    V Charles E., b. Mar. 10, 1832; m. Mar. 23,
       1855, Sarah A. Gott.

  Of the second wife:

    VI Died in infancy; not named.

    VII Lydia, born May 6, 1834; married (1)
       Jan. 26, 1853, James M. Tippin; (2)
       June 6, 1875, Charles S. Crowner.
       Children, five by the first husband,
       three girls and two boys. Lived, in
       1876, at LaGrange, O.

VIII Mary, born June 30, 1835; married Dec. 25, 1851, Manford B. Ripley, of the State of New York. Eight children. Lived, in 1878, at Charlotte, Eaton Co., Mich.

268 IX David Clark, Jr., b. Apr. 16, 1837; m. Oct. 29, 1858, Ellen Williams.

268 X James Kelley, b. Mar. 26, 1839; m. July 28, 1864, Phœbe A. Gott.

269 XI John, b. Aug. 26, 1842; m. Feb. 11, 1863, Julia Randall.

XII Grosvenor, born Aug. 6, 1844; served in Co. I, 103d Regt. of Ohio Vol. in the war of the Rebellion, and died in the U. S. service Oct. 15, 1863, of typhoid pneumonia at Hickman's Bridge, Ky.

XIII Adaline, born Sept. 2, 1846; married July 4, 1866, John Anderson, of LaGrange, O. One child. Lived, in 1878, at Ovid, Clinton Co., Mich.

XIV Hannah, born July 15, 1848; married Oct. 10, 1864, Thos. Cornell, of Charlotte, Mich. Four children. Lived, in 1878, at Charlotte, Eaton Co., Mich.

XV Elizabeth, born Dec. 17, 1849; married Dec. 12, 1869, Abraham Stevens, of Charlotte, Mich. Lived, in 1878, at Ovid, Clinton Co., Mich.

269 XVI Winfield, b. May 17, 1852; m. Apr. 2, 1871, Gertrude Cornell.

Of the third wife:

XVII Died in infancy.

XVIII Sylvester, born June 27, 1855; died Feb. 23, 1865.

XIX Clarissa, born July 15, 1857; married

35

Dec. 26, 1873, Augustus Van Linda,
of the State of New York. Lived, in
1878, at Rensselaer Falls, St. Lawrence
Co., N. Y. One child.
XX Frederic, born May 8, 1858; died Oct.
28, 1865.
XXI Floyd, born June 18, 1860.
NOTE.— The members of this family are tall, some
of them being over six feet in height.

**266. Charles E. Pelton**, second son of David
C.¹, James⁶, Phineas⁵, James⁴, John³, Samuel², John¹,
born at LaGrange, Lorain Co., O., March 10, 1832;
married there, March 23, 1855, Sarah A. Gott (born
Jan. 18, 1833), daughter of James Gott of that place.
Residence, in 1890, address Essex, Kankakee Co.,
Ill.   Children:
I Stephen, born Dec. 28, 1857; died Feb.
28, 1865.
II James, born Apr. 8, 1859.
III Lenora, born Feb. 6, 1860.
IV Maud, born June 11, 1869.

**266. David Clark Pelton⁸, Jr.**, third son of
David C.⁷, James⁶, Phineas⁵, James⁴, John³, Samuel²,
John¹, born at LaGrange, O., April 16, 1837; married
at Benona, Mich., October 29, 1858, Ellen Williams,
daughter of Hezekiah P. Williams, of Hampshire,
Kane Co., Ill.  Lumberman.  Lived, in 1878, at
Free Soil, Grant Township, Mason Co., Mich.  In
1891 at Cheboygan, Mich.   Child.
I Julia Ette, born May 6, 1861.

**266. James Kelley Pelton⁸**, fourth son of David
C.⁷, James⁶, Phineas⁵, James⁴, John³, Samuel², John¹,
born at LaGrange, O., March 26, 1839; married

Elyria, O., July 28, 1864, Phœbe A. Gott, daughter of James Gott, of LaGrange. Railroad conductor. Lived, in 1878, at Springfield, Walworth Co, Wis. Children:

    I James, born Aug. 30, 1867; died Sept. 1, 1867.
    II Charles W., born Racine, Wis., Apr. 8, 1872.
    III George M., born at Dwight, Ill., Dec. 19, 1876.

**266. John Pelton**, fifth son of David C.[7], James[6], Phineas[5], James[4], John[3], Samuel[2], John[1], born La-Grange, Lorain Co., O., Aug. 26, 1842; married at Findley, O., February 11, 1863, Julia Randall, daughter of Jacob Israel Randall, of Wood Co., O. General workman. Lived, in 1878, at Freeport, Wood Co., O. Children (all born in Wood Co., O.):

    I Isadora, born March 27, 1864.
    II Charles, born March 11, 1866.
    III Daniel, born Feb. 8, 1869.
    IV George, born Sept. 24, 1871.
    V John, born March 17, 1873.
    VI Curtis, born Jan. 28, 1875.
    VII ——, born March —, 1878.

**266. Winfield Pelton**, seventh son of David C.[7], James[6], Phineas[5], James[4], John[3], Samuel[2], John[1], born at LaGrange, O., May 17, 1852; married April 2, 1871, at Olivet, Eaton Co., Mich., Gertrude Cornell, daughter of Thomas Cornell, of Charlotte, Eaton Co., Mich. Farmer. Lived, in 1878, at Charlotte, Mich. Children, all born in Walton, Eaton Co., Mich.

    I Lena V., born Dec. 4, 1871.

II  Paulina, born Dec. 24, 1872.
III  Hattie, born July 26, 1877.


**269. James Kelley Pelton**, second son of James⁵, Phineas⁵, James⁴, John³, Samuel², John¹, born at Champion, Jefferson Co., N. Y., Feb. 4, 1810; married at LaGrange, Lorain Co., O., Oct. 11, 1834, Sarah E. Loomis, daughter of Russell Loomis, of that place.  Physician.  Lived, in 1877, at Columbus Grove, Putnam Co., O., and afterward at Toledo, O.  Children:

        I  Mary E., born at LaGrange, O., May 11, 1835; married there, May 28, 1853, Joshua E. Curtice (b. Oct., 1858), merchant, living in 1877 at Millbury, Wood Co., O.  Children: Alva, Malita and James Edward.

270    II  James R., b. July 26, 1838; m. Nov. 10, 1859, Lydia Beemot.

        III  Lucy E., born Aug. 30, 1842; married at Syracuse, N. Y., Dec. 9, 1867, John Ryan.  Living in 1877.  Children, none.

271    IV  David C., b. March 11, 1846; m. Oct. 3, 1871, Maggie M. Scudder.

        V  Richard F., born Sept. 5, 1848; unmarried in 1877.

271    VI  Erastus L., b. April 5, 1851; m. Nov. 13, 1873, Nettie E. Beach.


**270. James R. Pelton⁷**, first son of James K.⁶, James⁵, Phineas⁴, James⁴, John³, Samuel², John¹, born at LaGrange, Lorain Co., O., July 26, 1838; married at Grafton, O., November 10, 1859, Lydia Beemot, of LaGrange.  Machinist.  Lived, in 1877, at Gilboa, Putnam Co., O.  Children:

 I Anna S., born Aug. 14, 1860.
 II George A., born Feb. 24, 1862.
 III Jennie E., born Aug. 24, 1864.
 IV Frederic E., born Sept. 30, 1867.
 V Etta M., born June 30, 1872.
 VI Charles J., born Oct. 6, 1875.

**278. David C. Pelton**, second son of Jas. K.[7], James[6], Phineas[5], James[4], John[3], Samuel[2], John[1], born March 11, 1846; married, Ravenna, O., Oct. 3, 1871, Maggie M. Scudder. Living in 1877. Children, none.

**279. Erastus E. Pelton**, fourth son of Jas. K.[7], James[6], Phineas[5], James[4], John[3], Samuel[2], John[1], born April 5, 1851; married at Columbus Grove, O., November 13, 1873, Miss Nettie E. Beach. Living in 1877. Children, none reported.

**264. Phineas John Pelton**, third son of James[6], Phineas[5], James[4], John[3], Samuel, John[1], born at Champion, Jefferson Co., N. Y., September 6, 1812; married December 1, 1837, Electa Bentley (b. Sept. 12, 1813). Farmer. Lived, in 1877, at Fostoria, Seneca Co., O. He was a man of earnest piety, and an active member and class leader in the Methodist Episcopal church. Children:

 I Electa, born June 5, 1839; married Mr.
  A. O. Calvin, July 2, 1856. Lived, in
  1877, at Fostoria, O. Children: Jane
  M., b. Feb. 21, 1860; d. Sept. 19, 1873;
  William, b. March 23, 1866.
 II Harriet, born Feb. 24, 1841; married
  Sept. 12, 1868, W. H. Nelson; died
  Nov. 29, 1874. Children: Edna, George
  C., Mary, Oscar.

III Emeline, born Sept. 9, 1843; married
May 1, 1867, Ephraim Holopater.
Lived, in 1877, in Henry Co., O. Chil-
dren: 1. Georgiana; 2. Gertrude.

IV Lucy, born Feb. 4, 1845. Living, 1877,
at her father's, Fostoria, O.

V Melissa, born Jan. 22, 1847; died April
27, 1873.

VI Phineas, born June 4, 1850. Lived, in
1877, with his father.

VII Mary Jane, born April 4, 1853; died Aug.
8, 1874.

VIII John, born March 23, 1858. Lived, 1877,
with his father.


**264. Eurotas Albert Pelton**[7], fourth son of
James[6], Phineas[5], James[4], John[3], Samuel[2], John[1], born
in Champion, Jefferson Co., N. Y., December 15,
1814; married (1) La Grange, O., September 18,
1836, Harriet Jackson (d. 1852), daughter of Abner
Jackson, of Rutland, Vt.; (2) June 20, 1853, Mary
J. (Elvert) Smith. Farmer. Lived at Perry, Wood
Co., O., and there died, July 25, 1865. Children (by
the first wife):

I Francis E., born Oct. 26, 1837. P. O.,
1877, Millbury, Wood Co., O.

II Albert Elisha, born Oct. 21, 1839. Served
in the 1st Ohio Battery, and died in
the U. S. service from fever, at Bardstown, Ky., Oct. 23, 1862.

III Eliza Jane, born June 14, 1841. P. O.,
Millbury, Wood Co., O.

IV Sarah A., born Nov. 20, 1844. P. O.,
Millbury, Wood Co., O.

V Samuel, born Jan. 28, 1850. Address,
 1877, Millbury, O.
By the second wife:
 VI William C., born Oct. 1, 1854; died May
 15, 1872.
 VII Harriet M., born Oct. 6, 1856. P. O.,
 1877, Millgrove, O.
 VIII Charles B., born Aug. 2, 1859; died Nov.
 2, 1868.
 IX Franklin J., born Nov. 2, 1861. P. O..
 1877, Millgrove, O.
 X Melissa E., born July 30, 1865. P. O.,
 1877. Millgrove, O.


**261. Daniel S. Pelton**[7], fifth son of James[6],
Phineas[5], James[4], John[3], Samuel[2], John[1], born at Champion, Jefferson Co., N. Y., June 30, 1819; married
December 4, 1839, Eleanor Helm; died November
24, 1873. Children:
**272** I Henry, b. April 2, 1841; m. June 2, 1861,
 Sarah Amanda Baird.
**274** II Therian T., b. Nov. 15, 1849; m. Oct. 22,
 1871, Cassie A. Moore.
 III William L., born April 7, 1850.
 IV Phila S., born Oct. 13, 1853.
 V Mary C., born Oct. 30, 1855; married
 June 26, 1875, Nelson Low.
 VI Mary Matilda, born Aug. 23, 1857.
 VII Robert C., born Oct. 1, 1863.


**273. Henry Pelton**[8], first son of Daniel S.[7],
James[6], Phineas[5], James[4], John[3], Samuel[2], John[1], born
April 2, 1841; married June 2, 1861, Amanda Baird.
Lived, in 1877, in Perry township, Wood Co., O.
P. O., Millgrove, Wood Co., O. Children:

I Sarah Eleanor, born Feb. 9, 1862.
II Hartwell, born Aug. 20, 1867.
III Carrie M., born Oct. 27, 1870.
IV Elsie E., born Jan. 5, 1874.

**272. Therian T. Pelton**, second son of Daniel S., James, Phineas, James, John, Samuel, John, born November 15, 1849; married October 22, 1871, Cassie A. Moore. Lived, in 1877, at Millgrove, Wood Co., O. Children:

I Emma C., born June 2, 1872.
II Scott S., born May 2, 1874.

**202. Phineas Pelton, Jr.**, second son of Phineas, James, John, Samuel, John, born in Hartford, Conn., in 1788; removed with his father to Hartford, Washington Co., N. Y., and thence, with his father in 1801, to South Gower, Grenville Co., Canada; married there in 1816, Rachel Guernsey, daughter of Daniel Guernsey, of Mountain, Canada. Farmer. Died at South Gower, Ontario, Canada, February 25, 1853. Children, born at South Gower, Canada:

I Anna, born July 19, 1817; married there in 1834, John Cummings. Farmer of that place. Lived there in 1877. Nine children.
II Eliza, born May 15, 1819; married Apr. 20, 1834, James Carson. Lived, 1877, at Madrene Station, Santa Clara Co., Cal. Twelve children, eight living in 1877.
273 III Erastus G., b. May 3, 1821; m. June 15, 1853, Julia Ann Haskell.

IV Harriet, born in 1823; married Mar. 8, 1842, William Frazer of Mountain, County Dundee, Ontario; died Oct. 21, 1843, leaving one son, Alexander C. (b. July 12, 1843), now, 1877, in California.

V Rachel, born Aug. 11, 1827; married (1) Sept. 1, 1846, South Gower, Thomas Lonsdale, merchant; (2) Feb. 4, 1857, at Ottawa, Ont., Matthew Daugherty, farmer; (3) Feb., 1872, at Merricksville, Ont., to John Waddell, accountant. Lived, in 1877, at Oxford Mills, Ont. Children, two daughters, by the first husband.

275  VI Phineas C., b. Oct. 26, 1831; m. Feb. 6, 1855, Margaret E. Campbell.

276 VII Daniel G., b. Oct. 29, 1833; m. (1) Mar., 1864, Lucretia Olmsted; (2) Feb., 1877, Margaret Norton.

**274. Erastus Gates Felton**[7], first son of Phineas[6], Jr., Phineas[5], James[4], John[3], Samuel[2], John[1], born at South Gower, Ont., May 3, 1821; married at Madrid, N. Y., June 15, 1853, Julia Ann Haskell, daughter of Isaac P. Haskell of that place. Farmer. Lived, in 1877, at South Gower, Ont. Children, born at South Gower:

I Katharine, born Feb. 27, 1855; died Feb. 12, 1856.

II Haskell E., born May 13, 1860.

III Millburn D., born Jan. 27, 1862.

**275. Phineas C. Felton**[7], second son of Phineas[6], Phineas[5], James[4], John[3], Samuel[2], John[1], born at South

36

Gower, Ont., October 26, 1831; married Oxford, Ont., February 6, 1856, Margaret E. Campbell, daughter of William Campbell of that place. Farmer. Lived, in 1877, at Kemptonville, Grenville Co., Ont. Children:

    I William G., born Jan., 1857.
    II Daniel J., born Apr., 1859.
    III Elizabeth J., born Apr., 1861.
    IV Phineas Mc., born Mar., 1863.
    V Alexander C., born Sept., 1865.
    VI John G., born Nov., 1867.
    VII Emma K., born July, 1869.
    VIII Edwin C., born June, 1874.

**273. Daniel G. Pelton[7]**, third son of Phineas[6], Phineas[5], James[4], John[3], Samuel[2], John[1], born at South Gower, Ont., October 29, 1835; married (1) at South Gower, Ont., March 8, 1864, Lucretia Olmsted, daughter of Reuben Olmsted, of Scotland; (2) at Oxford Mills, Grenville Co., Ont., February 15, 1877, Margaret Norton, daughter of William Norton of Ireland. Farmer. Lived, in 1877, at Oxford Mills, Ont. Children, born at Oxford Mills, Ont.:

    I Lizzie, born Nov. 22, 1864.
    II Orpha, born Aug. 14, 1866; died Mar. 15, 1871.
    III Herbert, born Sept. 14, 1868.
    IV Eva, born June 8, 1873.
    V William, born Oct. 15, 1875; died Nov. 20, 1876.

**262. Elisha Pelton[7]**, third son of Phineas[6], James[4], John[3], Samuel[2], John[1], born at Hartford, Washington Co., N. Y., January 21, 1796; married at Madrid, St. Lawrence Co., N. Y., February 23, 1819, Mahala

Brintnell, daughter of John Brintnell of Vermont.
Farmer.   Lived at Madrid, N. Y., and there died
February 2, 1868.   Children, born at Madrid, N. Y.:
   I Elijah, born Jan. 18, 1820; died Sept. 2,
     1822.
   II Mary Ann, born June 17, 1821; married
     (1) Mar. 17, 1841, Jonathan Erwin, who
     died Feb., 1844; (2) Mar. 18, 1848,
     David Reed.
   III Laura L., born Dec. 19, 1822.
277 IV James E., b. Jan. 8, 1825; m. July 2,
     1850, Louisa Clark; d. April 9, 1877.
278 V Elisha C., b. Sept. 2, 1826; m. Jan. 4,
     1854, Ann P. Tilley; d. Sept. 16, 1862.
   VI Nancy L., born Oct. 2, 1831; married
     Jan. 5, 1856, Whitfield Watson; two
     sons, living in 1877; died Feb. 7, 1873.
278 VII George W., b. Sept. 29, 1835; m. May
     10, 1864, widow Ann P. (Tilley) Pelton.
279 VIII Henry E., b. Sept. 9, 1839; m. (1) March
     8, 1865, Adelphia Dixon; (2) Feb. 9,
     1874, Mary Etta Pelton.


276. **James E. Pelton**, second son of Elisha[6],
Phineas[5], James[4], John[3], Samuel[2], John[1], born at Mad-
rid, N. Y., January 8, 1825; married July 2, 1850,
Louisa Clark, died April 9, 1877.   Children:
   I Elmina L., born Nov. 11, 1851.
   II Lyman H., born July 11, 1855.
   III Ellen M., born Sept. 5, 1858.
   IV George E., born Feb. 14, 1861.
   V Frank L., born June 19, 1863.
   VI Betsy M., born Oct. 19, 1865.
   VII Clinton C., born Aug. 19, 1868.

**276. Elisha C. Pelton⁷**, third son of Elisha⁶, Phineas⁵, James⁴, John³, Samuel², John¹, born at Madrid, N. Y., September 2, 1826; married at Canton, St. Lawrence Co., N. Y., January 4, 1854, Ann P. Tilley, daughter of Walter Tilley, from Long Island, N. Y. Mechanic. Died at Madrid, N. Y., September 16, 1862. Children:

278 I Frederic M., b. Oct. 17, 1855; m. Sept. 22, 1876, Elizabeth M. Rutherford.
 II William H., born Aug. 30, 1861; died Nov. 2, 1863.
 III Carrie E., born April 25, 1863; died Nov. 16, 1863.

**278. Frederic M. Pelton⁸**, first son of Elisha C.⁷, Elisha⁶, Phineas⁵, James⁴, John³, Samuel², John¹, born at Madrid, N. Y., October 17, 1855; married at Potsdam, N. Y., September 22, 1876, Elizabeth M. Rutherford, daughter of Andrew Rutherford. Farmer. Lived, in 1877, at Madrid, N. Y. Children, none.

**276. George W. Pelton⁷**, fourth son of Elisha⁶, Phineas⁵, James⁴, John³, Samuel², John¹, born at Madrid, N. Y., September 29, 1835; married at Potsdam, N. Y., May 10, 1864, Ann P. (Tilley) Pelton, widow of his brother, Elisha C. Farmer. Lived, in 1877, at Madrid, N. Y. Children, none reported.

**276. Henry E. Pelton⁷**, fifth son of Elisha⁶, Phineas⁵, James⁴, John³, Samuel², John¹, born at Madrid, N. Y., September 9, 1839; married there (1), March 8, 1865, Adelphia P. Dixon, daughter of William Dixon, of Madrid, N. Y.; (2) February 9, 1874, Mary Etta Pelton, daughter of Elisha Boyd Pelton, of South Gower, Ont. Farmer. Lived, in 1877, at Madrid, N. Y. Children, born at Madrid :

By first wife:
      I Mary M., born Aug. 12, 1866.
      II Julia S., born April 30, 1871.
By second wife:
      III Martin H., born April 2, 1875.

**269. Elijah Pelton**[5], fourth son of Phineas[5], James[4], John[3], Samuel[2], John[1], born at Hartford, Washington Co., N. Y., June 23, 1798; married at South Gower, Ont., January 1, 1823, Peggy Brown, daughter of David Brown, of Mountain, Ont. Farmer. Removed, with his father, in 1810, to South Gower, and was living there in 1877. Children, born at South Gower:

    I Lucy, born Nov. 7, 1823; married Donald McIntyre, and lived, in 1877, at Mountain, Ont. Seven children.
    II Fanny, born Feb. 24, 1825; married Ephraim Hunter. Removed to Michigan, and there died, Sept. 2, 1871. Three children.
280  III Elisha Boyd, b. Mar. 11, 1827; m. Jan. 25, 1855, Martha J. Eldridge; d. July 6, 1876.
281  IV Phineas, b. Feb. 18, 1829; m., 1851, Miranda Gorham.
281  V Daniel Brown, b. March 18, 1832; m. Aug. 16, 1857, Elizabeth Cook.
281  VI Elijah, Jr., b. Aug. 23, 1834; m. Oct. 8, 1873, Elizabeth McNillage.
282  VII David, b. Dec. 30, 1836; m. Nov. 29, 1875, Eleanor E. Derrick.
    VIII Peggy, born Sept. 18, 1838; died Aug. 29, 1855.
283  IX Martin, b. Jan. 8, 1841; m. Mar. 2, 1871, Mary Louisa Doherty.

X Rebecca, born Feb. 28, 1843; married
Mar. 17, 1870, John A. Christie. Lived,
in 1877, at Oxford Mills, County Grenville, Ont.; in 1892 at Brandon, Man.
One child.

XI William John, born Sept. 18, 1845.
Farmer. Living, in 1877, in South
Gower, Ont.; unmarried.

XII Rachel, born Sept. 18, 1847; married
June 29, 1871, William Popham. Lived,
in 1877, at Osgood, Ont. No children.

XIII Nancy Mahala, born Dec. 16, 1850. In
1877 lived, unmarried, in South Gower,
Ont.

XIV Laura Ann, born May 16, 1852; died
Mar. 24, 1853.

XV James Kelley, born Jan. 20, 1854.
Farmer. In 1877 lived at Valley Ford,
Sonoma Co., Cal.; unmarried.

**279. Elisha Boyd Pelton[7]**, first son of Elijah[6],
Phineas[5], James[4], John[3], Samuel[2], John[1], born at South
Gower, Ont., March 11, 1827; married at Madrid,
N. Y., January 25, 1855, Martha Eldridge, daughter
of Henry Eldridge of Stockholm, N. Y. Farmer.
Lived at Madrid, N. Y., and there died, July 6, 1876.

Note.— He was a man of sterling integrity and
of ability, a lover of the right at all times; a Christian,
at first a Presbyterian, afterward a Baptist, a deacon
in each. An excellent, kind father, his children loved
and revered him. Children:

I Mary Etta, born Mar. 15, 1856; married
Feb. 9, 1874, to Henry E., son of Elisha
Pelton of Madrid, N. Y.

II Laura Ann, born Mar. 19, 1859; died
June 2, 1873.

III  Lizzie J., born Apr. 25, 1863.
IV  Nellie G., born Jan. 8, 1873.


**278.  Phineas Pelton[7]**, second son of Elijah[6],
Phineas[5], James[4], John[3], Samuel[2], John[1], born South
Gower, Ont., February 18, 1829; married in October,
1851, Miranda Gorham, daughter of Philo Gorham,
of Vermont.  Lumber dealer.  Living, in 1877, at
Martelle, Jones Co., and in 1891 at Persia, Harrison
Co., Ia.  Children:
     I  Amos J., born Sept. 2, 1851.
     II  Almeron P., born Mar. 12, 1854.
     III  Lucy M., born July 31, 1856.
     IV  Julia A., born July 22, 1859.
     V  William E., born May 19, 1862.
     VI  Daniel K., born July 27, 1866.
     VII  Horace H., born Dec. 19, 1868; died in
        1868.
     VIII  Emma E., born Jan. 19, 1870.
     IX  Nettie M., born Dec. 31, 1873.


**279.  Daniel Brown Pelton[7]**, third son of Elijah[6],
Phineas[5], James[4], John[3], Samuel[2], John[1], born at South
Gower, Ont., March 18, 1832; married there, August
16, 1857, Elizabeth Cook, daughter of Joseph Cook
of that place.  Commercial traveller.  Lived, in 1877,
at Kemptville, Ont.  Children:
     I  Emma Elizabeth, born Sept. 24, 1859.
     II  Ellnette Gertrude, born Sept. 23, 1865.
     III  Daniel Edson, born Nov. 9, 1869.
     IV  Charles Cook, born July 12, 1875.


**279.  Elijah Pelton[7], Jr.**, fourth son of Elijah[6],
Phineas[5], James[4], John[3], Samuel[2], John[1], born at South
Gower, Ont., Aug. 23, 1834; married at Oxford, Ont.,

October 8, 1873, Elizabeth McNillage, daughter of John McNillage of that place. Farmer. Lived, in 1877, at South Gower, Ont., and was clerk of the Township. Children:

    I Ida Maud, born Dec. 25, 1874.
    II Lucy Amelia, born Aug. 23, 1876.

**279. David Pelton⁷**, fifth son of Elijah⁶, Phineas⁵, James⁴, John³, Samuel², John¹, born at South Gower, Ont., December 30, 1836; married at Prescott, Ont., November 29, 1875, Eleanor E. Derrick, daughter of Andrew Derrick of Montague, Ont. Lived, 1877, at Burritt's Rapids, Ont. Farmer. Children, in 1877, none.

**279. Martin Pelton⁷**, sixth son of Elijah⁶, Phineas⁵, James⁴, John³, Samuel², John¹, born at South Gower, Ont., January 8, 1843; married at Burritt's Rapids, Ont., March 2, 1871, Mary Lousia Doherty, daughter of Matthew Doherty of that place. In 1877 a farmer, living at Burritt's Rapids, Ont. Children:

    I Charles Adrian, born Feb. 9, 1873; died Sept. 7, 1873.
    II Carrie Louisa, born Aug. 19, 1874.

**55. Phineas Pelton³**, third son of John³, Samuel², John¹, born (as deduced from his tombstone) in 1712; place and exact date unknown. Married (1) Middletown, Conn., May 22, 1740, Mary McKay, who "died Sept. 28, 1749, æ. 26 years." Married (2), but the place, date and name of the second wife are unknown. Farmer. Lived at Chatham, Conn., and as appears from the church records, was a church member, baptizing his children in infancy.   Indeed, it is from these records that we deduce his second marriage.   He died May 24, 1799, and was buried in the Chatham burying ground, where his tombstone states that he was æ. 87 years, and that he suffered from "numb palsey" for twenty-three years before his death."   His homestead is now, 1890, occupied by his great-grandson, Moses F. Pelton.   Children:

    I A daughter, born 1741; no other record.
**284** II Ithamar, b. May, 1744 (bapt. May 19, 1744); m. July 23, 1767, Elizabeth Hall; d. Jan. 22, 1806.
   III Charles, born unknown; died aged about six years (Rev. Charles Pelton).
   IV Jesse, date of birth unknown; baptized Dec. 8, 1752 (Chatham Ch. Rec.); must have died young; no other record.
   V Lucy, date of birth unknown; bapt. June 8, 1755 (Chatham. Ch. Rec.); no further record.

Note. — As shown above, the records of the family of Phineas are but few and mostly gathered from church and township records.   He and his brother Johnson inherited from his father, as appears by the will of his father, John Pelton (see Appendix) "The one-half of my above-said four hundred acres, called the School lot, together with the one-half of my dwelling-house thereon," etc., to which he added other lands, the larger part of which is now occupied by his great-grandson, Moses F. Pelton.   This old homestead of John Pelton, 1st, of Saybrook, lies in what is now the township of Portland, which was cut from Chatham, as that had previously been cut from Middletown.

**282. Ithamar Pelton**, first son of Phineas⁵,
John⁴, Samuel³, John², born at Chatham, Conn., in
1744 (probably about May 1), (baptized May 19,
1744, Ch. Rec.); married at Portland, Conn., July 23,
1767, Elizabeth Hall (b. 1747), daughter of Capt.
Samuel and Elizabeth (Wilcox) Hall, of that place.
Lived in Chatham, now Portland, Conn. Sea captain
and farmer. Died in Chatham, January 22, 1806–7,
aged 68 years. He was a sea captain for years, commanding privateers and taking prizes during the
Revolutionary War, and still sailed the seas to English and to other foreign ports after peace was de-
clared. He was an enterprising business man, and
from 1767 to 1795 an active land operator, as the
Land Records of Chatham show. For the last years
of his life, however, he was an invalid. Children:

    I Elizabeth, born Jan. 19, 1768–9; married
        (1) Capt. (Sea), Walter Hilliard, of
        Killingsworth, Conn., who died young;
        one child only, Abby, who died in in-
        fancy; (2) May 20, 1811, Nathan
        Gillum, of Portland, Conn., who died
        Nov. 4, 1821; date of her death un-
        known.

286    II Cale, b. Oct. 27, 1769; m. Oct. 3, 1790,
        Esther Crittenden; d. Feb. 22, 1843.

    III Charles, born Jan. 14, 1772; died July 5,
        1776.

    IV Grace, born Oct. 27, 1773 (Town Rec.);
        married (Ch. Rec.) May 4, 1794, Capt.
        James Stewart (b. July 12, 1771), of
        Portland, Conn. Lived at Portland,
        Conn., and there died, July 4, 1806.
        Capt. Stewart died and was buried at
        sea. They had four children, descend-

ants of whom lived in Middle Haddam, Conn.

300 V William Pitt, b. July 25, 1775; m. Dec. 3, 1797, Sarah Davis; d. June 16, 1848.

VI Mary, born Oct. 30, 1777; married Oct. 20, 1796, William (b. Aug. 14, 1764 or '7; d. Mch. 21, 1831), son of Ozias Bidwell, of Eastbury, Conn. Lived at Farmington, Conn., and thence removed to Madison, Lake Co., O., in 1820, where she died, July 31, 1868. Children, six: Walter Hilliard, b. June 21, 1798; Emeline, July 13, 1800; William, March 21, 1805; Oliver B., May 16, 1810; Elizabeth, Sept. 16, 1812; Mary Ann, July 15, 1815.

VII Luther, born Oct. 7, 1779; joiner and cabinetmaker; died at sea, May, 1805, tradition says by violence, aged 26, while on a voyage to buy mahogany.

VIII Charles, born 1781; died at sea, Nov., 1803.

301 IX Samuel, b. Sept. 18, 1783; m. Nov. 5, 1808, Sarah Bailey; d. Aug. 8, 1862.

X Sarah, born in June, 1789; unmarried. Lived after about the age of twenty-four years with her aunt, Mrs. Ruth Hall Deane (Mrs. Phineas Deane), until that lady's death, then with her cousin, a daughter of Mrs. Deane, Mrs. Harriet Makinster (Mrs. Wm. Mackinster), until she, Sarah, died Sept. 4, 1870, aged 81 years. Buried in Mr. Mackinster's vault in Indian Hill cemetery at Middletown, Conn.

NOTE.— She had earned and saved about $2,000, the income of which she used to bring up two orphans, nephew and niece, of a man who died a New York millionaire, whose fortune went largely to lawyers in the usual contest over a large fortune. At her death she left a sum of money to pay for removing her father's remains from the old burying ground to a new one.

**284. Calo Pelton**, first son of Ithamar⁶, Phineas⁵, John⁴, Samuel³, John¹, born at Chatham (now Portland), Conn., October 27, 1769 (family record); married October 3, 1790, Esther Crittenden (b. March 18, 1768) of Colchester, Conn. Removed in 1794 to Buckland, Franklin Co., Mass., and there died, February 22, 1843. Farmer. His wife Esther died there, July 25, 1845. Children:

    I Albert, born in Conn. Sunday, Nov. 11, 1792; died Feb. 19, 1795.

287  II Charles, b. Sept. 16, 1794; m. Nov. 28, 1819, Lucinda Merrill; d. July 25, 1854.

288  III Albert, b. June 22, 1796; m. Oct. 16, 1833, Sarah Maria Cross; d. Sept. 14, 1874.

289  IV Walter Hilliard, b. Mar. 22, 1798; m. (1) in 1819, Elizabeth Ward; (2) in 1834, Sophia Hawks; (3) in Nov., 1854, Widow Eunice Bassett; d. Sept. 14, 1876.

    V Phineas, born Tuesday, Feb. 18, 1800; died Mar. 15, 1800.

    VI Elizabeth Hall, born Thursday, Mar. 30, 1801; married Dec. 16, 1824, Asa (b. Mar. 8, 1798), son of Josiah Davis of Buckland, Mass. Lived there and died,

Mr. Davis July 4, 1872, and Mrs. Davis Mar. 20, 1873.   Five children.

291   VII Luther E., b. May 25, 1803; m. Oct. 25, 1827, Eunice Dodge.

292  VIII Cyrus B., b. Apr. 1, 1805; m. Apr. 17, 1827, Thirza S. Merrill.

293   IX Hiram, b. in 1807; m. in Moscow, N. Y., date and name unknown; d. Aug., 1831.

294    X Elias S., b. Nov. 12, 1809; m. Jan. 1, 1835, Anna M. Judd; d. Oct. 2, 1852.

295   XI Cale, Jr., b. Sept., 1811; m. in 1842, Ann Ferrier Wood; d. Sept. 12, 1853.

296  XII John O., b. Sept. 25, 1814; m. Sept. 14, 1842, Lydia Wood.

**286. Charles Fellows**, second son of Cale⁶, Ithamar⁵, Phineas⁴, John³, Samuel², John¹, born in Buckland, Mass., Saturday, September 16, 1794; married at Shelburne Falls, Mass., November 28, 1819, Lucinda Merrill, daughter of Joseph Merrill of that place.   Carpenter.   Lived at Shelburne Falls, and there died, July 25, 1854.   His wife Lucinda died June 23, 1854.   Children:

I Esther, born Dec. 19, 1820; married at Shelburne Falls, Mass., July 7, 1841, Asa Baldwin, blacksmith.   She died Jan. 19, 1852.

II Lucinda, born Aug. 28, 1824; married at home, Nov., 1846, Chester Talman: died Aug. 17, 1859.   Children: (1) Emily, b. Apr. 6, 1848; m. Sept. 21, 1871, Charles M. Smith of Shelburne Falls, supt. of Gardner's cutlery works; children, Charles H. and Julian C. (2) Angelica, b. Apr. 26, 1850; d. July,

1851. (3) Francis, b. 1852; drowned
in 1857.
**288** III Charles O., b. Jan. 2, 1829; m. May 24,
1848, Persis Crittenden.
IV Melissa, born Aug. 5, 1834.

**287. Charles O. Pelton**[7], only son of Charles[6],
Cale[5], Ithamar[4], Phineas[3], John[2], Samuel[2], John[1], born
at Shelburne Falls, Mass., January 2, 1829; married
at Charlemont, Mass., May 24, 1848, Persis Crittenden, daughter of David Crittenden of that place.
Carpenter.    Lived, in 1878, at Shelburne Falls, Mass.
Children:

        I Cornelia, born Dec. 11, 1851; died Jan.
          8, 1856.
        II Charles Frederick, born June 22, 1862;
          died July 25, 1863.
        III C. Henry, born Jan., 1865; died Jan.,
          1865.
        IV Cornelia Luana, born March 13, 1868;
          died June 18, 1874.
        V Charles Frederick, 2, born Aug. 12, 1874;
          died Sept. 20, 1874.

**286. Albert Pelton**[6], third son of Cale[5], Ithamar[4],
Phineas[3], John[2], Samuel[2], John[1], born at Buckland,
Mass., Wednesday, June 22, 1796; married at Leyden, Mass., Oct. 16, 1833, Sarah Maria Cross,
daughter of John Cross, of that place.    Farmer.
Lived at Buckland, and there died, September 14,
1874.    Children:

        I Sarah Rhoda, born at Shelburne Falls,
          Mass., Aug. 13, 1834; married at Buck-
          land, Nov. 30, 1854, Jared, son of Jacob
          Gragg, of Colerain, Mass.    Lived, in
          1878, at Buckland, Mass.

11 Lucy A., born May 15, 1842; married at
Buckland, Mass., May 1, 1867, Rev.
Noble Fiske, of the M. E. church, son
of Daniel P. Fiske, of Heath, Mass.
Lived, in 1878, at Marlboro, N. H.
Children: Lucy Christine, b. Feb. 28,
1870; Lelia Maria, b. May 27, 1872;
Mary Albertine, b. Feb. 23, 1875.

**266. Walter Lillard Pelton²**, fourth son of
Cale⁵, Ithamar⁴, Phineas³, John², Samuel², John¹, born
at Buckland, Hampshire Co., Mass., Thursday, March
22, 1798; married (1) there in 1819, Elizabeth Ward
(d. 1834), daughter of John Ward, of Buckland;
(2) at Northampton, Mass., in 1837, Sophia Hawks,
daughter of Charles Hawks, of Deerfield, Mass., who
died September 15, 1853; (3) at Coldwater, Mich.,
in November, 1854, Eunice Bassett, widow of Scho-
field Bassett, and daughter of John Osborn, of the
State of New York. Lived in Buckland, Mass.;
thence, in 1837, removed to Leeds Corners, N. Y.,
for three years; thence to Moscow, N. Y., for three
years; to Mount Morris, Livingston Co., N. Y., and
to Coldwater, Mich., November 16, 1852, and finally,
in 1866, to Girard, Mich., where he died September
14, 1876. Children (by first wife):
I Mary, born at Buckland, Mass., in 1820;
married at Mt. Morris, N. Y., 1844,
John Hall, of Co. Tyrone, Castle Can-
field, Ireland; died Sept. 15, 1852. One
child, Henry Irving, b. Aug. 15, 1847,
South Livonia, N. Y. Lived, in 1878,
at Fillmore, Fillmore Co., Minn.
II Elizabeth, born Buckland, Mass., Sept.
16, 1822; married May 26, 1844, Daniel

> S. Avery, of Perry, Wyoming Co., N.
> Y., son of Jas. Avery, of Pike, N. Y.
> Lived, in 1878, at Colon, Mich. No
> children.

III Joseph, born in 1824; died in 1825.

**290** IV George Franklin, b. Jan. 9, 1829; m June
20, 1850, Ann Eliza Doland.

V Rhoda Angelica, born, Buckland, Mass.,
June 10, 1832; married Jan. 1, 1856,
John F. Flynn, son of Thos. Flynn, of
Co. Cork, Ireland. Children: Chas.
Irvin, b. Jan., 1857; Viola Estella, b. Dec.
25, 1858; Wm. Early, b. July 28, 1861;
Geo. Edward, b. May 1, 1864 (d. Sept. 11,
1865); Frank John, b. Sept. 21, 1868.
Lived, in 1878, at Coldwater, Mich.

By second wife:

VI Hattie, 1, born in 1840; died in 1841, æ.
14 mos.

VII Hattie, 2, born in 1843; died in 1844, æ.
17 mos.

By third wife:

VIII Jennie Florence, born April 27, 1856.

IX Theron Burt. No record given.

**290. George Franklin Pelton**[9], second son of
Walter H.[8], Cale[7], Ithamar[6], Phineas[5], John[4], Samuel[3],
John[2], born at North Adams, Mass., January 9, 1829;
married June 20, 1850, Ann Eliza Doland, daughter
of John Doland, of Rushford, N. Y. Boot and shoemaker. Lived, in 1888, at Rushford, Allegany Co.,
N. Y. Children:

I John Frederic, born Feb. 12, 1852; died
Jan. 24, 1857.

**291** II Charles Irving, b. Nov. 24, 1853: m. Oct.
8, 1878, Adaline Kimball.

III Duane Shedd, born Nov. 24, 1855; jeweler, at Duke Centre, McKean Co., Pa.

**280. Charles Irving Pelton⁹**, second son of George F.⁸, Walter H.⁷, Cale⁶, Ithamar⁵, Phineas⁴, John³, Samuel², John¹, born at Rushford, N. Y., November 24, 1853; married there, October 8, 1878, Adaline Kimball, daughter of Addison Kimball, of Rushford. Boot and shoemaker, Rushford, N. Y. Child:

 I Mary, born Oct. 20, 1881.

**286. Luther E. Pelton⁷**, sixth son of Cale⁶, Ithamar⁵, Phineas⁴, John³, Samuel², John¹, born at Buckland, Mass., Wednesday, May 25, 1803; married at Hawley, Mass., October 25, 1827, Eunice Dodge (b. Aug. 7, 1803; d. Sept. 17, 1843), daughter of Silas Dodge, of that place. Farmer. Lived, in 1876, at Perry, Wyoming Co., N. Y. After his marriage he immediately removed to Leicester, Livingston Co., N. Y., thence, in 1845, to Mt. Morris, N. Y., and six months after to Castile, N. Y. Children:

 I Elmina D., born at Leicester, N. Y., Apr. 12, 1833; married at Castile, N. Y., Apr. 6, 1856, John W. Barnes of that place. Lived, in 1878, at Genesee Falls, Wyoming Co., N. Y. Children, two sons.

**292** II Luther E., Jr., b. Mar. 11, 1835; m. July 14, 1863, Betsey E. Helmer.

 III Derastus L., born Feb. 14, 1837; died Aug. 19, 1840.

 IV Ann E., born in Leicester, N. Y., July 18, 1838; married at Castile, N. Y., Sept. 12, 1859, Daniel F. Saxton, of Wethersfield, Wyoming Co., N. Y.

38

Lived, in 1878, in Danby, Mich. Children, one son and one daughter.

V Mary A., born Feb. 13, 1840; married at Castile, N. Y., Feb. 5, 1870, Lorenzo Brainard of Gainesville, N. Y. Lived, in 1878, at Castile, N. Y. No children.

**281. Luther E. Pelton[6], Jr.**, only son of Luther E.[5], Cale[5], Ithamar[4], Phineas[3], John[2], Samuel[2], John[1], born at Leicester, N. Y., March 11, 1835; married at Castile, Wyoming Co., N. Y., July 14, 1863, Betsey E. Helmer, daughter of Zebulon Helmer, of Eagle, Wyoming Co., N. Y. Lived, in 1876, at Gainesville, Wyoming Co., N. Y. Postmaster. Children:

I Flora B., born Oct. 17, 1867.

II Ollie M., born July 2, 1872.

III Arthur D., born Sept. 23, 1876.

**286. Cyrus B. Pelton[5]**, seventh son of Cale[5], Ithamar[4], Phineas[3], John[2], Samuel[2], John[1], born at Buckland, Mass., on Monday, April 1, 1805; married at Halifax, Vt., April 17, 1827, Thirza S. Merrill, daughter of Capt. Thaddeus Merrill, of Shelburne Falls, Mass. Carpenter and joiner and farmer. Lived, in 1878, at Cuylersville, Livingston Co., N. Y. Children:

293    I Lauriston C., b. Oct. 6, 1828; m. July 8, 1850, Calista Smith.

293    II Marcus T. M., b. Sept. 25, 1830; m. (1) July 12, 1851, Mary Adams; (2) Catharine A. Wood.

III Hiram B., born Apr. 16, 1832. Carpenter; unmarried. Served in the war of the Rebellion in the 2d Ohio Cavalry, and died in hospital at Fort Scott, Kan., Dec. 30, 1862.

294 IV DeWitt Clinton, b. Jan 25, 1834; m. July 3, 1854, Eliza J. Sessions. Killed in battle, Mar. 14, 1865.

295 V Watts E., b. Feb. 23, 1837; uses Watson as his first name; m. Sept. 23, 1864, Anna N. McDivett.

296 VI Loammi C., b. Apr. 19, 1843; m. (1) Apr. 6, 1870, Alice N. Nichols; (2) June 24, 1873, Margarette D. Lowery.

  VII Achsah Melinda, born Mar. 17, 1846; married Joseph Peter Pierson, son of Bradley M. Pierson, farmer, of LeRoy, N. Y. Lived, in 1878, at Lima, N. Y. Widow. No children.

296 VIII Cyrus Strong, b. Sept. 11, 1841; m. Oct. 11, 1874, Elizabeth Frances Rawlings.

**292. Lauriston C. Pelton**, first son of Cyrus B.[7], Cale[6], Ithamar[5], Phineas[4], John[3], Samuel[2], John[1], born at Shelburne Falls, Mass., October 6, 1828; married at Moscow, Livingston Co., N. Y., July 8, 1850, Calista Smith, daughter of Noah Smith, of Dansville, N. Y. Lived, in 1878, at Canaseraga, N. Y. Dealer in groceries and provisions. Child:

  I Thirza A., born Sept. 27, 1853, at Oramel, Allegany Co., N. Y.

**293. Marcus E. M. Pelton**, second son of Cyrus B.[7], Cale[6], Ithamar[5], Phineas[4], John[3], Samuel[2], John[1], born at Shelburne Falls, Mass., September 25, 1830; married (1) at Moscow, Livingston Co., N. Y., July 12, 1851, Mary Adams, daughter of Cyrus Adams of Wyoming Co., N. Y., who was divorced; (2) at Mount Vernon, O., June 12, 1873, Mrs. Catharine A. Ward, daughter of Thomas D. Simpson, of Delaware, O.

General master mechanic at C. & G. Cooper & Co.'s machine shops at Mount Vernon, O. Children:

**294**    I Frederic M., b. July 13, 1852; m. Apr. 5, 1875, Catharine A. Ward.

II Sarah A., born June 3, 1854; married Mar. 17, 1873, Nathaniel Van Horn. Two children. Lived, in 1878, at Springfield, O.

III Mary, born Apr. 8, 1858; died May 13, 1859.

IV Adelaide, born May 25, 1860.

V Annie, born Dec. 10, 1861.

VI Charles, born March 5, 1863.

VII William, 1, born and died March 10, 1865.

VIII Mark, born April 14, 1866.

IX Hiram B., born March 15, 1869.

By second wife:

X William, 2, born March 16, 1874; died Aug. 20, 1874.

XI Arthur W., born July 17, 1875.

XII Elizabeth, born March 19, 1877.

**294. Frederic M. Pelton**[9], first son of Marcus T. M.[8], Cyrus B.[7], Cale[6], Ithamar[5], Phineas[4], John[3], Samuel[2], John[1], born July 13, 1852; married April 5, 1875, Miss Catharine A. Ward, daughter of John F. Ward, of Goldsborough (state not given). Engineer. Living, in 1878, at Mount Vernon, O. Child:

I Elizabeth, born Oct. 31, 1876.

**295. De Witt Clinton Pelton**[8], fourth son of Cyrus B.[7], Cale[6], Ithamar[5], Phineas[4], John[3], Samuel[2], John[1], born Buckland, Mass., January 25, 1834; married at Rushford, N. Y., July 3, 1854, Eliza J. Sessions, daughter of David Sessions, of that place. Shoemaker. Served in the War of the Rebellion, in

Company B, 2d Regiment New York Mounted Rifles.
He was wounded at the explosion of the great mine
at Petersburg, Va., July 30, 1864, and killed, upon his
horse, in front of that city, March 14, 1865. The
residence of the family, in 1878, was Hinsdale, Cattaraugus Co., N. Y.   Children:

> I Emma M., born May 26, 1855; married
> Sept. 11, 1871, Bela Webster.   Lived,
> in 1878, at Hinsdale, N. Y.   Children:
> De Witt D., b. June 4, 1874, and Cora
> M., b. Apr. 18, 1878.
> II Helen M., born Feb. 24, 1857; married
> Aug. 5, 1877, George Adams.   Resi-
> dence, in 1878, at Olean, N. Y.   One
> child, Blanche Eliza, b June 5, 1878.
> III Frank D., born Jan. 1, 1860.
> IV Cora G., born Sept. 12, 1861.
> V Ira D., born Feb. 4, 1864.

**262. Wallis E. Pelton**[7] (known as Watson),
fifth son of Cyrus B.[6], Cale[5], Ithamar[4], Phineas[3], John[3],
Samuel[2], John[1], born at Shelburne Falls, Mass., February 23, 1837; married at Cleveland, O., September
23, 1864, Anna N. McDivett, daughter of Wm. Mc-
Divett.   Lived, in 1878, at Cherokee, Cherokee Co.,
Iowa.   Merchant.   Wife, Anna N., died February
18, 1878.   Children:

> I De Witt L., born Dec. 10, 1867.
> II Berenice, born Feb. 18, 1869.
> III Walter S., born June 30, 1872.
> IV Stanley S., born April 1, 1875.

**263. Lonson C. Pelton**[7], sixth son of Cyrus B.[6],
Cale[5], Ithamar[4], Phineas[3], John[3], Samuel[2], John[1], born
at Moscow, Livingston Co., N. Y., April 19, 1843;

married (1), April 6, 1870, Alice N. Nichols, daughter of Jesse Nichols, of Cortland, N. Y.; (2) June 24, 1873, Margarette D. Lowery, daughter of Philip Lowery, of Sonyea, Livingston Co., N. Y. Residence at Cuylersville, N. Y. Children, none.

**292. Cyrus Strong Pelton⁸**, seventh son of Cyrus B.⁷, Cale⁶, Ithamar⁵, Phineas⁴, John³, Samuel², John¹, born in the township of Leicester, Livingston Co., N. Y., September 11, 1848; married at Canaseraga, N. Y., October 11, 1874, Elizabeth Frances Rawlings, of Stratford, Ont., daughter of William Rawlings, of Plymouth, England. Painter. Lived, in 1878, at Canaseraga, N. Y. Children:

    I Charles Strong, born March 15, 1875.

    II Emma Plough, born April 3, 1876.

    III Watson Emerson, born Oct. 5, 1877.

**285. Hiram Pelton⁷**, eighth son of Cale⁶, Ithamar⁵, Phineas⁴, John³, Samuel², John¹, born at Buckland, Mass., in 1807; married at Moscow, Livingston Co., N. Y. Lived at Leicester, Livingston Co., N. Y., and there died, in August, 1831. Children, none.

**286. Elias N. Pelton⁷**, ninth son of Cale⁶, Ithamar⁵, Phineas⁴, John³, Samuel², John¹, born at Buckland, Mass., November 12, 1809; married at Bethany, Genesee Co., N. Y., January 1, 1835, Anna M. Judd, daughter of Liberty Judd, from Vermont. Mason. Died at Alexander, N. Y., October 2, 1852. Wife, Anna M., married (2) William Spaulding, of Alexander, N. Y., and there died, May 14, 1878. Children:

    I Emily, born Nov. 22, 1835; died March 15, 1837.

**297**  II Lewis W., b. May 7, 1838; m. Dec. 25, 1858, Mary Palmer.

III Martha A., born Mar. 15, 1840; married
   Eugene Fillmore.  Residence, 1878, at
   Attica, N. Y.
IV Ellen F., born May 14, 1842, at Batavia,
   N. Y.; married there, July 11, 1874, to
   William Reed (b. July 4, 1827), son of
   Josiah and Phœbe Reed of Batavia.
   No children.
297  V Allen C., b. Aug. 18, 1848; m. Nov. 22,
     1876, Agnes Moore.
297  VI Elias S., Jr., b. Oct. 21, 1850; m. Oct. 21,
     1868, Catharine Boyle.


**296. Lewis W. Pelton⁷**, first son of Elias S.⁶,
Cale⁵, Ithamar⁴, Phineas⁴, John³, Samuel², John¹, born
at Batavia, N. Y., May 7, 1838; married at Attica,
N. Y., December 25, 1858, Mary Palmer, daughter
of Henry Palmer of that place.  Mason and contractor.  Lived, in 1878, at 615 Cottage Grove avenue, Chicago, Ill.  Children:
      I Eugenia, born Feb. 14, 1862; died Oct.
        14, 1862.
      II Lillian, born Mar. 10, 1868.


**296. Allen C. Pelton⁷**, second son of Elias S.⁶,
Cale⁵, Ithamar⁴, Phineas⁴, John³, Samuel², John¹, born
at Alexander, Genesee Co., N. Y., August 18, 1848;
married November 22, 1876, Agnes Moore, daughter
of Thane Moore of Ireland.  Farmer.  Living, in
1876, at Attica, N. Y.  Children, none.


**296. Elias S. Pelton⁷, Jr.**, third son of Elias S.⁶,
Cale⁵, Ithamar⁴, Phineas⁴, John³, Samuel², John¹, born
at Alexander, N. Y., October 21, 1850; married at
Attica, N. Y., October 21, 1868, Catharine Boyle,

daughter of Thomas Boyle of Ireland. Railroad man. In 1878 lived at Attica, N. Y. Children:

    I Mary A., born Aug. 27, 1869.
    II Martha F., born Sept. 1, 1872.
    III Alice, born Feb. 8, 1877.

**286. Cale Pelton⁷, Jr.,** tenth son of Cale⁶, Ithamar⁵, Phineas⁴, John³, Samuel², John¹, born at Buckland, Mass., September, 1811; graduated at Yale College, class of 1840, A. B.; received his degree of A. M. in 1843; teacher and author, teaching in Pennsylvania and in other States. He was the author of "Pelton's Outline Maps," published by Sower, Potts & Co. of Philadelphia, and extensively used in schools. In 1842 he married Ann Ferrier Wood, daughter of Mr. ——— Wood and Hannah (Rhaum) Wood, born Halifax Pa., March 3, 1818; died in childbirth in Philadelphia, Pa., February 20, 1846. Mr. Pelton was a tall, slender man, well educated and a good and successful teacher. He died September 12, 1853, of consumption, at the house of Mr. George W. Rhaum, uncle of his deceased wife, in Fox Chase, Philadelphia, Pa., and was buried with his wife and child, and his wife's mother, in Laurel Hill Cemetery, Philadelphia, in a vault in lot 53, section 1. Child:

    I Still born, Feb. 20, 1846.

**286. John O. Pelton⁷,** eleventh son of Cale⁶, Ithamar⁵, Phineas⁴, John³, Samuel², John¹, born at Buckland, Mass., September 25, 1814; married at Bethany, Genesee Co., N. Y., September 14, 1842, Lydia Wood, daughter of Ammon O. Wood of that place. Farmer. Removed soon after marriage to Ovid township, Branch Co., Mich., and thence, in 1845, to Coldwater, Mich., and there lived in 1878. Children:

**299**  I Arthur M., b. Feb. 17, 1844; m. Apr. 22,
1875, Eliza J. Avery.
II Ella L., born Coldwater, Mich., Feb. 10,
1850; married May 2, 1877, Charles D.
Wright, lawyer, son of George Wright
of Meredith. Delaware Co., N. Y.
Lived, in 1878, at Coldwater, Mich.
No children.

**298. Arthur M. Pelton**[8], only son of John O.[7],
Cale[6], Ithamar[5], Phineas[4], John[3], Samuel[2], John[1], born
in the township of Ovid, Branch Co., Mich., February
17, 1844; married at Indianola, Tex., April 22, 1875,
Eliza J. Avery, daughter of I. Avery of Durham,
Conn., whose ancestors lived in Groton, Conn.   At
the age of about one year he removed with his
parents to the then village of Coldwater, Mich.; in
the fall of 1861 he entered the high school at Ann
Arbor, Mich., preparatory to entering the University
of Michigan; the next year entered the medical
department, instead of the classical, and remained
until 1864, when he passed an examination before
the "Army Board of Medical Examiners," and was
appointed by the Secretary of War to the position
of Medical Cadet April 21, 1864, for the term of one
year.   Attached to the General Medical Staff, he
performed duty in the hospitals in St. Louis, Mo.,
in Jefferson Barracks, Mo., and in Chattanooga, Tenn.,
where he acted as assistant surgeon for six months.
At the end of the year he returned to the University
and graduated March 28, 1866.   Afterward he was
in Illinois, Kansas, Indiana, Michigan and Arkansas
until April, 1874, when he settled at Deming's
Bridge, Matagorda Co., Tex., where he lived in 1876.
Physician.

39

**284. William Pitt Pelton⁶**, third son of Ithamar⁵, Phineas⁴, John³, Samuel², John¹, born in Chatham (now Portland), Conn., July 25, 1775; married there, December 3, 1797, Sarah Davis, daughter of Charles Davis of that place (whose wife was Anna Pelton, daughter of Joseph Pelton of Chatham, Conn.). Farmer. He bought a farm adjoining that of his father, soon after his father's death, and lived at Upper Middletown, Conn., and there died, June 16, 1848. His wife Sarah died September 5, 1851, aged 72 years. Children:

301 I Oliver, b. Aug. 31, 1798; m. in 1827, Julia Stewart; d. Aug. 15, 1882.

302 II William Walter, b. March 23, 1801; m. (1) Nov. 8, 1829, Mary Sage; (2) Oct. 23, 1845, Sarah Smith.

  III Anna, born Sept. 14, 1803; married April 27, 1825, Miles Hull (Hall in Town Rec.), son of Comfort Hull. Lived in Middletown, Conn., and there died, Sept. 6, 1839. Four children: One son, in 1876, in Meriden, Conn., and one in Hyde Park, Mass.

303 IV Charles Frederick, b. Jan. 10, 1806; m. April 4, 1827, Julia Ann Chamberlain.

  V Mary, born Jan. 22, 1808; unmarried. Lived in Middletown, Conn., and there died, Nov. 18, 1841.

  VI Grace, born June 25, 1810; married Dec. 3, 1836, Daniel Wilcox, who died Feb. 15, 1869. Lived at Cromwell, Conn., and died March 10, 1878. One child, Sarah, who married Linus A. Williams, who had one son, Clarence, living, in 1878, at Cromwell, Conn.

EDWARD R. PELTON

VII Elizabeth, born Sept. 30, 1812; unmarried.   Lived at Middletown, Conn., and there died, March 12, 1835.
VIII Harriet Maria, born Feb. 5, 1815.   Lived, unmarried, at Middletown, Conn., Oct. 25, 1878.   She had the Family Record of Joseph, 1st, of Chatham.
IX Julia Sarah, born May 22, 1817; unmarried.   Lived at Middletown, Conn., and there died, Sept. 21, 1852.
X Alfred, born Oct. 18, 1819; died, while a student at Wesleyan University, Middletown, Conn., Aug. 29, 1841.
263 XI James A., b. Feb. 19, 1822; m. Nov. 16, 1843, Lydia Matilda Atherton.


**300. Oliver Pelton**[7], first son of William P.[6], Ithamar[5], Phineas[4], John[3], Samuel[2], John[1], born at Portland, Conn., August 31, 1798; married at East Hartford, Conn., in 1827, Julia Stewart. Steel engraver, Hartford, Conn.   Residence at East Hartford, where his wife, Julia, died, Saturday, Feb. 12, 1881, æ. 75 years.   Mr. Pelton died August 15, 1882.   Child:
301     1 Edward R., b. Jan. 25, 1840; m. Oct. 6, 1869, Katie Flanders.   Eight other children died in infancy.


**301. Edward R. Pelton**[8], son of Oliver[7], Wm. P.[6], Ithamar[5], Phineas[4], John[3], Samuel[2], John[1], born in Boston, Mass., January 25, 1840; educated at Cambridge, Mass.; married at Brooklyn, N. Y., October 6, 1869, Katie Flanders, daughter of B. F. Flanders, of Louisiana.   Publisher, 144 Eighth street, New York. Residence, 1893, Brooklyn, N. Y.   Children:

> I Katharine Isabel, born Brooklyn, N. Y.,
> Aug. 7, 1871.
> II Edward Franklin, born Flushing, Long
> Island, N. Y., Jan. 21, 1877.

**266. William Walter Pelton**, second son of William P.[5], Ithamar[4], Phineas[3], John[2], Samuel[2], John[1], born Portland, Conn., March 23, 1801; married (1) at Cromwell, Conn., November 8, 1829, Mary Sage, daughter of Alexander Sage of that place; (2) at Cromwell, October 23, 1845, Sarah Ann Smith, daughter of Seth Smith of that place. Farmer. Living, in 1878, at Cromwell, Conn. Wife Mary died May 6, 1839, and wife Sarah, April 14, 1860. Children:

> I Henry P., born Cromwell, Conn., Sept. 20,
> 1830. He went to Bridgeport, Conn.,
> to be married and died at the house of
> his intended bride, Jan. 10, 1861.
> II Wilbur S., born May 10, 1832; died Sept.
> 4, 1833.
> III Mary A., born at Cromwell, Conn., Oct.
> 29, 1847; married December 19, 1876,
> Caleb S. Pease of Cromwell, where
> they lived in 1878.
> IV Emily, born Apr. 5, 1850; died Sept. 21,
> 1851.

**300. Rev. Charles Frederick Pelton**, third son of William P.[5], Ithamar[4], Phineas[3], John[2], Samuel[2], John[1], born at Portland, Conn., January 10, 1806, in the old Phineas homestead; married in Philadelphia, Pa., April 4, 1827, Julia Ann Chamberlain, daughter of John Chamberlain of Austerlitz, N. Y. Minister of the Methodist Episcopal church. Residence from about 1856 at Mount Kisco, Westchester Co., N. Y.,

where he still lived in good health in 1890.   Died
Thursday, November 5, 1891.   Mrs. Julia Ann Pelton
died in 1880.   Children:

**862**      I Lewis F., b. Feb. 13, 1828; m. May 15,
                1855, Elizabeth C. Calhoun; d. Sept.
                17, 1883.
         II Harriet E., born at Nassau, Rensselaer
                Co., N. Y., Oct. 1, 1830; married Sept.
                7, 1852, Luther C. Ward.   Residence
                in 1878 at Newburgh, N. Y.   Children:
                Julius Pelton, b. Aug. 20, 1855; Mary
                C., b. Oct. 21, 1861.
         III William P., born Nassau, N. Y., Feb. 11,
                1832; died young.
         IV Charles F., Jr., born Rye, N. Y., Mar. 10,
                1842; died ———.


**862. Dr. Lewis F. Pelton**, first son of Charles
F.[7], William P.[6], Ithamar[5], Phineas[4], John[3], Samuel[2],
John[1], born at Westfield, Mass., February 13, 1828;
married at Pawling, Dutchess Co., N. Y., May 15,
1855, Elizabeth C. Calhoun, daughter of Daniel B.
Calhoun, of Pawling (from Washington, Litchfield
Co., Conn.).   Physician and surgeon.   Educated at
Wesleyan University, Middletown, Conn.   Lived
for the most of his life after marriage at or near
Mount Kisco, Westchester Co., N. Y., and there died,
September 17, 1883.   Mrs. Pelton died in March,
1885.   Children:
         I Frederic Calhoun, born Mar. 28, 1856.
         II Arthur Campbell, born May 16, 1872.


**863. James A. Pelton**[6], fifth son of William Pitt[5],
Ithamar[4], Phineas[3], John[2], Samuel[2], John[1], born at
Upper Middletown, Conn., February 19, 1822; mar-

ried Glastenbury, Conn., November 16, 1843, Lydia
Matilda Atherton, daughter of Almarin Atherton, of
that place. Dental surgeon. Residence, in 1893, at
Middletown, Conn. Children:

    I Mary Jane, born March 27, 1846; died
        Jan. 23, 1883.
    II Lilly, born Aug. 21, 1854; an artist of
        ability; died Feb. 3, 1872.

**284. Samuel Pelton[6]**, sixth and last son of Ithamar[5], Phineas[4], John[3], Samuel[2], John[1], born at Portland, then Chatham, Conn., September 18, 1873;
married there, November, 1808, Sarah Bailey, born
November 24, 1784, daughter of Jeremiah Bailey, of
Haddam, Conn. Farmer. He inherited and lived
upon the old homestead of his father, grandfather
and great-grandfather, and there died, August 8, 1862.
His wife, Sarah, died October 10, 1863. Children:

  **285**  I George E., b. Sept. 28, 1811; m. Nov. 1,
        1831, Caroline A. Cotton; d. Dec. 25,
        1855.
  **286**  II Henry A., b. Feb. 7, 1813; m. Oct. 12,
        1840, Elizabeth Lay Post; d. Feb. 9,
        1881.
  **287**  III Edwin A., b. Dec. 23, 1814; m. Nov. 5,
        1840, Almira Clark.
    IV Moses F., born Portland, Conn., on the
        old Phineas Pelton homestead, July 24,
        1817. Farmer. Living on the home-
        stead in 1890; unmarried.
    V Martha E., born Oct. 18, 1820; married
        Feb. 5, 1840, John McCleve (d. Oct.
        16, 1867), son of Robert McCleve,
        of Portland, Conn. Children: Ruth,
        Emma, Ella, Henry, William. Resi-
        dence, in 1879, at Portland, Conn.

VI Sarah Jane, born Sept. 19, 1822; unmarried; died May 21, 1847.
VII Clarissa B., born Feb. 17, 1825; died Sept. 30, 1826.

**864.** George E. Pelton[6], first son of Samuel[5], Ithamar[4], Phineas[3], John[3], Samuel[2], John[1], born at Portland, Conn., February 28, 1811; married Middletown, Conn., November 1, 1831, Caroline A. Cotton, daughter of Samuel Cotton, of that place. Silversmith; learned the business at Middletown; worked there about six years, but soon after marriage removed to Portland, Conn., and followed the sea; drowned December 25, 1855. Children:

 I Jane E., born Aug. 5, 1832; married at Portland, Conn., Oct. 21, 1844, Ansel Hurlbut, son of Seymour Hurlbut, of that place. Residence, 1879, 33 Congress avenue, New Haven, Conn. Dealer in provisions. Four children.
 II Henry, born July 4, 1834; died Dec. 4, 1834.
 III Samuel W., born Jan. 18, 1836. Sailor. Died, unmarried, March 24, 1876.
 IV Sarah E., born Feb. 26, 1841; married at Portland, Conn., Aug. 26, 1862, Francis Wheeler (b. Sept. 8, 1837), son of Ahira Wheeler, of Moodus, Conn. Photographer, at West Meriden, Conn. Children: Edith M., b. Sept. 18, 1864; Alfred, b. Sept. 24, 1871.
**866** V Alfred H., b. Feb. 21, 1847; m. April 26, 1871, Mary E. Heustis.
 VI Emma E., born April 22, 1849.
 VII Charles H., born Feb. 21, 1854; died Oct. 15, 1854.

**803. Alfred E. Pelton**, third son of George E.[8], Samuel[7], Ithamar[6], Phineas[4], John[3], Samuel[2], John[1], born at Portland, Conn., Feb. 21, 1847; married Cold Spring, N. Y., April 26, 1871, Mary E. Heustis, daughter of Elijah Heustis, of that place. Farmer, in 1879, at Cold Spring, N. Y. Child:

    1 Carrie A., born Aug. 31, 1872.

**804. Henry A. Pelton**, second son of Samuel[7], Ithamar[6], Phineas[4], John[3], Samuel[2], John[1], born at Portland, Conn., on the Phineas Pelton homestead, February 7, 1813; married at Essex, Conn., by Bishop Vail, October 12, 1840, Eliza Lay Post (born Oct. 5, 1816), daughter of Russell Post and Jemima Pelton Post, daughter of John Pelton[4], 2d, of Essex, Conn. Merchant. Lived at Brooklyn, N. Y.; at Cold Spring, N. Y., and removed, about 1869, to Newfield, N. J., for a milder climate, and there died, February 9, 1881. — *Hartford Post.* Children:

    I ——. No record.
    II Adliza Crosby, born Essex, Conn., June
        17, 1841, daughter of Capt. E. F.
        Crosby, of Barnstable, Mass., and Miss
        Post, sister to Mrs. Pelton, was, after
        the loss of her father, Capt. Crosby, at
        sea, in the spring of 1844, adopted by
        Mr. and Mrs. Pelton. She was mar-
        ried in Brooklyn, N. Y., Feb. 13, 1864,
        to Col. Crawford, of Pennsylvania.
        Children: 1. Ada Clay, born Brooklyn,
        N. Y., Jan. 19, 1865; d. Aug. 5, 1865;
        2. Robert Ward, b. Eddington, Pa.,
        July 13, 1868; 3. Louisa Ada, b. Oct.
        2, 1869; 4. Arthur Pelton, b. in Mary-
        land, Nov. 23, 1871. In 1871 Col.

Crawford brought his family on a visit to Mr. Pelton's, and after some time disappeared.

**304. Edwin A. Pelton[7]**, third son of Samuel[6], Ithamar[5], Phineas[4], John[3], Samuel[2], John[1], born at Portland, Conn., December 23, 1814; married at Middletown, Conn., November 5, 1840, Almira Clark, born in 1816, daughter of Abel Clark, of East Hartford, Conn. Manufacturer and merchant, at Cold Spring, N. Y. He served for two terms, in 1855 and in 1860, in the New York Legislature. Children:

    I Mattie, born Sept. 2, 1841; died Feb. 7, 1862.
    II Jennie A., born at Cold Spring, N. Y., May 31, 1849; married there, June 14, 1870, Monroe L. Hayward (b. Dec. 22, 1840). Lawyer. Son of William J. Hayward, of Willsboro, N. Y. Residence, 1879, at Nebraska City, Neb. Children: Edwin P., b. Nebraska City, Neb., May 29, 1872; Mattie Almira, b. Cold Spring, N. Y., April 29, 1877; William H., b. Nebraska City, April 29, 1877.

**55. Johnson Pelton[4]**, fourth son of John[3], Samuel[2], John[1], born probably in Haddam, Conn., in 1714, as deduced from his tombstone; married March 3, 1748, Keziah Freeman, probably of Chatham, Conn. Farmer. He was left by his father's will a one-quarter interest in the four-hundred-acre tract of land bought of the School Commissioners of Middletown, Conn.; he and his older brother Phineas together having been left a one-half of said tract.

40

To this he, as appears by the Land Records, added other land by purchase. He lived in what is now Portland, Conn., and there died, December 13, 1804, aged 90, as appears from his tombstone. Buried in Chatham burying ground. The house, built by him, and the old homestead of 175 acres are now, in 1890, owned and occupied by his great-grandson, Hosmer Pelton. Children:

   I Hannah, 1, born Jan. 10, 1749, bap. Jan. 15, 1749; died May 28, 1753.

   II Susannah, born Aug. 9, 1750. No other record.

   III Eunice, born Apr. 12, 1753. No other record.

808 IV Johnson, Jr., b. Dec. 3, 1754; m. Feb. 17, 1780, Rachel Penfield; died Feb. 7, 1839.

   V Hannah, 2, born Nov. 7, 1756. No other record.

810 VI Freeman, b. Jan. 2, 1759; m. Nov. 30, 1783, Prudence Russell; d. Jan. 13, 1847.

812 VII Jesse, b. Feb. 8, 1761; m. Sept. 23, 1784, Phœbe Penfield; d. in 1795.

813 VIII Samuel, b. Aug. 7, 1767; m. —— Joanna ——; d. date unknown.

813 IX Seth, b. July 12, 1770; m. May 17, 1792, Abigail Hooker Brace; d. Apr. 19, 1855.


**807. Johnson Pelton, Jr.,** first son of Johnson⁴, John³, Samuel², John¹, born at Chatham, Conn. (now Portland), December 3, 1754; married there, February 17, 1780, Rachel Penfield (b. 1757). Farmer. About 1778 he removed to Ashfield, Franklin Co., Mass., and bought land. He began to clear it, carrying his grain on horseback thirty miles to mill. After some

years he returned to his father's homestead and there
lived to the time of his death, February 7, 1839 (Ch.
Rec.).    He was a large, strong man, very genial and
cheerful, and fond of good horses, good company and
a good story.    Rachel, his wife, by Church Record,
died March 6; by her tombstone, "March 9, 1843,
aged 86 years."   Children:

     I Lucy, born Dec. 7, 1780.    Lived on the
        homestead unmarried, and there died,
        June 2, 1857.

     II Chauncey, born Jan. 30, 1783.    A large,
        strong man; was a sea captain.    On his
        last voyage to Savannah, Ga., he was
        taken with yellow fever and died at sea,
        Aug. 29, 1808.

     III Polly, born May 3. 1785; married Daniel
        Shepard, of Portland, Conn.

     IV Ruth, born Nov. 17, 1787; married Oct.
        14, 1807, David Ames, of Portland,
        Conn.

     V Julia, born Feb. 17, 1790; died unmarried,
        Sept. 3, 1813 (Ch. Rec.).

     VI Fanny, born Mar. 2, 1792; unmarried.

**308** VII Sanford, b. July 1, 1794; m. Jan. 22, 1818,
        Phœbe Hurlburt; d. Jan. 11, 1870.

**308. Sanford Pelton**[6], second son of Johnson[5],
Johnson[4], John[3], Samuel[2], John[1], born at Portland,
Conn., July 1, 1794; married there, January 22, 1818,
Phœbe Hurlburt, daughter of Jesse Hurlburt of that
place.    Farmer.    He occupied the Johnson Pelton
homestead and had his father's jovial spirit.    Died
January 11, 1870.    Children:

     I Almira, born about 1819; married May 3,
        1838 (Town Rec.), Portland, Conn.,
        Franklin Payne.

310　II Chauncey, b. Mar. 31, 1821; m. Dec. 10, 1846, Maria C. Clark.

310　III Hosmer, b. Aug. 6, 1828; m. Dec. 1, 1870, Ida E. Hurlburt.

**309. Chauncey Pelton**[7], first son of Sanford[6], Johnson[5], Johnson[4], John[3], Samuel[2], John[1], born at Portland, Conn., March 31, 1821; married at Plainfield, Mich., Dec. 10, 1846, Maria C. Clark, daughter of James Clark, of that place. Residence, in 1876, at No. 83 Fountain street, Grand Rapids, Mich. Manufacturer of lumber and shingles at Cedar Springs, Kent Co., Mich. Children:

I Lucy Almira, born Oct. 4, 1854; died Nov. 25, 1855.

II Tenella Viola, born Feb. 24, 1858.

**308. Hosmer Pelton**[7], second son of Sanford[6], Johnson[5], Johnson[4], John[3], Samuel[2], John[1], born at Portland, Conn., August 6, 1828; married there, December 1, 1870, Ida E. Hurlburt, daughter of Alanson Hurlburt, of that place. Farmer. Living, in 1890, on the homestead of five generations. Children:

I Arthur H., born March 25, 1872; died July 1, 1873.

II H. Floyd, born May 28, 1875.

**307. Freeman Pelton**[5], second son of Johnson[4], John[3], Samuel[2], John[1], born at Portland, Conn., January 2, 1759; married November 30, 1783, Prudence Russell. Farmer. Removed to Lyme, N. H., about 1790, thence to Cavendish and to Plymouth, Windsor Co., Vt., where he died, January 13, 1847. Children, born at Cavendish, Vt.:

I Betsey E., born March 16, 1785; married
Joel, son of Timothy Davis, of that
place; lived and died at Haverhill, N.
H.  One child, Alanson Davis.

II Hannah, born May 16, 1787; lived at
Plymouth, Vt., and died unmarried,
April 4, 1862.

**311** III Martin, b. July 31, 1789; m. Jan., 1828,
Rebecca Kendrick; d. Nov. 16, 1866.

IV Persis, born March 25, 1792; married in
1814, Josiah Pelton, son of Joseph
Pelton, of Lyme, N. H.  Lived and
died at Lyme, N. H.

**311**   V Seymour, b. May 11, 1795; m. March 25,
1818, Melinda Burt; d. Sept. 23, 1873.


**310. Martin Pelton⁶**, first son of Freeman⁵,
Johnson⁴, John³, Samuel², John¹, born at Cavendish,
Vt., July 31, 1789; married January ——, 1828, Rebecca
Kendrick, daughter of Nathaniel Kendrick, of Hanover, N. H.  Lived at Plymouth, Vt.  In his older
days he was defrauded of his property, and lived and
died with Mr. Alanson Bates, who had lived with him
in his youth.  Mr. Pelton died November 16, 1866.
No children.


**310. Seymour Pelton⁶**, second son of Freeman⁵,
Johnson⁴, John³, Samuel², John¹, born at Cavendish,
Vt., May 11, 1795; married at Plymouth, Vt., March
25, 1818, Melinda Burt, daughter of David Burt, of
that place.  Lived at Cavendish and Plymouth, Vt.,
and thence removed to Bethany, Genesee Co., N. Y.,
where he lived, and there died, September 23, 1873.
Shoemaker and farmer.  Mrs. Melinda Pelton died
April 8, 1872.  Children:

    I Prudence, born Feb. 11, 1819; died March
       7, 1819.
    II Abigail, born May 13, 1820; married June
       30, 1853, David S. Russell, of Caven-
       dish, Vt.; lived there in 1878. No
       children. Husband, David S., died
       June 24, 1877.
812 III Albin, b. June 17, 1822; m. Sept. 1, 1870,
       M. Fidelia Rogers.
    IV Gratia Ann, born Dec. 5, 1823; died un-
       married, Dec. 28, 1869.

**811. Albin Pelton**, only son of Seymour, Freeman, Johnson, John, Samuel, John, born at Plymouth, Vt., June 17, 1822; married at Bethany, N.
Y., September 1, 1870, M. Fidelia Rogers, daughter
of Ezekiel Rogers, of Lyme, Conn. Farmer. Lived,
in 1878, at Bethany, N. Y. Children:
    I Infant, born and died May 17, 1872.
    II Infant, born and died Oct. 18, 1873.
    III Mary M., born Aug. 10, 1876.

**807. Jesse Pelton**, third son of Johnson, John,
Samuel, John, born at Chatham, Conn., February 8,
1761; married there, September 23, 1784, Phœbe
Penfield, of that place. Lived at Chatham, and also
owned land in Hartford, Conn., and there died, in
1795, letters of administration having been granted
his widow, April 20, 1795. His widow married (2),
September 10, 1818, Esquire James Bill. Child:
    I Frances, born about 1786; fate unknown.

**807. Samuel Pelton**, fourth son of Johnson,
John, Samuel, John, born Chatham, Conn., August
7, 1767; married —— ——, Joanna ——. Lived at

Hartford, Conn., and there died previous to 1822. A search through the Family and other Town Records of Hartford shows them to be in such an unsatisfactory state that little can be learned from them. After her husband's death the widow and the family, save one married daughter, removed to New York city, about 1829 or 1830, her name appearing in the city directory, from 1830 to 1854, as the proprietor of a store of fancy goods. Children:

    I Joanna; no further record; died in New York probably.

    II Emily, born ————; married a man who was a baker and confectioner, and removed to Providence, R. I.

**313** III Frederic S., b. about 1811; m., date and name of wife unknown; died Sept. 3, 1874.

**312. Frederic S. Pelton⁵**, born about 1811; date of marriage and name of wife unknown. Merchant tailor. He removed from Hartford, Conn., with his mother and sister Joanna, to New York city, about 1829 or 1830, where his name and place of business appears in the city directory from 1830 to 1854 as in or near Hudson street, New York. He gave up his store in 1864 and went to a Southern State about 1865 as a cutter; returning north to Bridgeport, Conn., in the same occupation, about 1870 to 1872, and there died, September 3, 1874, aged 63 years. His wife had died previously, date unknown.

**307. Seth Pelton⁵**, fifth son of Johnson⁴, John³, Samuel², John¹, born at Chatham, Conn., July 12, 1770; married at West Hartford, Conn., May 17, 1792, Abigail Hooker Brace (d. Dec. 28, 1775), daughter of Henry Brace, of that place. Farmer.

Lived at Chester, Mass., from 1792 to 1804, and thence removed to the Brace neighborhood in Litchfield, Herkimer Co., N. Y., in 1804.   He was a sailor in his younger days.   He died in Litchfield, N. Y., April 19, 1855.   Mrs. Pelton died April 24, 1849. Children:

  I Cynthia, born in Chester, Mass., May 25, 1793; married at Litchfield, N. Y., Josiah Marshall.   Lived in the township of Litchfield; died in Genesee Co., N. Y.   Children, thirteen, widely scattered.

  II Sylvia, born May 25, 1793; married Nathan Beardsley.   Lived in Litchfield, Herkimer Co., N. Y.   Children, fourteen, living mostly in Michigan, some in Ionia and others near Detroit, Mich.

815 III Brace, b. Sept. 23, 1795; m. Nov. 10, 1820, Lydia Harrington; d. Sept. 23, 1853.

818 IV Jesse, b. Apr. 18, 1798; m. Nov. 17, 1825, Alice Harrington; d. Sept. 12, 1878.

  V Susannah (went by the name of Susan), born at Hartford, Conn, Jan. 30, 1802; married at Batavia, N. Y., Mar. 18, 1825, Nathaniel Thompson Fish, son of Chas. Fish, of Augusta Center, Oneida Co., N. Y.   Lived at Batavia, N. Y.; removed to Grand Rapids, Mich.; died at Mohawk, Herkimer Co., N. Y., May 17, 1870.   Children, three.

  VI Abigail, born Apr. 11, 1804; married Benjamin Harrington, of Bridgewater, N. Y. Died in Ilion, N. Y., Nov. 19, 1872. Children, four.

VII  Louvina, born Oct. 20, 1806; married
       George Peck.   Lived, in 1878, at
       Waukegan, Ill.  Children, three.  Died
       Dec. 1, 1884.
**318** VIII Johnson, b. Nov. 8, 1808; m. Apr. 24,
       1831, Mary Ann Harrington.  Died
       May 23, 1879.
**319**  IX  Edmund H., b. Oct. 15, 1810; m. Nov. 25,
       1833, Lucretia E. Hodges; d. Mar. 22,
       1874.

**312. Brace Pelton**[6], first son of Seth[5], Johnson[4],
John[3], Samuel[2], John[1], born at Chester, Mass., September 23, 1795; married at Winfield, Herkimer Co.,
N. Y., November 10, 1820, Lydia Harrington (b.
Canterbury, Conn., April 16, 1799), daughter of
Heber Harrington, of Bridgewater, Oneida Co., N. Y.,
formerly of Canterbury, Conn.  Cooper and farmer.
Died on his father's homestead in Litchfield, Herkimer Co., N. Y., September 23, 1853 (another record
gives the date Sept. 3, 1853).  Mrs. Pelton still living
in 1890.  Children:
**313**    I  { Justus J., b. May 22 (20), 1822; m. Sept.
              23, 1843, Ruth Hayward.
          II { Justin Brace, 1, born Ilion, N. Y., May
              22 (20), 1822; died Dec. 29, 1830.
**317**  III  Justin Brace, 2, b. Sept. 12, 1837; m. Oct.
              24, 1861, Julia E. Warren.

**313. Justus J. Pelton**[6], first son of Brace[6], Seth[5],
Johnson[4], John[3], Samuel[2], John[1]. born at Ilion, N. Y.,
May 22, 1822; married at Smyrna, Chenango Co.,
N. Y., September 23, 1843, Ruth Hayward (b. Madi-
son, N. Y., Sept. 23, 1840), daughter of Benjamin
Hayward of that place.  Farmer.  In 1878 lived at
Ilion, N. Y.  Children:
   41

**316**   I Edgar J., b. Aug. 6, 1845; m. (1) Sept.
23, 1868, Mary J. Lewis; (2) Sept. 21,
1874, Mary Ann Haggerty; (3) Aug.
21, 1882, Ellen M. Casteel.

II Josephine A., born in Litchfield township,
Herkimer Co., N. Y., Jan. 16, 1848; mar-
ried (1) in Winfield, Herkimer Co., Jan.
1, 1867, Joseph Vickerman; one daugh-
ter, Nellie; (2) Lee Gaynor, in Utica,
N. Y., and in 1890 lived in Springfield,
Ohio.   Nellie Vickerman, above, born
June 24, 1868, in Litchfield, N. Y.,
married Mr. ―― Johnson.   Their son,
Raymond, born April 26, 1890, makes
the fifth of five generations now living,
Mrs. Lydia Harrington Pelton, relict of
Brace[5] Pelton, being the oldest.


**315. Edgar J. Pelton**[7], only son of Justus J.[6],
Brace[5], Seth[4], Johnson[3], John[3], Samuel[2], John[1], born
in the township of Winfield, Herkimer Co., N. Y.,
August 6, 1845; married (1) in the town of St.
Johnsville, N. Y., September 23, 1868, Mary J.
Lewis, born in Litchfield, N. Y., August 4, 1850, who
died; (2) in the township of Columbia, Herkimer
Co., N. Y., September 21, 1874, Mary Ann Haggerty,
born Litchfield, N. Y., in 1856, separated; (3) August
21, 1882, Ellen M. Casteel, born Mount Vernon,
Knox Co., O., May 24, 1855.   Mr. Pelton lived in
the State of New York down to 1875.   Since then
he has been a traveler for Amos Whiteley & Co., of
Springfield, O., manufacturers of harvesting machinery.   In the course of his business he has been over
most of the middle portion of the continent, has seen
life in most of its forms, can give a variety of ex-

periences, as to food and bills of fare, that will match almost any thing in Asia or Africa, excepting human flesh. He has been extremely well blessed with grandparents, he being the fifth in a line of five living generations, and having at one time ten living grandparents, all of whom he knew and remembers, excepting his grandmother, Whitford, who was of the Sweet family, who were the famous natural bonesetters of Connecticut in years agone, a trait that has followed down the line to Mr. Pelton, who is able to set bones by instinct and not by education. His place of business, in 1890, is still at Springfield, Ohio, with his family residence at Morrow, Warren Co., Ohio.  Children (by first wife):

    I Lydia May, born March 14, 1870, in Litchfield, Herkimer Co., N. Y.

By second wife:

    II Clarence I., born Litchfield, N. Y., Aug. 11, 1875; living with his mother at Cedarville, Herkimer Co., N. Y., in 1891.

**215. Justin Brace Pelton**[7], third son of Brace[6], Seth[5], Johnson[4], John[3], Samuel[2], John[1], born at Litchfield, Herkimer Co., N. Y., September 12, 1837; married there, October 24, 1861, Julia E. Warren, daughter of Julius C. Warren, of that place. Attended and taught school until he was of age, and then removed to Ilion, N. Y., where he entered the hardware business, and still, in 1878, continued therein.  Children:

    I Gilbert B., born March 11, 1864.

    II Lettie Mae, born Jan. 30, 1870.

    III Sarah Linette, born May 5, 1873.

    IV Jessie Warren, born Aug. 31, 1875.

**315. Jesse Pelton⁶**, second son of Seth⁵, Johnson⁴, John³, Samuel², John¹, born at Chester, Mass., April 18, 1798: married at Winfield, Herkimer Co., N. Y., November 7, 1825, Alice Harrington, born Canterbury, Conn., November 7, 1804, daughter of Heber Harrington and Hannah, of that place. Farmer.   Living, in 1878, at Bridgewater, Oneida Co., N. Y.   Died there, at the house of his son-in-law, Cornelius Conklin, after thirteen years of illness and suffering, September 12, 1878.   Mrs. Pelton still living, in 1890.   Children:

**318**    I Giles W., b. Aug. 13, 1826; m. Feb. 29, 1848, Sarah L. Goodier.

   II Abigail H., born Dec. 21, 1836; married Sept. 17, 1861, Cornelius Conklin. Lived, in 1878, at Bridgewater, Oneida Co., N. Y.

**318. Giles W. Pelton⁷**, only son of Jesse⁶, Seth⁵, Johnson⁴, John³, Samuel², John¹, born at Litchfield, Herkimer Co., N. Y., August 13, 1826; married there, February 29, 1848, Sarah L. Goodier, daughter of Aaron Goodier, of Litchfield, N. Y.   Farmer.   Living, in 1878, at New Hartford, Oneida Co., N. Y. Children:

   I Ammi G., born Oct. 21, 1850, at Richfield, Otsego Co., N. Y.   In 1878 a farmer, unmarried, living at Richfield, N. Y.

   II Attie L., born Nov. 10, 1852.

**313. Johnson Pelton⁶**, third son of Seth⁵, Johnson⁴, John³, Samuel², John¹. born at Litchfield, Herkimer Co., N. Y., November 8, 1808; married at Winfield, N. Y., Sunday, April 24, 1831, Mary Ann Harrington, daughter of Heber and Hannah (Whit-

ford) Harrington, formerly of Canterbury, Conn.*
Wheelwright. Lived, in 1878, at Cedarville, Herkimer Co., N. Y., where, May 23, 1879, in a fit of mental depression, caused by poor health, he committed suicide by shooting himself. He was a good citizen and highly respected. Mrs. Pelton still living in 1890. Children:

    I Mahala H., born Wednesday, Nov. 9, 1836; married Thursday, Nov. 4, 1852. George B. Tillson. Children: Carrie A., Anna M., Odie Johnson and George M. A widow in 1878, living in Utica, N. Y.

    II Miles J., born Sunday, April 23, 1840; died April 11, 1841.

    III Orlo A., born on Monday, April 1, 1850. Farmer, unmarried. Living, in 1878, at Cedarville, Herkimer Co., N. Y.

Note.— This branch of the family is generally of light complexion.


**313. Edmund E. Pelton**[6], fourth son of Seth[5], Johnson[4], John[3], Samuel[2], John[1], born at Litchfield, Herkimer Co., N. Y., October 15, 1810; married at Winfield, N. Y., November 25, 1833, Lucretia C. Hodges, daughter of Samuel Hodges of that place. Died at Ilion, N. Y., March 22, 1874. Occupation, mechanics and farming. Children:

    I Abbie L., born at Winfield, N. Y., May 23, 1836; married June 23, 1858, William J. Grimes. One child. In 1878 lived at Ilion, N. Y.

---

* Who was born there, son of David and Dorcas Harrington; his wife Hannah, daughter of David and Lydia Whitford, was born in W. Greenwich, R. I., Nov. 14, 1774. David Whitford was born W. Greenwich, R. I. Oct. 31, 1751. Lydia (Sweet) Whitford was born there, July 11, 1756.

329     II Seth C., b. June 3, 1839; m. June 25, 1862,
            Emma H. Bryant.
330     III J. Randolph, b. Oct. 17, 1845; m. May
            24, 1870, Florence M. Caswell.
        IV Lydia B., born March 20, 1848; married
            Nov. 19, 1868, S. W. Skinner, of Ilion,
            N. Y., where they lived in 1878.   Four
            children, three then living.


**329. Seth C. Pelton[7]**, first son of Edmund H.[6],
Seth[5], Johnson[4], John[3], Samuel[2], John[1], born at Winfield, Herkimer Co., N. Y., June 3, 1839; married at
Ilion, N. Y., June 25, 1862, Emma H. Bryant.  Salesman.  Residence, in 1878, at Utica, N. Y.  Child:
        I Minnie L., born at Utica, N. Y., April
            15, 1867.


**330. John Randolph Pelton[7]**, second son of
Edmund H.[6], Seth[5], Johnson[4], John[3], Samuel[2], John[1],
born at Winfield, Herkimer Co., N. Y., October 17,
1845; married at Ilion, N. Y., May 24, 1870, Florence
M. Caswell, daughter of Edwin C. Caswell, of that
place.  Mechanic.  Residence, in 1878, at Ilion,
N. Y.  Children:
        I Francis Edmund, born Oct. 17, 1875.
        II Edwin Caswell, born April 7, 1882.


**55. Josiah Pelton[4]**, fifth son of John[3], Samuel[2],
John[1], born probably in Haddam, Conn., in 1714 (as
deduced from his tombstone); married at Chatham,
Conn., about 1750, Hannah Churchill (b. 1728, bapt.
April 11, 1731), daughter of John and Bethia (Stocking) Churchill, of that place.  Farmer.  They lived
in that part of Chatham since set off as the township
of Portland, and there died —Josiah, February 2, 1792.

aged 78 (tombstone), and his wife Hannah June 12, 1810, aged 82. His farm in 1887 was occupied by his grandson, Mr. Ralph Pelton. Lived a short time in Medfield, Mass. On May 18, 1747, he sold land in Middletown, Conn., to Phineas Pelton, his brother (Middletown Records). Children, born in Portland, their exact order unknown:

> I Jemima, born about 1751; bapt. in the Cong. church at Portland, Conn., Sept., 1751; died May 14, 1774.
>
> II Josiah, born about 1753; bapt. Jan. 21, 1753; died young.
>
> III Prudence, born in 1755, baptized April 9, 1755; married Nov., 1778, her cousin, Joseph Pelton, son of John Pelton*, 2d, of Essex (Saybrook), Conn. Lived at Lyme, N. H., and there died, May 2, 1822. See p. 198.
>
> IV Unknown, born about 1757; died young.
>
> 322    V John, b. March 9, 1759; m. about 1784, Martha Pelton; d. Aug. 28, 1848.
>
> VI Hannah, born in 1760; m. (1) ———, Capt. Clark, who was lost at sea; one child, Amy; (2) about 1797, Capt. Charles Treat. Lived at Glastenbury, Conn.; died May 20, 1799, aged 39; one child, Elisha.
>
> 328 VII Moses, b. March 4, 1762; m. May 14, 1791, Mindwell Horsford; d. Feb. 5, 1842.
>
> VIII Phœbe, born July 4, 1764; married (1) Aug. 11, 1782, Capt. Stephen Hurlbut, who died at sea; children, Allen, Clarissa, Stephen, Harriet; (2) about 1800, Capt. Chas. Treat, second hus-

band of her sister Hannah.   Lived with
Capt. Treat at Glastenbury, Conn.;
died at East Windsor, Conn., Jan. 8,
1844, aged 80 years.

831   IX Marshall, b. Oct. 10, 1768; m. Jan. 3,
1793, Betsey Sage; died June 4, 1852.

840   X Josiah, Jr., b. March 5, 1772; m. Dec. 15,
1793, Lucy Shephard; d. July 9, 1834.


820. John Pelton[5], second son of Josiah[4], John[3],
Samuel[2], John[1], born at Portland, Conn., March 9,
1759; married at Essex, Conn., about 1782, Martha
Pelton, daughter of John[4] Pelton, 2d, of Essex, Conn.
Ship carpenter and farmer.   He lived at Portland,
Conn., removing to Lyme, N. H., before 1791; thence,
about 1818, to Cayuga Co., N. Y., and thence to
Conesus, Livingston Co., N. Y.   He died at the
house of his daughter, Mrs. Julia Whitney, at Springwater, Livingston Co., N. Y., August 28, 1848.   His
wife, Martha, also died there, February 16, 1846.
Children, all but the first two born in Lyme, N. H.,
the exact order of their birth unknown:

 I Martha, born at Portland, Conn., Aug. 11,
1783; married about 1801 or 1802, in
Lyme, N. H., by Rev. Mr. Conant, to
James Morrison (b. Londonderry, N.
H., Mar. 22, 1781), bridge builder,
who died Oct. 15, 1841, at Fairlee, Vt.,
where they had gone in 1804, and were
then living.   Mrs. M. died at Fairlee,
Vt., July 14, 1870.   Her descendants
live in New Hampshire, one of whom
is Judge George W. Morrison.   Ten
children.

 II Josiah, born about 1785; died about 1787.

III Hannah, born March 21, 1789; married
   at Fairlee, Vt., April 6, 1812, Ira Parker,
   son of Deacon Amos Parker, of Sharon,
   Vt. Twelve children. She lived in
   Vermont until her children were born,
   and then removed to Long Meadow,
   Mass., and there died, June 18, 1850.
   Mrs. Geo. Ferre, daughter, lived in
   1880, at 86 Bliss street, Springfield,
   Mass.; another daughter, Mrs. Martha
   Haskins, then lived at No. 11 Douglass
   street, Brooklyn, N. Y.

IV Ruth, born about 1791; married (1) Salmon Bigsbee (or Bixby), at Lyme, N. H.,
   who was killed by the fall of a tree,
   leaving two sons; (2) at Madrid, St.
   Lawrence Co., N. Y., Barnabas Ames.

V Betsey, born about 1792; married Jacob
   De Groff, at Aurelius, Cayuga Co.,
   N. Y., where she lived, and there died,
   Aug. 15, 1814. Two children, who
   died before their mother.

VI Phila, born Dec. 3, 1794; married, Cayuga
   Co., N. Y., Joshua Jones, of Dutchess
   Co., N. Y. (b. Oct. 23, 1792; d. Jan. 10,
   1858), son of Gershom Jones. Lived
   at Springwater, Livingston Co., N. Y.,
   and there died, Sept. 26, 1853. Eleven
   children.

VII Joanna, born Aug. 31, 1797; married at
   Aurelius, N. Y., Dudley Chapman (b.
   1796; d. North Bristol, O., Mar. 22,
   1876); died at West Farmington,
   Trumbull Co., O., Aug. 3, 1872. Eight
   children.

42

**322** VIII Josiah Johnson, b. June 25, 1798; m.
March 29, 1818, Eunice Geer.

**326** IX John, Jr., b. Jan. 16, 1800; m. in 1828,
Susan Gilman; d. Jan., 1857.

X Julia, born Jan. 10, 1804; married in the
fall of 1822, in Livingston Co., N. Y.,
Ezra Whitney (who died at Pavilion,
Kalamazoo Co., Mich., April 26, 1851).
Lived at Livonia, N. Y., down to 1848,
and then removed to Spring Arbor,
Jackson Co., Mich., and there died,
June 25, 1849, leaving six children.

NOTE. — Mr. John Pelton was tall and slender,
about six feet high, complexion light and eyes blue,
disposition amiable and of excellent character. His
wife, Martha, was thick-set, of medium height, and a
fine-looking brunette. She was a member of the
Presbyterian church. Her daughters were brunettes
and handsome women.


**322. Josiah Johnson Pelton**, second son of
John⁶, Josiah⁵, John⁴, Samuel³, John¹, born Lyme,
N. H., June 25, 1798; married at Aurelius, Cayuga
Co., N. Y., March 29, 1818, Eunice Geer, daughter
of Ezra Geer, of Delaware. Farmer. Removed to
Pennsylvania about 1837, and thence to Ohio.
Residence, in 1879, at Mecca, Trumbull Co., O.
Mrs. Eunice (Geer) Pelton died October 31, 1878.
Children:

**323** I Isaiah F., b. Feb. 15, 1820; m. Jan. 1,
1843, Caroline Ellsworth.

**325** II Christopher C., b. May 20, 1822; m. April
7, 1844, Matilda Randall.

**324. Isaiah F. Pelton**, first son of Josiah Johnson[6], John[5], Josiah[4], John[3], Samuel[2], John[1], born in Cayuga Co., N. Y., February 15, 1820; married January 1, 1843, at Albion, Erie Co., Pa., Caroline Ellsworth (b. July 14, 1823), daughter of Stephen Ellsworth, formerly of Scipio, Cayuga Co., N. Y. Farmer. Lived, in 1876, at Albion, Erie Co., Pa. Children:

> 1 Mary E., born Nov. 13, 1843; married July 4, 1866, W. A. Pratt. Children, 1876, Carrie M., b. Sept. 20, 1868; Gertrude M., b. Jan. 16, 1870.

325 > II James G., b. Jan. 27, 1848; m. Dec. 19, 1872, Ella E. Devore.

> III Hugh M., born April 26, 1852; died May 30, 1874.

**325. James G. Pelton**, first son of Isaiah F.[7], Josiah Johnson[6], John[5], Josiah[4], John[3], Samuel[2], John[1], born at Albion, Erie Co., Pa., January 27, 1848; married December 19, 1872, Ella E. Devore. Child, in 1876:

> I Alice M., born Mar. 20, 1876.

**324. Christopher C. Pelton**, second son of Josiah Johnson[6], John[5], Josiah[4], John[3], Samuel[2], John[1], born in Cayuga Co., N. Y., May 20, 1822; married in Erie Co., Pa., April 7, 1844, Matilda Randall, daughter of William Randall, of that county. Farmer and mason. Lived, in 1876, at Keepville, Erie Co., Pa. Children:

> 1 Sabra E., born Oct. 15, 1845, at Spring, Crawford Co., Pa.; married Aug. 31, 1863, Lloyd Luce, of Enterprise, Pa., where they lived in 1878. Children: Alta M., b. Dec. 11, 1868, and Birdie, b. Feb. 9, 1872.

336    II Josiah Johnson, b. Aug. 28, 1848; m. Oct.
          4, 1874, Eunice Wickwire.
      III Mary Ida, born Aug. 26, 1851; married
          Dec. 18, 1867, Matthew Groff, of Keep-
          ville, Erie Co., Pa.   One child, Chris-
          topher, b. Oct. 2, 1868.   Residence, in
          1878, at Meadville, Pa.
      VI Eunice A., born Aug. 29, 1860.


   335.  Josiah Johnson Pelton⁸, only son of Christopher C.⁷, Josiah Johnson⁶, John⁵, Josiah⁴, John³, Samuel², John¹, born at Keepville, Erie Co., Pa., August 28,
1848; married there, October 4, 1874, Eunice Wickwire, daughter of H. H. Wickwire, of that place.
Blacksmith.   Residence, 1878, at Foxburg, Clarion
Co., Pa.   Child, in 1876:
      I Etta, born Nov. 8, 1876.


   336.  John Pelton⁶, Jr., third son of John⁵,
Josiah⁴, John³, Samuel², John¹, born at Lyme, N. H.,
January 16, 1880; removed to Cayuga Co. about
1818; married in 1828 in Livingston Co., N. Y.,
Susannah Gilman (b. Sparta, N. Y., 1814), daughter
of Michael Gilman, of that county.   Removed in
1834 or 1835 to Michigan.   Lived in Stockbridge,
Ingham Co., and afterward in Bradley, Allegan Co.,
Mich., and there died in January, 1857.   Farmer.
Children (exact order of birth unknown):
337    I George W., b. March 4, 1832; m. June 23,
          1857, M. J. McQuade.
      II Sarah, born ——; married Myron Briggs.
          Lived, in 1879, in Sydney, Shelby Co.,
          O.   No report.
      III Joanna, died young.   No record.

IV Martha, born ——, at Stockbridge, Ingham Co., Mich.; married (1) Amos
Sharp; children two: (2) ——? Lived
in Allegan Co., Mich., and there died,
date unknown.

327 V Henry Johnson, b. April 10, 1842; m.
Oct. 29, 1870, Julia Davis.

VI Mary, born at Eaton Rapids, Mich., Jan.
22, 1846; married at Middleville, Dec.
30, 1864, William C. Williams (b. 1838),
son of John H. Williams, of Lorain Co.,
O. Farmer. In 1880 she lived at
Oregon City, Ore. Children: Horace,
Frederic and Laura.

**325. George W. Pelton**, first son of John⁶, Jr.,
John⁵, Josiah⁴, John³, Samuel², John¹, born at Mount
Morris, Livingston Co., N. Y., March 4, 1832; mar-
ried at Attica, Fountain Co., Ind., June 23, 1857,
Miss M. J. McQuade (b. 1833), daughter of John
McQuade, of County Armagh, Ireland. Farmer and
dealer in agricultural implements. Lived, in 1879,
at Fairhaven, St. Clair Co., Mich. Children:

I Anna, born May 18, 1858; died May 21,
1872.
II George G., born Aug. 29, 1859.
III Lillian C., born April 21, 1861; married
Feb. 25, 1879; no further record.
IV Minnie, born 1862; died June 3, 1872.
V John, born 1868; died June 7, 1872.

**326. Henry Johnson Pelton**, second son of
John⁶, Jr., John⁵, Josiah⁴, John³, Samuel², John¹, born
at Stockbridge, Ingham Co., Mich., April 10, 1842;

married at Eaton Rapids, Eaton Co., Mich., October
29, 1870, Julia Davis, daughter of Jonas S. Davis, of
Springport, Jackson Co., Mich.  Farmer.  Living,
in 1879, at Wheeler, Gratiot Co., Mich.  Children:

>I Edith, born at Springport, Mich., July 26,
>1871.
>II Benjamin, born in Saginaw Co., Mich.,
>April 14, 1874.

880. **Moses Pelton⁵**, third son of Josiah⁴, John³,
Samuel², John¹, born at Chatham, now Portland,
Conn., March 4, 1762; married at Marlborough,
Conn., May 14, 1791, Mindwell Horsford, daughter
of Daniel Horsford, of that place.  Sea captain in
his early life, and afterward a farmer.  He traded
with the West India islands and South American
ports, and made as many as twenty-two voyages to
Paramaribo, at the mouth of the River Surinam, to
Georgetown, at the mouth of the Demarara, and to
other ports on the continent of South America.  He
and his brother, Josiah, owned a vessel taken and
confiscated by the Spaniards during the war for
Mexican independence.  In 1820, he, with his family,
removed to Otisco, Onondaga Co., N. Y., where he
bought a farm, on which he lived and where he died,
February 5, 1842.  He was fair in complexion, with
clear, dark eyes and a Roman nose, thick-set and very
erect.  Children (all born at Marlboro, Conn.):

>1 Susannah, born March 30, 1793; married
>there, Feb. 21, 1814, Dr. Daniel Smith,
>of that place; removed to Beloit, Wis.,
>and there died, Jan. 31, 1871.  Chil-
>dren, five that grew up, of whom E. R.
>King, of Beloit, married a daughter.

**329**  II Elisha, b. April 26, 1795; m. March 18,
1824, Miss Betsey Ruth Gaylord; d.
Oct. 28, 1873.

**330**  III Frederic Hosford, b. Jan. 17, 1797; m.
Oct. 26, 1827, Eliza Davis.

IV David Miller Pelton, born Dec. 7, 1800;
removed to Otisco, N. Y., with his
father and family, thence to Turtle,
Rock Co., Wis. In 1878 he lived at
Beloit, Wis. He was not married, five
feet ten inches in height, hair and eyes
dark.

**328. Elisha Pelton[6]**, first son of Moses[5], Josiah[4],
John[3], Samuel[2], John[1], born at Marlboro, Conn., April
26, 1795; married at Otisco, N. Y., March 18, 1824,
Miss Betsey Ruth Gaylord, daughter of Lemon Gaylord, of that place. Removed, in 1820, with his father
and his family, to Otisco, Onondaga Co., N. Y., and
thence, in 1851, to Beloit, Wis., where he died, October 28, 1873. Farmer. Height, 5 ft. 8 in.; weight,
170 lbs. Mrs. Pelton died at Beloit, December 23,
1872. One child.

**329. Charles C. Pelton[7]**, only child of Elisha[6],
Moses[5], Josiah[4], John[3], Samuel[2], John[1], born in Onon-
daga Co., N. Y., May 25, 1825; married (1) there,
January 28, 1847, Cynthia Patterson, daughter of
James Patterson, of Otisco, N. Y., who died, Beloit,
Wis., January 29, 1857, leaving no children; (2) at
Rockton, Ill., February 23, 1858, Lydia A. Buffum,
daughter of Richard C. Buffum, of Colden, Erie Co.,
N. Y. Dentist. In 1878, living in Beloit, Wis., to
which town he removed in 1852. Height, 5 ft. 8 in.;
weight, 160 lbs. Children:

    I Ralph B., born June 25, 1861. Height,
      5 ft. 10 in.
    II Carrie Melinda, born Oct. 21, 1865.
    III Nellie Miranda, born Mar. 16, 1869.

**228. Frederic Hosford Pelton[6]**, second son of
Moses[5], Josiah[4], John[3], Samuel[2], John[1], born at Glastenbury or Marlboro, Conn., January 17, 1797; married (1) at Otisco, N. Y., October 26, 1827, Eliza
Davis, daughter of Elisha Davis, of Preble, N. Y.,
who died at Otisco, May 17, 1854, aged 54 years and
6 months; (2) in Preble, N. Y., March 5, 1856,
Miranda (Aldrich) Anderson, daughter of Asa Aldrich, of that place, and widow of J. M. Anderson.
Removed with his father from Connecticut to Otisco,
N. Y., in 1820, thence, in 1871, to Savannah, Wayne
Co., N. Y. Farmer. Resided, in 1878, at Savannah,
N. Y. Height, medium. Child:

**229. George Pelton[7]**, only child of Frederic H.[6],
Moses[5], Josiah[4], John[3], Samuel[2], John[1], born at Otisco,
Onondaga Co., N. Y., November 27, 1828; married
there, January 13, 1853, Fanny Bailey, daughter of
Solomon Bailey, of that place. Farmer. Living, in
1878, at Preble, Cortland Co., N. Y. Children:
    I Frank L., born at Otisco, N. Y., July 30,
      1854.
    II Florence E., born at Beloit, Wis., July 4,
      1856.
    III F. Estell, born at Otisco, N. Y., July 24,
      1860.

**230. Marshall Pelton[5]**, fourth son of Josiah[4],
John[3], Samuel[2], John[1], born at Chatham (now Portland), Conn., October 10, 1768; married at Portland,

Conn., January 3, 1793. Betsey Sage, daughter of Lemuel Sage, of Middletown, Conn. Farmer. Lived upon the Josiah Pelton homestead in Portland, and there died, June 4, 1852. Mrs. Pelton died September 1, 1855, aged 84 years. Children:

 I Betsey, born Aug. 15, 1793, at Portland, Conn.; married there, Feb. 12, 1815, Abram Phelps, of Marlboro, Conn. Lived in North Glastenbury, Conn., and there died, May 14, 1838. Children: Harriet, Phila, Francis, Ellen, Cynthia and Elizabeth.

 II Sally Maria, born July 31, 1795; married Sept. 20, 1821, George Stocking, of Middletown, Conn. Lived at Middletown, and there died, Aug. 5, 1878. Five children: Sarah, George, Elisha, Edwin and Ralph.

 III Cynthia, born July 19, 1797; not married but lived with her brother Ralph. She was thrown from a wagon on Wednesday, Sept. 22, 1880, and died on the 28th of that month.

332 IV Francis Sage, b. June 11, 1799; m. Aug. 20, 1823, Harriet Peet; d. Oct. 16, 1832.

 V Russell, 1, born Jan. 13, 1801; died Apr. 14, 1801.

333 VI Russell, 2, b. July 20, 1803; m. Aug. 21, 1821, Pamelia Abbey.

336 VII Henry M., b. Oct. 14, 1805; m. Nov. 22, 1828, Caroline Crittenden; d. Dec. 12, 1836.

 VIII Amy C., born Aug. 14, 1807; unmarried. Lived at Portland, Conn., and there died, July 28, 1836.

**337** IX Ralph, b. June 5, 1809; m. (1) May 6, 1834, Louisa L. Strickland; (2) April 18, 1865, Frances A. Strickland.

**338** X Lewis S., b. July 30, 1811; m. (1) Sept. 15, 1835, Sarah A. Payne; (2) Aug. 28, 1856, Betsey C. Post.

**339** XI Leverett S., b. June 6, 1814; m. (1) Jan. 17, 1837, Esther M. Strickland; (2) Sept. 27, 1845, Sarah H. Batchelder; (3) March 8, 1860, Mrs. Ruth (Brooks) Meach.

XII Still-born, between the 1st and 6th; probably between the 5th and 6th.

**226. Francis Sage Pelton**[6], first son of Marshall[5], Josiah[4], John[3], Samuel[2], John[1], born in Chatham, now Portland, Conn., June 11, 1799; married August 20, 1823, Harriet Peet (b. Dec. 7, 1801), of Canaan, Conn., only daughter of William Peet, of that place. Clothier at Canaan, and afterward in the stage and livery-stable business at Litchfield, Conn., where he died, April 16, 1832. Children, all born in Canaan, Conn.:

I Betsey Ann, born at Canaan, Conn., June 28, 1824; unmarried; residence, in 1879, with her brother at E. Canaan, Conn.

II William, born Jan. 23, 1826; living, in 1879, unmarried, on the Peet homestead at E. Canaan, Conn. Farmer.

III Edward Francis, born July 25, 1828; died Sept. 16, 1846.

# BROOKLYN VILLAGE AND CLEVELAND, O., BRANCH.

**320. Russell Pelton**, third son of Marshall[6], Josiah[4], John[3], Samuel[2], John[1], born at Chatham, now Portland, Conn., July 20, 1803; married at Portland, Conn., August 21, 1821, Pamelia Abbey, daughter of Asaph Abbey, of Chatham, Conn. Farmer. Lived at Chatham, and at Chester, Conn., where he and John Baldwin Pelton worked a granite quarry. On September 4, 1835, he removed to the township of Brooklyn, O., adjoining the city of Cleveland on the south. There he lived, and there died at the house of his daughter, Mrs. Elizabeth Fish, April 19, 1888. Children, all born in Connecticut:

> I Emily Frances, born Nov. 20, 1822; married at Brooklyn, O., July 3, 1848 (1838?) Philo Chamberlain, of Cleveland, O., where she lived, and there died, Mar. 4, 1861. Eleven children. One daughter, Mrs. Helen J. C. Butler, lived in No. Adams, Mass., 1891. Mr. Chamberlain, under the name of the Northern Transportation Co., built up a line of twenty-one propellers, forming a daily line between Chicago, Ill., and Ogdensburg, N. Y.
>
> II William Henry, born Sept. 24, 1823; died Oct. 23, 1823.
>
> III Elizabeth A., born Dec. 17, 1824: married, Brooklyn, O., Dec. 3, 1840, Ozias Fish, of that place, where she lived in 1888. Four children, one only, Dwight, living in 1878.
>
> **321** IV Frederick William, b. March 24, 1827; m. Aug. 25, 1848, Susan Anna Denison.

V Ella J., born Mar. 13, 1832; married Dec. 18, 1855, Samuel Sears, of Brooklyn, O., where she lived in 1879, with children, Miller, Rossie and Frederick.

**324** VI Francis Sage, b. June 8, 1833; m. Jan. 8, 1854, Mary Knight; d. Nov. 2, 1876.

**322. Frederic William Pelton⁷**, second son of Russell⁶, Marshall⁵, Josiah⁴, John³, Samuel², John¹, born at Chester, Conn., March 24, 1827; married at Brooklyn, Cuyahoga Co., O., August 25, 1848, Susan Anna Denison (b. Aug. 8, 1829, in Richfield, O.), daughter of John B. Denison, whose father, Daniel Denison, came to Ohio from Saybrook, Conn., about 1823–25. Residence, in 1890, in Cleveland, O. In 1878 he was County Treasurer, after having been Mayor of the city of Cleveland. Children:

    I Libbie Pamelia, born June 13, 1849; unmarried in 1878.

    II Lulu Ellen, born Feb. 5, 1852; married Oct. 8, 1874, A. A. Wenham. Residence, 1878, in Cleveland, O.

    III Clarence Frederick, born May 20, 1857; died Dec. 3, 1857.

    IV Clara Susan, born May 20, 1857; died Dec. 25, 1857.

    V Jennie Louisa, born June 28, 1860; died June 10, 1864.

    VI Emily Frances, born Nov. 10, 1862; died June 30, 1864.

    VII Susie May, born Sept. 19, 1866.

**323. Francis Sage Pelton⁷**, third son of Russell⁶, Marshall⁵, Josiah⁴, John³, Samuel², John¹, born at

Chester, Conn., June 8, 1833; married at Brooklyn Village, Cuyahoga Co., O., January 8, 1854, Mary Knight, daughter of Moses N. Knight, of Glens Falls, Warren Co., N. Y. Vessel owner. Lived in Cleveland, O., and there died at 288 Franklin avenue, November 2, 1876. Children:

   I Cora B., born Oct. 27, 1854.
835  II Russell K., b. Nov. 8, 1856; m. Aug. 15, 1877, Lillie B. Bouton.
   III Ellen M., born Oct. 13, 1858.
   IV Mary F., born May 21, 1862.
   V Noyes F., born Aug. 27, 1865; died Feb. 15, 1866.
   VI Esther L., born Nov. 1, 1867.
   VII Glenn W., born Jan. 20, 1869; died May 6, 1875.
   VIII Clarence B., born Aug. 19, 1870; died May 9, 1875.
   IX Emily G., born Nov. 21, 1872.
   X Francis Sage, Jr., born July 16, 1875.
   XI Lura A., born May 27, 1877; died Aug. 28, 1877.

**835. Russell K. Pelton**, second son of Francis S.[7], Russell[6], Marshall[5], Josiah[4], John[3], Samuel[2], John[1], born in or near Cleveland, O., November 8, 1856; married August 15, 1877, at Hudson, O., Lillie B. Bouton, daughter of Charles Bouton, of that place. Residence, in 1890, Cleveland, O.; in 1892, in Buffalo, N. Y. Business, transportation. Children:

   I Helen Mary, born Sept. 4, 1878.
   II Charles Frederick, born May 16, 1881; died July 11, 1881.
   III Roy Noyes, born Feb. 25, 1890.

**330. Henry M. Pelton**[6], fourth son of Marshall[5], Josiah[4], John[3], Samuel[2], John[1], born at Portland, Conn., October 14, 1805; married at Chatham, Conn., November 22, 1828, Caroline Crittenden, daughter of Daniel Crittenden, of that place. Lived at Barre, N. Y., thence removed to Sandstone, Mich., about 1830, and there died, December 12, 1836. Children:

 I Sarah, born probably at Barre, N. Y., in 1829; died at Sandstone, Mich., Feb. 28, 1837.

 II Lewis, b. May 2, 1835; m. Mar. 5, 1855, Julia B. Harrington.

**336. Lewis Pelton**[7], only son of Henry M.[6], Marshall[5], Josiah[4], John[3], Samuel[2], John[1], born May 2, 1835, at Sandstone, Mich.; married there, March 5, 1855, Julia B. Harrington, daughter of Porter Harrington, of that place. From previous to 1876 has resided in Jackson, Mich., to this date, 1893, save when absent in military service. Occupation, grocer. In 1861 he enlisted in Co. E, 8th Regiment, Michigan Volunteers Infantry, and was assigned to the 2d Brigade, 1st Division of the 9th Corps, under Gen. W. T. Sherman, Gen. Stevens Brigade Commander. Landed in South Carolina November 8, 1861; remained there until the summer of 1862, when in storming a breastwork on James Island, S. C., June 16, he was severely wounded in the wrist. After lying a week in the brigade hospital he was sent to the city hospital in New York city, where he stayed four months, and was then honorably discharged for physical disability, October 20, 1862. Child:

 I Carrie L., born in Sandstone, Mich., Mar. 1, 1856. In 1892 at home with her parents at Jackson, Mich.

**820. Ralph Pelton⁶**, fifth son of Marshall⁵, Josiah⁴, John³, Samuel², John¹, born in Chatham (now Portland), Conn., June 5, 1809; married (1) at Portland, May 6, 1834, Louisa L. Strickland, of that place (b. May 8, 1811; d. May 4, 1864); (2) April 18, 1865, Frances A. Strickland, sister of his first wife (b. May 24, 1823; d. Nov. 4, 1891), daughter of Noah Strickland (b. Jan. 9, 1776). Occupation, farming. Residence, Portland, Conn., until he died by La Grippe, at home, November 5, 1891, after a short illness. He was an excellent man and died in Christian faith, as he had thus lived since he was sixteen years old.

The writer is glad to acknowledge his cheerful and valuable assistance in gathering the records of the Chatham and Portland branch of the Pelton family. Children:

> I Frances M., born Mar. 16, 1835; married May 20, 1856, William H. Kelsey. Children: Elizabeth L., b. Mar. 10, 1857; d. Oct. 25, 1867; Frances Eugenia, b. June 11, 1860; Ralph Erastus, b. April 22, 1862; Wm. Hy., b. April 18, 1865; Frederic Marshall, b. Sept. 1, 1868; d. Feb. 15, 1870; Gracie May, b. Aug. 21, 1871; Julia Pelton, b. Nov. 21, 1872; Sarah Elizabeth, b. Mar. 25, 1875. Residence, in 1878, at Portland, Conn.
>
> II Julia Louisa, born Mar. 17, 1837; married (1) Dec. 14, 1856, Chas. Hy. Hall. Children: Frederic Edwin, b. Feb. 15, 1858; Clarence B., b. May 7, 1860; d. Aug. 30, 1862; Hy. Gilbert, b. Feb. 15, 1863; Julia Louisa, b. Sept. 29, 1865. Residence, in 1878, Portland, Conn.; (2) in New York city, Dec. 2, 1889, William

Dale (born in New York, Nov. 4, 1843).
No children. Residence, in 1893, New
York city.
III Frederick H., born Oct. 21, 1842.


**886. Lewis M. Pelton**[6], sixth son of Marshall[5],
Josiah[4], John[3], Samuel[2], John[1], born at Portland,
Conn., July 30, 1811; married (1) at South Glastenbury, Conn., September 15, 1835. Sarah A. Payne
(born Nov. 4, 1817), daughter of Alfred Payne, of
Portland, Conn.; (2) at Portland, Conn., August 28,
1886, Betsey C. Post, daughter of Wm. Post, of
Hebron, Conn. Farmer. Living, in 1878, in Portland, Conn. (P. O., Cobalt, Conn.) Children, born
at Portland, Conn.:

    I Amy Adelia, born Oct. 17, 1836; married
      April 5, 1865, Wellington G. Spencer,
      of Portland, Conn.; died Jan. 3, 1874.
      No children.

    II Sarah Jane, born Nov. 24, 1839; died
      Aug. 5, 1840.

    III Francis Lewis, born June 30, 1841; died
      Nov. 12, 1842.

    IV Mary Frances, born May 20, 1843; died
      Sept. 27, 1846.

    V Maria Elizabeth, born March 9, 1848;
      died Sept. 15, 1848.

    VI Lillie Elizabeth, born Nov. 15, 1849;
      married June 6, 1866, Henry F. Rams-
      dell, of Middle Haddam, Conn. Chil-
      dren: Emma E., b. April 12, 1867;
      Franklin H., b. July 22, 1869; Grace
      Spencer, b. July 28, 1873. Residence,
      in 1878, at Middletown, Conn.

589 VII Edward Waterhouse, b. Oct. 14, 1855;
        m. March 31, 1878, Miss Jenny Corn-
        wall; d. April 28, 1879.
    VIII Charles Henry, born Oct. 23, 1857. Lived,
        in 1878, in Portland, Conn.
    IX Nellie May, born Oct. 7, 1859; married
        Dec. 25, 1876, Norman C. Clark, of
        Cobalt, Conn.   Child: Amy Isabella,
        born July 16, 1877.   Lived, in 1878, at
        Middle Haddam, Conn.

**858. Edward Waterhouse Pelton**, first son of
Lewis S.', Marshall', Josiah', John', Samuel', John',
born at Portland, Conn., October 14, 1855; married
March 31, 1878, Miss Jennie Cornwall, daughter of
Charles Cornwall, of Portland, Conn., where he died,
April 28, 1879.   Child:
        1 Charles, born ——, 1879.   Mrs. Pelton
            married 2d James Rogers and lived,
            in 1890, near New Haven, Conn.

**860. Leverett S. Pelton**, seventh son of Marshall', Josiah', John', Samuel', John', born at Portland,
Conn., June 6, 1814; married (1) at Chatham, Conn.,
January 17, 1837, Esther M. Strickland, daughter
of Noah Strickland, of that place, who died at Vermillion, O., November 11, 1842; (2) at Londonderry,
N. H., September 27, 1845, Sarah H. Batchelder,
daughter of Nathan Batchelder, of that place, who
died there, April 3, 1858; (3) at Brooklyn, O., March
8, 1860, Mrs. Ruth (Brooks) Meach, daughter of
Elisha Brooks, of Parishville, St. Lawrence Co.,
N. Y.   Residence, in 1878, in Brooklyn Village, Cuyahoga Co., O.   Children:
        I Amy M., born at Brooklyn Village, O.,
            May 19, 1839; married at Londonderry,

44

N. H., J. C. Townes, and there lived,
in 1878. Three children.

II Sarah Jane G., born at Londonderry, N.
H., Dec. 16, 1846.

III Esther Frances, born May 17, 1852, at
Londonderry, N. H.; married at Brooklyn Village, O., Oct. 8, 1875, Edward
Stinchcomb. Lived, in 1878, at 523
Lorain street, Cleveland, O.

346 IV Leverett Francis, b. March 28, 1861,
at Brooklyn, O.; m. Jan. 19, 1882, Miss
Ida Van Ornum.

V Marshall Elisha, born at Brooklyn, O.,
Sept. 6, 1862.

VI Frederic Henry, born at Brooklyn, O.,
July 11, 1867.

**339. Leverett Francis Pelton**[7], first son of
Leverett S.[6], Marshall[5], Josiah[4], John[3], Samuel[2], John[1],
born at Brooklyn Village, Ohio, March 28, 1861;
married there, January 19, 1882, Miss Ida Van Ornum, daughter of F. S. Van Ornum, of that place.
Occupation, physician and dentist. Residence, 1891,
Berea, O. Children:

I Marshall Elisha, born Nov. 5, 1882.
II Ruth Effie, born May 22, 1884.
III Esther May, born February 7, 1888.

## VERMILLION, OHIO, BRANCH.

**320. Josiah Pelton, Jr.**[5], fourth son of Josiah[4],
John[3], Samuel[2], John[1], born at Chatham, now Portland, Conn., March 5, 1772; married there, December
19, 1793, Lucy Shepard. From 1787 to 1811 he followed the sea as cabin boy, sailor, captain and owner,

trading principally with the West Indies and the
Spanish Main, both in North and South America;
also with Brazil and the Guianas.  In 1811, during
the Mexican insurrection, under Hidalgo, he was
captured while commanding a vessel owned by himself and his brother, Moses, the vessel and $30,000
in specie confiscated and he held a captive.*  Released, after three years, he found his vessel sold and
all his papers destroyed, which prevented the recovery
of his property.  Abandoning the sea, he, in June,
1815, gathered up his family, and with a wagon drawn
by an ox team for a conveyance, started for Ohio,
and in August following arrived at Euclid, near
Cleveland, O., where a cousin, Jonathan Pelton, son
of Joseph Pelton, 1st, of Chatham, Conn., had settled
the year before.  Here he bought land, and here his
wife Lucy (b. Aug. 1 [or 11], 1775) died September
2, 1815.  In 1819 he bought land with a small clearing and a log house, of John Sherrarts, in Vermillion,
Huron (now Erie) Co., O., and removed to the new
farm.  At that time there was large game, deer,
bears, wolves and wild turkeys in plenty, with some
Indians still roaming the woods.  Here he was a
farmer.  But he could not forget the old vocation,
and soon after his arrival built a small vessel,
launched her upon Lake Erie, and called her the
"Franklin" after his youngest son.  At that time the
nearest mills were at Cleveland and Cold Creek.  He
died at Vermillion July 8 or 9, 1834.  Children, all
born in Chatham, Conn.:

> I Lucy, born Nov. 2, 1794; married Wil-
> liam Treat, of Glastenbury, Conn., who
> removed to Euclid, O., where he built
> many vessels.  Children, three.  Mrs.

---

* Another account says he was taken and held captive by pirates.

Treat died in 1819, Mr. Treat in 1872
or 1873.

II Phœbe, born Aug. 10, 1796; married Sept.
28, 1816, at Euclid, O., Anson Cooper,
of Stockbridge, Mass. Lived at Brownhelm, Lorain Co., O.; was living in
1875. Children: George, Lucy, Josiah,
Mary, Allen P., Henrietta B., Henry,
Julia Ann, Sarah M., Charlotte. Mr.
Cooper died July 26, 1846. Mrs.
Cooper, in 1878, lived within four miles
of Vermillion. She died at Brownhelm,
O., July 27, 1883.

843 III Josiah Shepard, b. Mar. 22, 1799; m. May
22, 1825, Sophia (Allen) Leonard; d.
Jan. 5, 1886.

IV Nathaniel, born Dec. 14, 1800; died Apr.
7, 1801.

845 V Allen, b. Apr. 25 (or 28), 1802; m. Mar.
25, 1827, Fanny Cuddeback; d. Jan. 27,
1882.

VI Charlotte, born Mar. 29, 1804; married
Levi Parsons, merchant, of New Haven,
Conn. Children: William Nelson and
Sarah. Lived at Vermillion, O., where
she died, Dec. 4, 1834.

846 VII Sylvester Augustin, b. Mar. 25, 1806; m.
Dec. 31, 1828, Eunice O. Sturges; d.
Jan., 1891.

847 VIII Austin, b. Mar. 10, 1808; m. (1) Aug. 11,
1834, Sarah Sturgis; (2) July 1, 1858,
Caroline (Durand) Nye; d. May 27,
1888.

IX Julia Ann, born Oct. 6, 1810; married
John Miller, a farmer, from Conn., who

died about 1835. One child, John.
Lived at Vermillion, O., and there died,
Oct. 6 (Feb. 16), 1832.

350 X Franklin, b. Nov. 13, 1814; m. (1) Dec.
13, 1838, Eliza Davis; (2) Dec. 24,
1854, Mary Elizabeth Cummings.

NOTE.— The sons of this family, excepting Austin,
were tall; their children are short.

**346. Josiah Shepard Pelton**, first son of Josiah⁵,
Josiah⁴, John³, Samuel², John¹, born at Portland, Conn.,
March 22, 1799; married at Vermillion, O., May 22,
1825, Sophia (Allen) Leonard, daughter of Holden
Alden from New Hampshire. Lived, in 1878, at
Vermillion, O. Farmer and vessel owner. Mrs.
Pelton, born in Connecticut, in infancy removed to
near Cherry Valley, N. Y., and there married a Mr.
Leonard, and by him had two children, Orange A.
and Jane Leonard, both dead. She died at Vermil-
lion, March 5, 1878, and Mr. Pelton died January 5,
1886. Children, born at Vermillion, O.:

      I Lucy C., born Mar. 16, 1826; married
          Dec. 28, 1848, William Pike, of the
          State of New York. Lived at Ver-
          million and died of paralysis, Oct. 20,
          1877. Children: Elwell Levi and
          Mary Sophia.

344   II Josiah Shepard, Jr., b. Mar. 16, 1828; m.
          Dec. 28, 1853, Jane Stone.

344   III Levi A., b. Sept. 24, 1830; m. Mar. 20,
          1859, Frances Nye.

      IV Mary A., born Sept. 28, 1832; married at
          Vermillion, Nov. 9, 1853, Charles B.
          Summers, of Vermillion, and lived there
          in 1878; in 1891 at Oakland, Cal.
          Farmer. Children: Roland and Bertha.

**844** V George W., b. Aug. 23, 1835; m. July 5, 1858, Adelia Klady.

**843. Josiah Shepard Pelton, Jr.,** first son of Josiah S.⁶, Josiah⁵, Josiah⁴, John³, Samuel², John¹, born Vermillion, O., March 16, 1828; married there, December 28, 1853, Jane Stone, daughter of William Stone, of Vermillion. Lived, in 1878, at Berlin Heights, Erie Co., O. Farmer. Died at Berlin Heights, O., July 27, 1882. Mrs. Pelton died April 8, 1891. Children:

> I Jennie E., born June 26, 1855; married Birmington, O., Aug. 21, 1882, Charles H. Cummings, of Youngstown, N. Y. Children: Josiah P., b. July 19, 1883; Clarence, b. Aug. 27, 1886. Residence, 1891, Geneva, O.
>
> II Annie M., born Apr. 7, 1858; d. Jan. 26, 1885.
>
> III Ruth, born Dec. 12, 1861; died Feb. 26, 1862 (3).
>
> IV Leonard L., born Apr. 21, 1867.

**842. Levi A. Pelton⁷,** second son of Josiah S.⁶, Josiah⁵, Josiah⁴, John³, Samuel², John¹, born at Vermillion, O., September 24, 1830; married there, March 20, 1859, Frances Nye, daughter of Benjamin Nye, of Syracuse, N. Y. Vineyardist and manufacturer of pure native wines. Died October, 1882. No children.

**843. George W. Pelton⁷,** third son of Josiah S.⁶, Josiah⁵, Josiah⁴, John³, Samuel², John¹, born at Vermillion, O., August 23, 1835; married there, July 5, 1858, Adelia Klady, daughter of Isaac Klady, of

Florence, Erie Co., O.  Residence, in 1878, at Vermillion, O.  Farmer.  Child:

    I Josiah Eugene, born June 21, 1865.

**339. Allen Pelton**, second son of Josiah, Josiah, John, Samuel, John, born at Portland, Conn., April 25, 1802; married at Vermillion, Ohio (where he had removed with his father in 1819), March 25, 1827, Fanny Cuddeback, daughter of Peter Cuddeback, of Marcellus, N. Y.  Residence, in 1878, in Vermillion, O.  Farmer.  He died in Vermillion, O., January 27, 1882.  Mrs. Pelton died there, January 18, 1883.  Children, born in Vermillion:

    I Lester A., born Sept. 5, 1829.  A millwright.*  In 1878, unmarried, and living in Comptonville, Yuba Co., California.  In 1891, residence at Oakland, Cal.

    II Sarah, born Oct. 10, 1831.

    III Leverett Franklin, born Dec. 29, 1835; died Sept. 20, 1838.

    IV Julia Antoinette, born Aug. 11, 1840; married Nov. 24, 1860, Henry Wagner, formerly of New Haven, Conn.  Residence, in 1878, at Vermillion, O.  Children: Fanny A., Nelson D. and Ruth A.

**340. Sylvester Augustin Pelton**, third son of Josiah, Josiah, John, Samuel, John, born at Portland, Conn., March 25, 1806; removed with his father, in 1815, to Ohio, and in 1819, to Vermillion, Erie Co., O.; married there, December 31, 1828, Eunice O. Sturgis, daughter of Frederic Sturgis, of that place, formerly of Roxbury, Delaware Co., N. Y.  Farmer.  In 1890 was still living at Vermillion, hale and hearty.  His wife, Eunice, died July 25, 1873.  Children:

---

* Inventor of the "Pelton water-wheel."

I Anna Maria, born Aug. 22, 1831; married
  March 16, 1853, William Bird Goodell,
  who died at Port Angelus, Washington
  Ter., Dec. 16, 1863. Children: Fred-
  eric Augustin, b. Feb. 18, 1854; Walter
  Gates, b. April 22, 1856, and Charlotte
  E., b. July 14, 1862. Residence, in
  1878, Vermillion, O.

II Sylvester A., Jr., born June 19, 1833;
  died Sept. 5, 1834.

815 III Frederic Josiah, b. Aug. 20, 1835; m.
  Sept. 28, 1873, Frances A. Cady.

IV Phœbe Cooper, born Jan. 14, 1838; married Oct. 18, 1854, Resolvent Case, of
  Sennet, Cayuga Co., N. Y. Residence,
  1878, at Vermillion, O. Children:
  Mary Dell, b. Mar. 23, 1857; m. Dec.
  11, 1877, Jno. Reifort, of Vermillion.

V Harriet Newell, born May 26, 1840; died
  Dec. 12, 1841.

817 VI Munson Miller, b. Oct. 23, 1842; m. July
  27, 1864, Melissa E. Call.

VII Amelia Elizabeth, born Feb. 4, 1845;
  married Dec. 25, 1864, Lawson Augustin Pierce, of Vermillion, O. Wholesale grocer at Chicago, Ill. Children:
  Lewis Burton, b. Nov. 8, 1870, and
  Warren Augustin, b. Oct. 8, 1871.

VIII Eunice Augusta, born Sept. 29, 1848;
  died Nov. 7, 1858.


**815. Frederic Josiah Pelton**, second son of
Sylvester A.[7], Josiah[6], Josiah[5], John[4], Samuel[2], John[1],
born at Vermillion, Erie Co., O., August 20, 1835;
married there, September 28, 1873, Frances A. Cady,

daughter of Jerome Cady. Captain of lake-going vessels. Residence, in 1878, at Vermillion, O. No children reported.

**815. Watson Miller Pelton**[7], third son of Sylvester A.[6], Josiah[5], Josiah[4], John[3], Samuel[2], John[1], born at Vermillion, O., October 23, 1842; married there, July 27, 1864, Melissa E. Call, daughter of Stephen Call, of Hartland, Vt. Farmer. Residence, 1878, at Vermillion, O. Children:

 I Sylvester A., born June 26, 1866.
 II Sarah Elizabeth, born Dec. 20, 1868.
 III Eunice Osborn, born Apr. 21, 1871.

**816. Austin Pelton**[6], fourth son of Josiah[5], Josiah[4], John[3], Samuel[2], John[1], born at Portland, Conn., March 10, 1814; removed to Euclid, O., and to Vermillion, O., with his father; married at Vermillion, August 11, 1834, Sarah Sturgis, daughter of Frederick Sturgis, formerly of Fairfield, Conn., and Roxbury, Delaware Co., N. Y. (b. March 30, 1790; d. April 29, 1818); Mrs. Sarah Pelton died January 16, 1853; (2) at Sandusky City, O., July 1, 1858, Mrs. Caroline (Durand) Nye, widow of Ebenezer Nye, and daughter of Simeon Durand, of Henrietta, Lorain Co., O. Farmer. Lived at Vermillion, O., and at Berlin Heights, Lorain Co., O. Removed to Kansas November 9, 1885, and died at Ford City, Ford Co., Kan., May 27, 1888, at which time his second wife was still living. Children, all born at Vermillion, O.:

 I Mamre Ann, born June 23, 1836; married there, Sept. 20, 1855, Albert S. Backus, lumberman, son of Absalom Backus, of Auburn, N. Y. Children: 1. Eunice Elizabeth, b. 1859; m. Apr. 17, 1883,

Ed. F. Lawrence; 2. Hattie, b. 1864;
d. June 2, 1865; 3. Albert Absalom, b.
1872; 4. Frederick Hildreth, b. 1875.
In 1888, post-office address Green Cove
Springs, Clay Co., Fla.

349    II Alonzo Shepard, b. May 15, 1838; m.
May 18, 1861, Lydia Handy.

III Diantha B., born Apr. 23, 1840; married
at Berlin Heights, Lorain Co., O.,
James Goldsmith, son of Isaac Goldsmith, of Vermillion, O. Residence, in
1888, at Vermillion. Children: Sarah
E. and Nellie A.

IV Sarah Austria, born Nov. 21, 1843; married (1) at Vermillion, O., about 1865,
William Gibson, who died Aug. 19,
1873. Children: 1. William Hy., b.
Dec. 1, 1866; 2. Nelson S., b. Sept. 16,
1868. Married (2) at Vermillion, Nov.
24, 1877, James Henry Reed, son of
Joseph Reed, of Ceylon, Erie Co., O.
Carpenter. No children.

349    V Nelson Austin, b. May 30, 1846; m. May
8, 1870, Mary Josephine Spear.

350    VI Henry J., b. Mar. 26, 1849; m. ——;
separated.

350    VII Levi Bliss, b. Feb. 21, 1852; m. Dec. 30,
1875, Hattie M. Johnson.

350    VIII Charles J., b. Oct. 27, 1859; m. Dec. 31,
1881, Emma A. Petty.

IX Lucinda Adele, born Nov. 11, 1861; removed to Kansas, Apr. 13, 1885; married at Ford, Ford Co., Kan., Mar. 14,
1887, George C. Pinkney, of Yorkshire,
Eng. Farmer. Child: Joseph, born
Dec. 12, 1887.

**347. Alonzo Shepard Pelton¹**, first son of Austin⁶, Josiah⁵, Josiah⁴, John³, Samuel², John¹, born at Vermillion, Erie Co., O., May 15, 1838; married there, May 18, 1861, Lydia J. Handy, daughter of Thomas Handy, of New London, Conn. Mariner. Residence, in 1888, at Vermillion, O. Children, born at Vermillion and Ceylon, O.:

 I Luna L., born June 25, 1863.
 II Millie, born Aug. 27, 1866.
 III Henry A., born at Ceylon, O., Oct. 5, 1875.

**348. Nelson Austin Pelton¹**, second son of Austin⁶, Josiah⁵, Josiah⁴, John³, Samuel², John¹, born at Vermillion, Erie Co., O., May 30, 1846; married May 8, 1870, at Vermillion, Mary Josephine Spear (b. Apr. 9, 1852), daughter of Ira Spear, of that place. Farmer. Residence, in 1890, at Caseville, Huron Co., Mich. Children:

 I Mary Lovinia, born July 5, 1871.
 II Maud Bell, born March 30, 1873.
 III Gertie Mamre, born July 8, 1875.
 IV { Nelson Austin, born July 3, 1877.
 V { William Henry, born July 3, 1877.
 VI Charles Hiram, born Sept. 13, 1880, at L'Anse, Baraga Co., Mich.
 VII Winnie Josephine, born May 8, 1882, at L'Anse, Mich.
 VIII Ira Russell, born Sept. 13, 1884, at Vermillion, O.
 IX Sarah Sturges, born Aug. 31, 1886, at Caseville, Huron Co., Mich.; died Oct. 20, 1888.
 X Margie Albertie, born Sept. 18, 1888, at Caseville, Mich.

**847. Henry J. Pelton**, third son of Austin[6], Josiah[5], Josiah[4], John[3], Samuel[2], John[1], born at Vermillion, Erie Co., O., March 26, 1849; married ———. Residence, 1890, Cleveland, O. Address, Center street, cor. W. River street. No children.

**847. Levi Ellis Pelton**, fourth son of Austin[6], Josiah[5], Josiah[4], John[3], Samuel[2], John[1], born at Vermillion, Erie Co., O., February 21, 1852; married there, December 30, 1875, Hattie M. Johnson, daughter of John M. Johnson, of Vermillion. Fisherman on the Great Lakes. Residence, in 1890, at Vermillion, O. Children:

> I Albert Leon, born Dec. 18, 1876; died Dec. 4, 1884.
> II Ernest Warren, born Nov. 4, 1878.
> III Jesse Urban, born March 7, 1883.

**847. Charles J. Pelton**, fifth son of Austin[6], Josiah[5], Josiah[4], John[3], Samuel[2], John[1], born at Vermillion, O., October 27, 1859; married at Elyria, O., December 31, 1881, Emma A. Petty (aged 25), daughter of John Petty, of Henrietta, O. Removed to Kansas, November 9, 1885. Farmer. Residence, in 1888, at Ford, Ford Co., Kan. Children:

> I Ellotta Blanche, born March 4, 1883.
> II Mary Adele, born Aug. 25, 1885.
> III Frederic Austin, born Aug. 15, 1887.

**840. Franklin Pelton**, fifth son of Josiah[5], Jr., Josiah[4], John[3], Samuel[2], John[1], born at Portland, Conn., November 13, 1814; removed, in 1815, to Euclid, O., and thence, in 1819, to Vermillion, with his father and his family; married (1) in Vermillion, December 13, 1838, Eliza Davis, daughter of James Davis, of that place, who died April 11, 1859; (2) December 24, 1859, Mary Elizabeth Cummings, daughter of John Cummings, of Avon, O. Farmer and vessel owner. Lived, in 1890, at Vermillion, O. Children, all born in Vermillion, O.:

**351**   I Edwin Richard, b. Sept. 16, 1839; m. Oct. 18, 1863, Hannah Brown.

**352**   II James Russell, b. Sept. 26, 1841; m. Aug. 28, 1865, Jenny S. Brown.

**353**   III Benjamin Franklin, b. Feb. 19, 1844; m. Dec. 25, 1869, Louisa Hoffner.

IV Francis Vivian, born May 15, 1846; in 1878, living, unmarried, at Vermillion, O. Lake captain.

V Alphonso Prentice, born July 1, 1851; died March 9, 1852.

VI Sarah M., born May 18, 1853; died Feb. 19, 1854.

VII Ella Gertrude, born April 2, 1855; married Nov. 18, 1876, Dr. Allen Cross, of Amherst, O.

VIII Mary Eliza, born Feb. 7, 1861.

IX Wesley, born July 8, 1862.

X Agnes Alida, born April 21, 1864.

XI Josephine J., born Nov. 8, 1865; died July 26, 1866.

**350. Edwin Richard Pelton**[6], first son of Franklin[6], Josiah[5], Josiah[4], John[3], Samuel[2], John[1], born at Vermillion, Erie Co., O., September 16, 1839; married there, October 18, 1863, Hannah Brown, daughter of Charles Brown, of Vermillion, O. Lake captain. Residence, in 1878, at Vermillion, O. Children:

I Grace A., born May 15, 1865.

II Russell A., born Aug. 28, 1867.

**350. James Russell Pelton⁷**, second son of Franklin⁶, Josiah⁵, Josiah⁴, John³, Samuel², John¹, born at Vermillion, O., September 26, 1841; married there, August 28, 1865, Jenny S. Brown, daughter of Charles Brown, of that place. Lake captain. Residence, in 1878, at Vermillion, O. Child:

    I Ernest, born Apr. 15, 1873.

**350. Benjamin Franklin Pelton⁷**, third son of Franklin⁶, Josiah⁵, Josiah⁴, John³, Samuel², John¹, born at Vermillion, O., February 19, 1844; married at Sandusky, O., December 25, 1869, Louisa Hoffner, daughter of Henry Hoffner, of Vermillion. Sailor. Residence, in 1878, at Vermillion, O. Child:

    I Pearly Hattie, born Nov. 25, 1872.

**55. Joseph Pelton⁴**, sixth and youngest son of John³ 1st of Saybrook, Samuel², John¹, born probably in Lyme, Conn., April 15, 1722; married in Chatham, Conn., September 27, 1744, Anna Penfield (b. Oct. 26-27, 1728). Farmer. Lived in Chatham (now Portland), Conn., and there died, December 31, 1804, "in the 83d year of his age" (tombstone). His wife Anna died May 19, 1797. In 1878 his homestead was occupied by his great-grandson, Nelson Pelton. Children, born in Chatham, Conn.:

    I Elizabeth, 1, born Nov. 19, 1745; bapt. Nov. 24, 1745; died Sept. 28, 1749.
    II Sarah, born Jan. 15, 1748; married Jan. 21, 1773, Jonathan Brown, of Portland, Conn., where she lived, and there died, Aug. 21, 1841. Children, none.
    III Jonathan, 1, born Mar. 23, 1750; died Sept. 16, 1750.
    IV Joseph, 1, born Nov. 15, 1751; d. Dec. 3, 1751.

**354**   V Joseph, 2, b. Oct. 30, 1752; m. (1) (Ch.
Rec.) Feb., 1776, Mary Shephard; (2)
(Ch. Rec.) Mar., 1798, Widow Lucinda
(Kneeland) Bidwell; d. May 13, 1820.

**365**   VI Abner, b. Mar. 4, 1755; m. (1) May 18,
1775, Sarah Bidwell; (2) Apr. 28, 1796,
Widow Dorothy Bagley; d. Jan. 17,
1846.

VII Anna, born Mar. 25, 1757; married at
Portland, Conn., Nov. 15, 1774, Charles
Davis, of that place. Children: Buck-
ley, Charles, Sarah, Anna.

**377** VIII Jonathan, 2, b. June 10, 1859; m. about
1782, Elizabeth Doane; d. Sept. 22,
1830.

IX Elizabeth, 2, born June 13, 1762; married
Nov. 17, 1785, Moses Stocking, and
removed to Sheffield, Berkshire Co.,
Mass. Children, three, of whom two
died young, and one, Phœbe, married
a Mr. Stillman and lived in Erie, Pa.

X Azubah, born July 24, 1764; married (Ch.
Rec.) in 1783, Amos Nathaniel Roberts
(b. Nov. 25, 1759), and removed to
Norwalk, Conn., to Paris, Oneida Co.,
N. Y., to Bridgewater, N. Y., and thence
to Waterloo, N. Y., where she died
about 1840, at a very advanced age.
Children: 1. Daniel, b. Mar. 27, 1784;
2. Amos, b. July 2, 1786; 3. Anna, b.
June 5, 1789; 4. Joseph P., b. Apr. 5,
1792; 5. Nabby, b. Jan. 9, 1794; 6.
Azubah, b. June 9, 1796; 7. Philo, b.
Apr. 28, 1798; 8. Asahel, b. Nov. 22,
1800; 9 and 10. Lyman Erastus and

Luman Augustus, twins, b. Feb. 14, 1804. Mr. Roberts was an excellent Christian man. One son, Philo Roberts, married Ruth Lord Pelton, daughter of Phineas Pelton, son of John Pelton[6], 2d of Saybrook, Conn., and lived at Cuba, N. Y. (See pp. 203, 205.)

386 XI Asahel, b. June 17, 1768; m. Dec. 5, 1790, Nabby Ranney; d. July 26, 1843.

389 XII Reuel, b. May 30, 1770; m. Apr. 9, 1792, Lucy Barnes; d. Nov. 1, 1851.

397 XIII Hatsiel, b. Oct. 23, 1772; m. about 1793, Hannah Stiles; d. Sept., 1806.

# GREAT BARRINGTON, MASS., BRANCH.

**353. Captain Joseph Pelton**[6], third son of Joseph[5], John[4], Samuel[2], John[1], born at Chatham (now Portland), Conn., October 30, 1752; married there (1) (Ch. Rec.), February, 1776, Mary Shephard, of Chatham, Conn., who died September 8, 1797, aged 39; (2) in Chatham (Ch. Rec.), March, 1798, Widow Lucinda (Kneeland) Bidwell, of Ellington, Conn. He was a cooper and farmer. He lived for years in Chatham. March 7, 1782, he bought in Colchester, Conn., of Samuel Wood, for £140, land on which was a "corn mill" and a dwelling, which he sold August 20, 1785, to Nathaniel Warner, and in 1801 removed to Great Barrington, Berkshire Co., Mass., where he died, May 13, 1820. His wife Lucinda died at New Marlborough, Mass., October 30, 1841, aged 74 years. Tradition says that Mr. Pelton was an austere man, showing good puritan descent. Children, all born in Chatham, Conn., but we have no authentic record:

355    I Timothy, b. Apr. 27, 1777; m. (1) Freedom Carter; (2) Huldah Royce; d. Dec. 29, 1817.

II Roswell, born, date unknown; not known to have been married; he lived, after 1802, in New York city, and there died at a date unknown, but probably after 1810. He was admitted to the church in Chatham, Conn., August 15, 1802, and he conveyed land in Chatham, January 6, 1802. Tradition makes Roswell the oldest child, but is probably wrong as to that.

NOTE.— Roswell Pelton was doubtless the " Roosevelt Pelton, combmaker," of the New York City Directory, of 1810.

III Anna, born, date unknown; married (1) a Mr. Crane; (2) a Mr. Clark, and removed to Union, Broome Co., N. Y., and there died.   Two children.

IV William; no record.   Said to have lived for a time in South Carolina, and to have there died, about or before 1801; probably before the removal to Great Barrington.

362    V Joseph Kneeland, b. Nov. 23, 1801; m. (1) Feb. 27, 1822, Harriet Ray; (2) Nov., 1857, Miss Dolly Prescott Baker; d. July 26, 1873.

VI Mary (Molly), born, as supposed, in 1804, and died Jan. 10, 1818, aged 14 years.

VII Infant, born ——; died (Ch. Rec.), in 1782.


362. **Timothy Pelton**, first son of Joseph[5], Joseph[4], John[3], Samuel[2], John[1], born at Chatham, Conn.,

46

April 29, 1777; married (1) Marlboro, Conn., about
1801, Freedom Carter, daughter of Ezra Carter, of
that place; (2) Huldah Royce, of Sandisfield, Mass.
Cooper and farmer. Lived at Great Barrington,
Mass., and there died, December 29, 1817. His wife,
Freedom (b. June 14, 1782), died in July, 1813; and
his wife, Huldah, died at Wyoming, N. Y., October
26, 1841, aged 55 years. Children:

       I Mary Shephard, born Oct. 25, 1802; mar-
ried at Great Barrington, Mass., November 22, 1826, Homer Bronson, son of
Dr. Abel Bronson, of Waterbury, Conn.
Children: Harriet Electa, b. Mar. 3,
1828; Jos. Perry, b. Apr. 3, 1831; Mary
Pelton, b. Oct. 6, 1833; d. Sept. 23,
1865. In 1875 lived in Springfield,
Mass., 41 Vernon street.

**256**  II Asa Carter, b. Aug. 23, 1804; m. April,
1832, Ophelia Austin.

**361**  III William, b. July 4, 1807; m. Feb. 2, 1836,
Jane Haight; d. Aug. 14, 1852.

**361**  IV Henry Franklin, b. May 12, 1816; m.
Aug. 3, 1843, Martha A. Gill; d. Sept.
21, 1877.

      V Elizabeth Royce, born 1818; died at Cold-
water, Mich., July 25, 1840, aged 22
years.

**255. Asa Carter Pelton,** first son of Timothy[6],
Joseph[5], Joseph[4], John[3], Samuel[2], John[1], born at Great
Barrington, Mass., August 23, 1804; married at Sheffield, Mass., in April, 1832, Ophelia Austin, daughter
of H. D. Austin, of that place. Farmer and jeweller.
Residence at Great Barrington, and in 1875, at Sheffield, Mass. Children:

357    I George Austin, born at Great Barrington, Mass., Apr. 15, 1833; m. Apr. 27, 1864, Miss C. Sarah Brownson. Congregational minister.

    II Mary Almira, born Feb. 10, 1835; married Sept. 4, 1861, Wm. P. Strickland, clerk of courts at Northampton, Mass.; judge in 1882. Six children. Lived, in 1893, at Northampton, Mass.

358    III William Henry, b. Apr. 9, 1837; m. Jan. 28, 1860, Cornelia Evelyn Philip.

    IV Harriet L., born May 20, 1839; married at Great Barrington, Mass., Nov. 23, 1859, Albern I. Do Silva, of the Island of Madeira. Lived at Lee, Mass., and there died, Apr. 2, 1862. One child, a son.

359    V Edward E., b. Aug. 18, 1841; m. Mar. 9, 1870, Emily Alice Fillow.

360    VI Timothy R., b. July 18, 1844; m. Nov. 4, 1874, Mary G. Arnold; d. Dec. 10, 1877.

    VII Charles A., born Apr. 10, 1847. In 1878, a farmer, unmarried, and living at Gilman, Marshall Co., Iowa.

**356. George Austin Pelton**[8], first son of Asa Carter[7], Timothy[6]. Joseph[5], Joseph[4], John[3], Samuel[2], John[1], born at Stockbridge, Mass. (family residence at Great Barrington, Mass.), April 15, 1833; married at New Haven, Conn., April 27, 1864, Miss Sarah C. Brownson, daughter of Seth Warner and Catherine (Post) Brownson, of that place. Congregational minister. Educated, preparatory. at Williston Seminary, East Hampton, Mass., class of 1857; Yale College, class of 1861; Theological Seminary, New Haven, Conn., and at Andover, Mass., class of 1864.    Licensed, February, 1864; ordained to the ministry at Franklin, Mass., August 9, 1865.    Served as minister at Franklin, Mass.; Bethel, Conn.; Candor, Groton, Morrisville, Greene and Sandy Creek, N. Y.; Shelburne Falls and Groton, Mass., and at Watertown, Conn.; a faithful, active pastor and evangelist.    Served in the first triennial council of Congregational churches, at Oberlin, O., in 1871, as one of the delegates from the General Association of New York, and was secretary of the New York Education Society of the Congregational churches, 1871-1876, in connection with his other work.    Residence, 1890, 41 High street, New Haven, Conn.    Child:

> 1 Mary Ophelia, born at Franklin, Mass., Aug. 14, 1865; died at Candor, N. Y., Jan. 16, 1870.

**856. William Henry Pelton**, second son of Asa Carter, Timothy, Joseph, Joseph, John, Samuel, John, born at Sheffield, Berkshire Co., Mass., April 9, 1837; married at Great Barrington, Mass., January 28, 1860, Cornelia Evelyn Philip, daughter of Daniel H. Philip, of that place. *War Record:* Mr. Pelton, one of three brothers who served in the War of the Great Rebellion, was first lieutenant, Squadron H, Sixth Massachusetts Cavalry, from the beginning to the end of the war.    Embarking at Boston, Mass., he entered the mouth of the Mississippi river, helped to take Forts Jackson and St. Philip and New Orleans, then on to Bonnet Carrie, to Baton Rouge, and twenty-seven days at the taking of Port Hudson, thence up the Red river and back, with an honorable discharge at the end of the war, and was presented with a fine steel engraving for bravery and good conduct. In 1878 a drygoods salesman in New York city; in 1890, still in mercantile business, in Brooklyn, N. Y., Mrs. Pelton having died in the meantime. Children:

    I Florence Evelyn, born Dec. 22, 1860.

    II Henry Victor, born Feb. 8, 1872; died July 1, 1872.

    III Raymond Howard Charles, born Nov. 20, 1874.

**846. Edward Ensign Pelton**, third son of Asa Carter[7], Timothy[6], Joseph[5], Joseph[4], John[3], Samuel[2], John[1], born at Great Barrington, Berkshire Co., Mass., August 18, 1841; married at Brewster's Station, N. Y., March 9, 1870, Emily Alice Fillow (b. Feb. 1, 1849, at Newtown, Conn.), daughter of Elijah N. Fillow, of Bethel, Conn. Hatter. *War Record:* Mr. Pelton enlisted for service in the War of the Great Rebellion at Meriden, Conn., September 23, 1861, in Capt. Chas. L. Upham's Co. K, Eighth Regiment of Connecticut Volunteer Infantry. Assigned to Gen. Burnside's Ninth Army Corps, they served through the North Carolina campaign until the taking of Fort Macon, Beaufort Harbor, N. C.; then with Gen. Burnside in Virginia, where they joined the Army of the Potomac, being made a part of the Eighteenth Corps. At Antietam, September 17, 1862, he was severely wounded, shot through the left thigh; was taken prisoner and paroled on the field. Exchanged in November following, he, for reason of his wound, was discharged March 4, 1863. Recovering, he again enlisted, February 9, 1865, in the Sixth United States Regular Cavalry, in which, August 12, following, he was appointed first sergeant of Co. E. The Rebellion over, they were sent to the Texas